STRICTLY LOVE

Julia Williams has always made up stories in her head, and until recently she thought everyone else did too. She grew up in London, one of eight children, including a twin sister. She was a children's editor at Scholastic for several years before going freelance after the birth of her second child. It was then she decided to try her hand at writing. The result, her debut novel *Pastures New*, was a bestseller and has sold across Europe.

As research for *Strictly Love*, Julia learned to ballroom dance. See the results of her labour at www.strictlycomedancing-not.blogspot.com and visit www.juliawilliamsauthor.com and www.AuthorTracker.co.uk for further information on her.

By the same author:

Pastures New

JULIA WILLIAMS

Strictly Love

WITHDRAWN

AVON

AVON

A division of HarperCollins*Publishers*
77–85 Fulham Palace Road,
London W6 8JB

www.harpercollins.co.uk

A Paperback Original 2008

First published in Great Britain by
HarperCollins*Publishers* 2008

Copyright © Julia Williams 2008

Julia Williams asserts the moral right to
be identified as the author of this work

A catalogue record for this book is
available from the British Library

ISBN-13: 978-1-84756-016-2

Set in Minion by Palimpsest Book Production Limited,
Grangemouth, Stirlingshire

Printed and bound in Great Britain by
Clays Ltd, St Ives plc

Mixed Sources
Product group from well-managed
forests and other controlled sources
www.fsc.org Cert no. SW-COC-1806
© 1996 Forest Stewardship Council

FSC is a non-profit international organisation established to promote the
responsible management of the world's forests. Products carrying the FSC
label are independently certified to assure consumers that they come
from forests that are managed to meet the social, economic and
ecological needs of present and future generations.

Find out more about HarperCollins and the environment at
www.harpercollins.co.uk/green

I am immensely lucky to have had help from a number of people when writing *Strictly Love* and would like to thank the following for their stonking support.

For Maxine Hitchcock, Keshini Naidoo, Sammia Rafique, Caroline Ridding and all the Avon crew, I don't think thanks will ever cover it properly, but I'll say it again anyway!

For Dot Lumley, thanks as ever for all your help.

My friends in the RNA, especially those on the Friends and Writers e-group, continue to be a source of strength, and have been joined now by a new bunch of writing e-buddies. Thanks are also due to the Bloggers with Book Deals who make my online life such fun.

I nearly came a cropper several times over legal points, so I would like to say a very grateful and heartfelt thank you to: Indira Hann (again!), Paula Moffatt and James Wilson for putting me right. Any mistakes are entirely my own.

I'd also like to thank Danuta Kean for introducing me to the fabulous word "zedlebrity" and my lovely sister Lucy Moffatt for the last-minute Spanish lessons.

Thanks are due to David Gard for giving me useful insights into the murky world of advertising.

I'd also like to thank Michael Ware for sharing his thoughts on being a single dad, which were immensely useful.

Sarah Iles and Jackie O'Neill shared their hilarious experiences of mothering boys with me over cups of tea at the tennis club. You'll both be glad to know that the pond dipping made the final cut.

I had a steep learning curve on the dancing aspects of the book, and I was hugely helped in this by Dot Lumley, who set me on my path and was an invaluable source of information, Anita Maciejewski, who generously shared her dancing experiences and Izabela Hannah, who is a fabulous dance teacher.

And a special thanks goes to the incomparable Marie Philips, whose hilarious blogging about *Strictly Come Dancing*, kept me up to speed when I didn't have time to watch.

And finally . . . without my husband's help on all matters dental, this book could never have been written.

For Dave – I owe it all to you.

Prologue

Dusk was falling as Emily got off the train at Thurfield. She looked about her and breathed a sigh of relief. Welcome and all as the Christmas break had been, it was good to be home.

Home. And where exactly was that? Not in Wales any more, that was for sure, where the absence of her father had been a permanent feature of Christmas, during which they had all tried very hard to pretend that things really hadn't changed. But could she yet call Thurfield home? In the year and a half she'd lived here, patiently (foolishly, her sister Sarah maintained) waiting for Callum to make a move to put their relationship on a more even footing, she had seen it more as a holding station – a place for her to temporarily rest while she waited for her life to begin.

But now, looking around her as she emerged from the station onto a snowy High Street, she realised with a jolt that she did feel at home here. Perhaps it was just that she knew her friend Katie was only up the road, or that Callum and his rich parents lived tantalisingly close. Or perhaps it was simply the little country cottage she had fallen in love with the summer before last, despite its desperate need for DIY. Being cramped in her mum's council flat over the Christmas period had made her long for the serenity and peace of the view from her window, looking out onto the common. Not that the rolling foothills of the South Downs compared to the more dramatic Pembrokeshire coastline of her birthplace, but they were hills nonetheless, and Emily was always comforted by them. Particularly now, as they gleamed and sparkled white in the late winter sunlight. They looked heavenly. And it felt heavenly to be back.

It was good to be here, away from the frantic guilt that accompanied the discovery that her mum had somehow got herself into huge debt thanks to a rather unhealthy addiction to scratch cards, or the feeling that her sisters Mary and Sarah were now more burdened than she was by the care of their mother. And it was a relief to get away from Sarah's nagging strictures about Callum.

'When are you going to get him to commit to you?' Sarah had insisted on knowing, but Emily couldn't answer that one. She wasn't even sure she wanted him to anyway. Part of the fun of Callum was the lack of commitment, and his ability to surprise, shinning up her drainpipe late at night, turning up at the office with champagne when she was working late, making her fizz over with pleasure when he made it all too clear how sexy he found her. Who needed commitment when he gave her all that?

Emily pulled her rucksack further onto her shoulders, and made her way down the High Street as snowflakes fell softly. The splendid Christmas tree in front of the imposing Victorian mansion that housed the council offices twinkled with a warm bright light. The grounds of the mansion were thronging with people: children shrieked and whooped as they spun round on a carousel while their parents looked on, and teenage couples straggled their way round the temporary ice rink the council had erected for the festive season. Emily belatedly remembered the leaflet that had been shoved through her door, promising a New Year's Eve Victorian Extravaganza. They were even roasting chestnuts. The smell was delicious, and took Emily back to the cosy warm Christmases of her childhood. So different from the barren coldness of this year.

Emily watched the skating couples, the laughing families, the elderly grandparents, for a few moments, before setting off again.

She walked on down the High Street. Though dusk hadn't yet fallen, the rather tacky decorations were already blinking on and off. Emily smiled at the sight. The beauty of what she'd just witnessed and the tackiness of the decorations summed up the incongruity that was Thurfield.

The long High Street went from posh to poor in almost a hair's breadth. The train station from where Emily had emerged was at the poor end of town – the chavvy part, which Katie cattily referred to as Turdfield. But walking towards the top end of town, the cheap nail bars and pound-saver shops, with their competing gaudy Christmas lights, were soon replaced by upmarket hair salons and chichi shops that would have done Covent Garden proud. By the time you got to the top end you could purchase your groceries from M&S and Waitrose, rather then Lidl. Thurfield even possessed a family department store, which resembled something out of *Are You Being Served*, and in keeping with the Victorian theme was currently displaying a tableau from *A Christmas Carol* in its front window. The staff had all joined in the spirit of the thing and were dressed in Victorian garb, handing out mulled wine and mince pies to anyone who wanted them. Emily was tempted for a moment, but she was cold and tired, and really just wanted to get home.

To reach her cottage, Emily had to cut through the park that ran behind the department store. The snow was falling harder now and she couldn't help but stare at the families strolling through the park. Men pushing buggies, couples laughing together, children running with unbridled joy through the snow. It was no good her looking with longing. She knew that was not what Callum was about, and she had never been either till now. Funny how things changed. More and more she looked at pregnant women with an envy she hadn't ever experienced before. Wistfully, she wondered what it would be like to hold a baby of her own in her arms. Her nieces and nephews just didn't count.

While you're with Callum you'll never know, Sarah admonished her from afar.

Shut up, sis, said Emily. *It's my life, not yours.*

She turned down the tiny lane that led to her cottage, but then took time to stop and watch the families sledging on the lower reaches of the downs. There was one dad with two girls, one dark, one fair, who were all wet and snowy, shrieking with laughter. Emily wondered if she'd ever have fun like that. She envied the man's wife. He looked like such a devoted dad. She tried and failed to picture Callum larking about like that, without worrying about his hair being ruined.

Shaking her head, she made her way down the lane to her house. It was time to take control of things. A new year soon. A new start. The purity of the snow seemed like an omen. Somehow her life seemed to have got bogged down in a way she couldn't have imagined. Perhaps she needed some purity too. She should take Callum in hand, get their relationship on track, and start to plan a future.

First things first, though. She opened the front door, switched on the light and looked at her cosy little lounge with pleasure. She was back. And for the first time since she'd lived here, it felt like she'd come home.

Part One

Dance Like No One's Looking

Chapter One

'Remind me what I'm doing here again?' Emily stared into the mirror with a frown as she applied some lippy.

'Emily Henderson, what are you like? Because there's free booze, we get to meet famous people and it's a laugh,' Ffion assured her. 'Come on, you know you'll enjoy it.'

'Oh, right,' said Emily, staring at herself critically. God, she was a mess. Her normally sleek dark bob was uncharacteristically unkempt, and she had dark circles under her pale blue eyes. She was looking gaunt. Even her mum had commented on it at Christmas. No wonder, with so many late nights since she'd been back at work. Working hard and playing hard. It was one way of not thinking about things, she supposed.

'Besides,' added Ffion, with characteristic thoughtlessness, 'you've been as miserable as sin since Christmas. You need cheering up.'

And why would that be, I wonder? Emily thought to herself. She really had tried to keep her resolution of looking on the New Year as a new beginning, but the grey cold of January had sapped away all her resolve, and she felt more miserable then ever. And less clear than ever about Callum. Like an idiot, Emily had mistaken the tenderness Callum had shown her briefly as they shared brunch together on New Year's Day for something else. Then she'd further compounded the mistake by mentioning babies. Callum had been pretty elusive since.

Emily followed her friend reluctantly out to the trendy bar, jammed full of Z-listers and their acolytes eager to buy copies of Jasmine Symonds's autobiography, *Jasmine: My Story So Far*. All Ffion cared about, with her endless invites to celebrity functions, launch parties, tickets for the Brits and the like, was hanging out with famous people. As if some of that shiny stuff would rub off on her. It was only a matter of time before she appeared on some crap reality TV programme.

'Hey, look.' Ffion dug Emily in the ribs as they picked up their free glass of dubious chardonnay from a bored-looking waiter. Crackers was the trendy bar much beloved of the celebrity set (or zedlebrities, as she and Ffion had taken to calling them. Mind you, such sarcasm didn't stop Ffion from wanting to join their ranks), and the place was heaving.

'What?' Emily had a headache and was thinking longingly of a long, hot bath and the Margaret Atwood she'd been given for Christmas. The thought of Jasmine writing anything was risible, let alone such an impossibly thick volume for someone who was a mere twenty-two years old.

'There's Twinkletoes Tone,' said Ffion. 'They must have made it up again.'

As Twinkletoes Tone went over to kiss Jasmine – a small, dumpy, rather cowlike creature – full on the mouth, the fact that they had indeed made up was plain for all to see.

'Tony babe,' Jasmine purred. 'Get me another chardonnay, will you?'

'Maybe they're just snogging for the cameras,' said Emily, thinking, '*like, do we care?*'

'Of course we care,' Ffion scolded her.

Damn it. Emily's annoying habit of thinking aloud had snuck out again. One day it would get her into serious trouble. Luckily Ffion was too preoccupied with the various permutations of Jasmine's love life to take much notice.

'But yes, you could be right, they could be just doing it for the PR.' Ffion's beady little eyes lit up with excitement. How she got so titillated by all this stuff was beyond Emily. 'Word on the street is that ever since Tony got ditched from his club, Jasmine's been looking for ways to get rid.'

'That's a bit rich, isn't it?' laughed Emily. 'For someone whose sole claim to fame is being the first person in *Love Shack* ever to have performed live fellatio on TV, she's hardly famous for her own merits. At least Tony has talent.'

'Hmm, tell that to his team mates,' said Ffion. 'Wasn't it his *lack* of talent that caused them to go crashing out of the FA Cup?' Twinkletoes Tone had earned his moniker by scoring an own goal in last year's FA Cup final, thereby earning the never-to-be-forgotten *Sun* headline: '*IT'S ALL GONE TITS UP FOR TWINKLETOES TONE!*'

'Well, I feel sorry for him,' said Emily. 'I mean, what has Jasmine got that is so wonderful?'

They watched as Jasmine scrawled her illegible signature across the front of an adoring fan's book.

'Ooh, Jasmine, I want to be just like you,' the girl, a spotty fifteen-year-old, gushed.

'It's easy,' said Jasmine with a lascivious wink, 'all you need to do is get your tits out on TV and you can do anything.'

'Jeez, there's an ambition,' muttered Emily.

'I dunno,' said Ffion. 'Jasmine's just signed a mega-deal with that cosmetic dental chain *Smile, Please!*' Ffion's PR firm, A-Listers, represented Jasmine so she knew these things. '*Smile, Please!* are going to be huge, you know. Everyone wants cosmetic surgery these days. And if that works out, who knows? According to *OK!* magazine, her aim is to be the face of L'Oréal.'

'Jasmine?' Emily snorted into her glass. 'I didn't know they were planning to put heifers in their ads.'

'Okay,' admitted Ffion, 'her looks are more bovine then elfin. But you don't know how she'll look after *Smile, Please!* have finished with her. And you've got to admit, those teeth . . . now *they* do look fantastic.'

They watched as Jasmine flashed her brilliant smile at another sappy group of fans.

'Well, I think without the smile she wouldn't be the face of anything,' replied Emily. 'God, the world's gone mad!'

'Maybe so,' said Ffion, 'but it sure as hell beats going to work for a living. If I had a chance to appear on *Love Shack*, I'd bite your hand off.'

'I'm sure you would,' answered Emily. 'Listen, I'm knackered, I think I'm going to call it a day.'

'Don't you want to come to Macy's?' Ffion looked disappointed. Up until relatively recently, a night like this would always end up with them visiting Macy's. But Emily was tiring of sitting bored in the roped-off VIP area, drinking tasteless cocktails for exorbitant prices. She'd blown Ffion out several times recently, and she had a feeling her friend was none too pleased with her.

'Not tonight,' said Emily, 'I've got an early start tomorrow.'

Despite Ffion's efforts to make her change her mind, Emily refused to back down. Once, the thought of a night out on the tiles would have appealed, but recently, even as a means to drown her sorrows, it was losing its allure. Besides, Callum had hinted he might call. She hated being so in thrall to him, but sometimes she missed him with an intensity that was nearly physical.

Indeed, as she sat on the train, making the long journey home, watching London racing away from her in the dark, Emily realised that she had at least made progress in one area of her life. More and more, Thurfield was feeling like a refuge from the nightmarish world she seemed to be trapped in. Katie had been telling her for years she needed to get out of her job. Emily wished it were that simple. If only her mortgage wasn't so big, the cottage didn't need so much work, her mum didn't owe so much money, and her firm didn't pay quite so well. If only.

Her mobile bleeped and she saw a message from Callum.

Where r u babe? Hope yr hot & waiting fr me.

In yr dreams, she texted back, experiencing the familiar feelings of lust coupled with irritation that Callum always engendered in her. She hoped he wasn't drunk. Or high. Though he had a penthouse flat in town, he had grown up in the town next to Thurfield, and his best mates still lived nearby. There'd been a football match on this evening. No doubt he'd spent the evening tanked up with them, and was now looking for a bed for the night. She leaned against the window and stared into the dark as the countryside flitted past her. She should probably teach him a lesson and not let him into her bed. But knowing what she should do and actually doing it were two very different things. Two very different things indeed . . .

Rob checked the steps again as they were laid out on the website he'd brought up on his laptop. Then he went to stand in front of the full-length mirror in the lounge, secure in the knowledge that Mark wouldn't be home for at least an hour. He flicked the button on the CD remote and the sound of South American music filled the room.

'One,' Rob counted under his breath, 'remember those snake-hips, two . . .'

He took a small step forward. What was it Isabella had said last week? Step forward on the ball of your foot, take the weight onto the flat foot, and swing your hips to the left. Easier said than done, of course, but he'd just about got the hang of it by the end of the lesson. And he had his silly little diagrams to refer to.

'. . . three, right foot remains in place, transfer weight onto it,' Rob muttered. '. . . four – then one, left foot to side, swing hips to left. Fuck this is difficult.'

He stopped, switched off the music and then peered myopically at the computer screen again. He really ought to get glasses, but Rob knew he was way too vain for them. And too lazy to keep changing contacts.

'Okay, so it's forward, rest, side, back, rest, side. Swing those hips. Right, I get it . . . I think,' Rob said. He switched the music back on and started again. This time it seemed to work, and before long he actually felt he was getting the hang of those 'sssssnake-hips' that Carlo, the hilariously camp Latin American dance teacher he'd found in an online dancing video, had talked about.

'I am the *man*!' Rob declared proudly as he pirouetted round the room. He even felt he'd got the hold right, left hand held high, holding the lady's hand, right hand (the bit that Rob particularly liked) snaked round the lady's back.

He had to crack the rumba. Since he'd started learning to dance, the tally on his bedpost had been the highest since his student days. He felt sure the rumba would only add to his allure.

'John Travolta eat your heart out,' he said, before spinning rather madly out of control and crashing headlong into Mark's oak dresser. Getting up, he rubbed his hip ruefully. 'On the other hand, maybe not.'

'I don't know how you do it,' Mark Davies laughed at his flat-mate later that evening, as Rob bustled into the kitchen to provide drinks for his latest conquest. 'Here you are, thirty-five, plump, those famous curly locks receding faster than the tide, and still you pull them. I can't think what's sadder – the thought of you practising the waltz, or the stupidity of the women prepared to fall for your lines.'

Mark had been on his way to bed, but Rob couldn't resist showing off his prize, an over-made-up girl whom he had picked up at his ballroom dancing.

'Well, you either have it or you don't, mate,' Rob winked knowingly.

'Mind you,' continued Mark, loading the last of the dirty plates into the dishwasher – living with Rob was like revisiting their student days, only more depressing; at least they had a dishwasher now – 'it's always been a mystery how you do it. I've never known what women see in you.'

'Treat 'em mean, keep them keen,' said Rob with a wink.

'Yeah, right,' said Mark. 'That explains why they never last more than a week.'

'Well, have you got a hot babe waiting next door for you?'

'No,' said Mark.

'And, of course, there's my natural charm,' continued Rob.

'Of course,' snorted Mark. Rob's mop of unruly curly hair and cute grin seemed to be what got the girls hooked, but his love 'em and leave 'em reputation should have been enough for them to run a mile. But somehow it never was. Presumably, each and every one of his hapless victims thought they would be the one to change him. And of course they never were.

'You should watch and learn from the master,' continued Rob.

'You know there's only one woman for me,' said Mark miserably.

'Yes, but she's nobbing a lawyer,' Rob reminded him.

Mark pulled a face.

'I'm going to bed,' he said. 'Don't do anything I wouldn't.'

'Now that I *can* guarantee,' smirked Rob.

As Mark climbed into bed minutes later, he could hear the telltale sounds of Rob getting his rocks off. Great, that was all he needed. Mark sighed and put Whitesnake on his iPod and turned it up loud. Heavy metal always made him think of Sam, the most unlikely headbanger in the world. Mark lay in the dark, trying to drown out thoughts of Sam. Pictures of Sam. Wishing things had turned out differently.

What had happened to his life? One minute he was happily married to the woman of his dreams, with two beautiful children, and now here he was: thirty-five, a single dad, living in a grotty three-bed semi with his best friend from uni. While undoubtedly there were advantages in rediscovering a bachelor lifestyle after so many years of domestic bliss (not having anyone nagging about leaving the toilet seat up was a real plus), they didn't outweigh the disadvantages, or the vast gaping chasm that Sam had left behind when she had dumped him unceremoniously for Kevin.

And, to add to the ignominy, he'd been left for a lawyer. Mark had never been keen on lawyers. He'd encountered a fair few smarmy law students when he was at dental school, but his hatred for them had been cemented when he'd watched Spike Sutcliffe, a close friend from dental school, being crucified by a patient who claimed Spike had been inappropriate with her. He hadn't, and eventually he was cleared, but not before he'd been dragged through a bruising court case in which the lawyers had dragged up all sorts of insalubrious details about Spike's rather colourful past, or before Spike had spent vast sums of money on his own defence. The costs that he was awarded just about covered the legal expenses, but they didn't make up for the stress of it all. Sam falling for Kevin had just given Mark another excuse to hate lawyers, only now his hatred was so passionate he knew it wasn't entirely rational.

'What the bloody hell does Kevin have that I don't?' Mark spoke aloud into the darkness. It wasn't the first time he'd asked that question and it wouldn't be the last.

'You never listen to a word I say,' had been Sam's constant refrain during their marriage.

'That's not true,' Mark had protested on more than one occasion. He had listened. Or tried to. He'd always been putty in Sam's hands. Ever since the first night he'd seen her, at his first-year dental ball: a tiny blonde vision in a red strapless dress, strutting her funky stuff to Motorhead of all things. He had been smitten in an instant and knew not just that he wanted to take her home with him, but after she'd amazingly said yes to his offer of a dance that he wanted to spend the rest of his life with her.

And at first everything had been fine. More than fine, it had been brilliant. True, it hadn't been part of the game plan to have children so soon, but he wouldn't be without Gemma and Beth now. Sometimes he wondered guiltily if he'd supported Sam enough when the kids were small. Mark had found it difficult to adjust to fatherhood, especially when Sam appeared to be such a great and totally in-control mum. He'd often felt like a spare part in those days – maybe that was what he'd done wrong. Although she'd never actually said that he wasn't a good dad. Or that he'd failed her as a husband.

Mark had been so content; it had been a shock to hear that Sam wasn't. A year ago (had it only been a year?) she had turned to him clear-eyed and brittle and announced she was leaving him.

'But why?' Mark had asked, in a state of profound disbelief.

'Isn't it obvious?' Her bitterness had stunned him.

'Not to me,' said Mark. 'If it's something I've done, let me put it right.'

But she had shaken her head, and said, rather sadly, he felt afterwards, though at the time he had been too blinded by fury to see it, 'It's too late, Mark. I tried to tell you, but you didn't want to know.'

And now, here he was, sixteen years after he first set eyes on Sam, alone in bed in his bachelor pad. This wasn't how it was meant to be at all.

Emily walked down the little footpath that led to her country cottage. Despite the lack of street lighting, and the fact that the common was only a few moments away, she never felt frightened coming down here by herself. The dark comforted her. It hid her and made her feel safe. Although tonight the clear winter sky and the full moon lit her path quite well enough. She let

15

herself in with a relieved sigh. It was gone midnight, she had an early start tomorrow, and with the way the trains had been lately she was going to need to be up at the crack of dawn. But she was home at last.

Ffion still didn't get why Emily had moved so far out 'into the sticks', as she put it.

'I like it,' Emily constantly said. 'It's cheaper than London and I get to have fresh air.'

Fresh air was important to Emily, having spent her childhood climbing all the hills she could find in her home county of Pembrokeshire. Besides, Katie had moved here first and had then persuaded her it was worth leaving London for the sight of green fields every morning. Mind you, that was before Katie had gone all 'desperate housewife' on her. Now she frequently referred to Thurfield as a fishbowl, and Emily got the impression that her friend missed the bright city lights. Not that Katie ever said as much. Trying to prise a confidence out of her had become somewhat harder than prising an oyster from a clam. But of late, Emily had begun to wonder how happy Katie actually was.

There was laughter coming from the lounge. Loud, raucous laughter. Oh God. Callum had done it again. Decided to bring his mates back to hers. She only hoped they weren't shoving white stuff up their noses. He hadn't yet done it in her home, but she couldn't be sure he wouldn't. Callum liked to live dangerously.

Which, of course, had been part of the original appeal. She still had to pinch herself that someone as gorgeous as Callum was interested in her, the original wallflower. Emily's teenage years had been punctuated by watching her friends cop off with all the good-looking guys, while she, knowing her place as a plain Jane, was left with the geeks. So when Ffion had introduced her to Callum at a PR bash and he showed in interest in her – Emily Four Eyes (an epithet from youth which she could never quite shake off despite having worn contacts for years) Henderson –

she was unable to resist. Even though she knew he was spinning lines. Even though he spelled trouble with every single one of them. There was something about Callum that was just – irresistible.

Which is how he had come into her life. And somehow remained there, never progressing beyond the Occasional Screw label Emily had given him from their early days of courtship. If courtship was what it could be called. Callum had never met her parents. Nor she his. They didn't always even see each other on a weekly basis. He had yet to remember a birthday or Valentine's, although he was always charmingly apologetic every time he forgot. And it was difficult not to respond to the dozen red roses that would appear like magic. And the sex. Well, the sex was dynamite.

She knew he was no good for her. Not long term. And not now, when her body clock was beginning to tick rather too loudly for comfort. While in her wildest fantasies she imagined how Callum would react joyfully if she told him she was pregnant, Emily was far too much of a realist not to know this was a pipe dream. And the more she tried to conjure up pictures in her head of Callum holding a baby à la Athena man, the less she was able to envisage it. She had to face it – if she wanted a suitable dad for her baby, Callum wasn't it.

Reluctantly, she pushed open the lounge door to find Callum with his two side-kicks, Jez and Danny, roaring with laughter at – jeez, what were they watching? Emily didn't like to stare, but it seemed to involve animals and naked people. Lots of naked people. It was compelling in an utterly gross kind of way. Someone had spilled beer over one of the cream sofa cushions. There was a fuggy smell of smoke in the air. Smoke with a very definite scent.

'Hey, babe,' said Callum, drawing on a spliff.

Callum always said Emily was over-anxious about his pot-smoking, but she was a lawyer and the consequences of being caught with drugs in her house weren't worth thinking about.

17

She knew dope was the least of Callum's vices, but she squared it with herself that if he wasn't taking drugs in her house, then what he did in his own place wasn't her business.

'Callum, what the fuck are you up to?' Emily was furious. It was late. They'd trashed her lounge and the three of them were giggling inanely at her. She didn't have the energy for this.

'Just brought Jez and Danny back for a quick drink,' said Callum. 'I didn't think you'd mind.'

'Well, I do,' said Emily shortly, ignoring Jez and Danny's muffled giggles.

'Right, you two, out,' she yelled.

'Don't be such a spoilsport.' Callum turned his smile on her. That devastating smile usually worked so well. But not tonight. Tonight she'd had enough.

'Callum, I've had a long day, I've got an early start, and I need my beauty sleep,' protested Emily.

'Too right you do,' sniggered Jez, who was immediately stopped dead with an icy look.

'Just go, will you,' said Emily tiredly. 'All of you. I need to go to bed.'

'Me too,' said Callum.

'Alone,' said Emily. 'Call a cab and you can just piss off home. I've warned you, Callum. I cannot have you smoking dope in my flat.'

'You know your problem, babe,' said Callum, as he eventually swaggered out of the door. 'You take things too seriously.'

'And you don't take them seriously enough,' said Emily. 'Now go, before –'

'Before what? You change your mind and say I can stay?' He was like a puppy begging for a treat. But for once Emily wasn't in the mood for giving in.

'No, before I say something I might regret. Now go on, get out of here,' she said, practically pushing him out of the door before she weakened.

She slammed it behind her and leaned back against it, sighing deeply.

Damn it! She blinked away angry tears. She was not going to go on like this with Callum taking advantage of her. She was going to take control of her life and start making some changes.

Emily walked slowly into the lounge and stared in dismay at the chaos in front of her. She was too tired to deal with it now, she'd sort it out in the morning.

Take control of her life? She couldn't even take control of her lounge.

Chapter Two

'Mark, you have to take the girls in for me.'

Mark had been shaving on Monday morning when the door-bell rang, and he found Sam and the kids at the front door.

'But I'll be late for work,' Mark protested. Why the hell did Sam always do this to him?

'And so will I. My boss has called an urgent meeting and I have to get up to town.' Sam worked for an American-based cosmetic-surgery company called *Smile, Please!*. It was a far cry from her humble beginnings as a dental nurse, but presumably the pay and perks were what she'd been after all along. The downside, as far as Mark was concerned, was that as he worked locally, she felt the school run was now his God-given duty.

'Besides,' as she frequently told him, 'you owe me. I stayed at home all those years with the kids. Now it's *my* turn.'

Quite why it being 'my turn' meant Mark had to drop every-thing every time Sam asked him to, he hadn't yet worked out, but knowing she could get arsy about access if he made too much fuss, he went along with it.

'Remind me again why Gemma needs a lift?' Mark asked. 'I used to cycle to school at her age.' Gemma, at thirteen, was more than capable of getting to school under her own steam. Her school was at the other end of town from Beth's, which meant a round trip of half an hour. There was no way he was going to make it to work on time.

'We're not in the Dark Ages now, Dad,' muttered Gemma from underneath her dark spiky fringe.

Sam gave him a withering look.

'Gemma's right,' she said. 'You do live in the past. Things are different now. It's not safe for kids to cycle. Or walk. There are all sorts of weirdos about. She just wouldn't be safe on her own.'

And it's nothing to do with you worrying that Gemma can't be trusted to actually go to school, is it? Mark thought to himself. Sam would never admit it, but though Gemma had never actually bunked off school to their knowledge, she was probably the most likely candidate to. Taking her in every day meant Sam knew Gemma had actually got there. Mark blamed the influence of Gemma's new best friend Shelly. Shelly was the reason Gemma had adopted her goth-like stance, eschewing all other colours in favour of black, and listening to bloody miserable music, which Mark had discovered was known as 'emo', whatever that was.

Sam had been quite frantic about it for a time, claiming that all kids who were into emo either committed suicide young or self-harmed. So far there was no evidence of either, but Gemma was displaying a singular reluctance to go to school. And while Mark was all in favour of his daughter getting a decent education, there were days when he hoped Sam would finally trust Gemma to make it to school on her own. The thought of Sam going to prison for Gemma's non-compliance in matters educational was one of the few things that had made him smile in recent months.

Sam dashed off in a flurry of self-importance while Mark went to finish shaving and ring Diana, his wonderfully efficient area manager, to say he'd be late. Then he bundled the kids in the car and drove as quickly as possible to Gemma's school.

He watched Gemma going in (if she did bunk off, he didn't want Sam accusing him of negligence), shoulders hunched, head down, bag slung loosely over her shoulder, presenting a glowering presence, and wondered with dismay what had happened to his cute little girl. Gemma was definitely not cute now, with her punky hairstyle, dyed a different colour every week – Mark frequently pointed out to her that what she thought was groundbreaking was in fact only the style his girl-friends had adopted twenty years previously, but he was always silenced with a, 'Whatever, Dad. It's just different now. You wouldn't understand.'

No, of course not. To Gemma, he'd never been young.

Once Gemma had been dispatched it was on to school with Beth. An entirely different proposition. Though she was ten, Beth was still cuddly enough to remind him what he enjoyed about fatherhood, not yet too embarrassed to kiss him goodbye. He felt vaguely guilty about comparing his children, but it was restful to be with Beth, whose sunny disposition made a nice contrast to Gemma's spikiness.

Then he drove like a maniac to the surgery. Despite the phone call to Diana, Mark still felt stressed. He hated being late and he hoped that anyone waiting wouldn't be too grumpy – some of his patients had a tendency to think that, as their dentist, his sole function in life was to be ready and waiting for them at all times. The fact that he might have an existence, a family, a *life* even, outside the narrow confines of his surgery seemed to be beyond them.

Mark squeezed his ageing Volvo into the one remaining parking space outside the surgery and got out to the distinctive wail of the alarm going off. That was all he needed.

He ran into the surgery and found Maya standing looking helpless, while three patients sat around looking pained.

'I'm so sorry,' she said. 'I was here first and there were patients waiting so I opened the door, but I had forgotten about the alarm and I don't know the code.'

Mark keyed in the right number and thankfully the alarm fell silent. It wasn't Maya's fault, she'd only started working at the practice two weeks ago, and as a newly qualified dentist it shouldn't be her job to make sure the surgery was open on time. That's why they had a practice manageress. Talking of which –

'Where the bloody hell is Kerry?' asked Mark.

Maya shrugged her shoulders.

'I was the first one here,' she said.

There was no sign of either of the nurses who were supposed to be working with them today. Mark sighed. It was going to be one of those days.

He apologised to the bemused patients sitting in the waiting room, answered the phone to Lorna's (nurse number one's) mum, whose defiant explanation that 'Lorna had a stomach ache, innit' didn't fool him for a second, and called in the first of his patients.

By the time he'd seen the second, Kerry had swanned in breezily. 'Sorry I'm late, the trains were bad.'

'But you drive,' replied Mark.

'Oh, not today, I was out last night.' She leered lasciviously and bent down over the desk to reveal a rather lacy thong peeping out of a somewhat less than sexy behind. It was more than a man could take first thing in the morning.

'I think that's what you call a whale tail,' whispered Maya, who had come out to get her next patient.

Mark snorted, before insisting that Kerry went and nursed for Maya, who needed the help more than he did. While he was phoning Diana, who unfortunately today was working at another surgery, in order to get her to find some cover for them, Sasha (nurse number two) walked in. Sasha, their latest recruit, seemed to be the only Eastern European in the country who didn't understand the value of hard work. Mark considered admonishing her, but, mindful that there were still patients in the waiting room, and aware that she probably wouldn't understand him anyway, he decided that, like much of his life, there really was No Point.

He looked down at his day roster to see what else lay in store for him, and groaned out loud. Jasmine Symonds – a so-called celebrity who was famous for shagging on some god-awful reality TV show, and, if the rumours were true, was the new face of *Smile, Please!* – was coming in. It was one more indication that someone somewhere didn't like him. Not only had Jasmine and her ghastly mother Kayla been his patients for years, but despite her newfound fame she wouldn't go to any other dentist. Trust him to have the misfortune to have Jasmine as his most loyal patient . . .

Katie Caldwell was standing at the school gates and watching her ten-year-old son, George, walk mournfully away from her. It cut her heart to the quick to watch his misery and be unable to help. But what could she do when any questions about what was upsetting him were just met with a shrug? George had been in a foul mood this morning, still sore about the fact that he'd spent the previous day on the subs bench – again. He and Charlie had both been peculiarly reticent about why George, the team's best striker, seemed to spend more time off the pitch than on it, but Katie had the deepest suspicion that there was something Charlie wasn't telling her.

It was probably nothing, but Katie knew if she did ask Charlie about it, he would just do that annoying trick of touching his nose and saying 'A Caldwell never blabs' – a phrase no doubt passed on to him by his mother. Was it rather pathetic, she wondered, to have been married for ten years and still be frightened of your mother-in-law?

She sighed, and kissed her younger son, Aidan, goodbye. At least she had no worries on that score. Aidan was a happy-go-lucky child who rarely cried and seemed to shrug off life's slings and arrows with an insouciance she envied, and which she longed for her older, more sensitive son to have too.

'Charlie been winding them up at football again?' Katie turned away from waving Aidan goodbye to see the tall shadow of Mandy Allwick, school gossip extraordinaire, framed in the early-morning sunshine. That was all she needed.

'What do you mean?' Katie squinted up at Mandy, who, as usual, looked perfectly (if a little tartily) manicured and well turned out for first thing in the morning. With her tight leather miniskirt and crop top (revealing as it did a ridiculously well-toned stomach for someone with three children), her high heels, painted nails and even more painted face, a casual observer might have fancied she was on the pull. Though the choice among the stay-at-home dads was hardly wonderful. Still, tarty or not, Mandy always had the knack of making Katie feel wrong-footed.

'Oh, you know Charlie,' Mandy laughed heartily. 'He's always giving that poncy coach a mouthful. And quite right too. That guy goes on and on about being fair to all the kids when it's obvious that your George is one of the best players. And your Charlie is only sticking up for George.'

'How exactly is Charlie sticking up for George?' Katie had a sinking feeling in her stomach. What had Charlie done now? Katie had given up going to football when Molly arrived, using the excuse that it was too cold to be out with a baby, but really it was because she couldn't stand the embarrassment anymore of listening to Charlie's roars of disappointment from the touch-line when George missed a shot at goal, or succumbed to a tackle. George always looked embarrassed at this, and Katie felt for him, but being unwilling to undermine his father's authority in front of him, she never said anything. And, in the end, she just stopped going.

Still, in all other aspects of their life, she couldn't complain. If it was inevitable that their early feelings of lustful desire had settled down into something more sensible and solid, she knew Charlie loved her, and she loved him. They were comfortable together. Despite the stress of being dragged over to his parents'

25

once a month and having to endure Marilyn's withering scorn as to why Charlie still hadn't made it to the top of his firm of accountants: 'His father was at the top in his thirties, though, of course, not everyone can be as talented as him.' But other than that, she was happy enough.

Of late, though, Katie had been getting the feeling that Charlie perhaps wasn't so happy. He hadn't said anything, but she wondered if he was getting twitchy about his fortieth birthday later in the year. He seemed a bit down about it. Or maybe it was that combined with the vasectomy he'd insisted on having after Molly was born. He'd certainly changed lately. He could be moody and difficult. Making a spectacle of himself on the touchline was probably just a symptom of a wider malaise.

'Only doing what any dad should,' said Mandy. 'Shouting for George, yelling at the opposition. It's what I always do.'

I bet you do, thought Katie silently.

'It's that arse Bill who's at fault,' Mandy continued as they made their way out of the school grounds.

'How so?' asked Katie, thinking, *poor bloody Bill, someone has to stand up to the hecklers.*

'Oh, you know what he's like,' said Mandy, tossing her long fair mane back. 'He goes on and on about not being too competitive and not putting pressure on our kids. But the way we all see it, it's a competitive world, innit? They've got to learn sometime.'

Have they? thought Katie. *Do they* have *to learn this way?*

'So why was George put on the subs bench?' Katie asked, but deep down she knew what the answer would be.

'Bill said your Charlie was putting the other players off, and George was taken off as a punishment.'

Katie frowned. It didn't seem at all fair to George to make him suffer for Charlie's bad behaviour. But then it wasn't the first time Bill had warned Charlie off.

Charlie would be bound to shrug it off if she raised the subject. Maybe it was time she started going to football again to see for herself.

A squawk from the buggy indicated that Molly was getting tetchy, so Katie made her excuses and was slowly pushing her way home when she had a better idea. Sod going to football. Who wanted to get their feet cold? What Charlie needed was cheering up. And that was her job. So that's what she'd do. She'd start tonight by cooking him a nice meal. Who knew where it might lead . . .

Emily arrived into work late. She'd spent the night at Callum's, despite her best intentions. But weekends on her own in Thurfield were so lonely. She could have gone to see Katie, but she felt she'd imposed on Katie's friendship too much of late. Besides, despite acknowledging to herself the meanness of the thought, Emily couldn't help feeling a twinge of jealousy when she spent time in Katie's perfect house with her perfect family. It only highlighted the complete and utter mess her own life had become.

The trouble was, Emily thought moodily, she was always so busy at work, and her weekday social life revolved around London, so at the weekend there was nothing for her to do. Or, rather, there was plenty. If she didn't work such long hours, she might have made some friends here other then Katie. Then she could spend her weekends with friends on long walks and cycle rides on the Downs, or going to the cinema or out for a meal. Normal stuff. Like other people did.

Instead of which she was practically chained to her desk, and when she wasn't, she was out late schmoozing people she was coming to despise, or partying like there was no tomorrow with so-called friends with whom she had increasingly little in common.

This wasn't how she'd planned things, back when she'd started law school in Cardiff, all those years ago. Then she'd been full of naïve optimism about how she was going to take on cases like her dad's (languishing at home a semi-invalid thanks to the incompetence of the firm he'd given most of his life to). She felt ashamed that she'd ended up at Mire & Innit – a small media law firm which specialised in defending the low-level famous, in cases which, in the main, were pretty indefensible. Her boss Mel had promised her the earth at her interview seven years ago.

'This is a small firm,' she'd purred silkily, 'but we are going places, and for the right person the rewards are high.'

The rewards had certainly been high financially. Emily was earning far more than in her previous job, but the mortgage on the cottage was correspondingly high too. And the promised promotion to senior associate seemed as elusive as ever, while Mel continued to pile on the work. One thing she'd failed to mention at interview was that, being a small firm, they were constantly short-staffed. Great in one way, as it had given Emily opportunities she would never have had elsewhere, but not so good in terms of having any kind of decent life outside the workplace.

Emily sighed. It had all seemed so glamorous when she'd first come to London. Now it just seemed tawdry to be raking through the muck of zedlebrity lives.

Callum, too, had seemed the height of glamour when she first met him – the gorgeous public school boy with the golden tongue had bowled her over from the start, and though she'd always known he was incredibly bad for her, now he was like a bad habit she couldn't quite shake. When Callum deigned to let her, she was allowed into his world, in small bite-sized pieces. He had perfected the knack of just keeping her interested. She hated herself for giving in to him.

Take this weekend, for instance. She had resolutely ignored his calls all day Friday, cried off a party that Ffion was going to, claiming a headache, and crashed out in front of the TV with a pizza and a bottle of wine.

But come Saturday, after a desultory morning spent catching up on household chores, and a dull afternoon alone trailing round the shops in Crawley, Emily had let herself into the flat to find three messages from Callum on the answerphone. When she switched on her mobile (which she had purposely left behind), she discovered he'd inundated her with messages.

'*Come on, babe*,' the last message had urged her, '*what else do you have to do tonight but come out clubbing with me?*'

What else indeed? In the end, she'd given in and driven up to his flat in town, where they had made up over a bottle of wine, before dancing the night away at a local grungy club that Callum and his less salubrious friends liked to frequent.

'I promise to be good,' Callum had said as they left the flat. He'd looked so solemn and schoolboyish when he'd said it, Emily couldn't help but laugh.

'You better had be,' she'd said. And then he'd kissed her, and she'd forgotten why she'd been so cross with him in the dizzying intoxication she always felt when he was near.

Callum had been as good as his word, in that he hadn't taken any drugs in her presence, which wasn't to say that he hadn't taken any at all, but it was enough for her to maintain the fiction that all was right with the world.

They had got up late on Sunday, gone for a pub lunch, and though Emily had known she should really have headed back home on Sunday evening, Callum's urgent plea of, 'Stay, babe,' coupled with the thought of another long, lonely evening, was enough to keep her from going back. Maybe that was why she couldn't quite let Callum out of her life. She knew he was bad for her, but he was pure escapism. Maybe she needed that right now. Perhaps it was worth it to avoid the pain of thinking about Dad, though it never felt worth it when the downside was being late for work.

Emily's nerves were jangling as she walked through the door. Mel didn't tolerate slackers on her team, as she put it.

Luckily, Mel was late too this morning, which allowed Emily enough time to get herself a latte and calm down before she started work. She sat down to a pile of paperwork and opened her emails, to find there were still hundreds she hadn't responded to from last week, including one from an ex soap star whose efforts to revive her career by applying for the next series of *Love Shack* looked doomed since she'd got into a racism row with another would-be contestant. Emily groaned loudly. She could feel another late one coming on. It was too bad they were so short-staffed and the secretary she had shared with her colleague had left, but at least working long hours kept her from thinking too much about everything. It was another form of escapism, she supposed, but not quite as satisfactory as shagging an unsuitable boyfriend.

'So that tooth we root-treated last time is still giving you gyp?' Mark asked once Jasmine was ensconced on his dental chair. Her crop top was hitched halfway over her stomach and her hipster jeans sagged below it. She had less of a muffin top and more of a meringue mountain . . . God, it amazed him that someone so foul-mouthed, foully dressed and generally appalling as Jasmine could be deemed worthy of being in the public eye. Once upon a time people actually did something *worthwhile* to be famous. Not any more.

'Too right it is,' whined Jasmine. 'It's bloody painful all the time. Those antibiotics were useless.'

'You do realise that if I can't sort it out this time, I shall have to take the tooth out,' Mark said.

'No way!' Jasmine was horrified.

'I'm sorry,' said Mark, a little nonplussed. 'I did warn you.'

'You can't mess with my teeth,' shrieked Jasmine. 'I've got a contract which says my teeth are all me own.'

'She's got a contract,' growled Jasmine's mother from the sofa. Kayla followed Jasmine everywhere and, Rottweiler-like, was always on hand to defend her daughter's interests.

'Well, if you want a second opinion . . .' This was Mark's get-out clause for all his difficult patients. Sadly, Jasmine had never yet taken him up on the offer, and she wasn't about to now.

'Oh go on then,' she said sulkily.

Mark felt his way round Jasmine's mouth. Despite her brilliant white smile, her teeth were shot to pieces. The dazzling grin covered a multitude of sins to all except her dentist. The rate Jasmine was carrying on, it wouldn't be too long before he provided her with dentures. He prodded around for a while. Jasmine responded when he poked the molar two doors down, but the tooth she was moaning about didn't evince a single response. Which meant it was as dead as a doornail.

'I'm really sorry,' he said. 'Your tooth's died. I'm going to have to pull it out.'

'You can't!' Jasmine shrieked.

'What about her contract?' Kayla demanded. 'You must be able to do something.'

'I'm touched by your faith in me,' said Mark, knowing that sarcasm was completely wasted on these two, 'but even I can't work miracles.'

Jasmine winced dramatically as he gave her the strongest injection he could. Her pain threshold was notoriously low, and this was a back tooth which would take a fair amount of work to get out. Mark toyed with asking Sasha for the right instruments, but as she leaned back against the sink, looking bored and playing with her nails in between taking text messages (even though he had asked her hundreds of times not to), he figured that in the time it would take to explain what he needed, he could have got it all himself. One day, God would take pity on him and send him a decent nurse.

'I can't lose a tooth,' Jasmine wailed. She was clearly not going to take this lying down. 'What about my contract?'

'I'm very sorry,' he said. 'But the tooth has got to come out. I'll make you a bridging unit, which I'll attach to the adjacent teeth. No one will ever know the difference.'

'Are you sure?' Jasmine eyed him suspiciously. 'What if someone finds out?'

'No one will find out,' said Mark. 'Your records are completely confidential.'

'You sure about that?' the Rottweiler jumped in, looking uncertain.

'Yes,' said Mark. 'Now, I have to do something about this tooth. I can't leave it like this.'

Eventually, Jasmine agreed. Luckily, the tooth came out relatively easily, and Mark took some impressions for her crown.

'What if someone sees the gap?' Jasmine demanded as she got down from the chair.

'It's pretty unlikely,' said Mark, 'it's a back tooth, no one is likely to be looking. You could always try not to get photographed for a bit.'

Which was as unlikely as him getting back with Sam, he realised. Jasmine was always splashed over one tabloid or another.

'You'd better be right,' Jasmine said, 'or there will be trouble.'

'I'll bear it in mind,' Mark replied, before showing Jasmine and Kayla out to the desk, where Kerry was chatting animatedly to Tony, Jasmine's third-division footballer boyfriend. Jasmine shot Kerry a dirty look, clicked her fingers at Tony, and swept out imperiously, leaving Kayla to pay. Mark made a mental note to remind Kerry that it wasn't done to flirt with the clientele, before calling his next patient.

Great. It was Mrs O'Leary, or Granny O'Leary as the girls had christened her: an ancient crone and toothless wonder who steadfastly clung to the ill-fitting dentures that her original butcher of a dentist had given her eons ago.

Mark reflected that he must have done something *really* bad in a previous life to deserve Jasmine and Granny O'Leary on the same day. But he couldn't for the life of him think what.

Chapter Three

'You're late,' Katie said as Charlie came through the door. She didn't mean to sound accusing, but she was worn down by a hard day coping with the kids. The boys had been really naughty at bedtime and Molly had only just gone to sleep. The kitchen was still in chaos from tea, and she hadn't even managed to get into the lounge yet to tidy up. She could feel all her good intentions to rekindle their spark leaching out of her. Her plan to cook a candlelit dinner had gone completely to pot.

'What's for tea?' Charlie asked, ignoring her. She *hated* it when he did that.

'Beans on toast.' Katie felt wrong-footed.

'You used to love cooking. You'd always have dinner ready for me,' said Charlie.

'Well, that was before we had Molly,' snapped Katie.

Katie would be the first to admit she was a control freak extraordinaire who wanted everything to be so perfect she made Anthea Turner look positively sluttish. She was the sort of woman who rose at six to clean out her kitchen cupboards, or iron and fold laundry. Charlie always teased her that her favourite room in the house was the large walk-in airing cupboard on the landing, where sheets, pillow cases, towels and blankets all sat neatly side by side in carefully orchestrated rows. White single sheets next to white doubles, coloured singles next to coloured doubles. Everything in its place, and everything easy to find.

It always smelled fresh and wholesome, and Katie would never admit to anyone the illicit pleasure she felt in running her hand over the smooth surfaces of freshly ironed sheets. But it was hard work maintaining such high standards with children in the house, although, by and large, till Molly had come along she had managed. Of late, Katie could feel those standards slipping. She had been so desperate for a third baby, despite Charlie's reservations. Now there were days when even she wondered why.

Charlie had touched a nerve, damn him. In the past Katie *would* have had the house tidy and tea on the table when Charlie walked in. To her that was part of the deal. She was the one at home, after all, it only seemed reasonable to cook the bacon for the person who provided it.

Emily had never got on with that attitude. 'It just seems so regressive,' she'd frequently said to Katie over a glass of wine when Charlie was away on business.

Katie had shrugged her shoulders.

'I don't expect you to understand,' she'd said. 'But if you knew my mum, you would. She put her career above everything: her marriage, her family. It tore our family apart. I'm never going to do that.'

Katie had had feminism shoved down her throat from an early age, and was sufficiently her mother's daughter to buy into the career dream until she'd met and fallen for Charlie. The minute she knew she wanted to have children with him was the day Katie said goodbye to her career. She was not going to make the same mistakes as her mum. Her children and husband would always come first. The trouble was, no one had told her how hard that would be. Or that she'd feel a small part of herself dying every day, subsumed into becoming someone's wife, someone's mother. What had happened to Katie? No one really cared any more . . .

'Let me know when it's ready,' said Charlie, grabbing an apple

35

from the fruit bowl. 'I've just got to go online and check some deals out.'

'What now?' Katie was dismayed. She was rather hoping that Charlie might join her in the kitchen and share a glass of wine with her as she cooked, like they used to do. She knew she should be glad about Charlie's recent promotion, as it meant more money and security, but his job was beginning to take over their life. The company seemed to be expanding at an alarming rate. Charlie's whole topic of conversation these days seemed to be about acquisitions and mergers, and he was away on business more than he was home.

'Five minutes, tops,' he said, already heading for the stairs.

Katie sighed. The chances were she wouldn't see him for another hour.

'I'll just get on with the tea, then,' she said disconsolately.

'Okay,' said Charlie. 'At least it's not chips.'

'Why?' Katie had a feeling she knew where this was going. Charlie had been having little digs for weeks now.

'Oh, nothing,' said Charlie sheepishly, stopping on the half-landing

'Don't do that,' retorted Katie. 'Tell me what you meant.'

Charlie looked a little embarrassed. 'I was only joking.'

'About what?' Katie's tone was icy. Even Charlie, who had the skin of a rhino, picked up on it.

'It's just . . . Since Molly . . .' Charlie was looking like he'd rather be anywhere than here. 'You didn't used to be – it's just that – well, you're looking a bit more cuddly these days.'

'You mean I'm fat.' Kate felt as if she had been punched in the stomach.

'No. No. Not fat.' Charlie was desperately trying to recover the situation. 'It's – well, I mean, after the boys you lost weight much more quickly. Anyway, cuddly's good. You know I don't like skinny women.'

His voice trailed off. And it was true. In the past she had

36

managed to shed the baby weight in a few months, but this time around it seemed not to want to budge.

'You think I'm fat.' It was a statement. Not a question.

'Nooo – not fat exactly, but you have to admit it, love, you're a – a tad on the lardy side. Nothing that a few weeks on a diet won't cure.'

The comment was delivered in a manner that was clearly intended to be light and humorous, but the result was anything but.

Katie stood open-mouthed as Charlie disappeared upstairs. Not for the first time she wondered if workload was the thing that really kept him late at the office . . .

'How was your day?' Rob greeted Mark as he came through the front door.

It had been a long day and Mark was glad to be home, even if it wasn't quite the home he wanted.

'Bloody awful. You?'

'Oh, you know. Kids running riot. Kids taking drugs. Kids being suspended. The usual.' Rob's job as head of history at the local comp gave him nearly as much pleasure as Mark's job gave him.

'Fancy a beer?' Mark kept resolving that he wasn't going to drink this early in the week. And kept giving in.

'Thought you'd never ask,' said Rob. 'Pint at the Hookers?'

The Hookers' real name was The Boxer's Arms, but because of the propensity of rugby players who went in there, it was commonly known as the Hookers. Although urban myth had it that it was once a knocking shop – a myth that Barry, the urbane landlord, did very little to dispel.

'Just let me wash my patients' spit off my face and get changed,' said Mark, 'and then I'm all yours.'

Ten minutes later they were propping up the bar and putting the world to rights.

'The usual, gentlemen?' Barry already had their pints lined up for them. 'You're a bit late tonight, if I may say so.'

Bloody hell, Mark thought in dismay, I'm becoming such a regular the barman knows what time I usually come in. How the hell did that happen?

'If we're not careful, we're going to end up becoming permanent fixtures,' Mark said glumly, looking round to see the usual regulars transfixed to their usual spots. Is that how people already saw them?

'So?' said Rob. 'I like it here. It's my kind of pub.'

'You know what's going to happen to us,' Mark said moodily, staring into his pint.

'No, what?' Rob was scanning the bar for possible talent. Rather a waste of effort considering most of the regulars were middle-aged men, but, ever the optimist, Rob never liked to miss out on any opportunity that came his way. Mark envied that optimism and the confidence that went along with it.

'We're still going to be sitting here in ten years' time,' said Mark. He paused to listen to a song on the jukebox. 'It's like this song – the laughs in the late-night lock-in will fade away and we'll have nothing left but sad, pathetic memories.'

'And your point is?' said Rob.

'Well, look at us. We've already been drinking in here for years. We stay here any longer, we'll end up fossilised.'

'You know your trouble?' asked Rob.

'Nope, but I have a feeling you're going to tell me,' replied Mark.

'You need to get out more. It's time you faced up to the truth. You're wasting your time with Sam. She's gone for good. Time you moved on, mate.'

'Yeah, right,' Mark responded with a wry smile. 'And this is really the place to do that.'

'It has been known to happen,' said Rob, tapping his nose and looking smug.

'When was that then?' teased Barry, earwigging their conversation as he wiped down the bar. 'The dark ages?'

'You remember those two art students who used to come in here a while back?' Rob said.

'What, the short tarty one and the goth?' Barry looked impressed.

'Yup,' said Rob. 'Didn't you wonder why they stopped coming in?'

'I thought they'd just finished their course,' said Barry.

'Nope,' said Rob, 'they just couldn't cope with the rejection. Once you've had a taste of the Robster, everything else pales by comparison.'

'That's right, Rob,' said Mark, 'and it's got nothing to do with the fact they found out what a bastard you are and never want to see you again.'

'You're just jealous,' laughed Rob.

'I keep telling you,' said Mark, 'I'm happy to be single.'

'Now that's where you are so wrong,' said Rob. 'It's not normal for someone to be celibate as long as you have been. You need to listen up and hone your seduction skills.'

'And how should I do that?' said Mark with amusement as he glanced round the pub. 'Now you've chased the art students away, I don't exactly see them queuing up.'

'Not here,' said Rob. 'You really must pay attention to your Uncle Rob and learn from a master. Dancing classes is where it's all at. There are tons of single women there. Come ballroom dancing with me and I *guarantee* you'll get laid.'

'I do want to actually like a woman when I go to bed with her,' said Mark. 'Besides, I don't want anyone but Sam.'

'Yes, you do,' said Rob. 'You just don't know it yet. Come on. Live dangerously for once.'

Mark sipped his pint and looked round the Hookers. Warning signs littered the pub. Paranoid Pete (catchphrase: 'They're watching us, you know') was swaying ominously over a pint. He

39

appeared to be talking to a wall. In another corner he spotted Jim 'n' John, who were so well-known in the Hookers, people had forgotten which was which now. Their beer bellies (twice the size they'd been when Mark first met them) were the fruits of the time they'd both been drinking there. Oh God. This was his and Rob's fate if they weren't careful.

'Oh go on then,' said Mark. 'I suppose it will make a change from a night in the pub.'

'That's the attitude,' said Rob, 'and you're wrong about the song, you know.'

'I am?'

'Yup. I've got a much better theme tune for us.'

'Which is?'

'"The Boys are Back in Town",' said Rob, raising his pint.

Katie paused from cleaning the bath, keeping a weather ear out for Molly, who could still just about be relied on to nap in the morning, allowing Katie to get on with some household chores. She looked around at the chaos of the bathroom (one day her sons would eventually learn not to miss) and sighed.

Katie had neglected the bathroom of late, and it showed. Another by-product of living with a mother with her head in the clouds had been a childhood spent in chaos. Katie, a type-A personality if ever there was one, hated the messy disorder of the place she had called home, and had spent the best part of her adult life ensuring she didn't replicate it.

Katie had just about managed to keep ahead of the game with two children, but the arrival of Molly had made it that much harder. Sometimes she was up at six in order to get the vacuuming done, and she frequently went to bed at 1 a.m. having got stuck into mopping the kitchen floor. The sheer exhaustion of keeping up with it all was taking its toll, mainly in the bedroom, where she frequently crawled in so dog-tired that even if Charlie had shown any interest, she would have been completely unable to rise to the challenge. No wonder he'd lost interest. Perhaps all that they needed was for Katie to initiate things a bit more. Trying to cook a candlelit meal the other night hadn't worked, it was true, but that was because it had been a spur-of-the-moment thing. She should have planned it properly. She'd try to do it again, on a Saturday night, when the kids were in bed and Charlie didn't have to worry so much about work.

Feeling a bit better, Katie got up from her kneeling position and went to pick up the bleach so she could start cleaning the loo. Damn. She'd run out. She ran downstairs to the loo there, but that was empty too. When Molly got up, she'd have to go and get some more.

Molly conveniently chose that moment to wake up so Katie wrapped her up warmly, popped her in the buggy and walked down the road towards the High Street. She and Charlie hadn't quite afforded a house on the Hill, the posh part of town (much to Marilyn Caldwell's sniffy disgust). But Katie liked their house, it was homely and comfortable, and close to town, and even on cold February days like today she liked to walk.

The advantage of living in a small town like this was that you were never far from anywhere. The disadvantage was that sometimes it was like living under a microscope and everyone knew your business. Invariably, if Katie met someone she knew on the High Street she would be regaled with the sordid details of some petty scandal, or told where she and Charlie had just been on holiday. Once, an acquaintance had even come and congratulated her on a nonexistent pregnancy. It could be very stifling. There were days when she just longed to get on a train and go somewhere, anywhere. Just to get away from where she was.

It wasn't just the feeling of being trapped in domesticity that was bothering her either. Although Charlie had apologised for the comments he'd made about her weight, his words still rankled. Especially as she knew he was right. From a size ten in her pre-children days, Katie had ballooned up to sixteen at one point, and was just heading back towards a fourteen when she had fallen pregnant with Molly. Now, just over a year later, she was hovering around the sixteen mark, and her exhaustion meant the idea of ever getting any exercise in was a complete joke. Her smallish frame didn't help. If she had been tall and buxom, she could have carried the excess weight, but now she felt like a little round barrel. Her fair hair flopped languidly around her shoulders. For practical reasons it would be better to tie it up, but then she risked exposing her double chin. Charlie was right. She *had* let herself go.

As she approached the corner shop her eye was caught by a poster.

Tempted to Tango?
Ready to Rumba?
Can't wait to Waltz?
Come to Isabella's Dancing Classes on
Tuesday Evenings at 8–9.30 p.m.
Beginners welcome

Tempted? Was she ever. In her early twenties, Katie had spent a happy summer learning how to waltz. She had been young, carefree, in her first job in London, where she knew no one. Week after glorious week in a summer, filled in her memory only with sunshine and happiness, Katie had gone along to dance, and had discovered that she was rather good at it. Then she had met Charlie through a mutual acquaintance. Nothing much had happened between them till she'd persuaded him to come dancing too. Katie was fond of saying he literally whisked her off her feet. And when the summer ended in the tragic and sudden death of Katie's beloved father, it had seemed natural to fall into Charlie's arms and seek comfort there. Within the year they'd been married, but somehow they'd never gone dancing again.

She stared at the notice. Perhaps she could give it a whirl.

Maybe she should ask Charlie if he wanted to come along. She knew her mum would babysit for them, and it was certainly a way of spending more time together. Besides, if he made any objection, she could always say she was doing it to lose weight. That should shut him up.

'Ballroom dancing? What, like on *Strictly Come Dancing*?' Emily collapsed in fits of giggles on Katie's comfortable sofa at the idea. It always did her good to come here. Katie's house was so serene, a haven of ordered domesticity which provided a sharp contrast to the chaos of Emily's own life. She had no idea how much effort went into keeping a four-bedroom house inhabited by three males so tidy, but given how much mess Callum always seemed to make in her place, Emily guessed it was rather a lot.

'Yes, why not?' said Katie.

'And you want me to come along?' asked Emily. 'What about Charlie?'

'I did ask him,' admitted Katie, 'but he didn't want to come. Will you come with me? I used to go years ago and it's great fun.'

'So you'll know what you're doing, then,' said Emily. 'Me, I've got two left feet.'

'Oh go on,' said Katie. 'I need someone to keep me company. Anyway, what else are you going to do on a dull February evening?'

What else indeed? Emily thought over her options. Tuesdays usually involved getting dragged to one of Ffion's PR bashes, but Emily had scarcely seen her since Jasmine's book launch. Ffion was notoriously touchy, and had clearly taken offence that Emily had gone home early on that occasion. Not that Emily minded all that much. To be honest, it made a nice change not to have to hang around sweaty nightclubs. There was always Callum, of course. Although, since their loved-up weekend she'd scarcely seen him either. That, too, she was finding peculiarly restful. It was always exciting being around Callum, but also incredibly stressful. You never knew what to expect. And of late the excitement didn't seem to be counteracting the stress all that much. Which only left –

'Is working late a good enough excuse?' Emily knew the answer to that question.

'No, it is not,' said Katie firmly. 'You've used that one on me far too often recently. It's about time you got a life.'

'Yeah, you're right,' replied Emily. 'I must admit, the thought of doing an all-nighter at work doesn't hold the same appeal it once did.'

'And what about Callum?' Katie asked. 'Does he hold the same appeal?'

Emily sighed and sipped her wine.

'Now there you have me,' she said. 'I just don't know any more. When I'm with him it's great – well, most of the time. Although he was absolutely useless about Dad. He says he doesn't do that kind of stuff very well.'

'Didn't that make you want to deck him?' Katie said. 'I don't think I could put up with that. Charlie was truly fantastic when my dad died. He took a week off work to be with me, and was really brilliant to my mum. And he spent weeks afterwards giving me little treats to cheer me up. Flowers, chocolates. That sort of thing. He even remembered the anniversary, and took time off to visit Dad's grave with me. I couldn't have got through it without him.'

'I know, I know,' said Emily. 'You're right. Callum uses me horribly. And when I'm not with him I'm fretting about him not texting me, or worrying that he's flirting with some other woman. And then we go out and I'm anxious the whole time in case he gets too drunk and does something stupid or comes to meet me from work high as a kite.'

'He hasn't, has he?' Katie looked suitably horrified.

'Once, although he promised not to do it again,' admitted Emily, 'but I can't really trust him not to.'

'What you need', declared Katie, 'is a change of scene. Come on, you're always banging on about how much you hate going up to town. Spend some proper time here once in a while. Get to know people round here. It might do you good.'

'I thought you hated it here,' said Emily with some surprise.

'Well, I'm here *too* much,' said Katie. 'I could do with an injection from the metropolis once in a while. But you, you need to take a break from all that. So come on, cut me some slack here. I'll feel too much like an idiot if I go to dance classes on my own. After all this time, I probably can't put one foot in front of the other any more. Please come with me.'

'I am *so* going to regret this,' said Emily. 'But go on, you've twisted my arm. I'll come.'

'Great,' said Katie. 'That's settled then.'

'Yes,' Emily agreed, taking another sip of wine, 'so it is.'

Chapter Four

'*Bienvenida*, welcome,' a small dark woman ushered them in. An off-the-shoulder top clung to the contours of her lean body and her red skirt swished and swirled as she moved on gold open-toed sandals with a heel, which Katie coveted immediately. With her long, raven-black hair tumbling down her back, and her gold hoop earrings, the woman resembled a glamorous gypsy queen. She motioned Katie and Emily to follow her into a large studio lined with tables and chairs. The lights were dimmed, the Blue Danube was playing in the background and couples were already dancing. Katie and Emily exchanged worried glances. They all looked scarily proficient.

'You must be Isabella,' said Katie. 'I'm Katie Caldwell and this is Emily Henderson.'

'Nice to meet you,' said Isabella, with the faintest hint of a foreign lilt. She looked part Spanish, or Portuguese perhaps. Katie already felt clumsy beside her, and wondered whether she'd made a terrible mistake. Charlie had teased her mercilessly about going dancing, conveniently seeming to forget that at one time he'd enjoyed going himself. He was spending the week at his company's headquarters in Amsterdam discussing a potential takeover bid, so Katie had organised a babysitter. At least she didn't have to put up with Charlie's ribbing tonight.

'Right, first things first,' said Isabella. 'Have either of you done any dancing before?'

'I can waltz after a fashion,' said Katie, 'and I know how to rumba. But it's been a long time.'

'Me, I can't dance to save my life,' admitted Emily cheerfully.

'*Excelente*. We'll put you both in the beginners' section for now. Katie, if you find it too easy there, we'll think of moving you on. Have you ever tried for any medals?'

'Oh God no,' said Katie. 'I'm more of an amateur enthusiast.'

'We cater for all sorts here,' Isabella reassured them. 'Though be warned, there are some who take it *very* seriously.'

Having extricated their fee for the evening, Isabella bustled off to deal with some other new arrivals.

The women sat down and looked around the room. Predictably, there were more women than men. The dearth of decent ones ensured they all at least had partners. The room was lined with women sitting alone.

'Oh God,' said Emily, 'this feels like the school disco all over again. I am so going to feel like a wallflower tonight.'

'You'll be fine,' Katie assured her. 'Though I'd be a bit cagey about what you tell people about yourself, if I were you. In my experience a lot of these things tend to be full of sad blokes on the pull.'

'What, you mean like those two?' Emily nodded towards the door where two men had just entered. One of them was rather plumpish and balding, though the other –

'Actually, the one on the left looks quite dishy, don't you think?' Katie nudged her friend. 'If I wasn't married already, I wouldn't say no.'

The one on the left was tall and dark, and looked ill at ease. Unlike his friend, who strutted confidently into the room and looked around him with a cheeky grin, eyeing up the talent. As if aware of the women's scrutiny he whispered to his friend then turned towards them and winked.

Katie and Emily snorted into their hands.

'I see what you mean,' said Emily. 'Right, my name is Amelia Earhart and I'm a pilot.'

'Aren't you a bit lost, then?' said Katie.

'You're not the first to say so,' Emily replied. 'Come on, I think it's time we got going.'

Isabella was busy rounding people up and organising them into groups. Katie and Emily followed her.

'God, I hope I don't make too much of a fool of myself,' said Emily. 'I have a feeling I might regret this.'

Mark had been having similar thoughts all day. He had very nearly cried off when he'd got home from a hideous day at work. Despite accepting his decision the previous week to pull out her tooth, Jasmine had put in a complaint to Head Office to say that not only was she unhappy with Mark's treatment, but he had been 'really brutal, know what I mean?' It wasn't the first time she'd made a complaint, and as she didn't really have any grounds to do so, Mark was intending to ignore it, but it was tedious nonetheless and he could have done without it.

However, Rob was having none of it when Mark tried to get out of going.

'You're coming out tonight, and that's that,' said Rob. 'So quit moaning and get your coat.'

Mark felt even more ill at ease when they walked through the door and saw the place was heaving with women, many of whom were dancing already. Rob had insisted Mark couldn't go in the jeans and trainers in which he felt comfortable, so he'd dug out a pair of smart trousers he barely ever wore and a pair of ancient brogues. Rob himself was dressed in black chinos, a dark blue shirt and tie, and black shoes with a Cuban heel. He had piled on the aftershave, evidently hoping to make a conquest. Mark looked around the room. There were hardly any other men there, so Rob wasn't likely to have much competition. But it made Mark feel more self-conscious than ever. He was going to stick out like a sore thumb.

Rob had no such worries. He swaggered through the room, smiling at the women he knew, and trying to catch the eyes of those he didn't. He nudged Mark.

'See those women over there,' he said. 'Gagging for it. They've been watching us since we came in the room.'

Mark glanced over at the women in question: a slim, dark brunette with a smart bob wearing a sleek black dress, and a rather plumper blonde, dressed in a frumpy skirt and baggy top. She was also quite pretty, and would have probably looked slimmer if she'd been standing up straight. Rob nodded over to them, and then turned back to Mark. 'Keep 'em keen, that's the trick of it. I've got them interested, and now I'm going to ignore them. They're *bound* to come running.'

Mark wasn't so sure. The women had gone off into peals of giggles, and he had the uncomfortable feeling that he was being laughed at.

'Oh, and a word of advice,' added Rob. 'If you do start chatting someone up, for God's sake don't tell her you've got kids. She'll run a mile.'

Thinking that the chance of even talking to a woman was about zero, Mark nodded absently. He wished he was anywhere but here.

'Ooh, I didn't have you down as a dancer,' a familiar voice squawked in his ear. Mark turned round. A tarty-looking blonde was eyeing him speculatively. Where did he know her from? Working in the same town he lived in meant he was always running into people he vaguely knew, and he could never work out if he had filled their root canal or met them over the fish counter in Sainsbury's.

'Your Beth looking forward to going to the Isle of Wight?' Oh. Right. School. Mark delved into the furthest recesses of his brain. She had a son in Beth's year. What was her name?

'Yes, I think so,' said Mark politely, though he couldn't remember Sam mentioning the trip.

'It's about time I made an appointment,' the woman continued. 'You'll be telling me off again about the state of my molars.'

Oh bugger. A patient as well.

'I'm a bit booked up at present,' said Mark, 'but give the surgery a ring. Diana may be able to find you a cancellation.'

Mandy Allwick. That was it. A single mum whose predatory nature was renowned. That was all he needed. Maybe he should palm her off on Rob. It would serve him right for getting Mark into this mess.

'Save a dance for me, Doctor Davies,' was Mandy's parting shot, as she wandered over to the double doors at the end of the room, where a petite dark-haired woman was sorting people into groups.

Forbearing to mention that he wasn't technically a doctor – calling dentists doctor was a stupid fashion that had come over from America, along with too much litigation – Mark got up and followed Rob into the crowd.

This was going to be a long evening.

'Tonight, *chicos*, we will start with the social foxtrot,' announced Isabella with a smile. 'For those of you who've come for the first time, it is quite simple and is danced in four/four time. Take your partners – if you are two women one of you will need to learn the man's steps, but remember it is always the man who leads.'

'That had better be you,' said Emily to Katie, who was suddenly feeling ridiculously nervous about the whole thing. 'After all, you've done it before.'

'For the social foxtrot, you need to learn the cuddle hold,' continued Isabella. 'The man places his right arm round the lady, and rests his hand under her right shoulder. The lady puts her left hand on the man's shoulder and holds the man's right hand in her left hand like so.' She demonstrated with a baby-faced lad who looked nearly young enough to be her son, before going round the room and checking everyone was in the right position.

'Now, the man leads off first with his left foot, to two beats of music, while the lady steps back with her right. Then the man takes a step to the right, the lady to the left, the man's left foot closes to the right, and the woman's right foot to the left.'

'I don't think I'll remember a word of that,' muttered Emily.

'It's okay,' said Katie, 'just follow me.'

Miraculously, mainly thanks to the fact that Katie clearly knew what she was doing, Emily did get it right, and was able to follow the next steps, which involved her stepping forward with her left foot, then stepping to the right, before closing with the left foot.

'Right, now we put it together,' announced Isabella with a clap. 'I will clap out the time and you dance the steps. Slow step forwards, quick to the side, quick and close, slow step backwards, quick to the side, quick and close.'

'I'll never get the hang of this,' said Emily, muddling up her lefts and rights and stepping on Katie's toes.

'Yes you will,' assured Katie, 'you just need practice, that's all.'

After twenty minutes, Emily wasn't convinced. Once they'd mastered the basic steps, Isabella had them trying it to music, and then she added in another set of steps which involved turns as well, and Emily got completely lost. Particularly as she'd had to change partners, and none of them bar one were as good as Katie, so she kept getting it wrong. She was sweating profusely and feeling like a total idiot. In her efforts to get it right, she had had her feet stamped on, and done her fair share of feet stamping too. She knew that dancing wasn't her thing, but she'd had no idea how little natural rhythm she actually had, or how hard it was keeping time to the music. That was until she was apprised of the fact in no uncertain terms by a gay dancer, who was training at the local dance school and had only come along to expand his repertoire. His were the only toes she'd trod on deliberately after hearing him mutter 'bloody amateurs!' one too many times under his breath.

Eventually the torture ended and Isabella announced it was time for social dancing, 'So you can put it all together.' Apparently this meant pairing up with just one other person. Emily looked at Katie, whom she'd been watching gliding around the room with a serenity she felt deeply envious of. Despite her post-baby weight gain, Katie had the natural poise and grace Emily lacked.

'I'd say I'd partner you,' she said, 'but I don't want to be the cause of hospitalising you.'

'You're not that bad,' Katie grinned.

'You know I am,' answered Emily. 'So stop being nice. We'll have to find someone else decent for you to dance with.'

'Ladies, would you care to dance?' The plumpish bloke from earlier on was pushing his way over, with his good-looking friend.

Katie and Emily looked at each other uncertainly.

'Please, we don't bite,' said the good-looking one. 'Besides, you have to take pity on us. I'm being chased by a raging nymphomaniac, and I need to seek sanctuary.'

Katie laughed. She had been watching Mandy Allwick in hot pursuit of their new companions all evening.

'Well, if you need rescuing from Mandy, I think we might be able to help,' she said.

'Oh, you know her?' Mark asked.

Katie pulled a face.

'For my sins.'

Mark was about to chip in with something about Beth being at school with Mandy's son, and then, remembering Rob's strictures, thought better of it.

'As it's your first time,' Rob whispered to Mark, 'I'll give you the pretty one, and I'll have the one with the fat thighs.'

Mark, who thought the not-so-pretty one had seemed rather nice, smiled awkwardly at Emily and said, 'Shall we?'

'If you like,' said Emily. She felt awkward too. The new arrival was even better-looking close up. He had rather soulful eyes, she thought. There was a kind of brooding intensity to him that she found appealing. She felt a brief flickering of interest, which she dismissed instantly. She was here for fun, not to pick up men.

Katie was fuming. She'd overheard Rob's whispered aside, and her poor opinion of him, based soundly as it was from two minutes' observation of his cockiness as he came into the room, had increased a hundredfold. She would have liked to tell him where to get off, but she thought Emily deserved a decent shot at his friend, who seemed altogether nicer.

'The one with the fat thighs heard you, by the way,' she said, as Rob took her by the hand and started to quickstep.

'Oh.' Rob had the grace to look sheepish. 'Did I say fat thighs? I meant to say gorgeous eyes.'

'Of course you did,' said Katie drily. The cheek of him. He was so sure a pathetic compliment would make up for insulting her. Still, he was so sure of himself, maybe she could have a bit of fun with that . . .

'Do you come here often?' Mark decided that a mocking approach was the best way to deal with the situation. It was so long since he'd asked a woman to dance, and the hour he had spent trying not to trip over people's feet had made him very aware that he was a contender for the most useless dancer in the room. But for the first time since Sam had left he felt the spark of interest in another woman. Mark wasn't sure if it was the determined look that had come across her face while she was listening to Isabella's instructions, or the rather panicky eye rolls that had set in when she had clearly forgotten them again. Or it might have been the way that she pealed with laughter when he stepped on her toes. He was so grateful that she hadn't slapped him.

'This is my first time,' she said, laughing again, her whole face lighting up. 'So be gentle with me.'

'If you're gentle in return,' Mark batted back. 'The name's Mark, by the way.'

'Emily,' she replied. 'You honestly can't be a worse dancer than I am,' she added, as Mark took hold of her. His hands were sweating, and despite trying to remember Isabella's admonitions about relaxing, he felt stiff and awkward.

'I don't know about that,' said Mark as he stepped on her toes once again. 'Sorry. You see what I mean.'

'It's okay, really,' she said, 'I think we're probably quits on that front.'

'This is horrible, though, isn't it?' said Mark, desperately trying to maintain a closed position and keep four/four time. 'I don't know why I'm here.'

Emily laughed again as she realised that once more they were out of step with each other.

'Just dance like no one's looking,' she said, as they both paused for breath.

'Do you think that will work?' asked Mark, looking around. 'I can't help feeling everyone's staring at us.'

'I'm sure they're not,' said Emily, 'but if we dance as if they're not, it doesn't matter, does it?'

'Dance like no one's looking,' said Mark. 'Where have I heard that before?'

'On *Green Wing*?' suggested Emily. 'That's where I heard it first.'

'Oh, I love *Green Wing*,' Mark replied.

'Me too,' said Emily. 'It's one of those proverb-type things. No one knows who wrote it. It goes like this:

Dance like no one's looking.

Love like you've never been hurt.

Work like you don't have to

Live like it's heaven on earth.

* * *

54

I think that's rather lovely, don't you?'

'Dancing like no one's looking is probably the best recipe I can think of for getting through this excruciating experience,' said Mark.

'Charming,' she replied.

'Oh God, that didn't come out right,' said Mark. 'It's not all.'

'It's not all what?' Emily teased.

'Excruciating,' said Mark. 'I mean, you're not.'

'Glad to hear it,' said Emily. She felt secretly flattered. She hadn't come here on the pull, but as they continued their awkward trotting around the room, she reflected that it was nice that someone other than Callum had showed an interest in her. However vague, it was a very welcome boost to her ego. Even if he did keep treading on her toes.

Chapter Five

'The name's Rob Dylan, by the way,' Rob said as he expertly led Katie round the room. Irritatingly he seemed to be rather a good dancer, 'as in Bob's younger, more good-looking brother.'

'Of course,' said Katie. 'I spotted the resemblance instantly.'

Rob was a bit of a revelation actually. Katie's previous experience of dancing lessons had been fun, but had not exactly filled her with confidence about the dancing abilities of the majority of the male of the species. Charlie wasn't bad, but their wedding day was probably the last time they'd danced together. Not only could Rob dance, but he knew how to lead her properly too. Which meant that, rusty as she was, she felt she was actually dancing the foxtrot the way it was meant to be danced. With Rob, she was gliding round the room with perfect confidence. For a few fleeting moments she felt graceful again. She was grateful to him for that at least, even if he was a bit of a twat.

'I'm Katie Caldwell,' she said. 'And I bet your brother doesn't dance as well as you do.'

'Nah,' said Rob. 'But he sings a bit better.'

Katie laughed. Dancing with Rob was turning out to be a lot more fun than she'd expected. Actually, she hadn't laughed so much in ages, she suddenly thought ruefully. When had she and Charlie stopped laughing together?

'Has anyone told you, you have a lovely smile,' said Rob, pulling her slightly closer than was strictly necessary.

'Yes,' said Katie firmly. 'You did.' She had been going to say, 'my husband', but then a mischievous desire stopped her. Rob clearly couldn't help himself. He was a serial flirt who thought he was God's gift to women. He really needed nipping in the bud instantly, but it wouldn't hurt to string him along a little bit. Just for fun.

'So I did,' said Rob. 'And did I mention your gorgeous eyes?'

'Hmm, I seem to remember you mentioning my thighs,' said Katie. What was this guy like? He couldn't seriously be thinking she'd have forgotten his earlier comments.

For a minute, Rob looked slightly nonplussed, but he recovered himself well.

'That was before I had stared into your gorgeous eyes,' he said, kissing her hand gallantly as the dance came to an end.

'Yes, that'll be it,' Katie said, with only the barest hint of sarcasm.

People were milling about chatting together, or heading for the pub next door. It was really time she got going. Katie wasn't used to staying out late midweek, and with Charlie away it was harder than normal to get herself out of bed in the morning and organise the kids. She needed an early night.

'You're coming next door for a drink.' It was a statement, not a question. Rob was steering Katie towards the door in a rather well-practised fashion. Despite herself, she couldn't help admiring his ridiculous self-confidence.

'I don't think so,' said Katie. 'I really have to get on.'

'Oh yes you are,' said Rob, 'you just don't know it yet. Expect the unexpected. That's my motto.'

'Well, how's this for unexpected?' said Katie. 'A woman saying no to you.'

'I wasn't chatting you up,' said Rob.

'You so were,' said Katie. 'And I'm not the slightest bit interested.'

'Don't flatter yourself, darling,' Rob replied. 'You're not my type.'

'And what's your type then?' Katie was furious. Which was ridiculous. Why should she care what he thought of her?

'Thin,' was the hurtful rejoinder.

Katie stood with her mouth open. The cheek of him.

'Well, you're hardly likely to win Mr Universe, are you?'

They glared at each other for a second.

'Are you coming next door for a drink?' Mark and Emily came up. Emily looked flushed and pretty. Her slimness accentuated Katie's curves. Katie wasn't normally the jealous type, but suddenly, next to Emily, she felt like a walrus.

'No, I don't think I am,' said Katie. 'It's time I was off.'

'Me too,' said Emily. 'I've got an early start in the morning.'

'Will we see you ladies here again next week?' Rob asked.

It was all Katie and Emily could do to keep straight faces. He was so ridiculously pompous. Despite her irritation, Katie realised it was hard to stay cross with someone who was clearly so deluded about his charms.

'Maybe,' said Katie. 'We'll have to see.'

'So you're not dancing again?' It was clear from the look on his face that this was not the answer Rob was expecting. He looked like a disappointed spaniel.

'Depends who's asking,' said Katie in an outrageously flirty, mischievous manner, before she and Emily made a bolt for it, laughing like demons.

'I think that went well,' said Rob, watching them go.

'And you've worked that out how?' said Mark. 'They've both just left. And they were laughing at us.'

'Sure sign they fancy us. Besides, you know my motto,' said Rob, touching his nose with a conspiratorial grin. 'Expect the unexpected. Don't you worry, they'll be back. Like I said, they're gagging for it. I can tell.'

*   *   *

'How dare he!' Katie was still apparently brooding on Rob's words about her weight the next day when Emily rang her to see if she'd calmed down yet. 'I mean, obviously I don't care what that idiot Rob thinks, but – first Charlie told me I'd put on weight and now that prat says I've got fat thighs. I must be enormous.'

Emily made soothing noises down the phone while glancing anxiously at her watch. She had a mountain of stuff to shift before the end of the day, and having rung her soap star and discovered what she'd *actually* said about the black girl she was meant to be sharing a room with on *Love Shack* was somewhat worse than even the papers had inferred, Emily had a feeling she might be up all night sorting out the mess. She really didn't have time for a long chat. But Katie always listened to her troubles, so it seemed mean not to do the same. The problem was, Katie had spent so long at home, she'd forgotten what it was like to be in a busy workplace and not have time to make personal calls. Emily looked across the corridor at her boss's office. In a moment, she felt sure that Mel would be on her like a ton of bricks for chatting during office time.

'Liar,' said Katie. 'Thanks for humouring your best friend. I do know I have to lose some weight. But it's not as if he's God's gift, is it?'

'Hardly,' said Emily.

'Mind you, his friend was nice,' said Katie. 'You looked *very* cosy together.'

'We were not, as you put it, cosy,' said Emily. 'Besides, I've got Callum. Why would I look elsewhere?'

'Why indeed?' said Katie with just the barest hint of irony.

'Oh shut up,' said Emily. 'Look, I've got to go, Mel is exiting her office and heading my way. So the burning questions is: are we going again next week?'

'I'll let you know,' said Katie, and put the phone down.

Katie stared out of the window at her neatly ordered garden. Why had she let Rob get under her skin? Was it because he'd said the same thing as Charlie had about her weight? Or was there something more to it? She shook her head. Thinking about it was a waste of energy. She had a house to clean, a baby to feed, children to pick up from school and dinner to cook. Besides, Charlie was going to be home on Friday, which gave her the perfect opportunity to have a romantic evening in with him. Time she got on and started planning it properly.

Rob wound up his Year Ten lesson on Hitler. Sometimes it felt like the only subject he taught was the Second World War. A whole generation of children were growing up to whom history simply meant the Tudors and Hitler. Oh, and the slave trade. It made him despair.

'Got a hot date tonight, sir?' Matt Sadler, one of Rob's more irritating students, piped up in the kerfuffle that followed the end of the lesson.

'None of your business,' said Rob, picking up his books.

'Ooh, are you sure?' Matt was one of those who just wouldn't leave it alone. He nudged one of his mates and whispered something they both clearly found funny. 'Only my mate's sister fancies you.'

'Well she's clearly a woman of taste,' said Rob, resisting the urge to throw a piece of chalk at him. When Rob had been at school, that's what his Maths teacher, Mr Coombs, would have done. But in these more touchy-feely times, should Rob even contemplate doing something that might cause a moment's misery to one of his charges, he'd end up explaining himself before some snotty tribunal. So instead he swept out of the classroom, ignoring the wolf-whistles and giggles that followed his departure.

Rob shivered. However irritating the likes of Matt Sadler might be, he would never dream of actually throwing the chalk. In the old days, the days when he was a student teacher and he and Suzie had been together, he would have been much more reckless. But that was then and this was now.

Suzie. He hadn't thought about her in years. Maybe Mark was right. That Levellers song in the pub the other night – "Fifteen Years", wasn't it? – should be their theme tune. He was going to end up a sad, lonely old drunk, sobbing into his pint.

Rob entered the staffroom feeling a bit odd. He wasn't normally this introspective, what had got into him this morning? What he needed was half an hour's sit down and a cup of coffee. He was actually gasping for a fag, but the whole school was now a smoke-free zone. Soon he'd be joining his Year Eights behind the bike sheds.

Rob made himself a coffee and sat down in an uncomfortable ancient chair shoved in the corner of the staffroom. Thanks to Matt he was too late to join in with the conversations already in progress. Not that he felt much like chatting with the twittering women who ran Modern Languages and spent most of their breaks moaning about how unfair it was that the PE department were always trying to muscle in on their lesson time. And he'd had one too many conversations about the latest views on the Big Bang theory with Andy Peacock, head of Physics, just recently.

In the good old days, when he'd first started teaching, you wouldn't have been able to see from one end of the room to the other through the fug of smoke. Now, of course, the diehards like him were among the two per cent of the population made to feel like pariahs.

He leaned back in his chair and shut his eyes for a moment. Katie's face floated in front of him. How odd was that? Why was he thinking about her? Her and her fat thighs. He tried to dismiss her from his thoughts, but Katie's face stubbornly refused to go away. Then it came to him.

Katie reminded him of Suzie. Granted, Katie was much plumper, but there was something about her that was so like Suzie it made him wince. Perhaps it was her fair hair – or her petite form. Maybe it was that bright, joyous laugh. Suzie had laughed like that. She had been full of fun and life and *joie de vivre*. Until that day. Then all the light and love had gone out of her. Gone out of them. Rob tried not to think about all that any more. But damn it, Katie had brought it back.

This would never do. Rob picked up a *Guardian* someone had left lying around. It wasn't like him to be so anal. And it didn't get him anywhere. Besides, he'd left all that stuff behind a long time ago. He turned to the crossword and had a go at that instead. Much better than dwelling on the past.

Mark was whistling as he entered the surgery that morning.

'You're cheerful today,' Diana greeted him.

Ah, good. That made the morning even better. If Diana was here it was much more likely that things would go smoothly for a change.

'Yes, I am rather,' said Mark. It was an odd feeling, to be this cheerful. He had spent so many months embroiled in gloom, it was a refreshing change. And one he could only put down to one thing.

Emily.

Mark had thought of nothing else all night long. He hadn't enjoyed being in the company of any women since Sam had left him. And now, suddenly, here was one who had made him sit up and take notice.

It wasn't that he fancied her exactly. Although she did have, as Rob would have put it, All That. But more than that, they had had a laugh. And they had seemed to find common ground really quickly. The time he had spent with her had been all too brief. He hoped that she'd be going along next week.

He had a quick look at his day list, where he could see three root treatments, endless amounts of drilling and filling, a bridge to repair and Granny O'Leary to boot. It would have normally sent him into the doldrums. But not today. He was in too much of a good mood. And thankfully, there was no sign of Jasmine.

62

'Have we heard any more about Jasmine's complaint?' Mark asked Diana at lunchtime.

'Not a dicky bird,' said Diana.

'Perhaps I should ring her?' Mark asked, not really relishing the task.

'Oh, you know what Jasmine's like,' said Diana, 'she'll be on to the next thing soon and it will all be forgotten. Particularly when she's in pain again.'

'Good,' said Mark. Diana was right. It would doubtless blow over.

As usual, he barely had time to pause for breath, and by the end of the day three cups of cold coffee were lined up on the side. It was only as he got into his car to go home that he allowed himself to think about Emily again. She was the most attractive woman he'd met since he'd been single and he didn't even know her surname. Or where she lived. Or her phone number.

There was no help for it: he was going to have to go dancing again.

Emily was coming to the end of a long day and feeling absolutely exhausted. She had enjoyed the previous evening much more than she would have thought possible. And it hadn't actually mattered that much that she was crap at dancing. Mark had been equally crap. And she had enjoyed dancing crappily with him. It had been fun. Plus he had been, well, so gentlemanly and attentive. She wasn't used to that after Callum.

She paused from filing away some case notes. Callum versus Mark. Callum was gorgeous, of course. And made her feel gorgeous. He was sexy. He made her feel sexy. He was dangerous, which gave him that edge.

Mark, on the other hand, didn't seem the dangerous type. He seemed sweet and kind and thoughtful. Could she do sweet and kind and thoughtful, after mad, bad and dangerous to know?

Emily laughed out loud. Listen to her. She'd spent, ooh, half an hour in the presence of a very attractive man, and already she was lining him up against Callum. She was being ridiculous. As if he was even interested.

The phone on her desk rang.

'Someone to see you down here,' drawled the bored-sounding receptionist.

Emily frowned. She wasn't expecting anyone.

Oh God, no. As she approached the front desk she vaguely remembered Callum had had a big pitch on today. Please don't let him be here and be drunk.

'Hey babe,' he said. 'Am I the dog's bollocks or what?'

'What, I think,' said Emily, squirming under the gaze of the supercilious receptionist.

'I just won the shittest, hottest pitch in town. You are looking at the new account handler of *Smile, Please!* I am *the* man.' Callum raised his hands above his head and practically beat his chest.

'Callum,' hissed Emily. 'I'm at work.'

'I just wanted to see you, babe,' he said, lighting up a cigarette.

'This is a non-smoking office,' said John Turnbull, one of Emily's more likeable colleagues, who'd just walked in.

'Sweets for my sweet,' said Callum, ignoring him and proffering a rather squashed box of chocolates.

'Thanks very much,' said Emily. 'But can you just leave now. I've got stuff to do.'

'Oh, babe, don't be like that,' Callum pleaded with her. For once it had no effect. She was furious. How dare he show her up here? How dare he?

'Callum, I'll be any way I like,' she said, her manner cold and stiff. 'Now just go, please.'

'Do you want any help escorting this waste of space off the premises?' said John.

'No, it's all right,' said Emily. 'Callum's just leaving, aren't you?'

Something of the coldness of her tone seemed to have pierced through Callum's skull because he shambled off with his cans of Stella. Jeez, he stank like a brewery.

'Sorry about that,' said Emily, shamefaced.

'No problem,' said John, 'but you're hot to trot, and he's a wanker. What on earth is a babe like you doing with a twat like that?'

What indeed, thought Emily, as she made her way back upstairs. *What indeed . . . ?*

Chapter Six

'You're going away *again*?' Katie sat and faced her husband across the table, laid with her white damask cloth, their Royal Doulton blue and white wedding china, their poshest Sheffield steel cutlery, a vase full of freesias and daffodils and two scented candles.

'Needs must,' said Charlie, tucking into the steak Diane that Katie had lovingly prepared. 'This is jolly good, by the way. I have to go. The takeover is turning out to be trickier than we thought. In fact,' he paused, as if uncertain as to what to say next, 'you may not like this, but there's a distinct possibility that I might have to be permanently in Amsterdam for a while.'

'No!' Katie put down the glass of Chablis she was sipping and stared at her husband in dismay.

'I'm afraid so,' said Charlie. 'So we'd better start looking for schools and things.'

'Woah!' Katie stood up and looked at him. 'Charlie, one thing at a time. When you say you have to be there for a while, how long is a while?'

'Six months – a year tops,' said Charlie.

'Don't you think,' Katie tried to choose her words carefully, knowing how capable Charlie was of twisting them, 'you might be jumping the gun a bit? We can't just pull the kids out of school. It will be so disruptive for them. When are you going?'

Besides, a little voice was hammering insistently in her brain, *we tried living abroad as a family before, and it was a disaster. And you promised . . .*

Charlie had relocated once before, in his previous job, and Katie had had to leave the job where she had met and made friends with Emily. She probably would have done so eventually anyway as she had found it increasingly difficult to manage a career and two young children, but having the decision forced on her hadn't helped. Katie had gone on to spend a miserable year in Frankfurt with a five-year-old and a toddler. She didn't speak the language, had no social network and found the other English wives dreary beyond belief. When he'd seen how unhappy it had made her, Charlie had switched jobs and sworn he'd never put her through that again.

'Oh, I didn't think of that,' admitted Charlie.

'No, you never do.' Shock and disappointment – that her romantic evening was being tainted by the prospect of changes that could only make her home life worse – made Katie's response more acidic than she'd intended.

'What's that supposed to mean?' Charlie looked belligerent.

'That you only think of what you need and want, and forget about the rest of us.'

'Don't be ridiculous,' he said. 'Why do you think I work the hours I do, if not for the family?'

Great. He'd done it again. He could always get her there. Charlie had always worked incredibly hard for them. Now Katie felt guilty. But she was still angry. How dare he just waltz in and assume they would all up sticks without a by-your-leave?

'I know,' said Katie, 'but I don't want to live abroad again. It was bad enough last time, and now we've got *three* kids. It's okay for Molly, she won't know the difference. But the boys have all their friends here. You can't expect them to uproot themselves.'

Charlie seemed to take a step back.

'So what do you suggest?'

'I don't know,' said Katie. 'Why not try commuting? You've

67

been away more than you've been home recently anyway. And if it's not for long, I'm sure I can manage here.'

'I'll think about it,' shrugged Charlie. 'It's not definite yet anyway.'

'Oh good,' said Katie. 'That's settled then.' But later, as she followed Charlie into the lounge and cuddled up with him to watch TV, she couldn't help dwelling on it. Neither choice was a great one. And Charlie didn't really seem as bothered as he ought to be about spending the week away from her . . .

'Dad, can we have Domino's tonight?'

Beth put on her special pleading look, but Mark was having none of it.

'Nope,' he said. 'Not tonight. Your mum will kill me if I give you a takeaway again.'

'Aw, that's so unfair,' said Beth, with a pretend pout. With her long fair curls and dimples, even at ten she was still able to make a bid for cutest kid on the block.

'Yup,' said Mark. 'But then so is life. Get used to it.'

Sam was always on at him to feed the kids healthily. Mark wasn't a brilliant cook, but he could rustle up spaghetti bolognaise or roast chicken (the kids' favourite) when he had to. And of late, he'd noticed that Rob's bad influence of late-night beers and takeaways were having a rather disastrous effect on his waistline. In order to make amends, Mark had bought a low-GI diet book and was busy trying to find out what constituted low-GI food. White bread, which he loved, alas did not. While rye bread, which he hated, did. One day someone would invent something that was good for him which he'd actually like . . .

The middle-age spread had come as a shock. Throughout his twenties, Mark had taken it for granted that he would retain his lean, rangy shape without too much difficulty. But when Sam had left him he hadn't bargained for the downward spiral of depression that would follow; a downward spiral which inevitably

68

sent him and Rob to the curry house late at night. Mark was at least grateful that he hadn't started smoking again, though the temptation had been great at times.

Recently he had made more of an effort to get to the gym or to go for the occasional run. He'd never get another woman interested in him if he looked too porky. Not that that seemed to stop Rob, but if Mark was sure of one thing, it was that he didn't want to end up like Rob. And somehow, he intuitively felt, Emily wasn't the sort of person who would want him to be either.

'How about I make us a stir fry?' Mark had discovered from his GI reading that this was apparently Good For Him, and Rob, who was a bit of a foodie, had moved in with a wok, so it couldn't be too hard.

'Can we have sweet and sour?' Gemma had mooched in from the room she shared with Beth.

'I think there's some in the cupboard,' said Mark. He had done a big shop the previous day, knowing that the kids were coming for the weekend. He loved having them and hated being apart from them. Something people often didn't understand. *Oh well*, they'd say, *at least your time is your own now*. Or, *You've got your freedom back*, nudge, nudge, wink, wink – the implication being, *You dirty old dog you, why not go and play the field?*

But playing the field wasn't as easy as all that. For a start, until meeting Emily, Mark hadn't had the slightest inclination to do so; but also, what people – even women – failed to understand was that Mark came as a package. It wasn't only him, it was his kids too. Love me, love my children. Not all the women you met were likely to want to do that. Mark wondered whether Emily would. He'd gone along with Rob's strictures not to mention the children, but it had felt a bit odd.

'Here it is.' Gemma passed over the jar. She hoisted herself onto the worktop. 'Da-ad,' she began in a wheedling tone Mark knew all too well.

'Whatever it is, I'm going to say no,' said Mark firmly as he cut up some peppers.

'But Da-ad. You don't know what it is yet!'

'Okay, what is it?' Mark turned the heat on and put the wok over the gas.

'Shelly's-invited-me-to-the-park-and-sleepover-tomorrow-night.' The words came out in a nervous gabble. Clearly rehearsed, and desperate to get his assent.

'Who's Shelly again?'

'You *know*. Shelly. The one who does dancing with me.'

Oh. That Shelly. The one with the tattoo. And the ring through her nose. And the one who Mark suspected had persuaded Gemma to smoke on at least one occasion.

'I don't think so, Gemma, do you?' Mark chucked the vegetables into the wok.

'Oh Da-a-ad,' said Gemma. 'Why not?'

'Because I don't want you hanging round the park after school,' said Mark with half an eye on the recipe. He had found a sachet of black bean sauce in the cupboard and tore it open with his teeth.

'But why can't I go to Shelly's?'

'Because I say so.' Mark hated himself the minute the words came out. He'd always sworn he wouldn't use that one on his kids. How parenthood makes hypocrites of us all, he thought. At least he hadn't done the one thing guaranteed to make sure she would stick to Shelly like a limpet, namely let Gemma know just how much he disapproved of her friend. 'Besides, it's a school night.'

'So?' Gemma wasn't going to give up that easily.

'So don't you have homework or something?'

Mark had chucked the sauce into the pan and turned the flame up a little – the stir fry didn't seem to be frying quite as quickly as it should.

'Homework sucks,' said Gemma sulkily.

Mark turned away to face her.

70

'So does going to work, but I still have to do it,' he said. Suddenly he was aware of the smell of burning. He turned round to see the pan had caught fire. 'Holy shit!' Mark turned the heat off and grabbed a lid to smother the flames, while simultaneously soothing Beth who had started to scream.

'But Da-ad –'

'Not now, Gemma.' Mark surveyed the charred content of the pan. Apparently stir fry was much harder than he'd imagined.

'You are so unfair!' Gemma stomped off to her room. It was only the third time she'd performed that trick that evening. 'Yup,' said Mark.

'What's up with Wednesday now?' Rob wandered in from the shower, rubbing a towel on his head. He'd christened Gemma 'Wednesday Addams' the first time she'd dyed her hair black. And, realising how much it annoyed her, he'd kept it up.

'Oh, the usual. I'm the meanest dad in the world for not letting her out with her mates.' Mark was scraping the remnants of his stir fry into the bin.

'What were you trying to do?' asked Rob. 'Burn the house down?'

'Ha bloody ha,' said Mark. 'Domino's anyone?'

Emily sipped her drink, stared around the glitzy nightclub and sighed. The tubthumping music blaring out from DJ Rappa, The Sugar Daddy, who, despite the moniker, was actually a former accountant called Tim Seiver, was giving her a major headache.

Jeez. She was too old for this. But it was the sort of happening place that Callum liked. Though she still hadn't figured out how he'd managed to persuade her to come here after the whole work debacle. Somehow he'd sweet-talked her into it, and a late night at her desk for the third night running hadn't been immensely appealing. So here she was.

Emily leaned her head against the wall. It was cool and felt like a haven in this dark maelstrom of sweating bodies and flashing lights. Once she'd have thought it was the height of cool to be here. She'd have been wowed by the bright city-lights appeal of it all; impressed by the zedlebs all crowding over each other in a desperate attempt to behave in a sufficiently outrageous manner to merit a picture in *Heat* magazine.

Once.

Now she wondered what had happened to her. When she had become a lawyer, Emily had been fired up with youthful idealism inspired by what had happened to her dad. He had never got the compensation owing to him after the accident, thanks to the fat cats who always covered their lardy arses. She would make up for that, and fight for all the little people: the ones like Dad who sat for years living a kind of half life breathing the shallow breaths of someone infected with asbestosis. An old man before his time. He'd been so proud of her when she'd told him.

Tears prickled the backs of her eyes. Oh God, no, not here. She still wasn't used to these overwhelming surges of grief that took her when she was least expecting them. They seemed to come at any moment, unannounced, like a huge shock wave, each one larger than the last. Would she ever get used to the fact that he wasn't here any more? She wondered if he had been disappointed in her. He'd never said if he was, but she wouldn't have blamed him. The idealistic Emily her dad had loved had turned into a shallow narcissistic creature, seduced by the false glamour of a fake lifestyle and ropey job. How had she let that happen?

'You are such a loser!' Jasmine Symonds came storming past with Twinkletoes Tone.

Tony looked, as ever, like a rat caught in a run.

'Oh, babe, don't be like that,' he whined. 'You know I love you.'

'Aw, do you?' said Jasmine. 'Well, I don't love you. It is so over.' She threw the contents of her bottle of Bacardi Breezer over his head, to the cheers of several bystanders. A couple of cameras flashed and Jasmine paused to pose – no doubt the whole scene would be being written about in next week's issue of *Heat*. Emily sighed. How had she ended up in this facile world? How?

'What you staring at?' Jasmine looked at her belligerently, and Emily quickly looked away. God, that woman was foul. Why on earth were so many people interested in her antics? Seeing she wasn't likely to get the fight she was clearly looking for, and to Emily's considerable relief, Jasmine turned round and disappeared into the crowd.

'Ready to dance, babe?' Callum came swaying up to her, no doubt stoked up after a visit to the gents. He was hyped and ready to keep partying all night. And she wasn't. With a moment of utter clarity, Emily knew that if she stayed with Callum for a hundred years, nothing was ever going to change. But she could take control of her life. She'd start here and now.

'No, actually,' said Emily, 'I'm a bit knackered. I've got an early start tomorrow. I'm going to make a move.'

'Oh.' Callum put on his little-boy-lost face. Once she'd have thought that endearing. Tonight it just irritated her. 'Please stay, pretty please.'

'Sorry, Callum,' said Emily, thrilled with the sudden realisation that, after all, this was going to be easy. She should have done it months ago. 'I've got to go.'

'Ring me,' he said, trying to give her a kiss on the mouth.

She brushed him aside. 'No,' she said. 'Sorry, Callum, but it's over. I won't be ringing you again.'

He looked gratifyingly open-mouthed at this news, but he didn't try to stop her from leaving. Instead, he shrugged and turned back towards the heaving crowd. No doubt by the end of the evening there would be a replacement. Emily made her way to the door, with an ever lighter heart. This really was the way the world ended, then, with not a bang, but the merest of whimpers. But even whimpers could feel great . . .

'So you've finally dumped Callum?'

Katie had persuaded Emily to join her in the park on Saturday

73

afternoon. It was a dull grey day, and with Charlie in Amsterdam, doing whatever he did to make sure that mergers happened and financial strategies were sorted, Katie didn't fancy being on her own and was feeling rather gloomy. Not that she would ever admit that to Emily. Katie had always found it hard to confide in people, even her closest friend.

If she were more suspicious, Katie might think Charlie was having an affair. But this was Charlie, Mr Ultra Conservative. He was so uptight and rigid in his views; he would never do anything to sully the reputation of the Caldwell Clan – or at least nothing to offend his domineering mother. Sometimes, Katie thought wistfully, he seemed more in awe and worried about his mother's feelings than he did about hers. But then Marilyn Caldwell was a formidable woman, and the whole family seemed to kowtow to her.

'Yup,' said Emily. 'I suddenly thought: what am I doing with my life? What am I doing with him? And I don't know. I just had the strongest feeling that my dad wouldn't have liked him. And suddenly I couldn't go on with it. Does that sound a bit weird? When Dad was alive I never thought twice about whether or not he liked my boyfriends.'

'No,' said Katie. 'Not weird at all. Grief does funny things to us sometimes. Either we see more clearly, or we don't see things at all. I think what's happened to you in the last few months has just woken you up to the fact that Callum was a complete tosser.'

'Oh, thanks,' said Emily. 'So glad to know you hold my boyfriends in such high esteem.'

'Only that one,' said Katie. 'And if you go out with him again, I promise to be a good girly friend and say of course it was completely wrong of me to call him a tosser.'

Aidan ran up at that moment, claiming that George had kicked him, so Katie decided maybe now was a good time to go home.

'Will you stay for a drink?' she asked, hoping she didn't sound too desperate for company.

'I'd love to,' said Emily. 'After all, I haven't got anything else on. We could have a really girly evening and watch *Fame* to get us in the mood for next week if you like.'

'So we're going again, next week?' While Katie had found Rob irritating, it had been so nice to go dancing again, but she had been unsure as to whether Emily wanted to repeat the experiment. But if she did then sod Charlie. If he could go swanning about in Europe, she didn't see why she had to live like a Wall Street widow.

'Of course,' said Emily. 'I'm a free agent now, remember. And I think Mark deserves another look, don't you?'

Chapter Seven

Emily stood nervously in the corner of the studio. As had happened the previous week, people seemed to be just grabbing partners and dancing. The music was Latin American, and the dancers seemed to be doing what she presumed was the rumba. She envied the relaxed way they all seemed to move their hips with such fluid, slinky ease, but, watching one couple getting incredibly intimate, she wondered if she would ever even have the nerve to dance like that in public, even if she did master the steps.

However, no one had yet asked her to dance. Which was probably just as well, as although she was watching the fancy foot-work of some of the more experienced dancers with fascination, she couldn't image ever being able to do it herself. Oh God . . . why on earth was she here?

She should have wimped out the minute that Katie rang up to cancel – Molly had been struck down by a tummy bug, apparently. Emily had been treated to a blow-by-blow account of every bowel evacuation that poor little Molly had had over the last twenty-four hours. She loved Katie dearly, but really. Sometimes you could have too much information.

Much as she envied Katie her family life, here was one reason she was immensely glad not to be shacked up with kids. Especially not with Cheerful Charlie. Emily had never warmed to him. He was pleasant enough, charming even, but there was something she couldn't quite put her finger on – it was as though he was only ever partly involved in his family. But as Katie always seemed so content, and claimed that her life was perfect in every way, Emily had always assumed that theirs was a happy marriage. So what if Charlie wasn't her cup of tea? If he ticked Katie's boxes, that was enough for her.

Emily frowned. Katie, who was the most repressed person she had ever met, would never ever admit that things weren't right, but Emily couldn't help feeling something was wrong. Katie had barely mentioned Charlie the last time they'd met, and the few times Emily saw them together Charlie seemed incredibly distant. In the meantime, Katie was developing a weird kind of cleaning fetish. Emily blamed Anthea Turner, whom Katie had actually started quoting as if she was Shakespeare.

'Penny for 'em?' Emily looked up and was surprised and pleased to see Mark standing next to her.

'Just wondering what I'm doing here, again,' she said. A warm glow suffused her. How stupid. She barely knew Mark.

'Me too,' said Mark. 'Rob was busy tonight. I wasn't going to come, but . . .'

There was a lot left in that *but*. Was it a *but* that said, I just thought it would be fun? Or a *but* that said, I wanted to see you again? Or maybe it was just a *but* that meant nothing at all. Poor little *but*, thought Emily, so very lonely . . .

'I'm sorry?' Mark looked puzzled. 'What *are* you talking about?'

Oh bloody hell, Emily must have let that last bit slip out loud.

'Oh, nothing,' she gabbled. 'Sometimes I have weird random thoughts. And sometimes in a weird random way they flow from my mouth, without me realising it. I think it's because I live on my own.'

'Oh,' said Mark. He looked around. 'Your friend not with you today?'

'Nope,' said Emily. She had been about to mention Molly being ill, but as Katie had been adamant she didn't want to give anything away about her private life, she said instead, 'She was busy this week.'

'But you came anyway?' That flash of a smile, utterly dazzling, had a rather unsettling effect on Emily.

'Oh, you know. I thought since I was so good last week, I'd come and show them all how it's done.'

'Me too,' agreed Mark.

'Actually,' confessed Emily, 'I didn't have anything else much on, so I thought, oh bloody hell, why not? What's the worst that can happen?'

'Dancing with me?' Mark was only semi-serious.

'You're on then,' said Emily. 'And I really will try not to step on your toes this time . . .'

'How does it go again?' Mark said as he tried and failed to perfect the open hold that Isabella had shown them earlier. Sweat was dripping off him, and his hands were clammy as hell. Hardly a way to get Emily to take the right kind of notice of him.

'Well, I think you're *supposed* to step forwards, while swinging your hips, while I step backwards,' said Emily, 'and then we're supposed to sway slightly and transfer our weight onto the other foot or something. Oh, and I think you need to hold your hand up higher.'

'I thought I'd got that wrong,' said Mark. 'Shall we stop and watch what everyone else is doing?'

'Perhaps we'd better,' said Emily, and they stood trying not to giggle as they watched the rest of the class sashaying round the floor to the Cuban music that was playing in the background.

'I have to say, it does get your toes tapping,' said Emily, unable to stop herself from swaying in time to the music, 'even if I can't go in step. Shall we have another go?'

'If we must,' said Mark. 'Okay, so it goes, one, two, step forward, three, transfer weight, four; one, step side, two, step back, three, transfer weight, four, step forward. Hey, I think we did it!'

Growing in confidence now, and by dint of watching their neighbours who seemed to be really in the swing, eventually Emily and Mark found themselves making a reasonable fist of the steps Isabella had shown them. Emboldened by their efforts, Mark decided to really push the boat out and attempted to fling Emily to one side as he had seen other people doing. Unfortunately, in doing so, her foot got entangled around his heel, and before he knew it the pair of them had tumbled unceremoniously to the floor.

'I don't think that's how it's meant to go,' said Mark ruefully.

'Me neither,' said Emily. 'I think someone is telling us something.'

'Like why don't we go next door for a pint?' said Mark with a cheeky grin.

'I thought you'd never ask,' said Emily.

It seemed an entirely natural thing to do until they actually got into the pub. It was only when they were facing each other over a pint that there was a sudden awkward silence.

'So what do you do when you're not picking up strange women at dance classes?' Emily broke the ice first.

Mark pulled a face. He hated telling people what he did for a living. Nine times out of ten they felt obliged to tell him all about their abscess, or their granny's dentures. 'I am that incredibly rare beast, an NHS dentist,' he said. 'And you?'

'Well –' said Emily. She felt the need to prevaricate. She wasn't quite sure why, but suddenly she felt rather ashamed of what she did for a living.

'I hope you're not going to say you're a lawyer,' Mark added. 'I can't stand them.'

'Oh, why not?'

'My wife ran off with one,' said Mark.

'You're married?' Emily looked disappointed.

'Divorced,' said Mark. 'She went off with the lawyer, and I didn't see much point in contesting it.'

'And you've not found anyone else?' Emily was determined to steer the conversation away from the subject of lawyers at all costs.

'Not yet,' said Mark. Again that dazzling smile. He paused briefly and then said, 'what about you? No significant other in your life?'

'Not any more,' said Emily, looking down.

'And no kids, I presume?' Mark was feeling his way. Perhaps if he could steer the conversation around to children, he could let slip he had a couple himself.

'Oh God, no,' said Emily. 'Why on earth would I want children? I've watched too many of my girlfriends turn from bright, intelligent women into poor demented creatures whose only topic of conversation is the content of their child's nappies. And *then* they expect you to be as entranced by their puking, shitting, squealing little bundles as they are. Children utterly ruin your life. Who in their right mind would ever want them?'

'Who indeed?' said Mark faintly. That put paid to that then. There was no way he could mention Gemma and Beth now. He scrambled around frantically for something else to say.

'So, you like *Green Wing*?' he said pathetically.

'I sooo love that programme,' said Emily, 'the scene where Statham kills the dwarf . . .'

'. . . is brilliant,' agreed Mark.

'I missed quite a bit of it, unfortunately,' Emily said, thinking back to all those nights when she'd been out aimlessly partying, or stuck at her desk trying to see an important deal through, and wondered why she hadn't been home more.

'Me too,' said Mark, thinking back to the days when he'd been so busy keeping Sam sweet that he'd had to watch all the crap she liked, which included drivel like *I'm a Celebrity Get Me Out of Here* and *Big Brother*. *Love Shack*, which had shot Jasmine to fame, had been on at the same time as the first series of *Green Wing*, so he'd pretty much missed the lot.

'I've just bought series one on DVD. I could lend it to you if you like.'

'Are you sure?' said Emily. 'I might never give them back. In fact, faced with the opportunity of being able to watch Julian Rhind-Tutt forever, I'll definitely never give them back.'

'Nope. I can't let you do that,' said Mark. 'In that case, we'll have to go for a full-on *Green Wing* fest at my place.'

'Oh.' Emily was slightly taken aback.

'There's nothing behind that,' said Mark hurriedly. 'I mean, it's just watching a DVD and having a beer if you want. Nothing more.'

'Of course,' said Emily, 'I never thought for a moment it was.' She ignored the voice in her head shouting *Liar!* at a thousand decibels.

'Good,' said Mark. 'Then that's settled. What are you up to at the weekend?'

Emily thought ahead. Without Callum to distract her, or some big do of Ffion's to attend, the time stretched out before her without end. A weekend watching *Green Wing* with Mark – especially with Mark – might be just the thing.

'Nothing much,' she said.

'Good,' said Mark. It was Sam's weekend with the kids. 'How about we kick off around two, then if you have something more exciting to do later, you'll still have time.'

'Sounds great,' Emily said. She lifted her glass. 'To dancing like no one's looking.'

'I thought you'd lost the plot when you started colour-coding my socks, but you're hoovering *now*?'

Charlie stood incredulously in the doorway with his suitcase. He was flying to Amsterdam that morning and seemed very bad-tempered about it. Katie had been up since five with the baby, and had decided, once Molly had finally gone back to sleep, that she might as well get the lounge cleaned while she was up. There would be precious little time later once the full onslaught of the day hit. But she hadn't factored in Charlie's bad temper, or thought very much about the fact that their bedroom was above the lounge.

'Sorry,' said Katie, feeling simultaneous twinges of guilt and resentment – her rejoinders of *if you were here more*, *if you helped out more*, were immediately cancelled out by, *who would pay for the house?* One of her mum's tricks had been to nag and nag and nag at her dad. Katie had always sworn she would never do that.

'Do you want a coffee before you go?' Katie asked, going for placation.

Charlie glanced at his watch.

'It's okay, the taxi will be here in a minute. I'll grab one at the airport.'

'Have you said goodbye to the boys?'

'They're still asleep.' Charlie was fiddling with a fridge magnet that bore the legend: *Hysteria is a state of mind. It has nothing to do with my womb.* He seemed very restless for some reason, and fidgety. Katie was feeling more than a little irritated. His evident annoyance at her cleaning had stopped her doing it, but now he wouldn't even sit down and talk to her. It was almost as though he couldn't look her in the eye.

'You got ants in your pants?' Katie enquired.

'Why would you say that?' Charlie looked like a startled rabbit caught in headlights.

'Because you've been pacing up and down the kitchen for the last five minutes. Are you sure you don't want a coffee?'

'Have I?' Charlie said. 'Sorry. I'm a bit distracted. What with this deal and everything.'

'Of course,' said Katie. It was understandable that he should be feeling wound up. She went over and gave him a hug. 'It will be all right,' she said.

'I don't deserve you,' he replied, kissing her lightly on the cheek.

Charlie continued to wander restlessly round the kitchen, picking up bits of paper and idly sifting through them, clicking a pen off and on incessantly. It was almost as if he was trying to work himself up to say something to her.

'This is hopeless,' he burst out suddenly. 'Katie, there's something I need to tell you –'

A beep from the front of the house indicated the taxi had arrived.

Katie looked at Charlie expectantly. There was a look of raw pain in his eyes, and he was trembling.

'Charlie, whatever's wrong?' she asked, genuinely worried now.

'Nothing,' he said. 'Nothing. I'm just wound up about this deal. Taxi's here, I'd better go.'

'Oh,' said Katie. 'Well, if you're sure you're okay?'

'I'm fine,' he said, 'I'll see you on Sunday.'

'Be good,' she said, going to kiss him on the lips.

'When aren't I?' It was said lightly, but she detected a faint look of strain in his eyes, and he turned away from her so her lips brushed his cheek instead. There was definitely something wrong. She felt sure of it. She watched him go off in the cab with a heavy heart. He looked lost and lonely sitting there. And she had the oddest feeling that nothing she could do was going to help him.

'So when's she coming then?' Rob was lounging on the sofa laughing like crazy as Mark frantically tried to remove all evidence of his children from the lounge.

'In about ten minutes,' said Mark. 'So could you please pass me the Sims game, which I know is hiding under your cushion, because that's Beth's favourite place to lose it.'

Rob whistled as he sat up and felt behind him, dragging out a plastic computer game and handing it to Mark.

'You're really not going to tell her about the kids?'

'You were the one who said I shouldn't,' said Mark.

'I know, but . . . it's going to be a bit hard to hide them from her if this *cosy DVD* thing becomes regular.'

'You didn't hear her going on about children. If she thinks I've got some, she'll never look at me twice.'

'So you do like her?' Rob could barely contain his delight. 'I knew it. I knew I could get you over Sam.'

'I'm not, as you put it, necessarily over Sam,' said Mark, 'but let's just say that meeting Emily has made me see I can keep my options open.'

'So long as you don't tell her you have children,' added Rob.

'There is that, of course,' said Mark, suddenly spotting a pair of Gemma's shoes in the corner. Honestly. It wasn't even as if the kids were with him all the time. How on earth did they manage to leave all their junk behind? He grabbed the shoes and shoved them in the kids' bedroom, slamming the door firmly shut. He toyed with locking it and then thought, no, that's paranoid. He flitted quickly into the bathroom to check that it was devoid of teen paraphernalia, but luckily, as Gemma could never go anywhere without a complete grooming kit, she tended to carry everything she needed with her.

Mark felt vaguely guilty about the subterfuge. He loved his kids, and didn't want anyone to think he was ashamed of them. But Emily was the first woman he'd been attracted to since Sam. And she had been so adamant about disliking kids, he didn't want to scupper his chances before they'd even got going. There'd be time enough to tell her the truth later. Chances were she wasn't the slightest bit interested anyway . . .

Emily stood on Mark's doorstep feeling incredibly stupid. It had seemed natural to say earlier in the week that she would come and watch a TV programme with him, but now it seemed a little odd. She liked him, certainly, and he had occupied rather a lot of her thoughts in the last few days, but apart from the fact they were both crap dancers and they liked *Green Wing*, what exactly did she know about him? He might be a serial killer or something. *Right.*

Rob answered the door. Which reassured her. At least she wouldn't be alone with Mark. But as she followed him into the lounge, she had a sudden panicky thought. Oh God, suppose they were into threesomes or something. Had she just walked into the lion's den?

'What did you just say?'

Shit. She'd done it again. This talking-out-loud thing was becoming a liability.

'Um, nothing,' said Emily, embarrassed.

'Yes, you did,' said Rob. 'Mark, you've picked a right nutter here. She talks to herself.'

Emily squirmed.

'Ignore him,' shouted Mark from a room upstairs. His bedroom? The thought made Emily go tingly all over. 'Anyway, I know.'

'Know what?'

The thunder of footsteps down the stairs heralded Mark's arrival. He poked his head round the door and said, 'I know Emily talks to herself. I find it endearing.'

Now Emily really wished the ground would swallow her up. She was less blushing and more completely puce. *But,* a little voice whispered in her head, *he thinks you're endearing.* Or mental.

'Cup of tea?' Rob asked.

'Yes, lovely, thanks,' Emily managed to squeak.

'Got it,' Mark said triumphantly, waving aloft a copy of the first series of *Green Wing* as he walked into the room. 'I was having a last-minute panic as I'd put the DVD somewhere so safe I couldn't find it.'

Emily sat down with a thump on the sofa, spilling the tea Rob had just handed her. Something had to give and it was her knees. Mark, walking in with his casual air and his laidback look, was utterly gorgeous, she realised. She almost forgot to breathe. Thank God his wife had left him.

'Well I'm glad someone's pleased about it,' said Mark, sitting next to her.

'What?' Oh God, please don't say she'd done it again? 'I'm glad someone's pleased my wife left me.'

She had.

Emily gripped the mug of tea for support. If it wasn't for the fact that it would seem rude to leave she'd go right now.

'And you?'

'Me what?'

'You're definitely single?'

Emily gripped the mug harder.

'Yes,' she said. 'I most definitely am.' If her heart beat any louder they'd hear it next door.

'I was hoping you'd say that,' said Mark.

Chapter Eight

'So you've got a date with the gorgeous Mark?' Katie teased Emily as they sat in the lounge watching *Dirty Dancing*, where Patrick Swayze was showing how the rumba should be done. Isabella had recommended it as useful background. So far, the combination of chasing children into bed, far too much wine and gossiping had led them to miss most of the film.

'Well, it's not a date,' said Emily. 'I went round to watch *Green Wing* and he's coming round to mine to watch some more. I'm cooking. It's not a date.'

'Nooooo, of course it isn't,' teased Katie. 'And he wants to come round for dinner with me too.'

'Well, you're married,' said Emily.

'Oh right, because I'm married with fat thighs, no man will ever look at me again?' said Katie.

'What?' said Emily.

'Well, you make it sound as if I'm some old has-been that no sane man would look at in a million years. I know I'm married, but it would be nice to think I might still have an ounce of attractiveness left. Besides, he doesn't know I'm married, and he still chose you. It's my fat thighs, I tell you.'

'Don't be daft,' said Emily. 'Of course it isn't.'

'So Rob's not the only one who thinks I have fat thighs, then?'

'Katie, will you stop going on about your fat thighs!' said

87

Emily. 'Anyway, why should you care about what Rob thinks? You've got it all. Charlie, the kids, the house. Your life's perfect.'

'Yes, of course,' muttered Katie. For a moment she was tempted to confide in Emily, but she had never been one for girly confidences, always feeling she should be able to sort her problems out by herself. No doubt something to do with having spent years growing up and not talking to anyone about the misery of her home life. Besides, Katie would rather have died than admit there was anything wrong with her marriage. Even to Emily. 'It's just with Charlie away so much I end up feeling quite sorry for myself. Which is ridiculous. Now, where were we? Isn't this the bit where Patrick Swayze dances with Jennifer Grey in the lake?'

Rob sat in the Hookers, drinking his pint and doing the crossword. The pub hadn't been the same since the smoking ban. It was too cold to go out for a fag under the canopy Barry had erected outside. *Smokers: the most ostracised members of modern society. Discuss.*

Rob had hoped Mark would be joining him, but Mark apparently had a date. Although the way Mark had put it was, 'I'm going round to Emily's to watch the next episode of *Green Wing*,' and then muttered something about her cooking him a meal. But it wasn't a date. Mark had been adamant on that point. Except that Rob evidently wasn't invited, so here he was, alone in the Hookers, trying to avoid the eye of Paranoid Pete, who needed no encouragement to leap in with, 'They're watching us, you know.' Rob knew of old that to answer 'Who?' would have Pete touching his nose briefly before muttering *sotto voce*, 'The others,' before proceeding to launch into a rant against aliens, New Labour and, bizarrely, scratch cards.

Oh God. And there was Dicey Derek, Thurfield's best used-car salesman. Rob had once made the mistake of buying a car from him. When he was hit from behind by a woman in a 4x4 on the school run, it more or less fell into two pieces. And yet still, Derek would come to tempt him with more goodies. Rob's salary was so pathetic, and Derek's prices so suspiciously good, it was horribly tempting sometimes.

Rob buried himself in his paper again. Good, Derek had found some pals in a corner. He could relax.

He looked around the bar again. The Hookers. So much a part of his life, it was like a second home. He came here every night of the week apart from Thursday. He had been known to spend the whole of Saturday here. Though now some of his ex-pupils were showing up, that was becoming slightly less appealing. Maybe Mark had a point. Perhaps he should think about coming in here less, and concentrate more on learning to dance, which, after all, he was enjoying. Rob shook his head. Apart from going to the pub and sex, what other interests did a man need?

Although Mark was definitely right about one thing. The Hookers was the lousiest pick-up joint in the world.

Or maybe not.

The flirty blonde from dancing was sitting in the corner with a friend, he noticed. They were giggling over their text messages. She was the one Mark had been so keen to get away from.

'Ding dong . . .' Rob muttered to himself, knocking back the rest of his pint. He picked up his paper and wandered over to them.

'I say, ladies, can I interest you in a drink?'

The flirty blonde looked at him provocatively.

'Mine's a double vodka,' she purred.

Cheeky cow, thought Rob. Still. It just goes to show you should always expect the unexpected. The evening was turning out promising after all.

'So how many episodes can we get through tonight?' Mark teased Emily as he came through the door.

The previous week, they had managed three. They had spent most of the evening in stitches.

'Well, if we're going to eat, maybe two?'

Mark followed Emily into her tiny little kitchen. It looked out onto a small but pretty garden, which had a beautiful view of the common, with the edge of the downs in the background. The first green shoots were coming up. Maybe spring was on the way. 'Nice view,' he said.

'Isn't it?' Emily agreed. 'It's the closest I'm going to get to the Hill.'

Mark laughed.

'You're not missing much,' he said. 'My ex-wife always wanted to live on the Hill. I think it's full of pretentious wankers myself.'

The Hill was full of massive properties, and at the top a fabulous gated community where rock stars were rumoured to live. Those who aspired to such things but couldn't afford the gated community (namely Sam and her lawyer lover) lived halfway up it. Mark had always resisted Sam's demands that they move onto the rather bland estate where she now lived, much preferring the tumbledown old house that they had bought in the Valley – where the normal people lived.

Mark had loved the house. Sam had hated it. But thanks to the property boom, when they'd sold it, it had made enough for her to go and live in the soulless zone when they split up. It helped, of course, that she was shacked up with a lawyer who'd just made partner. Mark's share had just about stretched to the three-bedroom cottage he'd bought for him and the girls. With Rob being between flats, it had seemed sensible to make some extra cash, if only to have something to put aside for the girls' futures. Sam and the lawyer were more of the 'spend today, think about tomorrow later' kind to worry about things like that.

'Say it like it is, why don't you?' Emily said, as she fried mushrooms in a pan. She was planning a steak flambé. She hoped it wasn't over-ambitious.

Mark pulled a face.

'Sorry,' he said. 'Sam always said I was very black and white.

It's just I can't stand pretentious people or snobs. And in my experience most of the people who live on the Hill are both.'

'I'd agree with you there,' said Emily. 'Although I'm not sure I agree with you about lawyers. I thought you were a bit hard on them.'

'I don't think I was,' said Mark. 'One of my best friends was sued by a patient once and, thanks to the lawyers, his life was hell.'

'Well you can't hold that against the whole legal profession,' said Emily as she carefully poured brandy onto a spoon.

'Don't tell me you're one.'

'Oh no, of course not. Laywers scum of the earth, that's what I always say.'

Emily waived the question away, as she tried to avoid singeing her eyebrows. What had she been thinking when she planned this meal? He seemed interested in her. She couldn't – mustn't – blow it. She'd just have to make sure she never mentioned the small fact that she was a lawyer.

'Mind you, I don't hate lawyers as much as I hate this crap.' Mark picked up a copy of *Heat* which was lying on the side. He sighed as he spotted the headline: *Jasmine and Tony All Loved Up – we go behind the scenes of their very own Love Shack*. Idly he flicked through it. 'I mean, *Pop Princess looks minging*; *Crap balding actor has fling*. It's not just vapid, it's downright nasty. Who actually cares? You don't really read this stuff, do you?'

'No, no, of course not. I had nothing to read on the train and someone had left it so I picked it up. You're right, it's utter nonsense. What idiot would read drivel like this?' Emily laughed a silly, high-pitched, slightly hysterical laugh. This was awful. The first really decent man she'd met in years and he hated everything she stood for. When he found out what she really did for a living he was never going to come anywhere near her.

'Good,' Mark said, leaning on the kitchen counter. 'Sam loved all that stuff. It drove me insane.'

'Absolutely,' said Emily, feeling rather hot. And it wasn't just from the frying pan.

'What about you?' Mark seemed to have changed tack, which was a relief. 'Anyone ever tempted you up the aisle?'

'Not so far,' said Emily. 'I've been concentrating on my career.'

'Which is?' Mark said.

'Um,' said Emily. After his rant about celebrities and lawyers, she couldn't possibly admit the truth. Not if she wanted to see him again. Christ, what could she do instead? She frantically scrabbled around for an alternative . . .

'I'm a teacher,' she gabbled, suddenly thinking about her oldest sister, Mary, stuck in the same comprehensive in Swansea for years.

'Oh, so's Rob,' said Mark. 'He teaches history. What about you?'

'Does he?' Emily's voice came out in a squeak. Trust her luck that Mark's flatmate was a sodding teacher. 'Um. I teach – er –' (think, Emily, think, favourite subject, best subject, only stupid subject you know anything about) 'English. I teach English.'

'Oh, that explains all the books.' Mark had already clocked that the downstairs of the cottage seemed to contain more books than furniture.

'Yes, books. Perfect thing for an English teacher,' said Emily, gabbling rather frantically. 'I love books, me.'

Mark pulled a face.

'I'm a bit rubbish at reading,' he confessed. 'Apart from thrillers, I don't read a lot. And I never did get Shakespeare.'

Emily acted semi-shocked. Despite getting distracted by the law, her love of books had remained undiminished since A-level English, when a charismatic English teacher had opened her eyes to the possibilities offered by literature. Up until then, Shakespeare had been a closed book, but after a trip to Stratford to see *Macbeth*, Emily had never looked back. From that moment on she had read as voraciously and widely as possible, and her love of books remained undiminished.

'You don't *get* Shakespeare?' Emily said. 'How can anyone not get Shakespeare? He's not only our greatest literary export, his plays are still hugely relevant today. The *Merchant of Venice* deals with racism, *Henry V* is about the horror of warfare.'

'Perhaps if *you'd* taught me Shakespeare, I might have listened more,' said Mark.

'Maybe I should take you in hand,' replied Emily laughingly.

'Maybe,' said Mark with a smile, as he expertly opened the bottle of Wolf Blass he'd brought round, 'maybe you should.'

Charlie was back from Amsterdam, and he seemed far more cheerful than he had of late. He kept whistling, which was driving Katie insane as she loaded the washing machine for the third time that evening. Charlie, meanwhile, was sitting at the kitchen table with a can of beer, doing *The Times* crossword.

'So, the meetings went well, I take it,' Katie said between gritted teeth. Why the bloody hell couldn't he see she needed help.

'Fine.' Charlie's response was only half there. For something that had been making him really wound up before he left, he was displaying a remarkable insouciance about it now.

'And the merger's gone ahead all right then?'

'Oh, there are a few teething problems,' said Charlie, 'but it should be okay.'

Normally Charlie was a bundle of nerves in the middle of an important deal. But he'd barely consulted his BlackBerry all evening.

'Good,' said Katie. 'What about the move? Any more news about that?'

Charlie folded the paper and put it down. He stretched languorously.

'I think you're right, Katie,' he said. 'We shouldn't rush things. It may not be necessary to move after all. Let's just play it by ear.'

Katie was dumbfounded. It was like she was talking to a different person.

'Well, if you're sure . . .'

'Absolutely,' said Charlie. 'The kids are the priority, we shouldn't uproot them. If I have to be in Amsterdam in the week, I can stay in the company flat.'

'The prospect seems to be making you very cheerful,' said Katie drily. Again, the thought briefly flitted through her head. Suppose he was having an affair? No. No. No. Not Charlie. Charlie wouldn't do that to her. Charlie would never do anything like that. Just picturing his mother's reaction would probably be enough to keep him on the straight and narrow for life. Wouldn't it?

'Well, I'm off for a bath,' said Charlie, putting the paper down.

'I could come and join you.' A little bit of harmless flirtation couldn't hurt. Maybe that was all their marriage needed. Some more excitement to spice it up.

'No, it's okay, thanks,' mumbled Charlie. 'I'm a bit cream-crackered to tell you the truth. I just thought I'd have a soak and crash out.'

He got up and kissed her briefly on the top of her head, and walked away as if nothing in the world was wrong. Katie folded a pair of his boxer shorts, and then buried her face in them in despair.

Oh God. Maybe, just maybe, he would.

Chapter Nine

'So you're an English teacher now?' Katie was hooting with laughter as she and Emily sat down. Isabella, dressed in a magnificent emerald-green dress dusted with silver sparkles that shimmered as she moved, was dancing with her partner Anton. They danced so fluidly together, they almost seemed to caress the floor, and it was hard to tell where one dancer ended and the other began.

The Jet Set, as Katie had decided to call them, the group of people who really knew what they were about, were dazzling their way round the room, switching from a flowing foxtrot to a thrilling tango in the blink of an eye. The women wearing floaty dresses and sparkly shoes, the men in their dark suits and polished shoes, they glided smoothly across the dance floor. Oh to dance like that, Katie thought enviously.

'Shut up!' Emily nudged Katie. Mark and Rob had just entered the room. 'Don't you dare say a bloody word.'

'Your secret's safe with me,' laughed Katie. 'Talk about subterfuge.'

'Says the woman who told me to lie,' said Emily. 'And it's not lying exactly. It's more, I don't know, living a fantasy life that's a damn sight better than my real one. Anyway, what about you? I haven't noticed you mentioning the fact you're married with three kids.'

'Yes, well, that's just to put off the weirdos,' said Katie.

'Who's a weirdo?' Rob came up with a cheeky grin.

'You, obviously,' remarked Katie.

'Cheers!' said Rob.

'However,' continued Katie, 'weird and all as you are, you are better than most of the prats I've danced with, so how about it?'

'Ah, Katie, you say the nicest things.'

'Well then?'

Rob looked around the room. He'd danced with most of the women on their own, more than danced with some of them. Most of them were rubbish dancers. Lots of them were rubbish in bed. Katie was a good dancer. The thought flitted into his head unbidden. What would she be like in bed? Which was ridiculous, as he didn't fancy her. Not at all.

'Oh, okay, Thunder Thighs,' he said, 'till I get a better offer.'

'Cheeky bugger,' said Katie, punching him lightly on the shoulder.

'Careful,' he said, 'I might start thinking you're flirting with me.'

'In your dreams, pal, in your dreams.'

'Expect the unexpected,' said Rob with a twinkle, and Katie couldn't help laughing as he led her to the dance floor. Rob might think she had fat thighs, he might be far too full of himself, but at least he was good company. And boy, she thought, as he whisked her round the room with practised ease, boy, could he dance.

'Shall we?' Mark smiled at Emily. 'I promise not to trip you up this time.'

'That was probably as much my fault as it was yours,' said Emily. 'Oh god,' she continued, watching Katie and Rob. 'Every time I look at them, they put me to shame. I just can't imagine I'm ever going to be able to dance properly.'

'Does that matter?' said Mark.

'Probably not,' laughed Emily, a thrill going through her as he took her hand.

Her heart seemed to be beating so erratically as he led her to the dance floor, she wondered how she could still be breathing. She hoped he hadn't noticed the stealthy blush that had crept across her face, as he pulled her close to him.

'I had a great time on Sunday,' said Mark as he clumsily tried to lead Emily in a foxtrot. It only took a couple of turns for him to muddle his lefts and his rights. 'Oh bugger, I've got that wrong again.'

'I think that was me,' said Emily, 'I led forward with my right instead of back.'

They started again, this time Mark managing to steer them smack bang into another couple.

'Sorry, sorry,' he and Emily said simultaneously, and they laughed.

Mark inexpertly attempted a spin turn that Isabella had shown them. Rather than ending up with Emily wrapped against his chest facing outwards, which was the effect he was after, their arms ended up twisted in opposite directions and she found herself crushed against his chest. Which was not a bad place to be.

'Fancy a drink afterwards?' Mark said.

'That would be great,' said Emily, as casually as she could muster.

This time, when they got to the pub there were no awkward silences, just easy and carefree conversation. Emily marvelled at how easy it was to talk to Mark. It felt like they had known each other forever. Before long they were comparing their likes and dislikes.

'Favourite film?' Mark challenged.

'*Some Like It Hot*,' said Emily. 'You?'

'*Shaun of the Dead*,' said Mark. 'And most comedy on TV, but I particularly like surreal stuff like *Spaced*.'

'Me too,' said Emily, 'perhaps we should go on to *Spaced* after *Green Wing*, I missed most of that one too.'

'I'm keen on political programmes, too,' added Mark. 'I never miss *Question Time* if I can.'

'I don't watch it as often as I should,' confessed Emily.

'What about music?' said Mark.

'Fairly eclectic,' said Emily. 'Pretty much anything but gangsta rap.'

'I'd probably say the same,' said Mark, 'though I retain an adolescent fondness for heavy metal.'

'Oh, and I am a real sucker for musicals,' added Emily. '*The Sound of Music* is my favourite.'

There was a pause while they both sipped their drinks.

'What else is there?' asked Mark. 'Oh, I know, we haven't done books yet.'

'I thought you didn't like books,' teased Emily.

'Well, not your kind of books, perhaps,' said Mark. 'But I'm a big fan of John Grisham.'

'Nothing wrong with that,' said Emily. 'Although I am going to make it my mission to get you into Shakespeare. I like nothing more than to curl up with a Terry Pratchett myself. But my favourite book of all time has to be *Brideshead Revisited*.'

'Wasn't that on TV when we were kids?' Mark asked. 'I vaguely remember something to do with a teddy bear.'

'That's the one,' said Emily. 'I studied it for A Level. My application to Oxford was entirely based on the fairytale depiction of Christ Church.'

'Did you get in?' asked Mark.

'Nope,' said Emily. 'I think a girl from a scraggy comp in South Wales was always going to have trouble, but I was so overawed to be there I completely fluffed the interview.'

'Do you know, I would never have guessed you're from Wales.'

'I cover it up well,' said Emily, feeling just a smidgeon of guilt. Since that experience at Oxford, when one of her interviewers had sneered at her accent, she'd worked hard to eradicate it. Sitting with Mark, who was clearly so unfazed by that kind of thing, made her feel that she had betrayed her roots somehow. And it made a change to be with someone who was so lacking in pretension. Particularly after Callum, whose *raison d'être* was to be seen in the right places, by the right people, wearing the right designer labels. She sipped her drink appreciatively. Maybe for once she had found herself a someone who was worth hanging on to.

'So when are you planning to tell her about your kids?' Rob demanded to know when Mark came through the door, later – unusually much later – than him.

Mark was singing 'The Hills Are Alive' loudly and tunelessly.

'Crikey, she must be good,' said Rob. 'She's achieved the impossible. For the first time since Sam, you're happy drunk rather than maudlin, you've come home later than me, and she's got you singing.'

'She likes *The Sound of Music*,' said Mark, falling against a wall. 'Rob. You're so right. I needed a kick up the backside. I think I'm in love.'

'Woah, cowboy,' said Rob, putting the kettle on for coffee. 'You're not meant to be in love. You're meant to be having fun. A shag. Blimey, you're hopeless.'

'But she's gorgeous.'

'She is a babe,' agreed Rob. 'Here. Drink your coffee and go to bed.'

'Oh yesh. Quite forgot. People to hurt in the morning.'

'So now you're in lurve,' said Rob, 'are you going to tell her the truth?'

'You were the one who said I shouldn't say anything about the kids,' protested Mark, suddenly sobering up.

'Yes, I did. But that was before I realised what a dipstick you are, and that you would fall for her big-time. You can lie all you like to the one-nighters, but if you're in it for the long haul, you have to be straight.'

'Rob, where do you get all this stuff from?'

'My Year Eleven girls, mainly,' confessed Rob. 'So what are you going to do?'

'Well, since Emily has made it perfectly plain to me that she hates kids, I'm not entirely sure.'

It was gone eight thirty before Mark screamed into surgery the next morning. Luckily, his first patient wasn't for a quarter of an hour. His head thumped and he was aware his eyes were bloodshot. He had swilled mouthwash – a perk of the job – round as much as possible, but he wasn't quite sure he'd covered up the smell of booze. But holy Christ, it had been years since he'd felt this good. Years and years.

He kept seeing Emily's mouth as she laughed, the way her eyes danced, her endearing habit of tucking stray strands of hair behind her ears. She was funny and sweet, and quoted poetry at him. He'd never been interested in poetry before, but when he'd been round at hers, she'd read him Shakespeare and Marvell and John Donne, and though he couldn't understand the half of it, he'd been utterly dazzled. He couldn't get enough.

'Good night, was it?' said Diana from behind the desk. She looked at him archly. Mark liked Diana. She was nearly old enough to be his mum, but kept up a healthy interest in his sex life – or lack of it.

'Fine, thanks,' said Mark.

'Pretty, is she?' Diana smiled, as Mark went behind the reception desk to check his day list.

'Diana, you're a witch,' Mark said. 'Oh, great. I see Jasmine's coming in for her last appointment.'

'At least it's done then,' said Diana. 'And you won't be seeing her for a while.'

Jasmine had been coming in intermittently to have the new crown fitted. She seemed to have got over her pique about the missing tooth enough to have withdrawn her complaint, but she was still grumpy and paranoid that someone would find out just how rotten her teeth were. Mark would be only too glad to be shot of her.

'True,' said Mark. 'And the sooner it's done, the better. By the way, where's Kerry?'

'She called in sick,' said Diana.

'What, again?' Mark frowned. That was the third time in as many weeks. 'Do you want me to say something to her?'

'It's okay,' said Diana. 'I'm on to it. I've spoken to HR, and next time she gets a verbal warning.'

It was always the same with the staff, particularly the sodding nurses, Mark thought as he went into his surgery. The good ones, the really good ones with a bit of nous and spark about them, went off to train to be hygienists so they could earn more money, which meant the surgery got left with the bottom-feeders who couldn't give a toss. Kerry had looked the ambitious sort to start with, and, frustratingly, was quite good at her job. But she was probably too busy having a good time to let a little thing like work get in the way. Thank God he had Diana to hold things together.

He went whistling into his surgery, hung up his coat and put on his lab coat and mask. There was no sign of Sasha, and nothing ready for his first patient, so Mark started to lay out the trays of instruments for himself. By the time he'd completed his third tray, Sasha had swanned in without the slightest notion that an apology might be in order.

The morning progressed reasonably smoothly, despite Mark's hangover. His good mood miraculously didn't evaporate when Jasmine came in. This time the Rottweiler had been left behind, but Twinkletoes Tone was sitting reading mags in the waiting room, looking bored.

'Right, all done,' said Mark, as he finally fitted the crown into place. 'Here, let me show you in a mirror. I doubt anyone will be able to tell the difference.'

'Ooh, you're right,' said Jasmine. 'Which one was it? No, let me guess. I know. It was this one.'

101

She pointed to a tooth in the bottom right of her jaw.

'No,' said Mark, showing her which tooth it really was, in the upper left of her mouth, right at the back. How stupid could she be? She would have been having kittens if it really had been a tooth so close to the front of her mouth.

'Ooh, that's fab,' gushed Jasmine. 'I'd never have known.'

'Really?' Mark replied, although he knew that sarcasm was wasted on her.

Jasmine was so enthusiastic about his repair work, for one ghastly moment he was worried that she was going to fling her arms around him and kiss him.

'Thanks so much,' she twittered as she went out of the room. 'You're the best dentist ever. I know people who go to Harley Street 'n all, and you're way better than that.'

'Glad to be of service,' said Mark, waving her out of the door. Thank God that was over. With any luck he wouldn't be seeing or hearing from Jasmine for a very long time.

Chapter Ten

'So,' said Katie. 'Go on, spill the beans. How was it?'

'Katie, I'm at work,' hissed Emily down the phone, as she saw Mel walking down the corridor towards her. Luckily, Mel wasn't coming her way, but took a left into one of her colleagues' offices.

'Oh come on,' said Katie, 'you can just tell me quickly. I've got to get Molly to the clinic anyway.'

Keeping a weather eye on the corridor, Emily got up to shut the door. She had a pile of correspondence to go through concerning the case of a zedlebrity who insisted that she was being stalked by a fan on the flimsiest of evidence. The poor sod who'd been thus accused just happened to have had the misfortune of living near the woman in question, and from what Emily could glean, all he'd done was ask for her autograph once and said hello another time. Honestly. These bloody people. Mark did have a point. Most of what she did was utterly shallow. Maybe it was time to start looking for another job.

'Okay,' said Emily, when she was settled, 'but there's not much to tell, really. We went for a drink, held hands, flirted a bit. No, a lot actually. He walked me home. And kissed me goodbye, and that was it.'

'That's it?' Katie was disappointed. 'Didn't you invite him in for a coffee?'

'I would have, but he seemed a bit shy. I didn't want to scare him off.'

'But you are seeing him again?'

'Yes, on Friday. We're meeting for a drink, and then he's going to take me out to dinner.'

'Way to go, girlfriend!' said Katie. 'So was it a full-on snog, or peck on the cheek?'

'Katie, what are you like?' Emily laughed. 'Peck on the cheek, but that's okay. I'm happy to go slow. It makes a nice change to be courted after Callum. My instincts were entirely lust-based last time, and look what good that did me.'

'So now you're getting on so well, when are you going to come clean about your job, then?' asked Katie. 'You can't keep this rubbish up about being a teacher forever.'

Emily looked around her office. It was piled high with case files on people seeking to make money for no good reason at all. She had a feeling that Mark would be appalled. And, what was more, she was becoming appalled by it too. It was as if she were looking at her world through his clear-sighted eyes, and she didn't like what she saw. This wasn't the person she had hoped to be. It certainly wasn't the person she wanted Mark to see. More than ever it seemed important to maintain the façade she'd built up.

'You can do anything if you put your mind to it,' said Emily. 'Besides, what the eye doesn't see, the heart doesn't grieve over. He's made it perfectly clear he hates lawyers, and he hates the celebrity culture even more. There's no way he's ever going to find out what I do for a living. No way at all.'

Mark was grinning to himself as he left work on Friday. He'd had a rare day full of happy patients, crowns that fitted first time, teeth that came out with one swift pull and, most satisfyingly, a patient who was ecstatic to have a bridge fitted to replace the two teeth that had been knocked out by a driver in a road rage incident. He and Emily had arranged to go out on a proper date and he had finished early for once. The only fly in the ointment was Kerry – who, after failing to turn up for several days in a row, had been summarily dismissed. She was supposed to have come in with her uniform and keys, but neither had materialised yet, so Diana had arranged for the locks to be changed. After an unfortunate incident with a nurse who had been breaking into the drugs cupboard after work and shooting herself up with Hypnovel, you couldn't be too careful.

As he made his way to the car, his mobile rang. Sam. Damn. What did she want with him now?

'Mark, you have to get the kids.' As usual she started with a demand. It would be so nice if just once she could ask him nicely.

'Hi Sam, yes, I'm fine, thanks, how are you?'

'Stressed,' said Sam. 'I've got caught up in a meeting and there's been a security alert at Clapham Junction so all the trains are up the spout. God knows what time I'm going to get home.'

'Where are the girls?' Mark glanced at his watch. Over two hours until he saw Emily. He could still pick up the girls and get them home without her knowing.

Sam was constantly doing this to him. Not that he minded. It meant he got extra time with the girls. He still couldn't get used to not seeing them every day. He missed Beth coming and bouncing on him to wake in the mornings, or Gemma (when she wasn't being grumpy) staying up to watch bad science-fiction movies with him.

Sometimes it was like a permanent ache not having them with him. Being flexible often worked in his favour. He just wished Sam had thought more about the implications of the big job in the city before she'd taken it. But, unfortunately, she had a lifestyle to maintain, and the big job in the city was part of that. He did worry about the effect it had on the kids, though. Gemma was so self-contained it was hard to know what was going on in her head, but Beth – she was so sensitive. On more than one occasion she had sobbed when her mother hadn't been there to pick them up.

'Beth's at her after-school club. She needs to be picked up by six. And Gemma's at Shelly's. Oh, and Beth needs to be dropped at scouts at seven p.m.'

'You'd better get a move on,' continued Sam. 'Beth's club finishes at six.'

Mark thought about making a cutting remark but Sam had already hung up. Bugger, Beth would be the last one in the hall again. He hated doing that to her. He couldn't understand how Sam could. So often. So easily. A picture of Emily swam before his eyes. For the first time since Sam had left him, he wondered what he'd ever seen in her in the first place.

Katie pulled into the poky car park belonging to the church hall, which housed the Thurfield 10th District Scouts Pack. As usual she was running late. Cars were already pulling out of the car park – everyone else evidently having arrived on time. It was hectic and dark and she had a pulsing headache at the thought of the effort it was going to take to extricate Molly, who'd fallen asleep, and Aidan, who was suffering from grumpy Friday-it is, out of the car while she got George inside. Normally she'd have let him run in, or left the others in the car while she saw him to the door, but there had been rumours of a stranger hanging round the scout hut and all the parents had been asked to escort the children directly to the door. Why did no activity involving the children ever seem to be straightforward these days? Katie couldn't remember her own mother transporting her round like this. If anything, Katie had been left pretty much to her own devices, and had taken herself off to Brownies more often than not.

Eventually, Katie pulled up next to a Volvo, got out, and went round to Molly's side to unclip her seat. As she was bending down she heard a familiar voice talking to someone. She looked up, and to her consternation saw Mark. Shit, what was he doing here? She busied herself with Molly and hoped he hadn't noticed her. Katie had been enjoying the glorious freedom of apparently being childfree that dancing classes had afforded her, and she wasn't quite ready to let the bubble burst.

'Yes, Sam, I am not entirely incapable. I've just dropped her off now,' Mark was saying. 'And you're sure you'll be back in time to pick her up? Only I am supposed to be going out, remember?'

Katie nearly dropped Molly in shock. Mark had kids? Emily had mentioned an ex-wife, but no kids, or none that he'd seen fit to mention to Emily. Maybe there was an explanation for it, but for the life of her Katie couldn't think what it was.

'Right, see you later. Try not to be too long.' Mark snapped his phone shut, got into his car and drove off, while Katie cowered behind hers, hoping he hadn't seen her. When he'd gone, she stood up and walked into the hut with the children, shaking her head in disbelief. She'd really had Mark taped as one of the good guys. But not only did he have kids, it looked like things might not be completely over with his ex. It just showed how wrong you could be about people. Emily was going to be livid.

Oh bloody hell. What a dilemma. Should she tell Emily before she met Mark tonight? Katie still hadn't made up her mind by the time she'd got back to the car. She had almost decided that she was going to tell Emily, then realised she'd left her mobile at home. She glanced at her watch: it had just gone seven. She thought Emily had said she was meeting Mark around eight – Katie should just have time to bathe Molly and get her into bed, then ring before Emily went out. Katie wasn't at all sure Emily would want to hear what she had to say, but as her closest friend she felt duty-bound to say it. Bugger. Why did life have to be so complicated?

Emily trudged up the hill from the station. She didn't have time to go home before she went to Mark's house. She'd just go straight there. Maybe they could dispense with the drink and just watch another episode of *Green Wing*. Heaven knows, she could do with a laugh.

It had been a hell of a day. Mel had been on her case all day long about the length of time it was taking to find out whether a soap star could really have been as sober as she claimed to be when she was picked up for drunk driving following five hours in a bar in Soho. The case for the defence was that she had been taking medication for a severe head cold which had interfered with the one drink she had had all evening. The trouble was, several barmen had spotted her staggering about the place, and there was CCTV footage of her downing shots of what looked like tequila.

It was pretty much cut and dried, but the soap star's agent had a lot of clients in similar situations on their books. Mel didn't want this one to go tits up. Never had Emily felt more despairing about her chosen career.

Emily grabbed an *Evening Standard* on her way home, and vaguely clocked that Jasmine was one of the lead stories, but she couldn't face reading about one of her lot tonight. Instead she concentrated on doing word searches and sudoku, and thinking about Mark. She couldn't wait to see him again. He was so refreshing after Callum. So kind and thoughtful and generous. Emily was enjoying his company more and more. She just hoped he felt the same.

Right. Mark took a deep breath. This should be simple. Sam was going to pick Gemma up at 8 p.m. and Beth up from scouts at 8.30 p.m. Emily need never know they'd been here. He could then take his time to tell her about the girls. Tonight had made him see that he had to let Emily know about them. It wasn't fair on any of them if Mark continued lying about it. At least he could finally tell Emily the truth. It was a relief, to be honest.

Gemma looked disinterested as he came through the door. She was lounging on the sofa watching *EastEnders*.

'Don't you have any homework?'

'Done it.' She barely acknowledged his presence. He wished he knew how to get through to her.

The phone rang.

Sam again.

'Look, I'm really sorry. There are still no trains from Victoria,' she said. 'I don't know what time I'm going to get in. Can the girls stay with you?'

'Well, I'm hardly going to say no, am I?' Mark said. 'Of course they can.'

'Great,' said Sam, and her phone snapped shut.

'Gem, you don't mind staying the night, do you?' Mark asked. 'Only your mum's stuck up in London.'

'Whatever,' said Gemma, looking bored.

Despite his outward calmness, Mark was in a flat spin. Now what was he going to do? Emily was going to be here any minute and he'd have to let her know that she was going to be sharing her evening with two children who until now she'd had no idea had existed.

The doorbell rang. Oh sod it, it was now or never.

'I've had a hell of a day,' said Emily, flying through the door like a whirlwind. She dumped her paper and bag in the hall. 'I hope you've got something to drink. I just got out of London before there was a security alert and my train home has been incredibly slow.'

'Er –' Mark's plan had been to stop Emily at the door and explain everything, but she was already barging past him to the lounge, saying, 'Am I ever in need of a laugh tonight –'

She stopped dead. And stared at Gemma. Then she stared back at Mark, her mouth wide open.

'Who –?' If he hadn't been so stressed, Mark might have pitied her bewilderment. She stared at Gemma again, and then back at Mark.

'Who are you?' said Gemma rudely. 'Dad, is this your *girlfriend?*'

'*Dad?*' Emily looked as if she'd lost the power of speech. 'You never said you had a daughter,' she continued after the silence.

Her bewilderment was growing into rage. 'When were you planning to tell me about this?'

Mark put his hands up. 'Look, Emily, I'm really sorry. I was going to tell you. Emily, this is my daughter, Gemma. Gemma, meet Emily.'

Gemma stared at Mark in disgust.

'You've got a new girlfriend and you hadn't bothered to tell her about *us*? That's nice. Really nice.' She threw the magazine she'd been reading onto the floor and stormed off to her room.

'Us?'

'Um – I have another daughter, Beth. She's at Scouts. I have to pick her up in a minute. Perhaps you could come –?' He left the question hanging and was rewarded with a withering stare. 'Or perhaps not.'

Emily looked at him blankly.

'I really thought you were different. But it turns out you're just like all the rest.'

'I'm not,' protested Mark. 'Look, I know I should have told you –' His voice trailed off in misery.

'How could you have lied to me like that?' she said, shaking her head in disbelief.

She stormed out of the lounge, and Mark followed her.

'I'm sorry, Emily, really I am. I never meant for you to find out like this.'

'Forget it,' said Emily, grabbing her bag and marching to the front door. 'And just so you know, you won't be seeing me again.'

She slammed the front door shut, leaving Mark feeling more bereft than at any point since Sam had left. In her hurry she'd left her paper behind. He picked it up idly, toying with the idea of running after her. He had been so looking forward to this evening, and it had all gone wrong. He didn't suppose it could get much worse.

A picture of Jasmine Symonds was splashed over the front

cover together with the headline: '*DON'T SMILE PLEASE! JASMINE'S TOOTH SHOCK*'.

He read on in mounting disbelief. Someone had got hold of the story about Jasmine's missing tooth. Someone had breached the practice confidentiality. When she saw this, Jasmine was going to hit the roof.

Apparently, things could get worse. Much, much worse.

Part Two

Love Like You've Never Been Hurt

Chapter Eleven

Emily slammed the front door behind her, stormed into the lounge and threw her bag on the floor. She wasn't going to cry. She. Wasn't. Going. To. Cry. She barely knew Mark. She wasn't going to waste her tears on him. Not now. Not ever. What kind of man lied about having two kids?

'A shitty one, that's what.' In the comfort of her own home Emily didn't need to worry whether or not the thoughts in her head were being spoken aloud. 'You got that one wrong big-time, *again*.'

The thought made her both angry and depressed. She slammed her way into the kitchen and got a bottle of wine out of the fridge. If it wasn't for the fact that she knew Charlie was home she'd have rung Katie. But it didn't seem fair to impose on them on a Friday night when they saw so little of each other.

She poured herself a big glass and stared out of her kitchen into the darkening gloom. Just when she thought her life was picking up, it had to go wrong all over again. What was it with her and men? She took a large swig of wine and took down the sheaf of takeaway leaflets she had pinned up by the cooker. Emily didn't feel like eating at all, but it was something to do, something to wait for. Something to make her think that she had a semblance of a life.

Taking the bottle of wine into the lounge, she went and

switched the TV on. There was nothing worth watching, so she went idly to the DVD player to put something else on. The *Green Wing* DVD was still in. She and Mark had had such a good time on Sunday, they had only watched two episodes and he'd told her to keep the DVD for next time. Now, of course, there wasn't going to be a next time.

Emily stared at the DVD. Mark or no Mark, at least it would make her laugh. She might as well watch it anyway. She could always send it back via Katie. She sat down, but it was no good. Without Mark by her side, nothing was going to seem remotely funny.

Mark headed to the scout hut to pick Beth up with something approaching despair. How could he have got it so spectacularly wrong? The only decent woman he'd met since splitting up from Sam and he'd lost her. He had left messages on both Emily's mobile and answerphone, but Mark had a feeling that he'd blown it. And he couldn't really say he blamed Emily if she never wanted to see him again. After all he had lied to her about something incredibly fundamental. But the worst thing of all, as bad as he felt about Emily, had been seeing the look in Gemma's eyes when she'd stormed out of the room. Not only was he a lousy potential partner, he'd turned out to be a lousy dad as well. And, on top of all that, Jasmine's story had somehow got in the paper. What an awful, awful day.

Mark searched for Beth in the crowds of kids and was rewarded by the sight of her racing towards him, arms outstretched, shouting, 'Dadd-eee!'

'Good time?' he asked Beth, cuddling her tight.

'It was great,' said Beth. 'Where's Mummy?'

'Slight change of plan, I'm afraid, sweetheart. Mummy's got stuck on the train, so you're having a sleepover at mine tonight, isn't that nice?' said Mark, with a cheerfulness he didn't feel.

'Brill, Daddy!' said Beth, squeezing his hand tightly. It made

Mark feel even more of a heel. He didn't deserve children. Not after what he'd done.

Emily came to suddenly on the sofa. The phone was ringing. Bugger, it was probably Mark again. He'd left three apologetic messages already. She, meanwhile, had downed the bottle of red, which had been a mistake of course. And, despite her determination not to cry, tears had eventually come.

The answerphone kicked in. As Emily sat up and looked ruefully at the empty bottle, her heart gave a sudden, unexpected lurch. It was Callum.

'Babe? Are you there? It's me.' There was a pause, as if he didn't quite know what to say, then his voice came out in a rush. 'ImissyouandImsorryandIthinkImightpossiblyhavemadeamistakeand . . .'

Emily listened in disbelief. She hadn't credited Callum with having that much soul, but he sounded both desperate and sincere.

He's a shit, said her head. *But he wants me back*, said her heart. *And if I'm going to make a fool of myself over a man, better the devil I know.*

Emily picked up the phone. She couldn't help the racing of her heart at the thought that, for once, she might possibly be able to have Callum on her own terms.

'I'm here,' she said.

There was a long pause.

'Look, Em,' Callum said, 'I know I've been crap, but . . . well . . . thing is. I'm not good at this stuff. But, well. Shit. I'm *really* not good at this stuff.'

There was a pregnant pause.

'Was there something you wanted to say to me?' enquired Emily gently.

'Oh fuck it. I miss you. I didn't think I would, but I do. Can I come over?'

Emily looked at her watch. It was gone ten.

'What, now?'

'No time like the present.'

Oh bugger it. In for a penny, in for a pound.

'You can come for a coffee,' she said. 'Nothing more.'

'I'll see you in a minute,' said Callum, with such alacrity it was hard to dispel the image of an overeager puppy from her mind.

'Wait a minute. Where are you?'

'Just outside your front door,' came the sheepish response.

Emily laughed as she went to open the door. The devil you know had to be better, didn't it? So why, when she let Callum in, did she feel disappointed he wasn't Mark?

Rob walked into the flat on Saturday morning and was struck by the brooding silence of the place. Mark didn't appear to be up yet, and the house seemed deathly. There had been a band on at the Hookers last night, and he and Mandy had danced till 1 a.m. before heading back to hers. Rob had figured that Mark and Emily needed some space. It was time Mark nailed himself a new woman, and Emily seemed just the ticket.

But if they were going at it like bunny rabbits, they were being awfully quiet. And, Rob noticed, there was only one can of beer on the table, not two. Perhaps Emily hadn't stayed after all. Really. He was going to have to take Mark in hand and remind him of *exactly* what was required when you invited a woman into your home.

Rob picked the can up from the lounge table and walked into the kitchen to make himself a cup of tea. He was feeling more cheerful than he had for some time. Mandy Allwick certainly knew how to give a guy a good time. Though there was the slight inconvenience of her lack of conversational abilities, her idea of an intellectual discussion centring around the relative merits of the two nail bars at the chavvy end of town. Still, he wasn't seeing her for that . . .

He walked back into the lounge with his cup of tea, ready to sit down with the newspaper he had purchased on his way home and –

'Holy shit, you startled me!'

Gemma had appeared, as if out of nowhere, like a silent pale ghost gliding across the room. Rob looked ruefully at his tea-stained trousers and then up at Gemma.

'What are you doing here, Wednesday? I thought you were at your mum's this weekend?'

Gemma paused and looked dramatic. She was good at that kind of thing.

'I've been abandoned,' she said. 'Mum couldn't be bothered to get home from work last night, so Dad had to have us.'

She spat the word 'Dad' out with such venom, Rob spilled his tea once more.

'Is everything okay?' Rob wasn't noted for his sensitivity but teaching had taught him a thing or two about teenage girls.

'No,' said Gemma. 'It is not. My life is terrible and my dad is worse.'

'Hey, come on,' said Rob, 'that's a bit unfair. Your dad would do anything for you. Whatever he's done to upset you, it can't be that bad.'

'Can't it?' Gemma looked less dramatic now, and more woeful. There was clearly something bothering her.

'Come on,' said Rob. 'Tell your Uncle Rob all about it. I'm sure we can sort it out, whatever it is.'

'It's – it's – Did you know he had a girlfriend?' burst out Gemma.

'Oh, you mean Emily,' said Rob.

'Is that what she's called?' Gemma gave a haughty sniff.

'She's not exactly his girlfriend,' said Rob. He had a feeling he knew what might be coming.

'Why did she come to see him then?' demanded Gemma.

'Your dad *is* entitled to have a girlfriend, you know,' said Rob.

119

'It's not the having a girlfriend I mind,' said Gemma, sitting down and looking suddenly deflated. 'It's the fact that he told her he didn't have kids.'

'Ah,' said Rob, feeling awkward. 'That may be partly my fault.'

'What? You told him to lie about us?'

'Not exactly,' said Rob. 'Look. It's complicated. Girls don't always like to meet boys who've got kids. I thought it would even up his chances of meeting someone if he pretended he didn't have children.'

'Well, thanks a bunch,' retorted Gemma.

'So, really, it's my fault, not your dad's,' said Rob.

'Oh,' said Gemma, but she appeared to be thawing a little.

Rob paused for a moment. She looked very young and vulnerable sitting there, without the armour of her make-up on, or the normal veneer she gave of downright hostility.

'It must be tough, your mum and dad splitting up,' he ventured.

'S'pose,' was the noncommittal reply. She paused and then said, 'I hate it most when Mum and Dad row. I wish they wouldn't.'

'Well, have you asked them not to?' said Rob.

'They wouldn't listen,' Gemma replied, and stared at the floor for a moment, before savagely kicking the coffee table. 'Why did they have to split up in the first place?' she burst out. 'It sucks.'

'Yes, it probably does,' said Rob. 'But I don't think you can change that now. I do think you should tell them how you feel, though. I think it might help.'

Gemma shook her head. 'I can't,' she said. 'And please don't say I said anything.'

'Scout's honour,' said Rob, saluting. 'I'm sure your dad didn't mean to upset you, you know.'

'I know.' For a moment Gemma looked as if she might crack, then the mask came right back on again. 'I think he should say sorry, though.'

'I'm sure he will,' said Rob. 'And I want to say sorry too. Because it was my stupid fault, really.'

'Oh, okay,' said Gemma.

'We friends again, then?' Rob asked, hoping that he'd said enough to put things right.

'All right,' muttered Gemma, retreating back into spiky teen mode.

'Good, then you can make me another cup of tea while I change my trousers,' said Rob.

Gemma stuck her tongue out in reply.

'Emily, are you okay?' Katie had tried several times the previous night to ring her friend, but her mobile had been switched off and her answerphone was on. Katie was reluctant to leave a message and eventually concluded that Emily must be with Mark, so things were out of her hands. 'Only I've been trying to get hold of you.'

'No. Yes. I don't know,' said Emily. 'I've just found out that Mark has kids.'

'I know,' said Katie. 'And it could be worse than that, from the way he was speaking on the phone, I think he's still seeing his ex.'

'You knew?' Emily practically shouted down the phone. 'Why didn't you tell me?'

'Woah,' said Katie. 'I only found out yesterday and I tried to ring, but you weren't answering.'

She explained what had happened the previous evening and Emily filled her in on events at Mark's.

'So that's it then?' Katie asked.

'That's it,' said Emily. 'I just can't believe he lied to me like that. I was so sure he was different.'

'Ahem,' said Katie. 'I hate to state the obvious here, but pots and kettles spring to mind. You've lied too.'

'Yeah, well, I only lied to him because he made it so patently clear how much he despised lawyers. I wouldn't have otherwise.

121

Besides, I was just doing what you were doing and creating a fantasy. I mean, it's not like it does any harm, does it? Well, at least I thought it didn't.'

Katie looked out of the window where she could see Charlie playing with the children in the spring sunshine, and felt vaguely guilty. He had showed so little interest in her dancing classes, she had neglected to mention that Rob was fast becoming her regular dancing partner. And Rob certainly didn't know about her domestic situation.

'No harm at all,' said Katie. Charlie was swinging Aidan over his head. It gave her such a warm tingly feeling to see him do that. It was a shame such moments happened so rarely.

There was another pause.

'There's something else,' said Emily.

'What?'

'Callum came round last night.'

'Oh, Emily, you didn't!' Katie couldn't contain her horror. 'No! No! No! Talk about frying pans and fires.'

'Well at least *he* hasn't lied to me,' said Emily. 'And he's missed me.'

'But can you trust him?' Emily didn't answer the question, so Katie continued. 'At least promise me you won't see him again.'

'I promise,' said Emily. 'It was a one-off.'

'Liar,' said Katie.

'It's true,' protested Emily. 'I'm not going to see him again.'

'Hmm,' said Katie, and put the phone down. Poor Emily. What a bloody mess. Really, her own problems were miniscule by comparison. She went to join the rest of the family in the garden, but as she came out, Charlie headed for the door.

'Oh good,' he said, 'you're off the phone. I've got some work to do. You don't mind taking over, do you?'

Katie tried to cover up her dismay.

'Oh, I thought when Molly woke up we might all go to the park together,' she said.

'Sorry,' said Charlie, 'this report I've got to write is really urgent. I did tell you.'

Katie went to join the boys in the garden, her heart heavy. Maybe she wasn't so lucky after all.

Chapter Twelve

'What do you think I should do about that?' Mark pointed out the article about Jasmine to Rob. It was late on Saturday afternoon, the girls had gone home (Gemma thankfully seemed to be at least speaking to him by the time she left), and he and Rob were about to sit down to watch the rugby. Mark had filled him in on the events of the previous evening, but it turned out he'd already gleaned most of it for himself from talking to Gemma.

Rob picked up the paper and glanced through it, guffawing loudly once or twice.

'"*JASMINE GOOFS IT UP – Jasmine Symonds, the celebrity winner of last year's* Love Shack, *looked tonight to be on the verge of losing her lucrative deal with world-famous cosmetic-surgery company* Smile, Please! *It seems, thanks to the ministrations of her as yet unknown dentist, the girl with the golden smile turns out to have teeth of clay.*" God, who comes up with this crap?'

He read on to the end, then chucked it on the table.

'I'd ignore it if I were you. I mean, it's hardly a big story. Some tarty celeb gets her name in the papers because it turns out she doesn't have a full set of gnashers. It's hardly headline, is it? It'll be forgotten tomorrow.'

'I suppose at least it doesn't mention my name,' said Mark, picking up the paper and scanning through it for the hundredth time. He was developing a morbid fascination with the story.

'It's a storm in a teacup, I tell you,' maintained Rob. 'Some other bimbo will be front page tomorrow.'

'I hope you're right,' said Mark, cracking a can of beer open and settling down to watch the Six Nations, which at this moment in time held no interest for him whatsoever. He hadn't stopped thinking about Emily all day. But he hadn't rung her again. If she wanted to find him, she knew where he was. The ball was in her court now.

Callum was screeching loudly in Emily's ear that there was no limit, really none at all, as they sweated and jumped semi-rhythmically to a hip hop version of a song Emily associated with a brief period of attending all-night raves in wet muddy fields in her late teens. Callum was a much better dancer than Mark. Much better. It should have felt great being with him. And six months ago it would have.

Was there no limit to her stupidity? Callum had talked the talk so convincingly the previous night, she had succumbed and let her own body talk back. So much easier and less awkward than actually having a proper conversation. And he still pressed all the right buttons.

But now she was actually out with him again – and, more importantly, out with him when sober – the surge of attraction she had felt the previous night seemed to be wavering. Emily had hoped that this turning-a-new-leaf thing might actually involve Callum doing something civilised like taking her out for a meal or to the cinema. Instead, she had waited all day to hear from him, only for him to pitch up at eight, announce they were heading up to town, and drag her into a series of pubs before ending up at the Cave, the dive to end all dives in seedy New Cross Gate. It was now too late to get home, so she had resigned herself to spending the night with Callum again, who, despite his protestations about getting clean, seemed pretty wired to her.

125

Mark wouldn't do this to you. The thought popped into her head. She ruthlessly shoved it down and, smiling with a confidence she didn't feel, started jiggling again with Callum. It was hot and humid and sweaty. Bodies heaved and pumped and thumped in and out of rhythm against a background of pulsating lights and loud music. Emily felt like she was in hell. Which is where, of course, the devil you knew took you . . .

'Hey, Emily!' A tap of the shoulder revealed Ffion beside her. It was weeks since they'd seen each other.

'Fancy a drink?' Ffion was mouthing over the music. Emily looked at Callum leaping about in a world of his own, fuelled by nostalgia and god knew what else.

'Sure do,' she said. She motioned to Callum, but he barely seemed to notice. 'Missing me already?' she muttered to herself, before following Ffion up to the poky bar.

It was a bit quieter at the bar, to Emily's relief, so she perched on a bar stool with Ffion and they caught up.

'It's been ages since I saw you,' Ffion said accusingly.

'Yeah, well, I've been busy.' Emily's tone was more defensive than she'd intended, but it didn't matter as Ffion barely noticed.

'Yeah, work's been manic for me this week too,' gushed Ffion. 'Did you hear about Jasmine?'

'Jasmine – who? Oh, Jasmine. What's she done now?' *Like do I really care?*

'Of course you care, Emily,' said Ffion. Damn she'd spoken her thoughts aloud again. 'Jasmine's teeth are as rotten as, apparently.'

'So?' Emily looked at Ffion blankly.

'So, she's the face of *Smile, Please!* and her teeth are supposed to be perfect.'

'And we know this how?'

'Because her dentist had to take a tooth out only last month. *Smile, Please!* found out and are hopping mad, and it looks like her career's going down the pan. Isn't that great?'

Emily looked at her friend and wondered what they had ever had in common. It seemed to her that Ffion was talking another language.

'I'm sorry. Run it by me again. How is that great?'

'Because, dummy, we're getting so many column inches out of this story. Jerry is getting me really involved in this one, and we're working out a way to see if we can sue the dentist for breach of confidentiality or something. Even if she loses the *Smile, Please!* contract, this might be just what Jasmine needs to make it to the proper big-time. This could be a great opportunity for me to start going places with A-Listers.'

'Oh.' Emily didn't know quite what else to say. 'Did the dentist breach confidentiality?'

'Who knows,' said Ffion with an airy wave of the hand. 'And who cares? Point is, *someone* breached it, and they can be sued. Which means Jasmine's career could be about to go stellar, and so might mine on the back of it.'

Emily looked at Ffion with distaste. How could she possibly get off on all this stuff?

'Well, I feel sorry for the dentist,' she said. 'It's not his fault Jasmine's got rotten teeth.'

'You're way too soft,' said Ffion. 'He'll be insured or something. Who cares about him?'

Emily felt a headache coming on. The music was thumping louder than ever. In the distance she could see Callum jumping higher than before. What was she doing here? Over these last few weeks with Mark she had been feeling cleaner somehow, as if the cancer that had got into her soul had been somehow washed out; but back here, listening to Ffion's greedy and small-minded chat, she felt polluted again. And watching Callum throwing himself around the dance floor just made her think about Mark and dancing like no one was looking. This place was all about everyone looking at *everything* you did. What was the next line? *Love like you've never been hurt.* Callum or Mark.

That was the choice she faced. But which one would hurt her the most?

'You saw the papers at the weekend.' Diana greeted Mark as he came into the surgery on Monday morning. It was a statement, not a question.

'Oh bugger. Was it in more than one? I only saw Friday's *Standard*.'

'There was a smallish piece in the *Mail*, but the News of the Screws went for it hell for leather,' said Diana. 'Do you want to see it?'

'Not particularly,' said Mark.

'Wise choice,' said Diana. 'Most of the article is taken up with pictures of Jasmine posing topless.'

Mark shuddered. 'I think I'll give that a miss,' he said with feeling. 'Did they mention any names?'

'Not so far, all they've said is "a dentist in South London". So they didn't even get that right. Don't worry. It will probably all blow over.'

Mark made himself a cup of coffee and wandered into his surgery ready to start the day. He was just putting on his lab coat when he heard a commotion by the front desk. Whoever was out there was becoming very agitated. He could hear Diana making soothing, placating sounds.

'You can't stop me seeing him!'

'I'm sorry, Mr Davies is busy –' he heard Diana say, before the door of his surgery was flung wide open and a red-faced and very angry-looking Jasmine marched right in. Snapping at her heels was the Rottweiler, and hovering apologetically behind her was Diana. 'Sorry, I tried to stop them,' she winced.

Jasmine thrust a copy of the *News of the World* in Mark's face. If he hadn't been so stressed, he might have laughed out loud.

'You said this wouldn't get in the papers,' she screeched. 'You promised.'

'And I have no idea how they got hold of it either,' said Mark, 'but coming in here being rude to my staff and upsetting the other patients doesn't help anyone. Why don't we all just calm down and talk about this sensibly.'

'Calm down? Calm down?' the Rottweiler screamed. 'Thanks to you she's lost her contract. How can she calm down?'

'I'm very sorry about that –' Mark attempted to say, but his words were drowned out. Both Jasmine and her mother were speaking loudly and incomprehensibly at him.

'You told the papers my teeth were rotten,' said Jasmine. 'Bastard.'

'I most certainly did not,' said Mark, 'and if you can't talk about this rationally, I'd like you to leave.'

'Liar!' spat out Jasmine.

Mark held the door open for them pointedly. 'Leave,' he demanded. 'Or I'm calling the police.'

'I'm going to 'ave you,' said Jasmine as she flounced out.

'Bloody hell,' said Mark as the door slammed shut. 'Now what am I going to do?'

'No Emily tonight?' Rob wandered over to Katie as Isabella, resplendent in shimmering turquoise, clapped to indicate the lesson was at an end and the social dancing had started. So far this evening he'd only partnered Katie once, much to her disappointment. He seemed to be all over Mandy Allwick instead. He couldn't be, could he? Katie shook her head. He probably could. She had the feeling that Rob wasn't all that fussy. But she was shocked by the twinge of jealousy she felt. She had got used to Rob partnering her, and hadn't enjoyed dancing the waltz with a very stiff fifty-something with sweaty palms and bad breath, who was clearly on the pull but lacked Rob's self-confidence. Katie would have felt sorry for him except he'd trodden on her toes three times and hadn't even noticed.

'No, she's still in the office,' said Katie, then kicked herself,

129

thinking how many teachers worked in an office? Luckily Rob didn't seem to have noticed. She looked around her. 'No Mark either?'

'I think he had a prior engagement.'

'Yeah, right.'

They looked at each other and laughed.

'So you know what happened on Friday, then, I take it?' Katie said.

'I gather things didn't go too well,' said Rob.

'That's the understatement of the century, I'd say,' replied Katie. 'I've never heard Emily so angry.'

Rob looked a little sheepish.

'Look, could you tell her from me, it's not really Mark's fault. I told him when we first started coming here that he should pretend he didn't have kids. I thought it would cramp his style. I just wanted him to get his end away. I hadn't factored in that the stupid sod might actually want a *relationship*.'

Rob said this with an air of such puzzled bewilderment that Katie roared with laughter.

'Thank God not all men are like you,' she said. 'Okay, I'll tell her. Though I don't know if it will make any difference.'

Katie wasn't at all sure that Emily would come to her senses, given that her latest emotional crisis seemed to have sent her straight back into the arms of Callum, but there didn't seem much point in telling Rob that.

The music had switched from waltz music to Latin American, and Katie was on the verge of suggesting they dance when Mandy chose that moment to swan up.

'Ready to rumba, babe?' she asked.

'Just you try stopping me,' Rob said. He winked at Katie, then whispered in her ear as he left, 'She bores me rigid, but she goes like a train.'

'What are you like?' said Katie, giving him a shove. Honestly. He was appalling.

And yet there was something ridiculously appealing about him.

Katie tried to put Rob out of her thoughts, but when she got home and found Charlie locked away in the study showing no signs of coming down soon, she wistfully wondered if this was all life had to offer. Her dancing lessons seem to whisk her away into a world that was infinitely more glamorous than the real life awaiting her at home. To countenance her gloom, Katie found herself digging out a couple of dresses that had been her favourites before the children came along. To her delight she could just about squeeze back into them. Dancing had done her some good then, as she'd clearly managed to shed a few pounds. Not that Charlie had noticed. She wondered if Rob had.

Chapter Thirteen

'Katie, what on earth are you doing?' Charlie was standing in the kitchen holding a wailing Molly and looking bleary-eyed.

Katie looked up from scrubbing the kitchen floor.

'Cleaning the floor. What does it look like?'

'It's six o clock on Sunday morning,' said Charlie. 'Who the bloody hell cleans the floor at this time?'

'I do,' said Katie. 'I couldn't sleep. It needed doing. And my mum's coming for lunch. You were fast asleep. Why on earth should it bother you so much?'

'Because our daughter woke me up,' said Charlie. 'Didn't you hear her yelling?'

'Not down here,' shot back Katie. Her back was aching, and she felt dog-tired. 'And it would be nice if you dealt with her for once.'

'I do help out,' said Charlie. 'But I can't do anything when I'm not here.'

'Well you're here now,' said Katie, for once letting her anger get the better of her. 'So you can help. I do everything for the kids. All the time. As well as keeping the house clean.'

Molly roared even louder at the sound of her mother's raised voice, and Katie guiltily chucked the sponge down, dried her hands and grabbed the baby from Charlie's arms. It was clear that he had no intention of doing anything useful like changing her nappy or giving her some milk.

'Yeah, well, I never asked you to martyr yourself on the altar of motherhood,' said Charlie. 'And you're the one obsessed with keeping the house clean.'

'Oh come on,' Katie protested. 'You always moan when the house is untidy.'

'I did,' said Charlie, 'until you started getting so nutty about it. I mean, look at you. Your mum is coming to lunch today, so that involves you getting up at some godforsaken hour to clean the floor, which, if I remember rightly, you cleaned two days ago.'

'Yes, but I didn't do it properly,' said Katie. 'And Anthea always reckons you should get things out of the way so you can be ahead of the game.'

'Just listen to yourself, Katie,' said Charlie. 'You're taking advice on housework from a woman on the TV. It isn't normal. Besides, it's not as if your mum is even going to notice how clean the house is.'

He had a point there, Katie thought. It was ridiculous the way she felt she had to constantly prove to her mother that she'd made the right choice in giving up her career for a family. She knew that, but she couldn't help herself. Katie was determined to show off her own happy home as a contrast to the discord she'd grown up with. Sometimes, she wished wistfully, it would be nice to put that pettiness aside and just relax with her mother and chat normally for once.

'It matters to me,' Katie said stubbornly. 'So I'm cleaning it. It's not hurting you, so go back to bed why don't you?'

'You do know you're bonkers, don't you?' Charlie turned round and stumped upstairs, while Katie settled down with a bottle of milk and Molly in front of the TV. She was fuming. Why should Charlie care when she cleaned the house? It wasn't as if he was in it very much.

Emily woke up in Callum's arms with a start. Her head ached, her throat was dry and she had the hangover from hell. The

133

room was thumping as loudly as the music at the party he had dragged her to last night. It had been the same for pretty much most nights over the last few weeks, since she had foolishly let him back into her life.

She rolled over and looked at Callum lying peacefully asleep beside her. In repose he was the picture of innocence, his mop of fair curls topping a baby-looking face – Callum often joked that he was never safe in the men's toilets – making him appear much less cynical than he did when out and about on the town. That, along with his lopsided grin and a look he had that made it appear he only had eyes for Emily, gave him a vulnerability which had appealed to her when they first met – although if she was honest she knew that Callum used that vulnerability to keep her hooked. How else had she let herself go back out with him? Though it had to be said, at least this time he was making more of an effort. He hadn't quite got to the giving-her-flowers stage, but he had been assiduously turning up to meet her after work, and they had even managed a couple of meals out. She'd barely been home all week, and Katie had taken to leaving her pointed text messages, which Emily was guiltily ignoring.

She buried her head in the pillow. She'd been ignoring a lot of things recently. Going out with Callum was one long party, but she yearned for more, and Mark had shown her that she could have it.

It wasn't just that she had connected with Mark through their shared sense of humour and fun, there had also been so much more depth to their conversations. She had never really spent much time around people who talked politics – or at least not since her student days. The lads in her office were too busy making ribald remarks, while friends like Ffion were too infatuated with the latest celebrity gossip; and Callum, apart from some loose and casually thought out leftist notions like being against the Iraq war and owning property (which was rich coming from someone whose parents appeared to own half of Sussex), barely had a conversation of any depth. The most profound she'd ever heard him be was the day after 7/7 when he'd admitted to being frightened when he found himself stuck in a tube train near Kings Cross.

Mark, on the other hand, always had something interesting to say. From the conversations they had had on the few occasions they had met alone, she had appreciated that his was a sharp intellect, which, coupled with a passionate sense of justice, she found incredibly attractive. In some ways Mark had reminded her of her dad, who had always been a champion of the little people and shared Mark's passion to stand up for what he believed was right. Mark genuinely seemed unfazed and unbothered by the razzmatazz and material things that were the stuff of Emily's daily life. It had made a refreshing change. *He* had made a refreshing change. Emily had persuaded herself that here was a person of great integrity, which had made it all the more galling to discover that he had lied to her about something so important.

Katie seemed to think Emily was overreacting the last time they had spoken about it. 'I haven't exactly been straight with Rob. You certainly haven't been straight with Mark. Besides, I told you, Rob said it was all his fault anyway. Don't you think you're being a bit hard on him?'

She and Katie had rowed about it and Emily hadn't seen her since. But maybe she was right, Emily thought.

Callum stirred beside her. He snuggled up against her back and caressed her shoulders sleepily.

'Hey, babe,' he said. 'I dreamed for a moment you weren't there. Come on, give me a cuddle.'

As she responded to his embrace, Emily wondered what Mark was doing, and why she was even thinking about him when she had Callum.

Mark sat on the edge of a very cold ice rink collapsed in hysterics. It seemed it wasn't just dating he was terrible at – he'd spent most of the past hour flat on his back. Beth wasn't much better, spending the whole time clinging on to him for dear life. On their last round they had both taken a tumble and Beth had ended up sitting on his head.

'You two are so *sad*.' Gemma skated up with the superiority of one who looked as if she had been born on ice. She and the dreaded Shelly were regulars at the skating rink, though up until now Mark had assumed they were merely coming to ogle boys. Apparently they had learned how to skate at the same time.

'Here, help us up,' said Mark, putting up his hand. Gemma leaned down and he pulled her down on top of him.

'I hate you!' she said, evidently irritated that the cool poise she'd been adopting had been ruined, but to his relief she was laughing. Gemma had perfected the art of giving him the strong silent treatment for the past few weeks, but here was a welcome sign of a slight thaw.

'Come on,' Mark said, getting them both up properly, 'why don't we go and have burgers?'

'Ooh yes, please!' Beth's eagerness as ever made up for Gemma's studied indifference. Mark wished he could break through that reserve but he didn't know how. It was at times like these that he missed having a woman around. Sam always knew the best way of getting through to Gemma, and he had relied on her heavily to communicate with his often problematic daughter. But now he was on his own. He sighed heavily. Mark had half hoped that Emily might have hung around long enough to get to know Gemma. But he hadn't heard from her at all, apart from receiving his *Green Wing* DVD back via Katie. There hadn't been a note attached. So that was that. Back to square one. A single dad spending lonely Sunday afternoons with his kids.

'Are you going to see that woman again?' Gemma shocked him into spilling his Coke with the directness of her question.

'What woman?' Beth piped up.

'You know,' said Gemma, 'Dad's girlfriend. The one he forgot to tell us about. And the one he forgot to tell he had kids.'

'Oh, that one,' said Beth, who seemed more interested in the contents of her burger then her dad's love life.

'I don't think so,' said Mark.

'I don't mind if you do,' said Gemma with uncustomary softness.

'Oh.' Mark was totally taken aback. It was the last thing he was expecting. 'What's brought this on?'

'Shelly said I was being stupid,' said Gemma. 'She thought I was making a fuss about nothing. Apparently her mum and dad have both had loads of girlfriends and boyfriends since they split up. She says that you have needs and I should understand that.'

'Oh does she indeed?' Mark, thinking he was never going to look at Shelly in quite the same way again.

'So, it's okay,' said Gemma. 'I don't mind if you want to see Emma.'

'Emily,' corrected Mark.

'Whatever,' said Gemma with an airy wave of her hand. 'And I forgive you for lying about us. Uncle Rob explained that it was all his fault.'

Thank you, Uncle Rob, thought Mark.

'So,' Gemma seemed to be warming to her theme now, 'are you going to see her again?'

'I think it's more a question of will she see me again?' said Mark. 'She's pretty cross with me right now.'

'If she fancies you, she'll get over that,' said Gemma. 'You just need to send her flowers or something.'

'Oh, it's that simple, is it?' Mark was amused now.

'Yes,' said Gemma. 'I read all about it in Mum's *Cosmo*. All you need to woo a woman is flowers and chocolates, a few multiple orgasms and then she'll be anybody's.'

Mark nearly choked on his burger.

'I'm not sure life is as simple as *Cosmo* makes it out to be,' he said. 'In fact, I'm not even sure you should be reading *Cosmo*, but thanks for the advice.'

Rob was practising his Cuban motion in front of the computer. The phrase always made Rob laugh, but according to Carlo it was only the hip movement he needed to dance rumba properly, not something rude.

'Remember,' exhorted Carlo (whom Rob had decided resembled a Colombian drug dealer) from the YouTube clip Rob had downloaded, 'it's *how* you move that matters. If you want to be sexy with your lady, you have to *move* her, baby. So let's get some hip action going.'

Getting sexy with his lady wasn't proving too easy at the moment. Things with Mandy seemed to have fizzled out. Not that he minded all that much. Apart from some sizzling sex, there hadn't been much else there.

It was funny, he thought, as he followed Carlo's instructions about bending and straightening alternate knees, when he'd started this dance-class malarkey it had been purely to meet women, but now (though he'd never admit it to anyone, least of all Mark) he was getting completely hooked. Since Mandy had lost interest there didn't appear to be a lot of other fish in the sea – Rob had by now managed to work his way round all the available attractive ones – but he was enjoying learning to dance so much, he didn't actually mind.

'As you step forward, remember to let your hip drop,' Carlo was saying, but when he started talking about contra-body action Rob lost him completely. He paused the clip and started it again.

There was always Katie, of course. Although it wasn't as though he *fancied* her or anything. She was way too plump for him, although he had noticed that in the last couple of weeks she did seem to be slimming out a little. But it did make a nice change to actually have an intelligent conversation with a woman.

After watching the bit about contra-body action for the third time, Rob finally worked out that it meant that his right arm should move forward at the same time as his left leg, while his left arm should move forward in time with his right leg. He had a practice go, but the lounge was so small he found himself banging his shins on the coffee table, so he decided to skip that bit.

The phone rang. Mark was out with the girls, which meant Rob had the house to himself. He hated to admit it but Sundays gave him that doomed, about-to-be-executed feeling that he remembered so well from his own schooldays. Some time around lunchtime he always started feeling that the weekend was already over, any possibility of fun or enjoyment gone. Perhaps it would be better if he had someone to share the dullness of Sundays with. Someone like Katie, maybe . . .

Stop it, Rob, he said to himself as he went to pick up the phone.

'Rob, hi, it's Jenny Masters, how are you doing?' Jenny was an ex-colleague of Rob's from the days when he had worked at the school Gemma now attended. There had been a time when she had also been something more, but they had settled in the end for an easy casual friendship. Besides, she was now living with a six-foot rugby player, which was one complication too many for Rob.

'Hi, Jen,' said Rob, 'to what do I owe the pleasure?'

'Well, I need a favour actually,' said Jen. 'You know I organise team-building courses for the Year Nines?'

'How could I forget?' Rob had spent the best part of three years finding excuses for not helping out at them.

'I've got one coming up in the autumn term,' Jen said. 'I can't get anyone to volunteer . . .'

'I wonder why not,' said Rob. He had a feeling he knew what was coming.

'So I was just wondering . . .'

'The answer's no, Jen,' Rob interrupted. He'd resolved years ago that he was never going to get involved in stuff like this again, and he wasn't about to make an exception, even for Jen. The memory of that night, so long ago, still haunted him, however much he tried to forget it. It was funny how since he'd met Katie, he found himself thinking about it more and more.

'Rob, please.' Jen was more pleading than he'd ever known her. 'If I can't get enough help I'm going to have to cancel. We use the team-building to help the kids prepare for SATs. It's only four Saturdays of your life. They look forward to it so much, it seems such a shame if they can't do it.'

She'd got him there. Despite his outward cynicism, Rob loved his job, and he liked it that kids got better opportunities these days. It wasn't his problem, but on the other hand he'd feel a bit lousy if he was the difference between the course happening or not. And what had happened in Wales was years ago. There was no reason at all to think such a thing could happen again.

'Are you sure you can't get anyone else?'

'I've tried everyone I can think of,' promised Jen. 'Honestly, I wouldn't ask if I didn't need to.'

Rob felt himself cracking. Maybe it would do him good to face up to his demons. And maybe he'd enjoy it anyway. The reason he'd gone to Wales was because he enjoyed that sort of thing. Perhaps it was time to reconnect with his past.

'Okay,' he said. 'I'll do it. But only on the understanding that if someone else puts their name forward I can drop out.'

'Rob, you're a star. Thanks so much,' said Jen. 'What can I do to repay you?'

'I can think of lots of things,' said Rob. 'But I don't think your boyfriend would like any of them.'

'I'll buy you a beer next time I see you,' laughed Jen.

'You'd better,' said Rob, and put the phone down.

What had he done? He'd spent the best part of fifteen years avoiding responsibility. It was why he'd lost Suzie. It was why he was spending yet another Sunday afternoon alone. He and Suzie had seemed so special, but it had not been enough to hold them together in the wake of the tragedy that had engulfed them. He wondered what she was doing now. He hoped she was happy.

But the face that kept swimming before him wasn't Suzie's at all. For some reason, he couldn't, just couldn't, get Katie out of his head.

Chapter Fourteen

'Are you dancin'?' Rob sidled up to Katie as she stood contemplating the room, wondering if she really had the guts to keep coming to dance classes when Emily clearly wasn't planning to return. The thing was, Katie wasn't sure if she could live without dancing now. When anyone ever asked her, she always maintained that she enjoyed her cosy domestic set-up so much she didn't miss having a social life. 'Being at home with the kids and Charlie is enough for me,' she'd always say earnestly, and with most people that worked. Apart from with her mum, who had scathingly said, 'I think the woman protests too much,' the last time Katie had waxed lyrical about the joys of domesticity.

And, increasingly, it wasn't true. The boys needed her, of course they did, but they were at school all day, leaving her with Molly, who was great and gorgeous and all of that, but Katie could hardly have a meaningful chat with her. And then there was the house. The effort of keeping it pristine was killing her. During the day when Molly slept, Katie would run round frantically trying to put things in cupboards, clean out loos, hoover bedroom floors, but there never seemed to be enough time to get it done before Molly awoke. Oh God, maybe Charlie was right, she thought. Perhaps she was going bonkers. She'd even found herself itemising her cupboards the other day, and, let's face it, who else would dream of ironing hankies and putting them in colour co-ordinated piles to match her husband's shirts? If she was like this now, what on earth would she be like when Molly started school?

And so her dance classes had become vital to her. It was the one time in the week when no one was demanding her attention, when she could be anyone she wanted to be. She could forget that she was a size sixteen, had three children and a failing marriage. Although, of late Katie had been pleased to notice that her clothes were getting a little bit looser. Perhaps the dancing was helping her to lose weight. She had also found that Isabella's strictures about standing tall meant she was walking straighter. She'd spent so many years crouched over a buggy, she'd begun to think hunchback was her natural position.

And once Rob was leading her on the dance floor, she felt less of an ugly duckling and more of a graceful swan. She needed what he gave her each week; the chance to escape from the dreary reality of her life, to believe she could go somewhere different, be someone different. It was intoxicating somehow.

'Are you askin'?' Katie laughed back. Why was it that with Rob she felt ridiculously alive in a way she never (if she was honest) had done with Charlie?

'I'm askin',' Rob said.

'Then I'm dancin',' Katie replied, following him onto the floor to do a quickstep they had practised last week.

There was no doubt about it, Rob was the most assured and polished dancer of all the men in the room. Unlike the terrified divorcé Katie had danced with the previous week, or the supercilious young dancer from the local theatre school who'd once taken it upon himself to spin her round the room while telling her everything she was doing wrong, or any of the Jet Set, who made her feel like a plank, dancing with Rob felt natural. Instinctively, she seemed to know where he was leading her, and her body automatically fell in step and rhythm with his.

'You not dancing with Mandy this week?' Katie couldn't help

143

teasing, as she counted slow, back, quick to the side, quick close, slow forward, while Rob whisked her round the room.

'Nope,' said Rob, deftly executing a quarter turn – so very different from the guy who'd nearly sent them spinning into a wall last week. 'I think you could safely say that Mandy isn't going to be on my Christmas-card list any more.'

'I wouldn't worry about it,' said Katie, 'I think she's got other fish to fry.'

They stopped dancing for a minute to watch as Mandy sashayed up to the divorcé (from whom Katie had managed to elicit the information that he was a rather wealthy stockbroker) and proceeded to guide him by the hand and throw him round the dance floor. The poor man looked terrified.

'That's a relief,' said Rob, as they attempted the Forward Lock step Isabella had shown them earlier. 'Sorry, I got that wrong, my right foot should have been to the left of your feet.'

'Ooh, Rob's actually made a mistake,' grinned Katie, as they started again.

Rob glanced over at Mandy and the divorcé again, who were dancing incredibly close, like something out of *Dirty Dancing*.

'At least I don't have to feel guilty that I didn't call her at the weekend,' he said, nodding towards Mandy, who was lasciviously trailing a hand down the divorcé's back and hooking a finger on his jeans. Her victim was coming out in a cold sweat and looking as if he was completely out of his comfort zone.

'I find it hard to imagine you *ever* feeling guilty when you don't call a woman,' said Katie as they completed a quarter turn.

'Oh ye of little faith,' said Rob. 'I do have my principles, you know.'

'Why do I find that hard to believe?' said Katie.

'Believe it,' Rob replied. He brought her close to him as the dance came to an end. She could feel the thump of his chest against her, and for a moment, as she stared into his eyes and looked at his cheeky grin, she did believe it. For a moment. Then she came quickly to. Rob was as much part of the fantasy as the dancing was. She knew him for what he was. It was all right to engage in harmless flirtation with him, but it could go no further. Even if she weren't married. She recognised a heartbreaker when she saw one.

'Are you coming to the pub this week?' said Rob. He asked every week, and every week she said no.

'Not this week,' Katie replied. 'Thanks for asking, though.'

'What is it with you?' Rob asked. 'I swear you turn into Cinderella when you leave here, you're in such a hurry.'

'Yup, Cinders, that's me,' Katie said, curtseying as she got to the end of the dance.

'I'll have to turn into Prince Charming to get you to stay then,' said Rob.

'I think it will take a little more than that,' said Katie, and made her excuses to leave, wishing that she didn't really feel like Cinders going back to her daily grind.

Mark had read the letter three times, and still he couldn't believe what he was reading.

'What is it?' Diana looked up from the reception desk, which she was busily trying to restore to some kind of order after mistakenly allowing Sasha loose on it the previous Friday.

'Jasmine's going to sue us. Well, me specifically.'

'No.' Diana put down the case notes she was holding, and looked at him aghast. 'She can't.'

'Apparently she can,' said Mark. 'She's been advised by her PR agency that the News of the Screws was given the story about her tooth by someone at this practice, which is tantamount to a breach of confidentiality. Without anyone else to point the finger at, they're blaming me.'

'Here, let me see,' said Diana.

Mark handed her the letter and she scanned it rapidly.

'It's not as if they can prove it's you. Shall I run it past my old boss, see what he thinks?'

145

In her previous incarnation, Diana had been a legal secretary.

'Would you?' Mark felt all at sea. Nothing like this had ever happened to him before, and he hadn't a clue what to do next.

'Have you informed Head Office?'

Mark grimaced. Since the practice had been bought out by a corporate dental group, there were precious few people at the top who knew the first thing about dentistry (their current CEO had been big in dog biscuits once, apparently), so he wasn't at all convinced anyone would even have a clue what he was up against, let alone think about supporting him. If anything they would be more likely to buy Jasmine off to shut her up, and leave him out to dry.

'I have already told them she might be complaining,' he said. 'So I suppose I'll have to tell them this too. Thank God I rang my union rep.'

The meeting was fortuitously scheduled for this week. He was relieved beyond measure that he had someone professional to talk about it with.

'I'm sure it will be all right,' said Diana. 'Judging from this letter, all they've got is hearsay. I doubt very much that it will go to court.'

'I hope you're right,' Mark replied, taking the letter back from her and going to his surgery to ring someone in HR. He had a nasty feeling, given Jasmine's propensity for wanting to be in the public eye, that this one was going to run and run.

Rob was suitably sympathetic when they met for a pint in the Hookers. But, like Diana, he thought it would all blow over.

'I mean, how can they prove it was you?' Rob wanted to know. 'Unless they have you on tape talking to a journo, I don't think they've got anything to go on.'

Mark looked into his pint despondently.

'I suppose,' he said. Why did everyone feel more optimistic about this than he did?

146

'You didn't, did you?' Rob suddenly looked a bit anxious.

'Didn't what?'

'Ring the News of the Screws?'

Mark threw a beer mat at him by way of reply.

'Don't be daft,' he said. 'I would never tell anyone anything about my patients. You of all people should know that.'

Rob had at one point tried to get Mark to divulge the address of a woman Rob had spotted in the waiting room while having his teeth checked, and had been most disappointed when Mark wouldn't oblige.

'Yeah, I didn't really think going to the tabloids was your style,' said Rob. 'But it was worth it to see your reaction.'

'Bugger off,' said Mark in response. 'Fancy a game of darts? I want to imagine the board is Jasmine's face.'

'Okay,' said Rob, and the pair of them ambled over to the dartboard.

'What's happened to your buxom lady friend?' Barry the barman shouted out.

'She couldn't keep up with me.' Rob affected a swagger then prepared to throw his first dart. As the dart bounced off the board and nearly hit Paranoid Pete (who was standing danger-ously close to the dartboard) on the head, the nonchalant effect he'd been after was rather lost.

'That's not what I heard,' said Barry.

'Oh, what did you hear?' Rob said.

'That she's found someone who's a better lay than you are,' said Barry. 'Not that that would be difficult.'

'And who told you that?'

'I have my sources,' said Barry, tapping his nose.

'Hmm, she may have found someone richer,' said Rob, aiming his second shot, and this time hitting a perfect ten, 'but I doubt she'll get as much satisfaction.'

He winked at Barry and threw his last shot, this time hitting the edge of the dartboard, the dart pinging off.

'Never mind,' consoled Mark, whose first throw had scored six, 'there's always Katie.'

'Puh-lease,' said Rob. 'I do have my standards, you know.'

'Yup. And you are such an Adonis.' Mark hit another six, followed by a ten. Anger seemed to be having a positive effect on his aim. 'Your round, I think.'

Emily felt sick to the pit of her stomach. Week five of her tentative reunion with Callum, and already he was demonstrating how little he cared for her, by sidling off into the loos to snort the contents of the little sachet of white powder she had seen him purchase from a man who had vanished as if by magic into the background of the so-called Fun Pub Callum had dragged her into. It was the sort of place she wouldn't have been seen dead in normally, and she couldn't understand why Callum had taken her here until, coming out of the girls' toilets, she had seen that brief exchange.

It hurt Emily far more than it should that Callum had clearly been hoping he could get away without her seeing anything untoward. And had she been a moment later he would have succeeded. Trust her luck to walk out at the wrong moment. The charade she had been keeping up for the last few weeks collapsed. With a sharply painful clarity, Emily realised that she was never going to be able to trust Callum.

'What? What have I done?' Even now, of course, he would deny it. Emily thought with despair of the piles of work waiting on her desk, piles that Callum had managed to persuade her could wait till tomorrow, and she wished she were there or back home in the cosy little house she had so neglected of late.

'Forget it, Callum,' she said. 'If you don't know by now, there's no point me trying to tell you.'

'You need to lighten up,' said Callum.

'And you need to grow up,' said Emily. 'I'm leaving. Don't bother trying to call me.'

Without waiting for his reaction, she headed for the train

station, with a lighter heart than she'd had for several weeks. It was a balmy April evening and spring was finally here. It was heading towards dusk as she got off the train in Thurfield. Birds were singing as she walked down the High Street, and in the distance the sight of the downs made her heart lift. There were worse places to live than this, worse places to be.

'Emily?' A familiar voice called to her from the shadows across the road. Her heart stopped for a moment.

'Hi Mark,' she said, feeling suddenly foolish. She hadn't seen him for weeks and suddenly up close she felt her face redden and her whole body tingle with anticipation.

'Where are you off to?'

'Home. You?'

'I've just popped out to the offie,' said Mark. 'Rob and I are putting the world to rights over a curry and a beer.'

Emily smiled. The picture of the two of them together in their bachelor pad was enormously cheering somehow.

'You – you don't fancy joining us, do you?' The words came out in a rush and Mark looked like a kid with his nose pressed up against the window of a sweetshop.

'Sorry, not tonight,' said Emily, 'I'm a bit tired.'

Tired? *Tired?* That sounded really lame. She didn't know why she'd said it.

'Oh.' Mark looked completely crestfallen.

'But you could ring me if you like,' said Emily. 'I might be free later in the week.'

'Great,' said Mark.

'Yes,' said Emily.

They stood for an awkward moment framed in the halo of the streetlight, then Mark said in a rush, 'I'm sorry about, you know – lying and everything. I didn't mean to. It all got a bit out of hand.'

'It's okay,' said Emily. 'Katie explained that it was partly Rob's fault.'

149

'So you don't mind me ringing?'

'Nope.'

'Good,' said Mark. He lingered for a moment, then said, 'Curry. Beer. Rob. You know. Must go.'

'Yes,' said Emily.

She watched as Mark headed for the offie. Just before he entered, she called after him, 'I know we nearly finished your *Green Wing* DVD, but we've still got the whole of *Spaced* to watch.'

Mark stood in the doorway and grinned.

Chapter Fifteen

'Hello stranger.' Katie greeted Emily with a hug as she came through the front door. 'Am I pleased to see you. George spent last night throwing up, Molly hasn't stopped screaming all day, and Aidan's throwing a paddy because I dared to suggest that he go in the bath.'

'How long's Charlie away for this time?' Emily asked sympathetically.

Katie shrugged. She didn't want to admit that Charlie hadn't actually said when he was going to be back. Nor that he had yet to ring her. When she'd tried both the work flat and his mobile all she'd got was the answerphone and a '*this mobile is switched off*' message.

'A week, I think,' she said vaguely. 'Ooh, flowers, lovely.'

'And chocolate, wine, and if we're having a girly evening I thought you might like to see *Grease*.'

'You shouldn't have,' said Katie.

'Oh, I think I should,' Emily replied. 'I've been a bit crap recently. In fact, a lot crap. I wanted to say sorry.'

'Don't be daft –' Katie was saying, when a yell from upstairs stopped her in her tracks. There followed the sound of thundering footsteps and Aidan appeared halfway down the stairs saying, 'George hit me!'

'Did not!' George stood indignantly behind him. 'Just because I wouldn't let him borrow my Xbox.'

151

'Children who've been throwing up half the night shouldn't actually be playing with their toys at bedtime, I think,' said Katie.

'But Mum –' the boys chorused in a desperate competition to get her on their side.

'But Mum nothing,' was the swift response. 'Bed! Or I'll tell Dad.'

'So?' shot back George. 'It's not as if he cares.'

'George, that is enough!' Katie was shouting now. 'You do not speak about your father that way, do you hear?'

'It's true,' muttered George, 'he cares more about that rotten job than us.'

'That rotten job pays for your Xbox,' said Katie. 'Now say goodnight to Emily and get back to bed the pair of you. And NO more fighting.'

The boys trotted dutifully back upstairs and Katie ran a hand through her hair. God, these fights with the boys were exhausting. And ever more so when she had to deal with them on their own. Charlie being away was taking a toll not just on her, but on the kids too.

'Sorry about the chaos,' said Katie, conscious that due to her energy levels being at rock bottom she hadn't even managed the twenty-minute frantic scoop-up of toys and the speedy hoovering of the lounge that she had planned before Emily's arrival.

'You should see my place,' consoled Emily. 'And there's only one of me.'

'But I bet you manage to plump up your cushions,' said Katie. 'And I'm sure your house is odour-free.'

She picked up a bottle of milk, which had rolled out from under the sofa when she had gone to straighten it after the boys had been using it for the Black Pearl in a game of *Pirates of the Caribbean*. God only knew how long the milk had been there. It smelled rank.

'Only when Callum isn't there,' said Emily.

'So, go on,' said Katie. 'Tell me how it's going? And I take it all back. I don't really think he's the most useless tosser in the world.'

'Yes you do,' said Emily. 'And you're right.'

'Oh,' said Katie. 'So what's happened now?'

'It's over,' Emily told her. 'For good. I caught him snorting coke again, and told him that was it.'

'Yes, right,' said Katie, trying to look as though she believed Emily.

'Don't look like that,' Emily replied.

'Like what?' protested Katie.

'As if you've swallowed a bad penny,' said Emily. 'I know. I know. I've said it before. But this time, I mean it. I'm really not going to have him back.'

Katie went to fetch some wine glasses and a corkscrew while Emily put the DVD in.

'So where does this leave you and Mark then?' Katie wanted to know as she poured them both a generous slug of wine.

'Nowhere,' said Emily, 'why should it?'

'Mark had *nothing* to do with your decision?' Katie left the question hanging.

There was a long pause.

'He might have had a bit,' admitted Emily eventually. 'I don't think he meant to upset me. Whereas Callum – Callum pretends to care for me, but all he's really interested in is himself and where his next fix is coming from.'

'And Mark?'

'He's just different, I guess.' Emily looked down at her hands, and paused again, as if she was finding it difficult to know what to say. 'Ever since Dad died, I've been fighting this feeling that what I do is just so pointless. That the world I'm in is so vacuous and facile. It's not where I thought I'd be right now.'

Katie grimaced.

'I think we all end up in places we don't expect to,' she said kindly. 'And it's understandable you should start questioning

153

things when your dad died. It's a major life event, and has probably made you reappraise everything. I know that's how it was for me.'

Katie thought back to how quickly she and Charlie had got engaged after Dad had died. At the time it had seemed so natural. Life is short. Seize the moment. Love doesn't come along every day. It was only now, looking back through the twenty-twenty vision of hindsight that she wondered if she had rushed headlong into making a terrible mistake?

'So, I'm reappraising,' said Emily. 'And I think Mark may be part of that. If he wants to be.'

'I can really see that,' said Katie as they settled down to watch the film. 'God, I'd forgotten how well John Travolta could dance. *Those hips.* They're something else, aren't they? I'd give anything to partner a man who danced like that.'

'Have you tried to persuade Charlie to come dancing with you?' Emily asked.

'Apart from it being a bit difficult to go out with someone who's never here, no,' said Katie, looking wistful. 'I haven't bothered. Charlie isn't too keen on dancing nowadays. More's the pity.'

'There's always Rob,' said Emily, singing along loudly and out of tune to 'Summer Lovin''.

'I'm not *that* desperate,' said Katie, throwing a cushion at her.

But as she settled down with her drink to watch the film, mesmerised by the sight of John Travolta's thrusting hips and the sheer joyous energy of the dancing, she couldn't help the picture of Rob dancing that popped unbidden into her head, and wondered what it would really be like to shimmy up to him. Was *he* the one that she wanted?

Mark was sitting on a train at Victoria, sipping a cup of coffee while staring vacantly at the *Evening Standard* he'd bought for no other reason than that there was a news stand by the entrance to his platform. Flicking through to the celebrity gossip section, he read that Jasmine was going to leave no stone unturned in her fight to discover the evil swine who had let the world know that her pearly gnashers weren't quite as pristine as she'd imagined. It appeared her multi-million pound contract with *Smile, Please*! really was in jeopardy, though, if the paper was to be believed, the ongoing column-inch value of her story seemed to be ensuring a steady stream of appearances on chat shows, and there was talk of her being signed up to front some ridiculous new programme all about cosmetic surgery.

Mark put the paper down and sighed. His meeting with James, the rep, had gone as well as could be expected. James had yet to see any evidence of wrongdoing from the other side, but had hooked Mark up with a lawyer.

'I'm sure when it comes to it, they'll back off,' James had assured him. 'They've got bugger all to link you to the leak. If we can find out who it was that let the press know, I'm sure we can sort this out easily.'

'And what about the General Dental Council?' In a way Mark was even more worried about that. If the GDC decided that he had seriously let down a patient, who knew what repercussions there could be for his career. He didn't always enjoy dentistry, but it was the only thing he knew.

'Unless Jasmine puts in a complaint about you, it probably won't be an issue,' said James.

Mark wished he could share James's confidence. But James had given up dentistry years ago in order to work on the legal side of the industry. He no longer remembered what it felt like at the coalface, nor could he probably imagine the cold weight of fear that had lodged deep in Mark's stomach. Mark knew he had done nothing wrong, but with the weight of a publicity-hungry celebrity hell-bent on revenge, what hope did he have of proving it?

The train was filling up rapidly. People were squashing in like

155

sardines. It made him grateful that he'd never been a commuter. He only hoped that Jasmine's antics weren't going to ensure that he joined their ranks.

'Is this seat taken?' A woman squeezed through the people jammed next to the doorway and grabbed the seat next to him with the ease of a seasoned commuter. Mark was always too polite to behave like that. Every time he came to London he marvelled that everyone reverted to stampeding animals.

'Mark! What a surprise!'

It was Emily. If anything was likely to lift him from his gloom, it was seeing her.

'Emily,' said Mark. Then he added stupidly, 'What are you doing here?'

'Going home from work. You?'

'Oh, just been to some boring dental thing,' he said. He felt reluctant to tell her about what was happening to him. After the debacle with the children, Mark was determined to regain Emily's good opinion of him.

'I thought you were a teacher,' he said. 'Don't you work locally?'

Emily blushed a deep scarlet.

'Oh God,' she said, 'I suppose you had to find out sometime.'

'Find out what?'

'Mark,' Emily said. 'I'm really, really sorry. You're not the only one who's not been telling the whole truth.'

'What do you mean?'

'I only said I was a teacher to get you to like me more,' Emily said.

'Why on earth would you do that?' Mark was genuinely puzzled.

'It was what you said about lawyers,' Emily confessed. 'You seemed to hate them so much.'

'I do,' said Mark, thinking *even more than I used to*. 'So what's that got to do with you?'

'Please don't hate me,' said Emily. 'But the thing is, I am one.'

'One what?'

'A lawyer,' said Emily.

'I hope you told her where to get off.' Rob was horrified when Mark told him later that night about the conversation he and Emily had had on the train.

'Actually, no,' said Mark. 'I laughed and said it didn't matter.'

'What? Are you mad? The woman lied to you, for fuck's sake. How do you know you can trust her?' Rob shook his head pityingly at his friend's folly. 'You've been out of this game too long, my friend. You need Uncle Rob to take you in hand.'

'And I lied to her,' said Mark. 'Point is, we were both hiding stuff from one another. And now we're not. So we've wiped the slate clean.'

'So when are you seeing her again?' Rob had the patient air of one who has seen it all before.

'Later in the week,' Mark told him. 'We're going out for a meal.'

'And will you both be gracing the dance floor again with your presence?' asked Rob.

'We might be,' said Mark. 'So long as that isn't going to cramp your style.'

'My style would take a lot more than you jumping around in your size twelves to cramp it,' said Rob. 'I still think you're being an idiot, though. There are plenty more fish in the sea.'

'Yes, but they're not Emily,' said Mark. 'She's the first woman who's meant anything to me since Sam. I can't just walk away.'

'Don't say I didn't warn you,' Rob cautioned. 'I just hope you're not about to make a prize tit of yourself. Again.'

'I may be sad,' Mark said, settling down in front of the TV, 'but it's better to be a tit than to spend my days flitting from woman to woman without ever committing to any one of them.'

'You only say that because you don't have it the way I do,' said

157

Rob with a lightness he suddenly didn't feel. Since Mandy had disappeared over the horizon he hadn't spotted any more potential at the ballroom-dancing classes. Maybe the supply was drying up. Or maybe he was losing his touch.

Rob told himself not to be so stupid. There were plenty of other women, and he'd never had difficulty pulling before. It was just that he'd hit a barren patch. Nothing had changed.

Except perhaps you, a little voice whispered. Rob had spent fifteen years running away from his past, running away from commitment. He'd always told himself that that was what he wanted. So why, now, did he feel so very lonely?

Chapter Sixteen

'*Muy bien, mis chicos.* You two are doing so well, I might have to think about moving you up to the intermediate group,' Isabella announced to Rob and Katie at their next dance class, as she helped them perfect their quickstep. 'If you wanted you could even try out for a medal.'

'What do you say, Katie?' Rob asked. 'You know how I'm longing to show you my best moves.'

'I'll think about it,' said Katie, as she pulled back laughing. She carried on laughing as Isabella clapped her hands to indicate that the music should start up again. Rob twirled her round the room and she felt light and pretty, and free. All the things she never felt normally.

She found less and less to laugh about at home these days; she was tense with the boys, miserable with Molly. Her perfect home was beginning to feel like a prison. Rob, it seemed, was the only person who could make her laugh. Charlie certainly didn't any more. When he was at home he barely communicated with her, spending hours in his upstairs office. Several times she had caught him in furtive whispered conversations on the telephone, which he'd cut short when she came in. Her suspicions were aroused, but it was proof of what exactly? Katie was enough of a realist to know that Charlie was displaying all the signs of a man with a mistress, but too much of an ostrich to want to really face up to the truth. She couldn't bear the fact that the carefully constructed edifice she had erected of a perfect family life might be crumbling apart. She hadn't even confided her suspicions to Emily.

The one person who had seen through her was her mum. Which had surprised Katie. It wasn't as if they were close. The last time Mum came to lunch, Charlie had snapped at Katie a couple of times and Mum had pursed her lips and looked askance in that infuriating superior way of hers, as if she could see something that Katie couldn't.

Tonight she'd come to babysit. Being Mum, she made a great fuss about the fact that she'd had to drive the full half an hour from Crawley to get there. 'Some of us still work, you know,' she'd bitched before she had even got her coat off.

Katie bit back a response, so practised was she in the art of not getting into fights with her mother, but it had got them off to an unsettled start. Mum had proceeded to tell her that she spoiled Molly (was it, Katie wondered, *really* possible to spoil a baby?) and should leave her to cry more often, and made loud remarks about women with over-tidy houses having too much time on their hands.

But the crunch had come when Katie came downstairs from putting Molly in her cot.

'I don't mean to pry,' began Mum, 'but is everything okay between you and Charlie?'

'What makes you say that?' Katie said waspishly. She knew she was being defensive.

'He does seem to be away on business rather a lot.'

'It's not his fault,' protested Katie. 'It's the way work is nowadays. At his level he has to be really involved in everything to do with this merger.'

'I'm sure you're right, dear,' said her mother, 'but I couldn't help wondering if –'

'Well don't,' said Katie with an air of finality. 'Don't wonder. Everything's fine.'

'If you say so,' her mum responded, in a tone which implied she didn't believe a word of it. 'You can always talk to me, you know, I would understand.'

'Thanks,' Katie had said shortly, 'but there's nothing *to* talk about.'

Besides, what could her mother possibly understand about her situation with Charlie? It was totally different from what had happened with Mum and Dad. It was Mum who'd deserted Dad, and left him in the lurch just short of his fifty-fifth birthday. He'd never recovered from the shock and less than two years later he was dead from a heart attack. Katie laid the blame squarely on her mother, and their relationship had never fully recovered.

'So you're going to give it a go?' Rob jerked her back into the present. Funny, how while dancing in his arms she could just drift off.

'Give what a go?'

'This medal thing,' said Rob. 'It might be a laugh.'

'You're right,' said Katie. 'It might be a laugh.'

And heaven knows, she could do with one of those.

Emily hovered nervously outside the King's Head pub, a cosy pub on the High Street, where she was meeting Mark before going for a curry. It was a warmish spring evening, but then it was nearly May. The cheerful sound of birdsong had accompanied her walk into town. It was lovely, the evenings were getting lighter, and Emily felt she was finally casting off the slough of despondency she'd felt over the winter. She loved this time of year, with its hint of new beginnings and promise, but she wondered if she'd made a mistake with the light strappy summer dress and cotton jacket she'd chosen. Her legs were certainly feeling the chill due to her having opted for sandals.

Maybe April was a little too soon to discard her boots. She

had felt the need to feel feminine, though. All the time she'd been with Callum, he'd barely noticed the way she looked, so unless she'd been coming from work she'd tended to go for the same jeans and T-shirt routine. Tonight she had spent a ridiculously long time choosing what to wear, and was regretting that she didn't have a convenient flatmate to check out how she looked. At one point she'd been so desperate for approval Emily had rung up Katie to ask if she could come round and model a couple of outfits, but hearing the sickness bug had now spread to Molly, she'd subsequently decided against it.

'Hi.' Suddenly Mark appeared as if from nowhere in all his heart-stopping gorgeousness.

'You look lovely too,' he said. 'Talking to yourself is the first sign of madness, you know.'

'Oh God,' said Emily, 'did I really say that heart-stopping gorgeous thing out loud?'

'You did,' said Mark, 'but I won't hold it against you.'

And then suddenly it didn't matter what she was wearing, or whether he'd notice that her heart was pounding and her hands were sweating, because she was out, alone with Mark. And there was no place she'd rather be.

'What'll you have?' asked Mark as he led her to the heaving bar.

'Vodka and tonic, thanks,' said Emily.

'I thought you drank beer?' Mark asked.

'I do in the week. But it's Friday, and I'm celebrating,' said Emily.

'Celebrating what?' Mark grinned.

'Ooh, I don't know, the fact that it's Friday?' She hoped that her own grin wasn't quite as goofy as she feared it was.

'We could of course celebrate a new beginning,' said Mark, as he skilfully guided her to an empty table nestled in the corner.

'That too,' said Emily, and chinked his glass.

There was a brief pause, before Emily said,

'I really do owe you an apology, though. I should have come clean about being a lawyer before. It was just that you seem to have such a downer on them. We're not all bad, you know.'

'And you seem to have such a downer on kids.'

'Touché,' said Emily. 'Actually, I don't. Have a downer on kids, I mean. I quite like them really. But experience has taught me that a woman of my age, body clock ticking and all that – men don't tend to want you to talk babies straight away.'

'Most men probably don't,' said Mark. 'But I'm not most men.'

'I'm beginning to realise that,' said Emily apologetically. 'Anyway, I'm sorry I overreacted. I can see if I'd been straight from the beginning you wouldn't have felt the need to lie in the first place.'

'I probably deserved it,' said Mark. 'Though, to be honest, I felt worse about deceiving the girls than I did you. Gemma has only just forgiven me.'

'Go on then,' said Emily, 'tell me all about them.'

'Are you sure?' asked Mark. 'There's nothing more boring than a proud parent.'

'And are you a proud parent?'

'Of course,' said Mark. 'Look, here's a picture of them. This is Gemma, who you've already met of course. She's thirteen, and here's Beth, who's ten.'

'Oh, aren't they lovely,' said Emily, feeling a peculiar mix of delight at Mark's obvious pride in his pretty daughters, who shared his arresting brown eyes, and a slight pang of envy that the little blonde one, certainly, took after the unknown mother, whom she hoped Mark had stopped thinking about.

'I think so,' said Mark, putting the photos away, 'but then I am biased. What about you? Tell me about your family.'

'Not much to tell,' said Emily. 'Mam, two sisters, all living near

Swansea. That's it.' She still found it hard to miss Dad out from the list.

'Are your parents divorced?'

'No,' Emily swallowed. 'My dad – he died six months ago.'

'Oh, I'm sorry,' said Mark, reaching for her hand.

'It's okay,' Emily said, trying to bite back the tears. 'He'd been ill for a long time. He worked for a building firm in the seventies who had, shall we say, a rather cavalier approach to health and safety. Dad ended up working on a site where there was asbestos. He was ill for most of my teens.'

'Emily, that's dreadful,' said Mark. 'I really am sorry.'

'At least he's not suffering any more,' she said.

'What was he like?'

'He was wonderful,' said Emily. 'As a kid he was always taking us out, giving us treats. He couldn't do that once he was ill, of course. But he was so brave. He's the reason I'm a lawyer, you know. I wanted to take on companies like his and get them to pay decent compensation . . .'

Her voice trailed off.

'But instead?'

'I seem to have got a bit sidetracked,' admitted Emily. 'The thing is, the firm I work for pays really well – I've got a huge mortgage and Mam got herself into a bit of a mess with scratch cards after Dad died. She's spent thousands on stupid offers, and calling those damned phone lines that promise you prizes. I'm helping her pay off her loan. I hate my job, but I can't afford to leave.'

'I have days like that,' said Mark. 'You never know, though, maybe the job of your dreams will turn up someday soon.'

'Maybe,' said Emily.

'Do you want another drink here, or one at the restaurant?'

'It's a bit noisy here,' said Emily, looking around at the pub, which was even busier than when they'd arrived.

'Okay, restaurant it is,' said Mark. He took her hand as they left the pub as if it were the most natural thing in the world. Emily's heart was singing. After all the angst and stress of the last few weeks she felt this was where she was meant to be. Here was a man who seemed to genuinely care for her; she'd be a fool to let him go.

'Are you sure you're okay with me having kids?' Mark asked as the waiter sat them down at their table. 'They are really important to me, and you do need to understand they have to come first. But I can see they could complicate things.'

Emily didn't say anything for a minute. Mark was right. The kids were a complication. One she had never factored in before. Perhaps she should walk away now. But then she'd never known anyone like Mark before. She instinctively felt he was worth a little complication. She took a deep breath.

'Yes, really, I am,' she said. 'I think it's great that you clearly have such a good relationship with them.'

'I couldn't honestly say I have that great a relationship with Gemma at the moment,' said Mark, 'as she's going through a bit of an awkward phase, but they do mean everything to me. And I need you to understand that, if we're to get anywhere with this – whatever *this* is.'

Emily took his hand and held it tightly.

'The kids are part of you. And I'll do my very best not to make that a problem.'

'Good,' said Mark. 'Love me, love my kids. That's the way it has to be.'

'Sounds good to me,' said Emily. 'Now, what wine do you recommend?'

'How did you manage to persuade me to do this?' Rob had just sat through a turgid presentation of the course he had found himself inveigled into helping on. 'I'm missing my dancing class for this.'

'Because I am wonderful and you love me deeply,' said Jen.

165

'Don't flatter yourself,' growled Rob. 'How am I going to keep with Mr Muscles over there?'

Mr Muscles was the highly toned and visibly hunky representative from Face the Fears, the activity company that was running the course. He had the innate confidence of the sporting jock, and Rob had loathed him instantly. Once upon a time, Rob had been active in adventures sports, enjoying climbing, hiking and canoeing, but since the accident he had dropped all of that. Watching Mr Muscles only highlighted how flabby and out of condition he really was. Perhaps he should start following Mark's lead and pop to the gym a bit more often rather than the pub.

'It's not a contest,' said Jen, laughing. 'Honestly, Rob. Don't you ever grow up?'

'Nope,' said Rob. 'So, this trip, then. Do you think it really helps the Year Nines to do team-building?'

'We think so,' said Jen. 'Don't you do anything similar at your school?'

'Nah, not really, but my lot are as apathetic as I am,' confessed Rob. 'The only reason I'm doing this is because of you.'

'I do appreciate it, really I do,' said Jen.

'How good on the old health and safety stuff are they?' Rob nodded at Mr Muscles. 'I mean, I know he talked the talk, but abseiling, climbing, canoeing . . . There's a lot of potential for things going wrong there.'

'I had you taped as a gung-ho adventuresome kind of guy,' said Jen, somewhat surprised. 'Surely you agree that some element of risk is worth it to broaden these kids' horizons.'

'I do,' said Rob, 'in principle. And I agree we've all got a bit obsessed with health and safety. But things can go wrong. I went on an adventure week very similar to this when I was at college and a kid died in a climbing accident. It was no one's fault, but it's left me very wary of doing this kind of thing.'

'I'm not surprised,' said Jen, 'but honestly, we've been using

Face Your Fears for years and they have an excellent safety record.'

'I'm sure they have,' said Rob. 'I'm just a bit paranoid about it, that's all.'

'Are you sure you still want to come?' asked Jen. 'You should have said – you know, about the accident.'

'It's fine,' said Rob lightly. 'It was a long time ago.'

'Well, if you're sure . . .' said Jen.

'I'm sure,' maintained Rob. 'After all, like you said, they've got a great safety record. What could possibly go wrong?'

Mark sank down into Emily's soft white sofa with a contented sigh. It had seemed natural to walk her home after the restaurant, and even more natural to follow her in for coffee.

'Actually, do you really want coffee?' Emily came in the room clutching a bottle of wine, a corkscrew and two glasses. 'I fancy some more wine myself.'

'I think I can cope,' said Mark. 'And I have the perfect accompaniment.'

'Oh?'

'Ta-da!' Mark waved aloft his *Green Wing* DVD. 'I think we still have a couple of episodes left to watch.'

Emily loaded the DVD and clicked on episode nine, before settling down beside Mark. He sat staring at her in silent awe. She was so gorgeous. He was overcome with an overwhelming need to kiss her.

'What?' she said, as if suddenly aware of his interest. 'Have I got a big zit on the end of my nose or something?'

'No,' said Mark, edging closer towards her. It had been eons since he'd been near a woman, since he'd been in a situation like this. And now he was here, he had a sudden urgent worry that Emily might not be interested after all. 'I was just thinking – well, wondering if you were thinking –'

'Thinking what?' she asked.

'What I was thinking?'

'Which is?' Emily gave him a look that made his heart flip over.

She was thinking what he was thinking.

'Only this,' said Mark, and kissed her.

Chapter Seventeen

'Dad, do we have to go out?' Gemma was whining as Mark rushed round the kitchen trying to throw things together for a picnic.

'Yes, we do,' said Mark. 'It's a bank holiday, the sun is shining – at the moment – and I thought a nice day out would be just the thing to break the ice between you and Emily.'

'Suppose I don't want the ice broken,' said Gemma sulkily. She was sporting a black T-shirt bearing the legend *Your worst nightmare*, a black miniskirt and leggings with skulls on. Her hair had been slicked and spiked into a hairstyle that would have looked alarming on the most determined of goths. He couldn't quite work out whether she resembled a porcupine or a spiny urchin. She was certainly spiky enough for both.

'Gemma,' Mark was getting a bit fed up with her attitude, 'I thought you were okay about me seeing Emily.'

'Yeah, well, I don't see why we have to see her.' Gemma was about to kick the table, but seeing Mark's look she fell short.

'I want to meet her,' Beth said as she came in. In his darker moments, Mark wondered whether she perfected this milk-of-human-kindness approach to curry favour, but dealing with Gemma was hard enough. If Beth was turning out to be as hideously manipulative as her mother, he wasn't at all sure he wanted to know.

'You would,' snarled Gemma – porcupine, definitely porcupine, Mark decided – before she stomped out of the room.

'What did I say?' Beth looked injured.

'Don't wind her up,' said Mark. 'You know it makes her worse.'

'You always take her side,' said Beth, 'it's so unfair!' And she too stormed off, slamming the door.

'Bloody hell,' Mark said aloud, 'what did I do to deserve this?'

'Insist that your new girlfriend met your kids,' said Rob, strolling in. 'I could have told you *that* was a bad idea.'

'They've got to meet her sometime,' Mark responded grumpily. The doorbell rang and his heart ratcheted up a few dozen notches. God, he hoped this was going to work.

'Shall we do something today?'

Katie had had the same idea as Mark. The sun was shining and Charlie was home for a rare weekend. They hadn't done anything as a family for ages. Perhaps all that was needed was some bonding time.

Charlie looked up from behind his copy of the previous day's *Financial Times*, which to her annoyance he always read at the breakfast table.

'How am I ever going to persuade the boys not to read at the table if you persist in doing it?'

'What about football?'

'It's not on today,' said Katie. 'Some of the schools have started their holidays early so Bill cancelled their session today. And there isn't a match this week. So, we have a free day. I thought we might go somewhere nice.'

'Oh. Right. Yes, I suppose it might be a good idea.' Charlie didn't sound wildly enthusiastic. 'I've got a bit of work to catch up on, though.'

'Dad, can't we go to Bodiam Castle?' George asked. 'Please. We haven't been to a castle for ages.'

'Oh, yes, please, Dad.' Aidan was jumping up and down now with excitement.

Surely even Charlie couldn't resist such blandishments, Katie thought.

170

Sighing deeply, he folded up his paper and said, 'Oh, all right then. But I do have to check my emails before we go. And we can't stay out long.'

'Dad, you're the best!' Aidan threw himself at Charlie, who hugged his son tightly.

'I won't be a tick,' he said, and shot off upstairs.

Good, thought Katie with satisfaction, as she went into the kitchen to prepare a picnic. She'd been right. A family day out was just what they needed.

Twenty minutes later, Katie was ready but there was no sign of Charlie.

'Charlie?' she called up the stairs. There was no reply. Sometimes it was so inconvenient having the office at the top of the house. She sent the boys to the loo, and carried Molly up the stairs. She could hear Charlie's tones very low.

'No . . . she doesn't. Look, I've told you I can't . . .' Charlie was having another of those furtive phone conversations. Katie's heart was hammering as she pushed open the door to see her husband crouched over the phone. He turned round and gave her a startled look.

'I've got to go,' said Charlie. 'We'll catch up about the Makepeace deal next week.'

He put the phone down with a guilty air.

'Sorry, just got caught up talking to the guy in our Amsterdam office.'

'What about?' Katie asked suspiciously.

'Nothing. Just boring work stuff. Come on, I'm all yours.' He kissed her on the top of her head, and headed for the stairs. Katie followed him with a heavy heart. Just what was he keeping from her?

'Dad, did you have to take us to a mouldy old castle?'

Gemma appeared determined to spoil the day. Ever since Emily had arrived she had whined and moaned and bitched about how boring everything was, and how she'd much rather be with Shelly, who she had spent most of the journey texting, until Mark had lost his rag and threatened to confiscate the phone. He had apologised profusely to Emily, who'd found it quite funny really. Mark didn't seem the type to get cross, and he was rather endearing when he did it, although it was quite clear to Emily that both his girls ran rings around him. And she didn't really blame Gemma for her bad behaviour. No doubt a thirteen-year-old Emily would have done similar in her shoes. Added to which, Gemma had spent the journey squashed up next to Rob, who on hearing they were going to visit a castle clamoured to join them too. 'I can check it out for my Year Sevens,' he explained. 'We could do with a new venue for our history trip next year.'

'Sorry, Gemma.' Emily turned round from the front passenger seat (another thing that had clearly annoyed Gemma, being ousted from her favourite spot), with what she hoped was a winning smile. 'That was my fault. I like castles, and I suggested it to your dad. I thought you might enjoy one too. Look, if it's really boring we can do something else instead.'

Gemma, clearly discomfited by this overture of friendship, retreated into a noncommittal shrug, and sulkily got out of the car.

'I like castles.' Beth came up and placed her hand in Emily's, in a gesture that nearly made her laugh out loud. One child was doing her best to alienate Emily, while the other was trying her hardest to win her over. It would be nice, she thought, if they were both eventually able to act normally with her.

'Good,' said Emily. 'We'll just have to persuade Gemma that it's fun, won't we?'

'You won't,' said Gemma as she stomped off.

As it turned out, even Gemma was hard pushed to keep up her indifference.

The views of the castle as they approached were spectacular. With its four round towers and square walls dominating the moat that surrounded it, it seemed the epitome of a medieval castle, so that Gemma, from affecting nonchalance, slipped instead to spouting information about portcullises and postern gates, half-remembered from her study of medieval history in Year Seven.

Emily suppressed a grin when she noticed that while Gemma was quite happy to tell everyone else about William the Conqueror, as soon as Emily asked a question Gemma couldn't seem to stop herself saying rudely, 'I wasn't talking to you.'

'Gemma!' Mark was scandalised, but Emily shook her head at him.

'Give her time,' she whispered, 'she'll come round.' Emily chatted to Beth instead, while Mark explained the function of a drawbridge to Gemma. In the meantime, Rob expounded to anyone who would listen the theory that while Bodiam might look the part, the chances were it wasn't a defensive castle at all.

'Walls are too thin, you see,' he said sagely, although by now they had entered the main courtyard and even Gemma was excited by the people dressed up as knights and the possibility of trying on medieval mail, which, as she was knowledgeably saying, wasn't actually called chain mail as most people thought.

'Well, I'll just talk to myself, then,' said Rob sulkily.

'Oh do shut up,' said Mark. 'And stop being such a know-all. We don't all have history degrees, you know.'

They wandered through to a tent and the boys had a happy ten minutes mucking about with swords and helmets, leaving Emily and the girls looking on.

'Dad, you are so embarrassing,' moaned Gemma. 'Don't you think you're a bit old for that now?'

'Nope,' said Mark, trying to parry and thrust with a sword that was lighter than he could have imagined.

'It's fun,' said Rob, breathlessly darting out of Mark's way, 'you should try it.'

'In your dreams,' snorted Gemma. 'Aren't you ever going to grow up?'

173

'Men never grow up,' said Emily, 'believe me.'

Gemma looked at Emily, and for the first time that morning gave her a grin that held a faint approximation of warmth.

'You know, Gemma,' said Emily, choosing her words carefully as she watched Gemma laughing at Rob's shenanigans, 'I can understand it's difficult for you. And I don't mind if you don't like me.'

'You're okay,' muttered Gemma.

Emily grinned. Perhaps they were getting somewhere after all.

Katie had a headache and was wishing they hadn't come. She couldn't get the sight of Charlie looking so guilty out of her head. They'd got stuck in traffic all the way to Bodiam, the boys had argued constantly about whose turn it was on the Nintendo DS, and Molly had thrown up in the car. Luckily most of it had gone on her clothes, and Katie had brought spares, but she could have done without it. Particularly as Charlie appeared to have completely zoned out, for all the notice he took of everything. He only seemed to stir temporarily to shout at the boys when their bickering got too much, and to make sarcastic comments about why Katie hadn't had the forethought not to give Molly milk in the car, because didn't she remember the last time?

Didn't you? was the resentful thought that lodged in Katie's brain, but it didn't, as usual, make it as far as her lips.

What had she been thinking? A day out together should have brought them together, but somehow, away from the house, doing something normal families did, just emphasised to her how far they had drifted. The boys deferred to her constantly, barely acknowledging their dad, and when they did so they appeared nervous, as if unsure of what his reaction would be. Which was fair enough, because Charlie's reactions were nothing if not unpredictable. One minute he'd be joking around and laughing and the next minute he'd be biting the kids' heads off for a triviality. Everyone was walking on eggshells around him. It was very wearing.

On discovering that it was raining as they arrived, Charlie was all for turning back.

'Let's have our lunch now,' Katie said as brightly as she could muster. 'It's probably an April shower. It'll blow over.'

And blow over it did, but not before George had managed to spill Ribena all over the tailgate of the car, where he and Aidan were perched while they were eating.

'Why are you so sodding clumsy?' Charlie bellowed at George, who promptly burst into tears.

'And why are you so sodding intolerant?' hissed Katie as she wiped up the mess and tried to calm George down.

Charlie had the grace to look embarrassed.

'Sorry, George, mate,' he said. 'I'm in a bit of a grump today. I'm not sure why.'

They hadn't even reached the castle yet and the trip was already turning into a disaster. Katie had a feeling it was going to be a long day.

Rob, on the other hand, was having a great time. He had chased Beth round the battlements, and had interesting conversations with Emily (who had turned out to be a bit of a history buff) about the numbers of archers really likely to have been involved in the Battle of Agincourt, and they had had their lunch on the castle lawn, watching a display of medieval archery. Even the brief shower and Gemma in full Wednesday Addams grumpy mode had failed to dampen Rob's spirits. He looked at Mark and Emily sitting together, close, but not too close, clearly doing their best not to touch too much and risk alienating the girls, and wondered idly what life would be like if he had stayed with Suzie, and gone on to have children with her. He'd probably be having more days like this for a start. Rob felt a rare pang of regret for the path untravelled. He wasn't used to feeling envious of his friend, but watching the girls mucking about with Mark and the stupid soppy smile on his face as he looked at Emily, for once,

175

Rob did feel envious. Mark had so much that he, Rob, had missed out on.

You don't have to miss out.

The sudden thought came into his head. Katie, despite her rejection of him, might after all be persuaded. And even if she couldn't be, there were other fish in the sea, and the Robster had a fine track record. If he set his mind to it, there was no reason on earth why he couldn't get himself out of the rut he was in. And it was a rut. He had spent ten years drinking in the Hookers already. And, much as he liked it there, the sudden vision of himself slumped at the bar with only Paranoid Pete for company didn't really appeal. Not any more. Perhaps it was finally time for the Robster to grow up.

'Hey, Mum, Dad, look at this!' Two boys came piling through the portcullis and ran past Rob, shouting and gesticulating at the archers. Their energy seemed boundless. What it must be like to be that young.

Walking behind them were a man and a woman, bending down to deal with a child in a buggy. His eyes lingered on the small fair-haired woman. There was something about the shape of her head . . . She looked up and started to push the buggy toward him.

Oh my God, it couldn't be –

But what was she doing here? And how come she had three children with her? Three children. And a man.

'Oh shit,' said Katie, as she walked up the path following the boys. 'What are you doing here?'

Chapter Eighteen

Rob couldn't explain the fury that engulfed him when he saw Katie was with her family. He had no right to feel that way. And yet he did.

'Expect the unexpected,' he said with icy coldness. 'Well, this is certainly unexpected.'

Katie darted an anxious look at the man she was with, who was now preoccupied with one of the boys who had fallen over.

'I warned you not to run,' the dad was saying angrily. 'Look what happens when you do.'

'Rob, look, I can explain –' Katie looked mortified.

'You just didn't think to mention that you were married – that is your husband, I take it?' Katie nodded miserably. 'And with what – three kids? It just slipped your mind. Christ, now I know why you're always in such a hurry to get home.'

'I didn't mean to lie,' said Katie. 'Things just sort of got out of hand. I mean, it's not like you've ever been interested in me or anything.'

'Too right it's not,' said Rob coldly.

'Why are you being like this then?' Katie asked, frantically looking at her husband, who was coming towards them, a wailing child in tow.

'Why do you think?' said Rob. 'You made me look like a pillock.'

'I'm sorry,' Katie replied. 'I never meant to.'

'You'd better get back to them,' Rob said.

'Yes,' said Katie. She looked down at the ground, and for a moment he thought she might have been crying.

'Who's this?' The greeting was peremptory and just short of rude. Katie threw Rob a pleading look and he bit back the sarcastic response that had been on his lips, about being Katie's secret lover. Though he was still inexplicably cross with her, he didn't want to land her in the shit.

Katie looked as though she wanted the ground to swallow her up whole, and muttered, 'Charlie, Rob. Rob, Charlie.' Then, by way of explanation, she added, 'Rob's my dancing partner. I told you about him, remember?'

'Oh, right,' said Charlie, in tones of studied disinterest.

Rob's fury transferred instantly from Katie to Charlie. What was this bloke's problem?

'Daddy, Daddy, can we climb the ramparts?' The older of Katie's two boys ran up and tried to drag Charlie by the arm.

'If we must,' said Charlie. 'Come on, Katie, we can't stand chatting all day. Nice to meet you, Bob.'

'You too, *Chris*,' said Rob between gritted teeth, rather wishing he had the nerve to deck Charlie.

'I'm sorry,' Katie whispered as Charlie stalked off. 'Charlie's not normally this rude.'

'A right charmer you have there,' said Rob.

'Don't be like that.' Katie looked as though she might cry, and Rob immediately felt guilty. Charlie was marching down the path, and turned back to call her. 'It's not as though you don't have dozens of women waiting for you. Why are you suddenly so bothered about me?'

'Don't flatter yourself,' said Rob.

He turned back to where Mark and Emily were sitting, still totally enrapt in each other, only wishing it were true.

'Was that Katie and Charlie I saw?' Emily said. 'Didn't they stop to say hello?'

178

'You never said Katie was married,' Rob accused.

'You never asked,' said Emily. 'Sorry, I didn't think it was such a big deal.'

'It isn't,' said Rob, but he looked grumpy. 'Christ, what an idiot. I don't know what she sees in him.'

'Charlie's not exactly my cup of tea,' said Emily tactfully, 'but they've always seemed happy enough to me.'

'Well, Katie doesn't look too happy today,' said Rob. 'In fact, she looked like a wet weekend in November. And I'm not surprised, going around with that miserable sod.'

'Don't tell me she's got under your skin,' laughed Mark. 'Well I never. Next thing you'll be rushing off on your white charger to rescue her from the dark knight.'

'Ooh, is Uncle Rob in lurve?' Gemma snorted with derision and she and Beth burst into a spontaneous round of 'Uncle Rob and his lady love sitting on a bench K- I- S- S- I-N-G.'

'As if I would go for Thunder Thighs,' snorted Rob.

'Children, children,' said Mark. 'Come on, let's go and watch the jousting.'

'Ooh la-la, Uncle Rob's wearing a bra,' chanted the girls, until Rob threatened to throw them from the top of the tower.

'But you do like that lady, don't you?' said Beth cheekily, before Mark threatened to clip her ear.

'I have no interest in Katie whatsoever,' Rob declared firmly. Now he just needed to believe it himself too.

Katie was shaking like a leaf as she followed her family around the castle walls. Realising that climbing to the ramparts was going to involve a trip up a very narrow spiral staircase, she opted to stay outside with Molly.

As Katie sat on a wall playing peekaboo with Molly, she felt sick to the pit of her stomach. What had seemed like a mad but entirely harmless fantasy when she'd been going to dance classes seemed a bit seedy in the cold light of day. She'd been enjoying flirting with Rob as she danced with him, knowing that although there was undoubtedly an attraction on her side, it didn't matter because Rob wasn't in the slightest bit interested in her. And there was no chance at all of him meeting Charlie. Now Katie was feeling uncomfortably aware that she had been leading him on. Maybe. Just a smidgeon. And even if Rob were a terrible flirt, she had toyed with him. And it wasn't a fair thing to do.

With a sudden shock Katie realised she had been looking at this purely from Rob's perspective. Not Charlie's. Why did she feel bad about Rob, but not Charlie? She should feel guilty that she'd been flirting with someone other than her husband, except on today's evidence she didn't think he'd give a monkey's. Plus, it was clear Charlie was keeping secrets from her as well. Instead of uniting them as a family, all the day had done was expose the shakiness of their marriage. Oh God, where was it going to end?

Molly giggled and gurgled in her buggy. How lovely to be a baby and not to have any cares, apart from where your next meal was coming from, or when your nappy needed changing. She smiled weakly at her daughter through watery eyes.

'Mummy! Look at us!' She shielded her eyes as she squinted up towards the top of the castle to see her sons and husband framed against the castellations, bathed in bright spring sunshine, looking down on her.

She waved.

'Look, Molly,' Katie said, 'see Daddy and the boys.'

'Dadda,' burbled Molly with her cute smile. 'Dadda.'

Katie looked up again. Charlie was waving down too. She and Charlie splitting up wasn't inevitable. It couldn't be. However bad things got between them, she couldn't deprive the kids of their father. She wouldn't. All marriages had rocky patches. She and Charlie could work through this one. There was no way she was going to give in the way her parents had. She would find a way through it. She had to.

* * *

'Are you up for some ritual humiliation tonight?' Mark laughed as he led Emily onto the dance floor. Rob was already strutting his stuff with a sleek svelte brunette, showing off a new Cuban salsa he'd been practising in the mirror, but there was no sign of Katie. Emily had tried to ring her earlier but had got the answerphone.

'Oh go on,' said Emily. 'I can't believe we're no better at this yet.'

'What you need, *chicos*, is more practice,' said Isabella, today wearing a pale turquoise dress with sequins that danced and shone in the reflected lights of the studio, as she came and put her arms around them both. 'And now you can. You see, here I have details of a dancing weekend in June which Anton arranges at his hotel in the New Forest. You get a three-course dinner every night and can take master classes in all your favourite dances. The hotel is *magnifico*, with beautiful grounds, a spa, a gym. You will have a fabulous time.'

'Don't look at me,' said Mark. 'I can just about cope with a dancing lesson once a week, but I think a weekend might be a bit much.'

'What, not even for me?' Emily asked.

'Not even for you,' said Mark.

Isabella had left them with a leaflet each, and Mark started to lead Emily round the floor in his rather shuffling and ungainly style. Emily tried to remember to count in her head, but got muddled after their second turn.

'Honestly,' she said, 'I wish I could get my head round this one, two, three, square step. I feel like I'm worse than when we started.'

'Perhaps you should go on that weekend after all,' teased Mark. 'Then you might stop stepping on my toes?'

'And it might do something about your grip – it's so tight I feel like I'm being held in a vice.'

'Sorry,' said Mark.

'I do think a weekend away would be good,' said Emily. 'Even

181

if I don't learn to dance, the hotel looks nice. And if you won't come I can always ask Katie.'

'Who says I won't come?' said Mark petulantly. 'Oh bugger, I don't believe I meant to walk you into that wall.'

'I don't believe you did,' said Emily, 'and from that performance, I think you need the practice more than I do.'

They broke away from each other laughing as the dance came to an end. Rob was still transporting his brunette across the floor as the music for the next dance started up, but Mark waved away Emily's offer of another spin.

'I need a pint,' he said. 'That was torture.'

'Thanks a lot!' said Emily. 'I think I'll have to go on that weekend alone after all.'

'Then you can come back and teach me all about it,' said Mark with mock solemnity.

'Who says I'll want to dance with you any more if I learn to dance properly?' was her rejoinder. 'You never know, I might meet a gorgeous Latin dancer who'll teach me more than the tango.'

'Oh sod it,' said Mark. 'Then I'll have to come. Maybe I can persuade Rob to join me.'

'If there are lots of women involved, I'm sure that won't be too hard,' said Emily, watching Rob flirting outrageously with his brunette. 'Come on, let's get that drink.'

'Is this a good moment?'

Emily had turned up at Katie's on her way back from work, to find Katie standing in her porch over Aidan, who was covered in wet, slimy mud. He was stripping off his clothes and Katie was sluicing him down.

'Aidan's been pond-dipping with cubs,' said Katie, by way of explanation. 'Except he decided to dip himself.'

'It was Tarak's idea,' protested Aidan.

'Hmm, and if Tarak said go and jump off a cliff I expect you'd do it, wouldn't you? Now hop it, run upstairs and get straight in the bath.'

Aidan hopped it, while Katie gingerly put his reeking clothes in a plastic bag.

'God, they smell rank,' she said. 'I am only grateful that it was Tarak's mum's turn to pick them up tonight. Her car must smell foul. Make sure you never ever have boys.'

Emily laughed and followed her into the house.

'Molly in bed?'

'Yup. But only just. I had to unpick the banana she had smeared all over her head out of her hair first. Thankfully, George hasn't got mucky yet, but as he's painting Warhammer models in his bedroom, it is probably only a matter of time.'

Katie looked tired, Emily noticed. And, unusually, the house was looking quite untidy. The kitchen was grubby and in the corner the floor was covered in some glutinous mass. Katie had obviously been attacking it because a large bucket and sponge were propped up there.

'Excuse me while I just finish mopping the floor,' said Katie. 'Anthea always says you should do it at least once a week, with vinegar diluted in warm water.'

'Anthea doesn't have three kids,' Emily pointed out. 'Shall I put the kettle on?'

'Excellent idea,' said Katie, getting to work on the floor with a vigour Emily admired but couldn't hope to emulate. Nor even wanted to.

'You look knackered. Is everything okay?' Emily asked as they sipped their tea a while later, Katie not being prepared to sit till the floor was scrubbed, lunch boxes were emptied, Aidan was chased from the bath and George was persuaded to put his precious Warhammer away.

'I am a bit,' admitted Katie. 'Molly doesn't do lying in bed in the mornings, and with Charlie being away so much I end up sitting up really late sorting stuff out.'

183

'Sounds like you could do with a break,' suggested Emily.

'Well that's not going to happen,' Katie replied. 'Charlie's never here to go away with, and who would look after the kids?'

'Couldn't your mum?'

Katie pulled a face. 'You've met her. She's hardly the maternal type. Anyway, where would I go? What would I do?'

'You could come away with me and Mark and Rob on a dancing weekend,' said Emily, waving the leaflet in Katie's face. 'Come on, it looks fun, and I'm sure you'd enjoy the dancing. Can't you persuade that husband of yours to come home for once and let you off the hook?'

Katie looked through the leaflet. There were master classes in rumba and street jazz, plus guest performances from a couple of the previous year's stars of *Strictly Come Dancing*. There was a Jacuzzi and a spa. She could almost feel the soft luxury of the cotton sheets on the impressive-looking four-poster beds in the brochure.

'It looks bliss,' she said, 'but I don't see how I can possibly do it.'

'Never say never,' said Emily. 'I'm sure we can find a way.'

'I wish I shared your optimism,' Katie answered wistfully. She looked at the leaflet again. It did sound wonderful, but somehow she couldn't see Charlie letting her go. Besides, she'd never left the children before. How would they cope without her?

'Oh go on,' said Emily. 'Of all the people I know you deserve to treat yourself a little.'

'I'll think about it,' said Katie, putting the leaflet down on the table. 'I'll have a chat with Charlie when he gets back.'

But she knew what the answer was going to be. Let's face it, when you were a mum you were worse than Cinderella. And there really was no chance of going to the ball.

Chapter Nineteen

'Oh bugger.' Mark had just finished for the day and was going through his mail and emails. He'd had a really hectic day which seemed to involve fitting an inordinate number of dentures. It seemed that Granny O'Leary had been down to the Day Centre singing his praises as he'd been inundated with patients over the age of seventy. On the plus side, one of them had taken a shine to him and left him a bottle of whiskey.

As usual, most of Mark's mail was junk. But sitting in his email box was a very unwelcome message.

'What's the matter?' asked Diana, who was sitting at reception tidying it up.

'This court case,' said Mark. 'Seems it's not going away. I've just had an email from my lawyer to say they've confirmed they're going to sue.'

'I'm sure it will be all right,' said Diana.

Mark smiled with a conviction he didn't feel. He hoped Diana was right, but every time he thought about it a lead weight settled on his chest and he found it hard to breathe. The thought of having to give evidence brought him out in a cold sweat. He knew he'd done nothing wrong, but somehow information about one of his patients had entered the public domain, and even though he was innocent, at the same time he felt absurdly guilty.

'Doing anything nice tonight?' Diana was putting her coat on, ready to go. She asked this question every night and normally Mark had nothing terribly exciting to say.

'I'm going out with Emily,' he said. 'It's one of her client gigs. It's some music awards thing I've never heard of.'

'Sounds fun,' said Diana.

'I think it sounds awful,' said Mark. 'We're going to some swanky – or should I say wanky? – bar, and seeing some crap boy band get an award. I only said I'd go because there's free drink.'

'It might not be so bad,' said Diana.

'It will be,' Mark replied gloomily. He stared once more at the computer screen.

Jasmine Symonds v Mark Davies.

It sounded so legal. So final. So bloody scary.

Katie was putting the boys to bed when she heard the key in the door. Charlie was home early for once. Her heart was pounding and she felt stupidly nervous. He was her husband, and all she was going to do was ask him if she could go away for the weekend. She'd spent the whole day working out what to say. Luckily, the dates coincided with George and Aidan being away on a cub/scout camp, which meant that Katie felt she could ask her mum to have Molly if necessary. She felt a rush of guilt. From the moment Emily had mentioned the weekend, Katie had not just wanted to go, but had felt a sense of desperation about the thought of *not* going that she didn't think was entirely normal. Her house, her home, her family were all suddenly hemming her in. It was such a long time since she'd had any time for Katie, she'd begun to forget who Katie was. A weekend away seemed tempting beyond measure.

'Hi.' Charlie had come up the stairs and wandered into Aidan's room, where Katie was folding clothes away while Aidan read a *Captain Underpants* book. Charlie bent over to kiss Katie lightly on the cheek, and went and ruffled Aidan's hair. A good sign, Katie felt.

'Good day?' she asked, getting up and bundling up all the stray socks, pants and other clutter that Aidan had left scattered around his room.

'Not bad,' said Charlie. 'You?'

'Nothing out of the ordinary,' said Katie. 'Aidan, lights out in ten minutes.' She always felt a little like a prison warder when she said that.

She kissed her son on the cheek, and went to check on Molly, while Charlie went into his study to check his emails. Molly was lying entangled in blankets, her thumb stuck firmly in her mouth and her curly hair plastered to the side of her head. She looked so peaceful and still lying there, Katie wanted to cover her in cotton wool and keep her like that forever. Hard work as it was having a baby, they grew up all too soon.

She went downstairs and watched ten minutes of a wildlife programme about snow leopards with George before chasing him off to bed. By the time Charlie had come down an hour later, Katie had put the lounge to rights after the chaos inflicted on it by her sons and was sorting out a chicken *alla cacciatore* as recommended by Nigella. She had decided to cook the dish because it was only supposed to take half an hour, but unlike Nigella her cupboard wasn't stocked with every kind of bean under the sun, and she'd spent a fruitless ten minutes searching for a replacement for cannellini beans before rereading the recipe and realising that rice was a suitable alternative. She'd also had to improvise and replace pancetta with bacon, but she doubted Charlie would notice.

'That smells nice,' said Charlie, coming into the kitchen and pouring himself a glass of wine.

'Shouldn't be too long now,' Katie told him. She was now used to Charlie not being there in the week, and it was ages since it had been just the two of them in the kitchen without the children distracting them. He seemed suddenly too big and awkward to fit in her cosy space, and, she realised with a jolt, she wasn't at all sure she wanted to share it with him.

They made perfunctory small talk while Katie stirred and seasoned, and Charlie sat flicking through the paper, but she was struck by how little they actually had to say to each other. Beyond asking how work was going – 'Fine' – and the merger – 'Boring, you wouldn't be interested' – Katie hadn't a clue what to say to him. Nor he to her. How had they become such strangers?

She could see his eyes glazing over as she mentioned silly little things that Molly had done that day, like clapping Aidan as he was strumming on his guitar, or dropping her favourite teddy in the bath. Although, to be fair, Charlie did show interest in how George's tutoring sessions for grammar school were going, but only, Katie felt, because it would reflect badly on the family somehow if Charlie had produced a dunce. Marilyn still hadn't forgiven them for not sending George to Charlie's alma mater – the one and only time Charlie had ever stood up to her. Katie suspected Marilyn didn't have a clue about how difficult it was to fund private education nowadays.

Katie sighed. She couldn't put the moment off any longer. The dancing weekend was only three weeks away.

'Charlie –' she began, hoping her voice wasn't wobbling too much. 'Would you mind – I mean, would it be a problem if –' She paused. Why was it so hard to ask? This was pathetic. If she were at work she'd probably be away on business from time to time and Charlie would have to cope. Nicola Horlick managed it, and so should she.

'Spit it out.' She could sense Charlie's impatience.

'I'dliketogoawayonadancingweekendwouldyouhavethekids?' The words came out in a rush.

'Okay,' said Charlie, barely looking up from his paper.

'Are you sure?' Katie could barely believe how easy it had been. 'The boys are going to be away at scout camp for part of

188

the time anyway. And I could get my mum to have Molly if you like.'

'No, no need,' said Charlie, putting the paper down. 'I know I've not been around much lately, and I'm sure the break will do you good.'

'Thanks,' said Katie, feeling absurdly uncomfortable. She went to kiss him on the cheek, but he almost flinched, so she patted him awkwardly on the shoulder instead. She went back to the stove feeling a sense of relief that it had been so easy, but it was coloured with disappointment that Charlie seemed so utterly uninterested in her.

The music was blaring out from a corner. Another DJ rapper was pumping out charming lyrics about living on an estate and blowing off the heads of your gangsta rivals. Emily felt old. Was there anyone here who actually liked this stuff? She supposed the young guns all did, but she had actually over-heard a *Guardian* journalist in the loos earnestly telling anyone who would listen that Gangstas 4 Guns was not only in tune with the zeitgeist but was such a telling and heartfelt satire on the state of gun crime in the UK today. And there had been Emily thinking they were just glorifying weaponry. Showed how little she knew.

She wondered whether she'd been right to drag Mark out to these awards. Emily's firm had been invited because they'd just drawn up the contracts for We Five, a new boy band who were taking the pop world by storm. Although the Krank Up the Volume awards had been unable to ignore this latest pop phenom-enon, they were in the main aimed at the indie bands and keen on musical icons, which is why she'd asked Mark. But now the thought of him coming into her world was bringing her out in a cold sweat.

Emily glanced over at the door, just at the moment when Mark walked through it. Their relationship was still new enough for her heart to skip a beat when she saw him. She'd forgotten the delicious dizzying sensations of early love – for love she was convinced this was, though she hadn't dared utter the L-word to him yet. Nice and all as Mark was, along with mentioning babies that was guaranteed to send even the most decent of blokes packing. But for the first time in a long while, she felt able to let herself fall hook, line and sinker.

Love like you've never been hurt.

There was no other way to do it.

'Hi.' Mark made his way through the crowds and gave her a light peck on the cheek, which was still enough to send a thrill through her.

'Hi yourself.' She suddenly felt absurdly shy now that Mark was on her territory. 'Would you like a drink?'

'I could murder a beer,' said Mark. 'I've had a hellish day.'

They pushed their way through the scrum at the bar – the Gangstas 4 Guns having been sufficiently unpopular to send the mass of the crowd out for a desperate drink. After a wait of at least ten minutes, they got served and then fought their way back towards the stage, where the Gangstas had been replaced by a bizarre-looking female who was trying and failing to emulate Amy Winehouse. Amy had also been slated to appear, but was another no show. Rumour had it that she was in rehab again, but then rumour would.

As the music pounded out, the lights flashed on and off, and no doubt in order to create atmosphere, strobe lighting was introduced in between bouts of dry ice.

'Just as well I'm not epileptic,' shouted Mark through the attempts of some thrash metal band, whom he recalled Gemma was keen on. That might earn him some brownie points.

'Me too,' said Emily. 'God, I feel old.'

The music wound down and the lights came up for the serious business of the evening, namely the awards ceremony. Being of the MySpace, Facebook, anything goes generation, the organisers of the Krank Up the Volume Awards didn't go for anything as establishment as tables, so the punters had to stand cradling their beer while they cheered wildly to each new award.

The award for best new talent inevitably went to Emily's clients.

'It's all right, we can go after this,' said Emily. 'I'll just go and get my coat.'

As they left, Mark paused to stare at a woman who was sitting in a darkened corner. He made as if to go over to speak to her, but as he moved forward the woman got up and left.

'Who's that? Someone you know?' Emily asked.

'I thought it was the useless receptionist who's just left us in the lurch, but I can't think why she'd be here,' said Mark. 'It's so dark in here. I must have been wrong.'

'Is it important?' asked Emily. Mark seemed a bit agitated.

'No, not really. If it was Kerry I only wanted to let her know how much she's dumped us in it,' he said. 'It doesn't matter. Come on, let's get home.'

'I can't believe we're really here.' Katie kept having to pinch herself as Emily drove up the driveway of the Hillcrest Hotel. It wasn't on much of a hill, but being in the middle of the New Forest it was surrounded by trees. They had driven through a picturesque little village to get here, with village green, stocks, and a pretty bridge overlooking a stream. To complete the picture-postcard scene there had been two New Forest ponies grazing by the side of the stream. Even if there was to be no dancing, Katie felt like she'd come to paradise. Every mile that she put between herself and her family – particularly Charlie – she had felt a lessening of burden and responsibility. True, she had been absolutely frantic up until the moment she'd left, packing and repacking the boys' kit for camp, but, to her surprise, once she'd waved them off (and after wiping away the surreptitious tears that they absolutely must not see) and gone home to pack her own stuff, she'd felt none of the guilt she'd been expecting. Just a lightening of the load.

It was the same when Charlie got back early to help with Molly. To her amazement he had even insisted that she hop in the bath while he put Molly to bed. He had been tender, kind, conciliatory – the way he had been early on in their relationship. It was a long time since he'd behaved like that towards her, but it was reassuring. Perhaps all they both needed was for Katie to get out more, and not sit at home brooding on nonexistent problems.

'What time are the boys going to get here?' Katie asked Emily. She wasn't at all sure how she felt about Rob coming along. A girly weekend away with Emily was one thing – and the way she had presented the weekend to Charlie, not quite having the nerve to mention that Rob was going to be there too. But a weekend where there was the possibility of dancing with Rob, spending proper time with him – well, that complicated things. Part of the attraction of coming away had been a continuation of the fantasy of dancing lessons – but Rob and Charlie meeting had made her realise how potentially dangerous the fantasy could be. It was time she stopped fantasising and started sorting out her problems. Rob being here might not be such a good way to do that.

'I don't know,' said Emily. 'I think Mark was rather hoping to get out of it, but Rob wouldn't let him.'

'I bet he's only coming because of you,' teased Katie as they made their way to the reception desk.

'He did say something along those lines,' said Emily.

The place was buzzing, with people checking in, tripping over each other's luggage, and the odd shriek of recognition as friends caught up with one another. The age range was vast, from people in their twenties to a dapper elderly couple who could have been in their eighties. There was a lot of excited chatter about the appearance of the *Strictly Come Dancing* couple, but despite hearing a giggly plump twenty-something blonde girl claiming she'd spotted them in the driveway, Katie couldn't see any evidence of anyone famous.

As she and Emily waited patiently in the queue for their rooms, the sounds of a waltz wafted from the elegant ballroom to the left of the reception area. Katie peered round the corner. Already there were couples dancing. Many of the women were wearing elegant floaty dresses. They looked like swans, or brightly coloured peacocks. She thought of the little black number she'd shoved in her suitcase at the last minute and wondered whether she was going to end up feeling like mutton dressed as lamb. At least she had lost weight enough for her to be able to wear a dress she hadn't worn since before Molly was born. Katie had been overcome with an absurd sense of pride when she'd realised she could fit into it again and had gone out and bought some new gold sandals and some make-up to celebrate.

The receptionist gave them the keys to their rooms, next to each other on the second floor. Katie and Emily were thrilled to discover they had been upgraded to adjacent large sweeping rooms with fantastic views of the grounds.

Music was still wafting from the ballroom and Katie's feet were starting to tap.

'Do you fancy a drink first, or would you like to dance?' she asked.

Emily pulled a face.

'Drink, no contest. Just look at them! They all look like they should be on *Strictly Come Dancing*. I'd feel too much of a prat,' said Emily firmly. 'I'm going to text Mark and see where the boys are, then sit here with my glass of wine until they arrive.'

'Spoilsport,' said Katie, making her way towards the dance floor. She stood a little uncertainly for a moment, but within minutes someone had asked her to dance. He was tall, dark, debonair, handsome. Nothing like Rob or Charlie, and he danced beautifully. She floated around the room with him, feeling that perhaps she too could be a swan. She never felt as confident anywhere else as she did on a dance floor. Katie shut her eyes and let herself drift into the music. Her troubles seemed so very far away. Her real life seemed the fantasy now. It was going to be a great weekend.

Chapter Twenty

'Do you think you might have had enough of dancing yet?' Mark enquired in a panting gasp, as he and Emily completed a set of the quickstep, at which he felt he was even worse than the waltz. He and Rob had arrived much later than the girls the previous evening, as neither of them had been able to get away from work that early, and though Rob had managed to strut his stuff on the dance floor till quite late, Mark had happily escaped with Emily for a quiet drink in the bar area. Of Katie there had not been much sign till the dancing had finished around 1 a.m., but she had emerged eventually, flushed and beaming. Rob seemed put out that she hadn't been dancing with him, but then again, Rob had wasted no time in finding the prettiest women in the room to dance with. He also appeared to have got over his anger with Katie, and today they were mucking about like they used to, sitting close together at breakfast and teasing each other mercilessly about who was the better dancer. They looked natural together in a way that Katie never did with Charlie, Emily thought. Katie never complained about Charlie or said she had problems, but she had been rather down of late, and, not for the first time, Emily wondered if everything in her friend's marriage was okay.

The morning session had involved either basic training in the waltz and quickstep, which Emily and Mark had opted for, or lessons in salsa and rumba, which had been Katie and Rob's choice.

'I think I might just have,' said Emily, in response to Mark's question. She came to a halt. 'Shall we go and see if Katie and Rob have finished and get some lunch?'

'Sounds good to me,' said Mark. Holding hands, they walked towards the room where they had last seen Rob and Katie, from whence the sounds of Latin music were drifting. They watched in awe for several minutes as Rob and Katie, along with everyone else in the room, seemingly executed the perfect cha cha cha. Katie and Rob seemed to move in perfect sinuous motion together. They looked almost made for each other, Emily mused.

'Now that's what I call synchronicity,' said Emily in admiration as Katie and Rob came up to them. 'I am never ever going to be able to do that.'

'Ah well, you can't all be as gifted as us,' said Rob. 'Though of course, in our case, Katie would get nowhere without my talent. It's men who are in charge on the dance floor, don't you know?'

'Oh do shut up,' said Katie. 'I had to correct your salsa steps, remember? You were dancing Cuban style and we were supposed to be doing Colombian.'

'We're going for lunch now,' said Mark, breaking up the squabble. 'What about you?'

'Sounds good,' said Katie, 'but I want to be quick because there's another Latin workshop this afternoon. I think they're going to be teaching the merengue and I've never done that before.'

'And I have to perfect my snake hips for this evening,' said Rob. 'Just to make sure I am indeed the sexiest man on the floor.'

'In your dreams,' laughed Katie.

'You two are gluttons for punishment,' said Emily. 'I think Mark and I are just going to go for a wander into the village this afternoon. I'm up for dancing this evening, but I think my feet have had enough for now.'

After lunch Katie and Rob disappeared back to the ballroom, and Mark and Emily set off down the drive.

It was a bright sunny day, and by the time they reached the village they were both parched.

'Fancy a drink?' asked Mark.

'Sounds great,' said Emily, and they made their way into the quaint little pub that stood by the bridge.

They sat in the afternoon sun drinking shandies, watching children feeding the ducks, and chatting about everything under the sun. It was so easy to talk to Emily, Mark thought. He'd never found it easy to talk to Sam. Not really. There were always undercurrents he didn't understand, and he had the knack of offending her in ways he found unfathomable. Emily, on the other hand, was much easier, more straightforward. And she seemed to be prepared to listen to him getting on his favourite hobby horse, of too much government interference in everyday life.

'If only politicians could just trust people to get on with it,' he said, idly chucking bits of bread at the ducks, 'I'm sure we'd all be much happier.'

'You're probably right,' said Emily. 'To be honest, I haven't given it that much thought before.'

'Really? Haven't you noticed the creeping bureaucratisation of petty-minded jobsworths?' he said. 'Surely in your line of work you must be getting ever more regulated and bound by stupid directives from Brussels. I know it's true in my business.'

'I guess,' said Emily. 'Actually, you're making me feel quite ashamed. I've been so caught up in the crap that is my work, I haven't really paid much attention to current affairs. Maybe I should.'

'Why do you stay?' Mark asked suddenly. 'You don't seem to be very happy in your work.'

Emily pulled a face.

'I'm not really,' she said. 'But it's hard. My company may prey on human misery, but they do pay well. And since my dad died, my mam needs all the financial help she can get. I live such a long way away from her, I can't do much else but help with money. I couldn't do that so easily if I changed jobs.'

'I sense a "but" there,' said Mark.

'I can't help but wonder what my dad would have thought,' admitted Emily. 'I think he'd be disappointed in me. I know I am.'

'What?'

'Disappointed in me,' she said. 'I had so many ideals and I feel I've betrayed them all.'

'Don't be,' said Mark, taking her hand. 'We all lose sight of our ideals from time to time. It's never too late to do something different.'

'True,' said Emily with a smile, and she sipped her drink and stared into the river. And as he watched her flicking back her dark sleek bob, Mark realised with a jolt that he was falling headlong in love with her.

He hadn't felt that combination of excitement, passion and tenderness in years. And it seemed miraculous to him that he should feel it now. When Sam left, he'd thought love would never find him again, and yet here he was, sitting by a river in the sunshine with the woman he now knew he loved. It was as if Emily had obliterated the pain that Sam had caused. Life really did move on.

'You look – stunning.'

For once Rob was almost speechless. He'd spent all day dancing, if not with Katie, in close proximity to her, and for most of it she'd been looking sweaty in loose-fitting baggy grey sweat pants and an oversized T-shirt. But she and Emily had emerged transformed from their rooms after hours doing whatever it was that women did to turn themselves into beauties. Katie was wearing a simple black strappy dress which accentuated her curves, and her fair hair was piled in her high curls on her head. Her dress was set off by a gold silk shawl and she wore a topaz locket and earrings. 'I almost didn't recognise you. Have you lost weight?'

'Why, thank you kindly, sir,' said Katie, performing a mock curtsey. 'Emily did my hair. I'd have made a right hash of it on my own.'

'You look lovely too, of course,' said Rob, feeling it was only polite to compliment Emily, who was wearing a sparkly red dress and whose black bob looked particularly sleek and sexy tonight.

'Thanks,' said Emily. 'Are we ready to go?'

The evening's entertainment consisted first of a three-course dinner and plenty of wine. Rob enjoyed the meal and teasing Emily and Mark about their lack of dancing ability, but he was itching to get on the dance floor and dance with this new, improved Katie. He couldn't take his eyes off her. It was perhaps time to admit to himself that he really was taken with her.

She's married. Rob shoved down the nagging voice in his head that pointed out the obvious. She had a husband. She had three kids. He shouldn't really be going there. But watching her laugh at something Emily had said, he badly wanted to.

Eventually the music started up and the crowd roared their approval as the *Strictly Come Dancing* couple did some exhibition dances. Then it was time to hit the dance floor with a vengeance. At first things felt rather stiff and formal, as the band started with a couple of waltzes. Katie was being most elusive. 'I'll dance with you later,' she kept saying. 'I'm promised to other people.'

'Which other people?' Rob growled at her.

'Never you mind,' Katie said vaguely and giggled.

'Are you drunk?' Rob asked. He'd never seen her this vivacious.

'I might be,' said Katie, getting up from the table and promptly falling over. 'But I'm still not going to dance with you – yet.' She got up, winked at him mischievously and disappeared into the crowd.

Emily and Mark hobbled their way around the room in fits of laughter – after dancing with Emily himself, Rob wasn't at all

199

surprised. Soon, though, the music changed and Rob found himself tangoing around the room with a variety of different women before taking part in a hilarious and chaotic merengue. At this point Emily and Mark dived out, making their excuses, which left Rob alone on the dance floor in desperate pursuit of Katie.

Eventually he pinned her down and extracted a promise of a dance so long as it was a salsa. After two more foxtrots, in which Rob's chosen partners both managed to step on his toes, the music switched to Latin once more and he grabbed Katie from where she was taking a break in the corner.

'Come on,' he said, grabbing her by the hand. 'I am going to dance with the loveliest lady in the room, even if it kills me.'

'I bet you say that to all the girls,' said Katie.

'No, I don't,' Rob replied, pulling her closer to him. He felt her freeze just the tiniest bit and relaxed his grip. He didn't want to push her away, not now he'd finally got her.

Katie didn't say anything as she danced with Rob. She just let herself float away on a sea of soft music, flashing lights and sparkly dresses. She was vaguely aware that she had had too much to drink, and that her initial instinct of avoiding Rob for the evening had probably been the right one. But it felt so right to be dancing a salsa with him. He was such a good dancer, he made her feel like she was someone else, not the Katie the world saw – mum of three and downtrodden wife – but Katie as she saw herself: the ugly duckling turned into a swan. However little confidence she lacked in her real life, once she was on the dance floor, Katie knew she became someone else entirely, someone gorgeous and sexy and vitally alive. Rob brought all that out in her. Was it so wrong for her to hold on to that bubble of fantasy and keep it for a little while, even if she knew it couldn't last? It was as though she were on a honeymoon from her real life.

As if in a dream, Katie was aware that the music had softened, the lights had dimmed, and Rob was facing her for a rumba.

He looked nervous, and suddenly so was she. They'd been practising this all afternoon, but it had been different in the afternoon, when they were dressed in their scraggiest clothes. Hard to feel sexy about someone when their T-shirt was covered in sweat. Not so when they were standing before you in a dinner jacket. The sexiest dance ever invented. Should she be doing this? Vaguely, somewhere, Katie knew the answer was no, but she wasn't quite ready for the bubble to burst. God. No wonder Baby fell for Johnny in *Dirty Dancing*. Who wouldn't be seduced by this dance?

'Are you up for this?' Rob asked as he pulled away from her and started counting the beat.

'If you are?'

Oh God. Katie swallowed slightly as she realised the song they were dancing to was *Body Talk*.

Rob was singing softly in her ear that he was searching for lust, and breath, and life, as he snaked up close and back. Quick, quick, slow. Quick, quick, slow, they danced to an exquisite beat. To begin with they barely touched, except to take each other's hands for the occasional turn.

As the music flowed sensuously around them, Katie was almost hypnotised by Rob whispering suggestively about the heat of passion. She knew she was on dangerous ground but she felt mesmerised by the music, the sensation of floating, the feeling that she was somewhere very far away. As the dance progressed they moved closer and closer together, and Katie had the weird sensation that they were the only two people in the room as they began to move together in single motion, their bodies talking without need for words: where his hand ended hers began; as he stepped forward, she pulled back.

She was vaguely aware that Rob was singing that they had become one, as he pulled her close. She felt a delicious thrill as he ran his hands up her body, before she pushed him away in a gesture of – defiance? Rejection? What? Even she didn't know.

The dance seemed to go on forever. Forward. Back. Side. Quick. Quick. Slow. The lights flashed intermittently as one minute Rob held her close to him, the next he pulled away. Katie had never experienced anything like it. And then it was over: he performed one last turn, and she lay back in his arms, laughing with delight.

'That was fantastic,' Katie sighed.

'Wasn't it,' Rob agreed, and he bent over and kissed her on the lips.

'Oh no!' Katie pushed him away from her. 'I didn't mean – oh God, I'm so sorry.' She grabbed her shawl from a nearby chair and ran away, close to tears. What on earth had she done?

Emily sat down next to Mark on the bank of the stream that ran at the far end of the hotel grounds, and leaned against him with a contented sigh. The sky was clear and bright and the evening warm and balmy.

'I love looking at the stars,' she said, 'don't you?'

'It's nice being able to see them,' said Mark. 'There are too many neon lights in Thurfield.'

'It's been a lovely weekend,' said Emily, snuggling up close. She felt more content than she had done in months. Mark made her feel so safe. So cared for. It was a long time since she'd felt like that.

'Hasn't it?' said Mark, caressing her hair.

'We could make it lovelier,' she added, laying her hand on his leg with careful deliberation.

'Are you sure?' Mark asked. 'I don't want to push you into doing anything you're not ready for.'

Emily thought back to her early days with Callum. His seduction technique had been a 'Are you up for this or what?'. With Mark she knew things would be different.

'I've never', she said, kissing him, 'been surer about anything.'

They walked slowly back to Emily's room, the brightness of the moon and the music from the ballroom making it seem even more magical. Yet even knowing there were all those people nearby, Emily felt as if they were the only two in the world.

In a daze, she let Mark into her room. For one moment they looked at each other stupidly, as if too hesitant to begin. But then they touched, and after that it was easy. Clothes were peeled away, caresses given, whispered promises made, and afterwards they lay silently holding one another, marvelling at what they had just done. While they might lack rhythm on the dance floor, there was no mistaking their compatibility in the bedroom. And when Mark eventually slept, Emily lay beside him clear-eyed and content, and watched the dawn rise, as close to heaven as she thought it was possible to be.

Part Three

Work Like You Don't Have To

Chapter Twenty-one

Katie ran and ran. Kicking off her heels – why had she worn the bloody things anyway? – she ran out of the ballroom and onto the patio area outside. She kept running across the lawn until she reached the little stream at the end of the gardens. It was only there that she stopped and flopped down on the ground in despair.

How could she have been so stupid? All evening she'd been aware of Rob looking at her. And she could admit now, sitting out here on her own, feeling like a fool, that she hadn't been able to take her eyes off him either. The black dinner jacket he'd been wearing had transformed him into someone debonair, sophisticated ... fanciable. She'd recognised the danger, which was why she'd avoided dancing with him for so long. Practising the rumba with him that afternoon, she'd resolutely ignored his snake-like hips. So Travolta-like. So desirable. So definitely, absolutely avoidable.

But in the end, fuelled by a sense of adventure and reckless-ness, which had had the unfortunate effect of kicking in just when Rob asked her to dance, she'd gone for it hook, line and bloody sinker. And how.

All those weeks of carefully maintaining the fantasy. That her home life was fine and dandy. That Rob was just a semi-harmless flirtation. And now she had to face up to facts. She fancied Rob. She fancied someone who wasn't her husband, and he (judging from the strength of that kiss) fancied her. Charlie had let her have a precious weekend away from the family and she'd betrayed him. And the children. What on earth had she done?

'Katie.' She looked up to see Rob standing over her. She stood up awkwardly.

'Katie, I'm sorry.' Rob took her arm and she let him hold her for a second. How could something that felt so right be so very wrong?

The tears fell then and she shook herself away from him.

'No, I am, Rob,' she said. 'I shouldn't have led you on. I'm married. I have kids. It was wrong of me.'

'It was my fault,' protested Rob. 'I got carried away. It's just you're the first person I've felt like this about for a very long time.'

'We can't,' said Katie, turning to go. 'I like you. I really do. But we can't.'

'I know,' said Rob, with a sadness that was slightly unexpected, and she found herself pausing. 'Despite what you think of me I'm not a *complete* bastard. And I don't generally make a habit of falling for married women.'

That elicited a small smile from Katie.

'And there was me thinking you were a serial commitment freak,' said Katie.

'I am,' said Rob. 'But I have my reasons.'

He sat down, and Katie sat back down next to him. She knew she should leave, go up to her room and pack, but she wanted so badly to stay.

Rob paused for a minute, and then put his head in his hands, and stared through his fingers for a bit. He had undone his shirt and bow tie, and he looked incredibly vulnerable sitting there. Waves of tenderness swept over Katie, which in a way were more terrifying than the lust she'd been feeling earlier. She couldn't let herself feel these things for Rob. She mustn't.

Eventually, Rob spoke.

'I was in love once,' he said. 'Her name was Suzie. And she was a lot like you. Feisty. Fun. Pretty.'

He thinks I'm all those things, Katie thought in awe. When had Charlie ever said anything like that to her? Never, was the answer. Or not for a very, very long time.

'What happened?' asked Katie.

Rob didn't say anything. He sat staring at his hands.

'It's difficult,' he said, looking up again. 'I've never really told any of this to anyone before. I don't know where to begin.'

'The beginning, perhaps?'

'Suzie and I met at college,' said Rob. 'We were interested in the same things – both studying history, keen on activity stuff, into the climbing wall, and both of us wanted to be teachers. So we got involved in the student community project group. We went into schools and did reading with kids who had literacy problems, set up team-building days for deprived children. That kind of thing.

'During our last summer, before we were due to go to teacher-training college, we volunteered to help on a week away, camping in Wales. There were walks and climbing things set up. We thought it would be fun. And we were so in love. So stupidly in love, the way you are when you're young . . .'

Rob's voice broke off for a minute and Katie felt almost jealous of Suzie for having inspired such feelings.

'Anyway,' he continued, sounding strained, 'to cut to the chase. One day we went on a long walk in the mountains. The terrain got more and more difficult, and I kept saying to the group leader that we should turn back. But she said they'd done the climb before and it was fine.'

Rob paused again and ran his hand through his hair. 'Christ, this is difficult.'

'Go on,' said Katie, slipping her hand into his and squeezing it.

'Then we got to this rocky outcrop. Suzie and I were ahead with one group, and I said we should wait for the rest to catch up. Suzie and I were distracted and mucking around with each other, so we didn't see the kid at first. He was determined to show off, and just ran off and climbed up the rock face.'

'Then what happened?' Katie asked.

Rob shook his head slowly.

'I tried to call him back but he ignored me. Suzie said I should go after him, and I started to, but then he began to climb down. And then he slipped and fell.' Rob stared into his hands, as if seeing the full horror of the moment for the first time. 'He died, Katie. He died and I could have saved him.'

'Oh Rob, that's awful,' said Katie, involuntarily covering her mouth with her hand.

'There was an inquiry, of course,' said Rob. 'But while they found the organisation had been negligent, they didn't attach blame to Suzie or me.'

'Well, it wasn't your fault,' said Katie.

'No? I've thought about it every day for the last fifteen years. Wondered if things could have been different. If I should have done something different. Suzie blamed me. She said I should have stopped him. Our relationship never recovered. And I've been on my own playing jack the lad ever since.'

'Sounds lonely,' said Katie.

'It is.' Rob looked at her intently. 'Which is why I need you.'

Katie let go of his hand as if it were red hot.

'No,' she said. 'You don't. You need *someone*. Have you ever thought of counselling?'

Rob pulled a face. 'I don't need counselling. I need you.'

'You can't have me,' said Katie. 'I'm sorry.'

'Me too,' said Rob. 'Me too.'

Katie got up, kissed him on the top of his head, and walked away. Her last sight of him was as he sat on the grass, looking so lonely and lost. She wanted to go back, to comfort him. But she couldn't. She mustn't. She had her family to consider.

*   *   *

Mark woke up and blinked as the sun shone through the blinds, in an unfamiliar room, with an unfamiliar feeling. One he'd forgotten had ever existed. That feeling of sheer luck and good fortune that came from having fantastic sex with a woman you loved.

Emily was curled up next to him, breathing softly. Her dark hair had fallen slightly over her face. She looked beautiful, vulnerable, completely wonderful lying there. He bent over and gently kissed her neck. She opened one eye sleepily and smiled at him.

'Hello you,' she said.

'Hello you,' Mark replied.

'You're still here then,' said Emily.

'Looks like it,' Mark agreed.

'Good,' she said. 'I'm glad.'

She snuggled up to him and he held her close. Two hearts beating as one. All the old romantic clichés came out at times like this; perhaps because they were true. Mark gave a deep sigh of contentment.

'I never *ever* thought I'd feel like this again,' he said.

'Like what?'

'Happy, content. Feeling that I'm the luckiest man in the world,' said Mark. 'I'd forgotten what being in love is like.'

'Wait a minute, did you just –?'

'Use the L-word?' Mark said. He pulled her close to him and kissed her on the mouth. 'Yes,' he said, 'I did. Emily Henderson, I think I love you.'

Emily looked shocked before responding, 'And I love you too.'

Mark hugged her tight. 'Life really doesn't get much better than this,' he whispered.

'No, it doesn't,' she whispered back. Then she said, 'Why are we whispering?'

'No idea,' said Mark, 'I just feel a bit like a naughty schoolboy.'

'And I feel like a naughty schoolgirl,' said Emily, giggling as an arm snaked its way down her back. 'A *very* naughty school-girl.'

'Now what do you suppose,' asked Mark, 'a naughty schoolboy might find to do first thing on a Sunday morning?'

'Ooh, I don't know,' said Emily teasingly as she traced a path down his spine with her fingers, 'but I think I can guess.'

As Mark let himself explore Emily's body again, he gave silent thanks for having found her. It still seemed a miracle that somehow he had.

Rob was silent on the journey home. Mark had come down for breakfast with a jaunty look in his eye, and it was clear from his and Emily's body language how things had panned out for them last night. Katie, on the other hand, had cried off breakfast and he had only seen her when they were checking out. She'd looked red-eyed and tired, and had avoided his gaze. He couldn't alto-gether blame her. Something had happened last night that neither of them had been expecting, and while he knew, had always known, that she wasn't the sort of woman to abandon respon-sibility lightly, Rob also wished beyond all measure that things could be different.

Christ, he hadn't even told Mark all that stuff about Suzie, and Mark had been around at the time. Mark knew about the accident, of course, but he had no idea of the effect it had had on Rob, or how it had destroyed his and Suzie's relationship. For years Rob had cultivated a devil-may-care attitude towards women and relationships. And for years it had worked. But Katie had brought all that tumbling down, and now Rob wanted her with a fierceness and a passion he hadn't realised he was capable of.

'You all right?' Mark glanced at Rob, who was gripping the steering wheel hard as he drove up the motorway.

'Yeah, fine,' said Rob. 'Just a bit tired. That's all.'

'So who was the lucky lady?' Mark asked.

'No one,' said Rob shortly.

'No one?' Mark laughed out loud. 'There's always a lucky lady.'

'Well there wasn't last night,' said Rob.

'There's no need to be shirty,' Mark retorted.

'I'm not being shirty,' Rob replied, knowing he was. 'I just sat up in the bar too late, having one too many.'

'Oh, right,' said Mark, 'only it's not like you to be so grumpy.'

'I'll be grumpy if I feel like it, so just leave it, will you,' said Rob with unaccustomed savagery. 'Would you look at that idiot?' Someone had just pulled out into the middle lane without indicating. Rob hooted him, before flooring it and taking off in the outside lane. There was nothing like driving fast to ease his damaged soul. A pity that the effect was only temporary.

Emily hummed as she walked into work on Tuesday morning. The weekend couldn't have been better. Despite a distinct lack of improvement in her dancing skills, in every other way it had been fantastic. On the way home, Katie had been peculiarly reticent about the events of the rest of her evening, but was kindly and politely thrilled for Emily in the way only the best girlfriends could be. Emily had spent the remainder of the weekend with Mark. It felt like a whole new world was opening up before her. They had cooked together on Sunday evening. Laughed uproariously together at *Spaced*. Fallen into bed together with the joyous abandon of new lovers. It had been wonderful. Perfect. Better than perfect.

'Good weekend?' John greeted her as she backed through the office door, trying not to spill her latte.

'The best, thanks, and you?'

'Not bad,' said John, 'but it would have been all the better for sharing it with you.'

'Flattery will get you nowhere,' said Emily, heading for her desk, which was piled high with files she'd not got round to clearing out on Friday. She didn't care.

'By the way, did you hear about Andrew?' John shouted as Emily started to pick her way through the chaos on her desk. Andrew was one of the partners who tended to handle all their most important media clients. He was away at present on a quad-biking holiday.

'No, what?'

'Apparently he's broken his leg,' said John. 'He's suing the firm he went with, of course.'

'Of course,' said Emily drily. Andrew was known for his propensity to sue anything that moved. The man didn't know the meaning of the term personal responsibility.

She turned back to the files on her desk. With Andrew away, presumably his workload would get shared out among them. As if she didn't have enough to do.

'Emily, can I have a word?' Mel popped her head round the door.

'Yeah, sure.' Emily followed her boss into the office, wondering what crap was coming her way due to the fallout from Andrew's accident.

'You've probably heard by now about Andrew's unfortunate accident,' Mel began.

'Yes, is he all right?' Emily asked.

'He'll be fine.' Mel waved away concerns about her colleague's health. 'However, he obviously can't work at the moment, and there are one or two pressing things coming up. I wondered if you'd be prepared to take them on.'

'Well, of course,' said Emily, her heart sinking. She was frantically busy as it was, but Mel was a hard person to resist.

'Of course, there may be something in it for you,' said Mel with a significant smile. 'We were all pleased with the outcome of the Brabham case, so who knows, maybe it's time you went up in the world.'

Emily saw the carrot. She'd fallen for this before, but maybe, just maybe, this time she could prove her worth and get on to the next rung of the ladder. Heaven knows, her shaky finances and ever-increasing mortgage costs could do with it.

'I'll be happy to help in any way I can,' she said.

'Right, then. Here's the first case I want you to work on,' said Mel. 'It's already been in the papers. That woman from *Love Shack* – is it Jade or –?'

'I think it's Jasmine,' Emily said. Oh great. Just the kind of high-profile case she didn't want.

'That's the one.' Mel snapped her fingers decisively. 'Her dentist pulled out a tooth and there's been a breach of confidentiality, so we're suing the pants off him. Here are the details.'

She shoved a file at Emily, and Emily opened it gloomily.

Jasmine Symonds v Mark Davies.

She did a double take. The page swam before her eyes.

Jasmine Symonds v Mark Davies.

It was there. In black and white.

Oh my god, she thought, *Mark was the dentist.* Now what was she going to do?

Chapter Twenty-two

'Sorry, did you say something?'

Shit, she must have spoken her thoughts out loud. Emily tried to gather what was left of her wits about her. Her heart was pounding. She couldn't take this case. There was no way she could prosecute Mark. But if she didn't and said why, Mel would immediately say she had a conflict of interests. Hell, she might even lose her job. And at the moment, she couldn't afford to. Why hadn't Mark mentioned the case to her? she wondered anxiously. What else might he be keeping from her?

'I don't think I can take this case after all,' said Emily, her voice coming out in a squeak. 'I mean, it's probably quite complex, and I do have a lot of other stuff on . . .' Her voice trailed off. She knew Mel would never buy it.

'I see. I take it you still want to be a senior associate,' Mel said with silky sweetness, her talons tapping the desk. 'We only want team players here. Are you a team player or not?'

Emily thought back over the months she'd spent working late while Mel swanned off to expensive dinners with clients. It was on the tip of her tongue to scream how unfair it all was, but she knew that would cut no ice with Mel. Mel didn't give a toss about things being unfair. She just cared about results and would get them in the most ruthless manner possible.

'So what are you saying?' asked Emily.

'If you want that promotion you take the case,' said Mel. 'I don't think you understand quite how important it is to us. Andrew managed to cock up on the last case involving a client of A-Listers, and they represent rather a large portion of our business. We cannot afford to lose them as clients. Do I make myself clear?'

'Crystal,' said Emily miserably.

'Good, because if you're not on side, I'm sure I can find someone else to fill your shoes.'

Emily stalled. Maybe there was a way around this. Maybe. Though God knew what it would be. 'Do I have to give you an answer now?'

'You have till tomorrow afternoon,' said Mel, waving her away.

Emily flew out of the room in a state of semi-incoherent rage. How could this be happening to her? How? All those years trying to haul herself up the ladder. All that hard work she'd put in. And now, when it was within her grasp, she was facing the worst moral dilemma of her life.

Of course she shouldn't take the case. She knew Mark was innocent of any wrongdoing. He must be. And she was hopelessly compromised. But there was the small matter of her financial situation, and the fact that her cosy little country cottage seemed to eat money. Last year she'd had to put in a damp course, and it was only a matter of time before she was going to have to replace the roof. Every time the wind blew, another tile seemed to come off. Morally she should say no, but practically it wasn't going to be easy.

She wondered how Mark would react. She knew what he'd want her to do. She knew what she wanted to do. But could she do it?

Katie was cleaning. She'd washed windows and dusted surfaces; she'd scrubbed baths and poured bleach down loos; she'd cleared out cupboards and hoovered carpets. She'd reorganised her cupboards – *again*. She'd been at it all week. The events of the weekend had made her feel out of control. Cleaning was a way of regaining that control. Molly solemnly watched her from her high chair where she was banging the saucepan and spoon that Katie had provided to keep her amused. It was giving Katie a headache, and she'd already picked the wretched things up half a dozen times, as for Molly part of the game also involved throwing them on the floor. So the kitchen surfaces that Katie was attempting to clean had taken twice as long to do as they should have.

She stood back and looked at her handiwork. The stainless-steel cooker and sink gleamed back at her, returned to their former glory after a weekend with Charlie's haphazard cooking and lack of cleaning.

'There,' she said with satisfaction. 'At least that looks better.'

A pity that it wasn't possible to clean out the parts of your life you wanted to run away from, she thought. She'd embarked on this orgy of cleaning partly to help her forget, to ensure she wasn't thinking about Rob twenty-four-seven, but it hadn't worked. Not one bit. Every time she shut her eyes his face swam before her. She could hear him laughing at her for her cleaning obsession. Charlie laughed too, but not so kindly. And all she could think of was that scene by the river, where she'd sat and held Rob's hand and comforted him. Or the look in his eyes at the end of the rumba. Charlie had *never* looked at her like that.

Stop it. Stop it. She had to get these thoughts out of her head. Rob was just a distraction. She'd let herself fall for someone who was paying her attention, instead of her husband who'd lost interest. It was up to her to regain that interest. Somehow she had to persuade Charlie that she was the sexy, beautiful woman Rob so clearly thought she was.

Molly threw the saucepan again and laughed gleefully as it hit the floor with a satisfying clang. Katie went to pick it up and knocked the calendar off the wall. She idly flicked through it,

218

noting birthdays she mustn't miss and appointments she had to keep. The answer was staring her in the face. It was Charlie's fortieth birthday in August. He'd been as miserable as sin about it, claiming not to want to celebrate. If she organised a surprise party for him, then surely Charlie would realise how much she really loved him, and everything would be all right. And if there was a voice in her head which insisted on telling her she was clutching at straws, well, she was just going to ignore it.

Rob sat in the staffroom marking his Year Eight essays on Elizabeth I and the Spanish Armada. If he had to read another essay which stated that Philip had dissed Elizabeth he was going to burst a blood vessel. He was all for taking a modern approach to his subject, but there were limits.

He sighed and put down the essay he was looking at, and stared out of the window at the Year Ten boys playing football and the girls trying to skive off netball. Rob couldn't have given a monkey's about Elizabeth I at the moment. All he could think about was Katie. All he had thought about since the weekend was Katie. He was still horrified by how much of his soul he had laid bare on Saturday night. Rob the prankster, Rob the joker. Christ, he'd nearly been in tears. All those years of not talking about it, and suddenly he'd had to blurt it all out. And now he felt all at sea.

What Rob wanted, with a feeling that was more painful than anything he'd ever experienced before – even losing Suzie – was for Katie not to be married. For years and years he had perfected the art of not falling in love – of leaving women as soon as his heart was even remotely compromised. And now he was putty in the hands of the one woman he couldn't have. Maybe Katie was right and he should think about counselling. He decided he would look into it at least.

Rob had never been in the business of breaking up marriages. He'd never needed to, having always found a steady source of willing singletons. But Katie was different. He was different when Katie was around. She'd got under his skin in a way that he could never have thought possible. After all those years of being determinedly single, suddenly he didn't want that any more. But was it too much to ask for at his age, to find a woman he loved and one who was prepared to love him? He'd watched Emily and Mark with considerable envy at the weekend. They had something that had eluded him for years. Something that, until he met Katie, he'd never thought he'd find again And now he had. But he couldn't have it. He felt like a kid in the toyshop with no money. Life was sometimes incredibly unfair.

'Emily, this is an unexpected surprise,' Mark said. Emily had said she would have to work late for the next couple of nights, so they had agreed to meet again later in the week to go out for a meal. Even though they'd only said goodbye that morning, he'd been missing her badly and wondering whether he should call on her. The minute they'd parted he'd been feeling stressed that she might have second thoughts. He desperately needed the reassurance of seeing her again. 'Do you want a drink? I could open a bottle of wine if you like.'

'That would be nice.' Emily looked different somehow. Awkward. Ill at ease. She responded stiffly to his embrace. Oh God. Maybe she'd come to tell him she'd changed her mind.

'Is everything all right?' Mark asked as he ushered her into the kitchen. His heart was pounding. The weekend had been so perfect, so special. He didn't think he could stand it if she'd come round to say it was all a ghastly mistake.

'Red or white?' asked Mark, picking up a bottle of each.

'So long as it's alcohol, I don't care,' Emily said.

She had picked up a bit of Blu Tack from the table, which she was twisting nervously round and round.

'Come into the lounge,' said Mark. Emily was so different, so on edge. It was making him nervous.

220

But when they sat down, and Mark persuaded her that they really had to watch another episode of *Spaced*, she seemed back to normal again. She snuggled up to him, and he felt himself relax. But after about half an hour, Emily wriggled out from under his arm, put her head in her hands and said, 'I can't do this.'

'What?' Mark was alarmed now. She looked desolate, and there was a slightly desperate look in her eye that didn't bode well.

She paused again, and said, 'Mark, I've got something to tell you.'

Here it is, thought Mark. Here's the moment when my dreams go up in smoke.

'Oh?' he said with pretended lightness.

'Well, the thing is,' Emily was twisting her hands round and round, 'I've got a dilemma. I went into work today and my boss gave me a new case. If I work on it, it could mean promotion. More money, maybe.'

'That's great, isn't it?' Mark looked puzzled. Maybe it was in the Outer Hebrides.

'Not really,' said Emily. 'She wants me to work on your case.'

'Oh.' A cold chill spread through Mark. She had to have said no. She must have said no. There couldn't be another response, could there?

'You've said no,' Mark said. 'Haven't you?'

'I haven't said anything yet,' said Emily. 'Why didn't you tell me about it?'

'Because that's the shitty, crappy part of my life, and you're the good bit of my life. Only you're not, are you? Not now.'

'Believe me, Mark, I didn't know,' Emily said. 'Well, I knew Jasmine was suing a dentist, but not who it was. Not until today. And I came straight here to talk to you about it.'

'What is there to talk about?' asked Mark. 'We're going out. You can't work on a case against me. It's unethical.'

221

'I haven't said no.' Emily looked thoroughly miserable now.

'Why the bloody hell not?' Mark was almost speechless.

'Because if I say no, I'm going to lose my job,' said Emily.

'Then get another one,' Mark told her. 'I don't know many lawyers who are out of work.'

'I'm getting top whack, though,' said Emily. 'I'd be hard pushed to find that elsewhere, and I'm struggling with the mortgage as it is. And there's my mam's loan. I can't just give up my job without anywhere to go.'

'Right,' said Mark. 'So you're not prepared to do this for me.'

'No, I mean, yes. Of course I don't want to work against you,' said Emily. 'But I can't afford to lose my job. I haven't got anything to fall back on.'

'Then find a way, Emily,' said Mark, getting up. 'If you really loved me, you would.'

'Of course I love you!' said Emily. 'How could you think I don't? Why do you think I'm so upset about this?'

'Are you? Really?' asked Mark. 'If you were, you wouldn't put money above me. I can't believe you're even considering taking this case. And after all that rubbish you gave me about your dad.'

'Don't you dare bring my dad into this.' Emily jumped to her feet angrily. 'It has nothing to do with the things I said about him.'

'Doesn't it?' Mark shot back. 'There you were telling me how shallow and crap you realised your job was, and it was only your dad dying that made you see the light. But you didn't change jobs for him, and now you won't for me.'

'If that's the way you feel, then perhaps I'd better go,' said Emily.

'Perhaps you'd better,' said Mark angrily.

Emily picked up her things and walked to the door. She looked absolutely shattered and a part of Mark wanted to stop her and say it would be all right. That they would get through it. But he didn't stop her. How could it possibly be all right now?

'You're wrong, you know,' she said as she left. 'Just because I'm thinking about practicalities, it doesn't mean I don't love you.'

And with that she was gone, and Mark was left staring at his wine glass, feeling like the biggest fool on the planet.

Chapter Twenty-three

Emily sat at her desk and looked blankly at the file before her. Her eyes felt raw and swollen from crying, her mouth was dry and her head was thumping. She had slept very little the night before and had already endured several comments from her colleagues about looking like she'd been dragged through a hedge backwards. She felt like it too.

Symonds v Davies.

Why did it have to come to her?

She opened the file, thinking she might as well get a feeling for what she was dealing with. After what Mark had said yesterday it didn't look like they had a future together. If he thought the worst of her, maybe she should live up to his expectations. And yet she felt heartsick as she read through the file and saw Jasmine's bleating self-justification about what was really something so deeply insignificant in the scheme of things as to be risible – if the consequences for the man she loved weren't so serious.

Because the more she read, the more Emily realised that Mark was in big, big trouble. Whoever had rung the News of the Screws had done so after-hours from the practice phone, and there was a statement from one of Mark's colleagues that he had been working late on the night in question. In another statement the same colleague claimed that Mark had been shooting his mouth off in the pub about how Jasmine didn't have perfect teeth at all. Emily frowned. Now that didn't sound a bit like Mark. But then again, although he'd been merry in her presence, she hadn't seen him that drunk. Maybe he *was* different then.

Jasmine's statement was to the effect that she had had trouble with Mark in the past, and had had to complain about a filling in a back tooth that had fallen out. She then went on to say that he had lied to her about needing a crown on her tooth. She'd gone along for a regular check-up and he'd told her she needed a root canal, but on the day in question he had just taken out her tooth without a by-your-leave, and had ignored her pleas to save the tooth for the sake of her career. With a sigh, Emily rang the number in the file for Jasmine's PA and set up a meeting. Maybe she could find something to help Mark if she ran through the statement one more time.

Reading further, Emily discovered there was also reason to believe that Mark Davies should have declared a conflict of interest as his ex-wife worked for *Smile, Please!*, Jasmine's sponsor, and there was a good chance the leak came out that way.

Emily frowned again. Mark hadn't said much about Sam, but she'd got the impression they weren't on the best of terms. What if she were around more than Mark had said? No, she shook her head, Mark wouldn't lie about something like that. He had too much integrity.

Wouldn't he? A nagging voice wouldn't go away. She couldn't help remembering the business with his kids. Mark had lied to her about that. Plus he hadn't mentioned the court case. After all, Emily had only known him for a few brief months. What did she *really* know about him? Had she any idea at all as to whether he was a good dentist or not?

True, the person making the complaint was the dumbest of dumb fame-seekers, but sheesh, everyone had to have a chance to have their voice heard. Just because she, Emily, didn't particularly like Jasmine, it didn't mean that Jasmine wasn't telling the truth.

Emily shut the file, her head spinning. She didn't want to think that Mark could be in the wrong, but Andrew had begun to build a fairly convincing case against him. And after yesterday it looked like she'd blown it anyway.

Boyfriend or job? Job or boyfriend? It looked as though she'd lost the boyfriend, so she might as well keep the job. However badly Mark thought of her, he couldn't hate her more than she hated herself right now.

'So Emilysh left you?'

Rob blinked over his fifth pint at Mark. He felt he might have asked this question before. And, bafflingly, his glass seemed empty again. 'I need another drink,' he said.

'Other way round,' said Mark. 'This one's mine.'

He was a bit behind Rob, who'd started early that evening, going straight from work to the Hookers. All week Rob had retained that feeling of being all at sea, and tonight he wanted to reach solid ground. If he was going to sit and be miserable, he might as well be miserable on his home turf.

'Don't you think you've had enough?' asked Barry.

'No,' said Rob. 'We're drowning our sorrows. Trying to forget women.'

'Women.' Mark looked sorrowfully into his pint. 'I don't think I'm ever going to understand them.'

'You don't want to waste your time trying to understand women,' said Barry, the veteran of two failed marriages, pouring out two more pints. 'Complete waste of time, that. So what's the problem?'

'Mine's married, his is a cow,' said Rob.

'No, she's not,' said Mark, 'she's just confused. I need to – to unconfuse her. Then everything will be all right.'

'You're too trusting, mate,' said Rob, 'you should have listened to your old Uncle Rob.'

'If I hadn't listened to you in the first place,' said Mark, 'I wouldn't have gone to those sodding dance lessons and I wouldn't be in this mess.'

'That is a slur,' said Rob, trying to defend himself, then having the oddest feeling that he didn't have a leg to stand on. In fact, when he tried to stand up he didn't have two legs to stand on and he slumped to the floor. He looked up to see Jim and John looking down at him.

'Did you mean to do that?' asked Jim – or maybe it was John – with interest.

Rob glared at them and tried to get up, but didn't seem to be able to.

'Do you know, Jim,' said John, 'I don't think he did.'

'I think you're right, John old boy,' said Jim, laughing. 'Do you need a hand, Rob?'

'I'm fine.' Rob gathered what remained of his dignity, pulled himself up and went to powder his nose. Moments later he was back with a vengeance. 'And another thing –' In the toilets he'd been hit by a blinding revelation. 'I'm giving up on women.'

'Me too,' said Mark moodily. 'They're bad for my health.'

'I'll second that,' said John, whose wife had left him for a limbo-dancing tattooist. '*Women*. They've caused me nothing but trouble.'

'I'll third it,' said Jim, who'd never had a wife in the first place.

Dicey Derek nodded from the corner. 'Women, who needs 'em?' he said. Derek's wife hadn't left him, yet, but rumour had it she was about to.

'It's all their fault,' chipped in Paranoid Pete, who would score highest in a least-likely-to–get-a-woman-this-decade competition. 'Take my advice. You should never ever trust a woman.'

'Oh my god,' said Rob, looking around him and seeing his future all too clearly. He buried his head in his hands. 'We're living that bloody song already. I'm not sure I can take any more.'

'Hello, Marilyn?' Katie felt the usual mixture of nerves and irritation that always accompanied phone calls to her mother in law. Doyenne of the local WI, Ladies' Captain of the golf club, leading light in the bridge club, organiser of charitable works, and naturally a paid-up blue-rinse member of the local Conservative party, Katie couldn't think of anyone she would rather not call for a chat.

The first time Katie had ever met her, over ten years ago now, newly pregnant with George (but sadly, in Marilyn's eyes, as yet unmarried to Charlie), Marilyn had looked her up and down as if appraising a prize racehorse. Katie had half-expected Marilyn to examine her teeth.

'Of course, the new arrival will be in illustrious company,' Marilyn had brayed when she'd got over the shock that she was to have an illegitimate grandchild, and proceeded to take Katie through the family tree, which could trace Caldwells back to the time of William the Conqueror and included a branch of the family said to be descended from Pitt the Younger.

Katie was left in no doubt that she had entered a family steeped in power, money and influence. She had as yet to recover from the sense of disadvantage that this realisation had engendered in her. Charlie, of course, missed such nuances, thinking Katie oversensitive when she mentioned that his mother made her feel inadequate. But she knew she wasn't imagining the disappointment that Marilyn felt in her son's choice of bride. For all Charlie's protestations, even after all these years she felt like a fish out of water, with their talk of stocks and shares, houses in Tuscany, the cost of public schools and expensive skiing holidays.

'Katie, how delightful to hear from you.' To Katie's oversensitive ears, it sounded as if her mother-in-law was anything but delighted. 'We so rarely see you these days.'

Biting back a retort that they had in fact paid a visit to the ancestral mansions deep in the heart of Sussex a mere two weeks ago (in fact they were lucky if a month went by without a visit taking place), Katie forced herself to smile and say, 'I've been thinking about Charlie's fortieth, and I was just wondering if you were free on the first Saturday in August. It's the nearest weekend to Charlie's birthday, and I thought it would be nice to organise a party. He's been working so hard recently, I thought I'd do it for him as a surprise.'

'That sounds wonderful, dear,' said Marilyn. 'Let me just see . . .' There was a pause while she clearly consulted her calendar. 'Yes, I think Stephen and I are free, I'll make a note of it. Would you like me to let the rest of the family know?'

'Er, yes, that would be great,' said Katie. 'Although I was thinking of something quite small.' Charlie wasn't big on birthdays and she didn't want to crowd him.

'And have you thought of a venue?' asked Marilyn, 'because I'm sure I can organise something at the golf club.'

'Oh, I was thinking of –' Katie began.

'Leave it to me, dear,' Marilyn interrupted. 'We'll invite the Price-Joneses of course, and the Pritchards. Let me know who you want out of Charlie's friends and I'll do the rest from here.'

'Er, thanks,' said Katie, 'but –'

'What a wonderful idea,' said Marilyn, 'I'll get on to it right away.'

Katie put the phone down with a heavy heart. It wasn't what she'd intended at all, but Marilyn wasn't used to resistance, and Katie knew better than to try.

'I suppose at least for once she's pleased with me,' Katie told Emily after the latter had dropped in on the way home from work. 'I can't ever recall her saying that before.'

'Is everything all right?' Emily asked, as she helped Katie to pick up the mess of toys the boys had left on the lounge floor, 'only you seem a bit hyped up.'

'Do I?' Katie replied. She sighed and stared out of the window at her perfect garden. She looked around her perfect (once it was tidy) lounge, and thought about her perfect life. It seemed like such an effort to keep it all going, and she badly wanted to confide in Emily that the whole thing was becoming more and more of a sham, but where to begin? Once she started talking she might never stop.

'I'm just tired,' said Katie. 'Charlie's away such a lot, and we have so little time together. That's why I decided on the party. I thought it would be a nice surprise. I just hope I can wrest some control back from my mother-in-law.'

Emily laughed. 'You're making me glad I don't have one,' she said.

'Well, that's probably about to change,' said Katie. 'You'll be meeting Mark's mum before too long.'

Now it was Emily's turn to look wistful.

'I don't think that's going to happen now,' she said. 'We've split up.'

'Oh, Emily,' said Katie, 'what's happened? You seemed so happy at the weekend.'

'We were,' said Emily, and then proceeded to explain her dilemma.

'I don't know what to say,' Katie told her, getting up to pick up a toy truck she'd just spotted under the bookshelf. 'But honestly, can you really sit there and do that to Mark?'

'I don't want to,' said Emily. 'Of course I don't. But I need the money and I'm not sure I'll get another job that pays as well. It's the old golden handcuffs thing. They rope you in, get you hooked, pay you fantastically well, and then you look around and think, yikes, I can't afford to change jobs. Besides, I have to pay back Mam's loan as well. I can't let her down.'

'Don't you think,' said Katie carefully, plumping up a cushion before she sat down again, 'that it's about more than money? What about principles?'

'What are they?' Emily looked bleak. 'I think I lost the right to have principles the day I started this job. And I'm not sure I'll ever get them back.'

* * *

'Oh for fuck's sake.'

Mark was beyond livid. He and Rob had spent the weekend on the wildest bender he'd had since his student days, his head was thumping and he was feeling like death warmed up. And now Rob had brought in the Sunday papers, and there, plastered all over the News of the Screws, was a story about Twinkletoes Tony with a mysterious blonde friend. Pages and pages seemed to be devoted to their shagathon sessions, which wouldn't have mattered at all, but the story was linked to Jasmine's troubles, and thereby led to him. They had even found a picture of him. It was from his student days and depicted him with spiky gelled hair wearing a loud striped shirt, and good God, was he wearing braces? Mark was only grateful that although it made him look like a goofy idiot, it was unlikely that anyone would recognise him from it.

But shit. He was in the Sunday papers, damn it. Through no fault of his own, but he knew how people's minds worked. They'd think him guilty of a breach of patient confidentiality just because he'd been in the papers, linked with the likes of Tony and Jasmine, both of whom would probably sell their grandmother to keep their spot in the limelight. His reputation could only suffer by association. Besides, Mark had an abhorrence of publicity. He preferred to keep his life private and out of sight. It appalled him that his name had been mentioned in the papers, even if only briefly.

The phone rang, and when he went to answer it his rage turned to ice-cold fury. Logically he knew it wasn't Emily's fault his picture was in the papers, but he wasn't feeling logical today, just hung over and angry.

'Oh, it's you,' he said. 'I hope you're proud of yourself.'

'What do you mean?' Emily sounded subdued.

'Have you seen the papers today? Thanks to your lot I'm splashed all over the Sundays.'

'Oh, Mark, I'm so sorry,' Emily said. It sounded genuine, and, for a moment, Mark softened. But then he looked back down at the paper. Even if Emily had had nothing to do with it, the people she worked for had. She, too, was guilty by association.

'I'll believe that when you tell me you're not taking this case,' said Mark.

There was a pause and what could have been a sob.

'Mark, you know I don't want to do this,' said Emily, 'but I don't have a choice.'

'Everyone has a choice,' said Mark. 'It's whether you make the right one or not.'

'You're so bloody black and white,' said Emily. 'Don't you ever live in shades of grey?'

'Not when my job's on the line,' Mark replied. 'Which, thanks to this case, it is.'

'And mine's on the line if I don't take the case,' said Emily. 'Can't you see how hard that is?'

'You could get another job if you wanted to,' Mark argued.

'And you could understand my position if you wanted to,' said Emily.

Mark stood for a minute holding the phone in his hand, with the feeling that what happened next would be irrevocable.

'You know I can't do that,' he said, the rage suddenly draining away, leaving him with a painful sadness.

'And neither can I,' said Emily. 'I'm sorry.'

She put the phone down but Mark held on to his end, unwilling to break the connection. He leaned back against the wall, unable to comprehend the gulf that had grown between them so quickly, and wondering if he would ever see a way to bridge it.

Chapter Twenty-four

'Marky, babe, was that you I saw in the papers last week?'

Mark groaned. He might have known that Spike Sutcliffe, his erstwhile friend from dental school, would have read about him in the tabloids. Spike had never been one for reading the broadsheets.

'Don't,' said Mark. 'I rue the day I ever set eyes on Jasmine Symonds.'

'So she's not a good lay then?' asked Spike.

'Do shut up,' said Mark. 'Are you ringing to remind me about Gorgeous Gus's stag weekend?'

Gorgeous Gus had borne the brunt of most of the mickey-taking in Mark's student days. He was a grade-A student who was also incredibly good looking, hence his epithet. Everyone should have hated him, but, annoyingly, Gus was also a good laugh, and a decent sport about the ribbing. Remarkably, he had escaped the marriage market so far, but now it was his turn to walk up the aisle, and some time back Spike had rung Mark to ensure that he joined in the fun. 'It will be a good reason to get the old gang back together,' he'd said, and at the time Mark had agreed. Now, with the current chaos, Mark was looking forward to a complete break from everything.

'You can still make it, can't you?' Spike reeled off a list of the other attendees. It seemed like most of Mark's year were going to be there. 'We're going kart racing in the morning and then we'll paint the town red that night.'

'Sounds great,' said Mark. 'I've arranged that Sam will have the kids this weekend. I have to say I am really looking forward to it.'

'Do you think it's a good idea to keep this party a surprise from Charlie?'

Katie's mum had called round unexpectedly to find Katie compiling lists and sorting out invitations. Katie was furious. Mum never just popped in, so why was she here now? Katie had barely had time to sweep up the mass of Molly's toys that were littering the lounge floor. She hated being wrong-footed. Why hadn't her mum rung first? And now she was sitting opining about things she knew nothing about, and getting dangerously close to topics Katie would have preferred to ignore.

'Of course,' said Katie. 'I'm sure he'll be delighted. From what Marilyn tells me half the Caldwell clan will be there, and I've managed to track down most of his school and university friends. I think it will be just what he needs. He works so hard.'

'Yes, doesn't he,' said her mum drily.

'What's that supposed to mean?' Katie was well versed in her mother's subtleties. She knew her mother hadn't called round accidentally. There was a reason for this visit.

'Nothing,' said her mum. 'I'm just wondering if Charlie always has to work quite as hard as he says.'

'Of course he does,' said Katie. 'Whatever gave you the idea he didn't?'

'It's only that I ran into him the other week up in town.' Her mum looked distinctly uncomfortable.

'And?' said Katie. 'Charlie works in town.'

'Well, it was the night you'd asked me to babysit because Charlie was working late and you were dancing and I couldn't,' said Mum. 'I was on my way back from a meeting and I saw Charlie. And it looked very much to me as if he were heading for the pub.'

Katie felt herself go cold all over. She remembered the night in question. Charlie had sprung an I'm-sorry-I-have-to-work-late on her. It was just before the weekend away, and Katie had felt so guilty about going away she'd said nothing about it. Her mum had been unable to babysit so she'd cried off.

'So?' asked Katie. 'Part of Charlie's job is to entertain clients.'

'If you say so.' Katie could hear the scepticism in her mother's voice and she understood where it was coming from. And the thing was, Charlie had told her that his meeting had only finished at nine. If he had lied about that, what else was he lying about?

Katie swallowed hard, and tried to portray a nonchalance she didn't really feel.

'They had a dinner early in the evening that night. Charlie told me all about it.'

'Right.' Her mother looked unconvinced. 'Only you would tell me, wouldn't you, if there was anything wrong?'

'There's nothing wrong,' Katie said firmly. 'And Charlie is going to have the best birthday ever. I'm going to make sure of that.'

'Well, if you're sure . . .'

'Sure,' said Katie. 'Everything is fine. Now why don't you play with Molly while I sort us out a cup of tea?'

Katie walked into the kitchen but her head was spinning. Charlie had lied to her. But why?

Emily was feeling a distinct sense of relief. Mark's court case had been adjourned, which meant, for the moment at least, she didn't need to think about it, or him. Perhaps she could have enough breathing space to extricate herself from this mess, by trying to sort out her finances enough so she could look at getting another job. It wasn't just Jasmine's case that had got her down, it was most of the work she had to do. The majority of her clients were people who were in the public eye for nothing more important than being in a soap, or having once appeared on the *X Factor*. They were constantly unhappy with their lot, and suing papers for scurrilous stories on the one hand, while on the other rushing out and making sure their faces were constantly photographed. Either that or they were being charged with possession of drugs, or of drink driving, or of happy-slapping. It was all so tawdry and tedious. And the more Emily worked on these cases, the more she felt she was struggling in primeval slime. Interviewing Jasmine had been a case in point.

'You are going to get 'im for me, aren't you?' she'd said. Emily had made her go through her statement again, and elicited the welcome information that Mark had actually warned her that the tooth would have to come out eventually (a fact borne out by the case notes that Mark's frosty-sounding case manager had sent her), but she was sticking to the rest of the story like glue.

'It 'ad to be Mr Davies,' she said. 'He was the only one wot knew. He's ruined my life, *and* he threatened me.'

'What? When?' Emily looked up in alarm at this.

'We went round to tell him what's what, didn't we?' Jasmine's spiteful mother, Kayla, who had tagged along with her, said. She spat venom with every breath, and Emily felt polluted by her presence.

'Well, that was rather foolish,' Emily replied, drawing a deep breath. Reading between the lines, she'd bet anything it was Jasmine and Kayla who'd done the threatening. 'Presumably you have witnesses to Mr Davies' behaviour? Would you like to register a formal complaint about that too?'

'Oh no, no.' Jasmine obviously realised the implications of what she'd said and backtracked wildly. 'Just make sure we get him for the confidingly thing,' she said, and Emily had had to promise she would.

How on earth had she got herself into this mess? Working on cases like this? When Emily started out it had been so different. She'd wanted to work on compensation cases, certainly, but the ones she'd wanted to do had involved people whose lives had been blighted by tragedy because of reckless firms who'd played fast and loose with safety considerations, or those where someone in charge had failed in a duty of care and as a result ordinary people had been hurt. It was people like her dad she'd wanted to help. And now here she was, helping people like Jasmine. She didn't blame Mark for hating her. Self-loathing was fairly high on her own agenda right now.

She hadn't seen or spoken to Mark since their last conversation. Emily had dropped dancing – there was no point now. The only reason for going had been Mark.

And despite her best efforts, she couldn't stop thinking about him. She'd chosen the job, not the boyfriend, but Emily wasn't convinced she'd made the right choice, and more than anything she wished she could turn the clock back.

Work like you don't have to.

Work, it seemed, was all that she had left.

'You come here often?'

Rob was at the gym. It seemed the only thing to do on a Saturday morning which he would otherwise have spent alone. Mark had gone off the night before on his stag weekend, and, unusually, Rob hadn't felt like going to the pub.

So he'd woken up early and decided that it was time he took his life in hand. He would go to the gym and start on an intensive exercise programme, aimed at reducing his pot belly and restoring him to all his Adonis-like glory. The women would be back falling at his feet, and he could forget all about Katie Caldwell. He decided to start with the woman next to him on the running machine. She wasn't exactly slim, but not too fat either. She was currently red-faced and panting beside him.

She didn't hear him at first, and then turned off her iPod.

'What did you say?' she asked above the thumping beat that reverberated round the gym.

'I asked if you come here often?' said Rob. He was having trouble with his own running machine, which didn't seem to want to speed up by the required amount. He wanted to impress this woman by showing her how easily he could pace his running. She didn't look all that impressed. In fact, she looked him up and down with the eyes of one who has just walked on a slug.

'It's none of your business,' she said, 'but if you really must know, I come here twice a week, with my husband.'

She gave him a withering glance and got off her machine, walking away in disgust.

At that moment Rob's machine decided it was going to speed things up, but he wasn't prepared for it and he shot backwards, landing on the floor with an ignominious thud. It was at that point that he decided maybe chatting up women in the gym wasn't the best idea he'd ever had.

After an hour and a half, during which Rob felt he'd used muscles he'd forgotten he had, Rob decided to call it a day and headed into town for some retail therapy. Not that he was all that keen on shopping, but it was something to do.

As he was coming out of WH Smiths, armed with fags and this week's copy of *Loaded*, he ran into Katie. She was with the kids, but there was no sign of the husband. Katie blushed when she saw him.

'Hi,' he said, ridiculously nervous.

'Hi,' said Katie.

'What are you up to?' Rob enquired, then kicked himself for asking such a daft question.

'Shopping,' said Katie. 'It's Charlie's fortieth soon. We're looking for a present for him.'

Lucky, lucky Charlie.

'Mummy's having a party for Daddy,' the older of Katie's boys piped up.

'But it's a secret,' added the younger one.

'Which means you aren't to tell anyone,' said Katie. 'Not even Rob.'

'Sounds fun,' said Rob, wishing he didn't feel such a horrible sensation of jealousy. It was an unusual emotion for him to feel, and not one he particularly liked.

Katie pulled a face.

'Actually, I'm rather wishing I hadn't started on this,' she said. 'There's so much to do, and I keep having to come up with all these lies. It's a nightmare.'

She looked flustered as she said this, and Rob was transported back to the moment by the river. How he wished he could sweep her up in his arms, but seeing her here, with her kids, in a purely domestic setting, he realised how wrong that would be. Katie was right, they couldn't be together. He couldn't be the reason why these kids became a statistic.

'Right,' he said. 'Best go. Things to do and all that.'

'Yes, of course,' said Katie. Had he imagined it, or was there the tiniest hint of regret? He hoped so, but couldn't afford the luxury of thinking that way. The sooner he got Katie out of his system, the better.

'Katie,' he said as she turned to leave.

'Yes?'

'About before.' Rob felt stupider than he ever had.

Katie looked embarrassed. 'What about it?'

'I'm really sorry,' said Rob, 'it shouldn't have happened. Can you forgive me?'

'Consider it done,' said Katie. 'Now, really, I must go.'

But she lingered briefly, casting him a look that tore at his heart. Because suddenly he knew that she was pretending. Pretending to herself. Pretending to him. What had happened by the stream wasn't one way. Katie clearly felt the same way he did. And he couldn't do a single thing about it.

Chapter Twenty-five

Robbie Williams was singing from the jukebox about the need to feel real love, as Mark got a round in. It had been a great day. They'd had a lot of fun at go-karting, at which it turned out Mark was rather good. Not good enough to beat Gorgeous Gus, of course, who naturally shone as he shone at everything else, but Mark had won a couple of races, which had been absurdly good for his fractured ego.

Now, as he carefully carried five pints to the table where his mates were sitting, he reflected that, like Robbie, he wasn't at all sure he understood the road he'd been given. But for the first time in ages, he'd come out and had a good laugh. The events of the last few weeks seemed to have happened in another lifetime. And though he missed Emily with an ache that pierced him right through, he knew he'd get over her eventually. He had to.

Just as he got to the table, someone brushed past him, causing his drink to go flying.

'Oh, sorry,' said the stranger, a funny-looking little man with the most protuberant eyes Mark had ever seen. He looked like a little blinking owl. Mark felt sure he'd seen the man some-where before. 'Can I get you another?'

'No, you're all right, mate,' said Mark. 'I've probably had enough anyway.'

He sat down with the others and joined in the merciless ribbing of Gus, all part and parcel of the ritual humiliation that was a stag night. Mark was only glad that he'd already been through the experience. Even if he were to marry again, he doubted he'd go for this a second time.

'So where are we off to after here?' Mark asked.

'A-ha,' said Spike, 'that's a secret. Gus isn't to know. We might have to blindfold him to take him there.'

'Right, so we're going to a lap-dancing club then,' said Mark. Earlier on Gus had said the only way to get him into one of those kinds of places would be if he were dragged in blindfold. Gus had managed to get to the tender age of thirty-five and still retain a degree of innocence. God only knew how, as none of his mates were exactly squeaky clean. Added to which, the wife-to-be was fiercely feminist and definitely would Not Approve, so Spike had told Mark gleefully. Which was red rag to a bull for him. The more trouble he could cause, the more he was likely to try.

'I've got this as well.' Spike produced a blow-up doll. 'Meet Mary. Before the end of the night, she's going to make Gus a very happy man.'

Mark roared with laughter and decided that another drink was on the cards after all.

Yes, undoubtedly, it was good to be here. And just what he needed.

Katie was in Charlie's office riffling about, not entirely sure what she was looking for. Or what she would do when she found it. So far she had found nothing to incriminate him. There were no dodgy emails to women abroad – if he had a mistress, Katie felt sure she must be in Amsterdam – and no incriminating visa stubs.

Perhaps she was barking up the wrong tree. Maybe it wasn't a woman he was hiding, but something else. Was it possible he'd got into drugs? It seemed unlikely, but maybe the atmosphere in Amsterdam had loosened him up a bit. She searched through

241

his drawers for evidence of small packets of white powder, before giving up in disgust. What was she *doing*? Maybe Charlie was hiding something from her, but this wasn't the way to find out. He was her husband. She should just come straight out with it and ask him when he got home.

She shut his desk drawer and got up to go downstairs, when she heard a cab pull up outside. Shit. Charlie must be back early. She slid out of his office and ran down the stairs, ready to greet him as he came through the door.

'Charlie, you're home, how lovely.' Katie hoped she didn't look obviously flustered. She'd thought Charlie would be back later that afternoon, and had left her lists of what to order for the party (if she was allowed to have her own way, that was, and not be obliged to use the exorbitant catering firm Marilyn was after), the invitation list, the number to ring for the cake, etc., all out on the dining-room table.

Charlie gave her a quick kiss and headed straight up to the office, so Katie quickly rushed into the dining room, gathered everything together and put it away. It made her feel secretive, sly somehow. That, coupled with her unexpected meeting with Rob, had left Katie feeling out of sorts. It had been so nice to see him again, and had made her realise how much she'd missed him in the last couple of weeks. Missed him, she realised, more than she missed Charlie when he was away.

Her mum was right. This party was probably going to be a disaster. Katie's husband was becoming ever more a stranger; they passed each other like ghosts in the house they shared. Nine times out of ten Charlie ended up crashing out on the sofa in his office. This wasn't a marriage, it was a house-share.

No, no, no. It wasn't. It couldn't be. Katie had worked so hard to try to hold it together. All it needed was some more effort on her part. Charlie was away such a lot, they had just forgotten how it was to be part of a couple, and if Charlie had lost the art of being part of a family, then it was up to her to help him recover it.

She realised when he'd walked in she hadn't even kissed Charlie. He'd been away for a whole week and she had barely acknowledged him. No wonder he was distant with her. Leaving Molly in her buggy, where she was fast asleep, and the boys watching television, Katie went upstairs and put her arms around Charlie, kissing him on the cheek.

'Welcome home,' she said. 'Do you fancy a fry-up for lunch?'

'Sounds great,' said Charlie, disentangling himself from her grasp, 'but I've just got to sort this thing out on the computer. I'll be down in a sec.'

Katie bit back her disappointment. But what had she expected, really? Charlie had been shrugging off her advances for months now.

Charlie looked up as if sensing her disappointment.

'Sorry,' he said. 'Lunch would be lovely. Then maybe I can take the boys to the cinema this afternoon.'

That was better. Katie smiled.

'Great,' she said. 'I'm sure they'd love it.'

All that they needed was more time. If they could only spend a bit more time together, everything would be fine, she was sure of it.

The evening was going with a swing. After the pub and a dodgy curry, Spike had got his wish and they had managed to inveigle Gus into a lap-dancing club. Mark had enjoyed the novelty of it to begin with – what red-blooded male wouldn't? But after a while, watching middle-aged blokes stuffing pound notes down the underwear of scantily clad women just seemed a bit seedy, and, well, to be quite frank, tedious. Mark looked at his watch. Midnight. It was yonks since he'd been out on the razzle for a whole day like this. His body wasn't up to it any more, so he'd been pacing himself. He retired to the bar, fully intending to make this his last one and then wander back to the Holiday Inn where they were staying.

'Stag night?' A chap at the bar nodded at him. It was the man Mark had bumped into earlier.

'How did you guess?' Mark said with amusement, as he watched Spike trying to force Gus into a rather rude position with Mary.

'Not yours, I take it?'

'No,' said Mark. 'Thank God. Been there, done that. Paying the alimony.'

'Ah, women,' said his new friend, 'can't live with 'em . . .'

'Can't live with 'em,' finished Mark. 'Do I know you?'

'I don't think so,' said his companion. 'But here, let me buy you a drink.'

Mark looked around the room and suddenly felt a maudlin surge of self-pity. If only things had worked out with Emily, he might be thinking about marrying again himself, or at least moving in with her. Now he was back to square one, destined to live a lonely bachelor life. Before long Mark was telling his new friend all about it. It was good to pour out his troubles to a complete stranger. Cathartic.

Time seemed to take on a different dimension, and suddenly Mark realised he had lost a great chunk of it. He was no longer by the bar, which now looked very far away, as if he was standing in the wrong end of a long tunnel. He realised belatedly he was actually standing in the middle of the dance floor with his trousers round his ankles, while Spike was leading the cry of, 'Get them off, get them off.'

Mark fought rather pathetically to avoid the debagging. But he couldn't delay the inevitable. It had been a standing joke in his student days that once he'd had a drink or three, he was putty in his mates' hands. And that he had a tendency to strip. On previous occasions Spike had left him tied up naked outside their hall of residence, and had once locked him out of their shared student flat and pelted him with flour and eggs.

Mark tried to focus his thoughts but they swam away from

244

him. Funny, he didn't think he'd had that much to drink, but now the room was spinning round and round . . .

He came to in a dark corridor. Something lay next to him. Something hard and plastic. He shivered. Why was he so cold? His head was pounding and he felt dizzy and sick.

'Smile, you're on candid camera!' A flash of light, the sight of two protuberant eyes staring down at him and a peal of unkind laughter rang in his ears, before footsteps disappeared down the corridor.

Mark sat up blearily. What had just happened to him? He was stark naked, and lying next to him, staring at him unblinkingly, was Mary.

Emily had been away for the weekend too. The thought of one more weekend in her lonely house had been enough to drive her out of it. It had been far too long since she'd made the trip home to Swansea. Her mum was lonely, she knew as much from their frequent conversations, but Emily had been guiltily putting off going to see her. The house hadn't felt the same since her dad had died. The chair he'd sat in for the past fifteen years, eking out what was left of his miserable existence, seemed to reproach her with its emptiness. Look, it seemed to say, I expected more of you than this, when are you going to stand up for the things you believe in?

But her mum was glad to see her, and so pathetically proud of Emily's flash life in London, as she liked to tell everyone, that Emily felt guiltier than ever. It must be nice to look at the world in the simplistic way Emily's mum did, to see the gleaming surfaces and not the grit and grime underneath.

It was only Sarah, who invited them both round for Sunday lunch, who saw through her.

'I see that Jasmine is in the papers again,' she said, serving out the Sunday roast, disapproval written all over her face.

'So what if she is,' Emily said defensively, though she knew she had no right to defend the indefensible.

'Isn't your firm defending her?' Sarah wheedled away.

'Yes,' said Emily.

'Don't you have more important things to do than sue some poor sod of a dentist who most likely hasn't done anything wrong. Honest to God, no one will go into public services if we carry on like this.'

This was a well-worn theme with Sarah, an NHS nurse whose Welsh lilt always seemed to get stronger whenever Emily came home, as if to berate her sister for abandoning her working-class roots. Sarah always managed to make Emily feel like a heel.

'Someone has to do it,' said Emily, blushing.

'Well, that someone doesn't need to be you, does it?' Sarah retorted.

'Don't be so hard on your sister,' said their mother. 'Now, come on and tell us all about those celebrities you keep meeting.'

But afterwards in the kitchen, Sarah took Emily aside and said, 'Did Mam tell you about her scratch cards?'

'Oh, not again,' said Emily heavily. 'How much does she owe this time?'

'I'm not sure,' said Sarah, 'but I think it's a couple of thousand.'

Emily groaned. 'I can't do the whole amount, but I can do some of it, and give her some more next month.'

It always came to this. Sarah hated what Emily did, but always turned to her younger sister when the family finances needed sorting out. And Emily, always guilty of not being around enough for her mother, had no option but to sign the cheque. There was no way she could leave her job right now. Not when her mum owed all this money. It was no use trying to talk to her either. Every single time Emily had tried it, her mum had promised she wouldn't do it again, and before Emily knew it they were back to square one. It was worse than dealing with a child.

As a result of her weekend away, Emily got to work late on Monday morning. She wasn't sleeping at all well, and had tossed and turned half the night. In the frantic space when she had slept, her dreams were half-remembered, anxious, and seemed to involve her wandering down corridors searching hopelessly for Mark.

A huge guffaw greeted her appearance. John and several of her other colleagues were gathered round a desk looking at the morning papers.

'You're going to have a load of fun with your new case,' said John.

'Why?' asked Emily.

'Haven't you seen the papers?'

'Not this morning,' Emily replied. 'Why? What's there to see?'

'Only this,' said John.

He handed her a copy of the *Sun*. Emily's hands shook as she saw the picture on the front. Under a headline of '*JASMINE DENTIST IN DEBAUCHED ORGY*' was a picture of Mark, stark bollock naked (only those bits were considerately covered up with a picture of a dental mask, this being, of course, a family newspaper) lying next to what looked like a blow-up doll.

Chapter Twenty-six

'Oh my god.' Rob opened the front door on Monday morning and shut it again. A sea of faces stood outside and he blinked as dozens of cameras flashed. 'Mark, have you seen how many reporters are in the front garden?'

'Oh shit.' Mark opened the door himself and was met with a barrage of questions. 'Have you anything to say about the weekend, Mr Davies?' 'What was her name?' 'Did she give good head?' The laughter was raucous, jeering. Mark slammed the door shut and sat down in the lounge in disbelief. How could this be happening to him? He looked out of the lounge window to see someone with a long-lens camera in the garden. Enraged, he raced to the back door, flung it wide open and yelled, 'Why don't you just piss off or I'll call the police.'

'You have to admit it's funny.' Rob hadn't stopped laughing since he'd seen Mark's picture all over the papers.

'No it bloody well isn't,' said Mark. 'I've got to get through that lot to get to work. Fuck knows what sort of trouble I'm going to be in there, but I'm really not looking forward to finding out.'

The phone rang. Mark snatched it up and yelled, 'If you're that runt of a journalist you can just bog off – oh, hi Sam.'

'How could you be such a prat?' Sam launched into a tirade. Mark held the phone away from his ear. She hadn't had so much to berate him with since before the divorce. '. . . And if

248

you think I am going to let the kids near you with all this going on, you can think again, Mark Davies,' she finished with a flourish.

'Sam, you can't do that –' protested Mark, but she'd put the phone down.

'What did she want?' asked Rob.

'To tell me what a prat I've been and ban me from seeing my children. Can this day get any worse?'

'Well, you have been a prat,' said Rob. 'I mean, how on earth did you get so drunk that you didn't see that one coming?'

'Actually, that's the weird thing,' said Mark. 'I honestly don't know. We didn't drink at all during the day because we were go-karting. And then we had a couple of pints in the pub, I had maybe three glasses of wine with my dinner, and then perhaps two more pints. It was hardly excessive – I should have been merry but not like that.'

Rob frowned. Despite his joshing, there was a serious point to this. He remembered all too well his own brush with the media after Wales. Luckily, he and Suzie had missed out on most of the aggro – that had fallen on the shoulders of Janet, the hapless organiser of the camp. But still, it hadn't been pleasant.

'You don't think someone could have spiked your drink?'

'I suppose it's possible,' said Mark. 'But I don't know who'd do such a thing. It's all a bit blurry after the pub. I remember going to the club, and chatting to some bloke. And the next thing I knew I was on the dance floor with my trousers round my ankles. After that it's blank again till I woke up with that sodding doll.'

'What did the rest of them say?'

'Well, according to Spike, who was the instigator of the joke, one minute I was fine and the next thing I was putty in their hands. You know how I used to get when we were students, when I'd get so drunk that anyone could do pretty much anything to me? Apparently I was just like that.'

Mark put his head in his hands.

'I just can't believe this is happening to me,' he said. 'It was bad enough being sued for breaching confidentiality, but now I could lose my job. No one will see this as blokes pratting about, which is what it pretty much was; not after the way they've stitched me up.'

'*Debauched dentist goes on rampant orgy* isn't truly indicative of your professionalism,' agreed Rob. 'Have you spoken to your rep yet?'

'I've arranged an urgent meeting with him this week,' said Mark. 'I just hope he can actually help me.'

'I'm curious, though,' said Rob. 'How did they get all that stuff about you and Emily? Or should I call her your "mystery woman"?'

'I don't know,' said Mark. 'I may have blabbed my mouth off. I wasn't exactly in any fit state to remember.'

He looked thoroughly woebegone.

'Oh God,' he said. 'I suppose I should also tell my parents what's going on before they read about it. I feel like I'm living a nightmare.'

Emily was reading the *Evening Standard* on the way home. She had read and reread every sordid detail, but still she felt compelled to read the *Standard*'s regurgitating of it.

> *Shamed dentist and dad of two, Mark Davies, wasted no time on Saturday night. After a hard day's drinking with his other dental chums, he went on to an evening of total debauchery, during which he:*
>
> *Visited a lap-dancing club.*
>
> *Stripped on the dance floor.*
>
> *Ended up naked next to a blow-up doll.*
>
> *He and his drinking partners are a disgrace to their profession.*

*Is there no end to his shame? Jasmine Symonds, who
is suing Davies over breach of confidentiality, says, 'This
confirms all my fears about Dr Davies. I always knew
there was something odd about him.'*

*Kayla Symonds, Jasmine's mother, agrees. 'I never
trusted him right from the start ...'*

Emily threw down the paper in disgust. It was more of the
same.

Part of her was absolutely horrified by what Mark had done.
That sort of behaviour she might have expected from Callum,
but surely not Mark. He didn't seem the type. But one of his
friends, Spike someone, was quoted as saying he was always like
this. And Emily was distraught over the way he had spoken about
her – although luckily she was only identified as his mysterious
lady friend, it must have been her to whom Mark was referring
when he said that he'd been badly let down and would never
trust another woman again.

And yet, between her shock and anger, Emily also felt appalled
on Mark's behalf. Someone had clearly set him up. He'd gone
out for an evening with his mates – a stag weekend, the papers
said – and someone had alerted the press to what was happening.
It was a pretty shitty thing to do, even if Mark had behaved badly.
Emily wanted to contact Mark, to let him know that she was
thinking about him, but she knew Maniac Mel wouldn't be
impressed if she did. And, given how much money Emily now
needed to send her mum on a regular basis, for the moment she
had no choice but to let it lie.

'So what are my options?' asked Mark as he sat down with James,
feeling that, quite frankly, things were so bad now they couldn't
get much worse. He'd definitely noted a cooling off in James's
hitherto friendly attitude. Mark couldn't say he blamed him
really. It was one thing representing someone who was being

251

sued by a patient who may or may not be telling the truth, but the events of the weekend had painted Mark's situation in a whole different light.

James looked very uncomfortable. 'Christ, Mark, what on earth were you thinking?' he said. 'Didn't you think about how your behaviour would come across? Have you never heard of the *Sun* rule?'

Mark looked blank.

'How would this look as a *Sun* headline?' James clarified. 'Well, now you know.'

'To be honest,' said Mark, 'by the time the blow-up doll incident happened I was well past the place of rational thought. But hell. I was on a weekend away with my mates. What the fuck were the press doing there in the first place? I'm a nobody, why should anyone be interested in me?'

'That is a very good point,' said James. 'We'll get someone to check that side of things out.'

'I know I don't have a leg to stand on,' said Mark, 'but seriously, I hadn't had that much to drink. I think someone spiked my drink.'

James looked sceptical, and Mark couldn't honestly blame him. He knew he was clutching at straws, but what other explanation was there?

'I'll look into that too,' said James. 'But, to be honest, it does sound a bit far-fetched.'

It was the best Mark could hope for, he supposed. All the way home on the train he felt absurdly self-conscious – as if at any moment someone would point him out and say, 'Look, it's the Debauched Dentist!'

Thankfully, his parents had been incredibly understanding – not exactly thrilled to have their son plastered all over the papers, but not overly worried either. After two days of doorstepping, in which Mark and Rob had had to run the gauntlet of press and photographers every morning, Mark had seriously considered going to stay with them for a bit, just till everything calmed down. He'd had to call the police when he found one reporter looking in his bins and another with their nose pressed against his front window. But, luckily, by the Wednesday the story had gone off the boil and though several reporters were still hanging around the house, none of them, thankfully, had followed him up to town.

It was different at the surgery, where most of his patients had read or heard about what had happened. Some of them appeared so shocked by the story that they had requested to see other dentists, which, Mark felt, was fair enough, but in the main he was relieved to see they were pretty tolerant. A fact that did go some way to restoring his faith in human nature. Granny O' Leary had been the most forthright about it: 'Those papers, they just print lies about people,' she said. 'We all know you wouldn't do anything wrong.' Mark was touched by her faith in him, but doubted Granny O' Leary's testimony would cut much ice if the powers that be hauled him up for a hearing, which James had warned him was a distinct possibility.

'All it will take is for one of your patients to make a complaint to them,' James had said, 'and then you'll be looking at a hearing for professional misconduct.'

Mark felt sick every time he thought about that. Suppose they found him guilty? What could he do if he was no longer a dentist?

Sam was also continuing to give him grief. She had rung him daily to berate him for his stupidity. Not, it turned out, with reference to the girls (who were Mark's main concern), though when it suited her Sam would throw in a 'How could you have put your daughters in such an embarrassing position?' to ensure he felt maximum guilt, but she was crosser, it seemed, about the fact that he might have caused complications in her job. 'Jasmine is the face of *Smile, Please!*' she said. 'Didn't you think how that would affect me?'

'Yes, that was just what I was thinking as my career went down the tubes,' was Mark's sarcastic response, 'and anyway, I thought you'd sacked Jasmine.'

'That was before all of this came out,' said Sam smartly. 'Your little efforts have meant Jasmine's been on the front page of the papers all week. There's considerable sympathy for her out there. We'd be mad to turn down such good publicity.'

'It's nice to know the fact that my life is in freefall is helping your publicity,' said Mark.

'Well, you've only yourself to blame,' Sam replied. 'I have serious reservations about letting the girls come and stay while this is going on.'

Mark had serious reservations too, but only because he didn't want the kids to be exposed to the media scrum that was currently camped outside his house, so he let the comment go. But he felt sick to the pit of his stomach. He'd lost his wife, his girlfriend, and now he was in danger of losing his job. Were his children about to follow?

Katie wasn't a great reader of the tabloids, and she hadn't seen Emily, so she wouldn't have picked up on Mark's plight if she hadn't run into Mandy Allwick at scouts.

'Ooh, did you hear the latest about Mark Davies?' asked Mandy.

'I can't say I did,' said Katie, casting a look at Mandy, who was bursting out of a tight-fitting top and leather miniskirt. 'What about him?'

Mandy happily obliged and filled in the gory details.

'I always knew there was something pervy about him,' said Mandy. 'You'd better tell that friend of yours to watch out. He's bad news. I always knew it. I'm changing dentists straight away.'

Katie was utterly appalled. How could anyone be so judgemental? Apart from the fact that the Mark she knew wasn't anything like that, this was all hearsay.

'I am sure there'll be an explanation for all of this,' she said. 'I just can't believe Mark would do anything like that. In fact, I'm sure he wouldn't.'

Mandy sniffed audibly and said nothing, but her body language said it all.

As she left, a hand tapped Katie on the shoulder, and she turned round to see Mark.

'I heard that,' he said. 'Thanks. It's nice to know someone believes me.'

'Apart from the fact that I would always take anything I heard from Mandy Allwick with huge dollops of salt,' said Katie, 'I never believe anything I read in the papers on principle. Particularly not the red-tops. So come on, tell me what happened. How on earth did you end up naked next to a blow-up doll?'

Mark sheepishly filled Katie in on the events of the weekend, and she roared with laughter when he finished.

'You're not shocked?' Mark asked. 'You wouldn't believe some of the comments I've had.'

'I live with someone who works in the City,' said Katie. 'I'm pretty unshockable. Besides, I dated a medic when I was a student. I know what you lot are like. I think it's funny.'

'You might not if your career was on the line,' said Mark. 'Or if your ex-wife was threatening to stop you seeing your children.'

'Oh no, she's not, is she?' Katie was horrified. 'Mark, I'm so sorry.'

'It's fair enough, I suppose,' said Mark, 'there's been a fair bit of press activity at my house this week. Which is why we're going to my parents in Surrey for the weekend. Gemma's still at her mum's and I'm going to pick her up after scouts.'

'Still,' said Katie, 'that's a bit steep. I'm sure this will all blow over eventually.'

'I hope so,' said Mark, but he looked uncertain and lonely. Katie felt immensely sorry for him.

'Have you spoken to Emily about any of this?' Mark asked.

'I knew nothing about it till just now,' said Katie. 'But I will if you like.'

'Thanks,' Mark said. 'I think I may have said one or two things about her that have been misquoted, and I don't want her thinking I'm some kind of weirdo.'

'I'm sure she won't,' said Katie. 'Say hi to Rob for me.'

'Will do,' Mark answered, and left, leaving Katie with an unspeakable feeling of sadness. Mark and Emily would probably never be together after this. What a pity, when they seemed so right for each other.

And you and Rob – are you right for each other? The question popped into her head, but she ruthlessly brushed it away.

Chapter Twenty-seven

The day of Charlie's party dawned bright and fair. Katie had been in an orgy of planning for weeks now, and was keyed up from the effort of keeping it under wraps. She was fairly sure Charlie didn't suspect a thing, though Marilyn had nearly given the game away by announcing something loudly about seeing them next week when they'd visited the other weekend. Luckily, Charlie, as usual these days, seemed too preoccupied to notice. In fact, the way he was just as preoccupied while with his parents as he was while with her was giving Katie hope. His distant air and lack of engagement in family life probably had less to do with her and more to do with a clearly impending midlife crisis. He had made several references over the last few weeks to the approach of his fortieth. The way he'd gone on about it anyone would have thought it was a death sentence.

'It's only your fortieth,' she'd joshed him. 'Don't you want to celebrate it?'

'Not particularly,' he'd said.

'Oh,' Katie had said in dismay. 'What, really? You don't want a party or anything?'

'You know I hate parties,' had been the response.

Katie had nearly told him at that point. But surely everyone liked parties, didn't they? No one could really be upset if the people they loved had sorted out a surprise party for them, could they? She sincerely hoped not.

Katie and Marilyn had cooked up the idea of telling Charlie they were going out for lunch with his parents to celebrate the birthday, but of course they were going straight to the golf club instead. In the end, Katie had been unable to organise the last-minute preparations her end, so had gratefully left the decoration of the room and the sorting out of the caterers to Marilyn and Charlie's sister, Lucy, who was cut from her mother's mould. She'd also invited Emily, who was bringing the cake, plus flowers for Marilyn, and Charlie's birthday present: a Red Letter day's racing at Brands Hatch. Katie thought they'd covered all bases, but she felt absurdly nervous as Charlie drove up the drive of Ranelagh Golf Club. She sent Marilyn a surreptitious text. *We're on our way.*

They were ushered from the plush reception area into a small anteroom.

'Wait a minute,' said Charlie. 'Where are Mum and Dad? I thought we'd be meeting them here?'

Just then his mother came in through one of the doors.

'Darling,' she said, 'happy birthday. We've got a little surprise for you.'

'I hate surprises,' said Charlie, shooting daggers at Katie.

Katie felt like she was going to be sick. She followed Charlie through to the main reception room.

'Surprise!' A hundred people leapt forward with party poppers and screams and shouts. A band (wait a minute, Marilyn had ordered a band?) started to play 'Happy Birthday'. And Charlie stood in the middle of it all, looking like thunder.

'What the bloody hell did you have to do this for?' he hissed. 'I said I didn't want a party. I said I didn't want to celebrate. But little Ms Organisation always has to butt her nose in where it's not wanted. Why the hell don't you ever listen?'

Emily walked into Charlie's fortieth birthday party with a feeling of impending doom. She was late with the cake, and felt that

Charlie's formidable-sounding mother might have something to say about that. The trouble was the Ranelagh Golf Club was so exclusive it didn't bother to signpost itself, so Emily had spent a fruitless half an hour driving round in circles before eventually finding a local to tell her the way.

There was music playing that sounded like it had been piped out of the 1950s. She hadn't had Charlie down as a sultan of swing. But then again, from what Katie said, it would be typically selfish of his mum to organise music on his birthday that she herself liked. There was a party going on, but the atmosphere didn't feel exactly party-ish. Emily snuck in quietly and looked round the room, hoping to spot Katie and discreetly offload the cake to her.

The room was fairly busy with the sort of people Emily couldn't imagine herself socialising with normally: greying stockbrokers talking loudly about their bonuses mingled with braying women talking even louder about horses. No wonder Katie hated coming down here. There was no sign of Katie, or Charlie, and Emily was beginning to feel slightly anxious, when someone tapped her on the shoulder and said, 'There you are. You must be Emily.'

Emily turned round to see a very well dressed, smart woman in her sixties with perfectly coiffured greying hair. She spoke as if Emily was some kind of insect beneath her feet. This, presumably, was the dreaded Marilyn. Marilyn held her hand out, and Emily felt at an immediate disadvantage, given that she was holding the cake and flowers.

'Sorry,' she said, trying to extricate her arm from under the cake box. In doing so, she knocked the box onto the floor. 'Oh sod,' she said, then, 'Sorry' again. Marilyn looked horrified, and Emily wished the floor would swallow her up.

'Let me take that,' said Marilyn in despairing tones, and opened the box. Emily watched in horror as she realised half the cream on the cake was now squashed against the lid. 'Really!' said Marilyn, and whisked it away, presumably for repairs.

Feeling at a loose end, Emily wandered aimlessly round the room, rather wishing Katie hadn't invited her. She didn't know anyone here at all. It looked like it was all Charlie's friends. Presumably, all Katie's friends, like Emily, would feel they stuck out like sore thumbs.

Eventually she saw Katie in the corner. She was wearing a flowing flowery summer dress, with gold sandals and a light cardigan. She looked lovely, and she'd lost more weight since the dancing weekend. Emily frowned. She hoped everything was all right. Katie, never forthcoming about her private life, had shut up like a clam recently. Emily felt sure it had something to do with Rob, but whatever it was, Katie wasn't telling.

'How's it going?' Emily said as she reached her friend. 'I met your dragon of a mother-in-law, and I'm really sorry but I dropped the cake –'

Emily stopped mid-sentence. Things were clearly not all right.

'Whatever's the matter?'

'Not here,' muttered Katie, and dragged her friend into the ladies, where she promptly burst into tears.

'Oh Katie,' said Emily, 'what is it?'

'It's everything,' said Katie. 'I thought giving Charlie a surprise party would make everything okay, but he hates it. He stormed off at the beginning and I haven't spoken to him since.'

'Oh,' said Emily, not knowing quite what to say. 'Maybe he just needs to calm down.'

'I don't think so,' said Katie, looking thoroughly miserable. 'Everything's been going wrong for ages. I don't know whether he's having some kind of midlife crisis or something, but we've barely had sex in months and we hardly talk any more. It's like I'm living with a stranger.'

'Katie, you should have said,' Emily told her, putting an arm round her friend. 'Why didn't you?'

Katie pulled a face.

'Fear of failure, I suppose. I've set so much store by my marriage, I didn't want to admit that it might be falling apart. I'm not very good about talking over my problems. Besides, I knew once I got started I wouldn't be able to stop.'

'Everyone has rough patches,' argued Emily. 'It will get better.'

Katie looked bleak.

'That's what I've been telling myself,' she said. 'But I can't really believe that any longer. I think I may have to face the truth. It's over. Or near as damn it.'

She wiped her eyes with a tissue.

'There's something I haven't told you,' she added.

'About Rob?' Emily hazarded a guess.

'Oh lord, is it that obvious?' Katie looked truly horrified.

'Well, I have no idea what went on, but it's clear that something happened the other week,' said Emily. 'Go on, spill the beans.'

'It was after we danced the rumba,' said Katie in a whisper. 'He kissed me.'

'Well, you know what he's like,' Emily replied.

'Yes, I do,' said Katie. 'But the thing is – I wanted him to.'

Katie floated through the rest of the party in a daze. Her crying in the loos had left her with a terrible headache. Luckily, with Emily's help she'd done a fairly decent job of repairing her face, and she was well-used to containing her feelings, especially where Charlie's family were concerned, so no one apart from Emily knew anything was wrong. Charlie had studiously avoided her all day, spending his time slapping the backs of boring blokes he knew from the City. Marilyn and Lucy were in full Caldwell Takeover mode, so there was nothing for Katie to do except wander about aimlessly, trying to engage the periphery relations like Charlie's aged deaf Auntie Glenda in conversation. It was so dull, in the end Katie persuaded Emily to go home. 'I have to be here,' she argued, 'but you don't.'

Wistfully, she wished she'd pushed Marilyn into letting the kids come, but Marilyn had been adamant that she didn't think the occasion was suitable for children. Katie had had to promise them a day in London with their dad to make up for the disappointment of not being there. Katie suspected the real reason Marilyn had barred her grandchildren was because she was worried how the Golf Club would stand up to the combined assault of George and Aidan. Katie's mum had stepped in and was looking after them. Katie wondered idly if this out-of-sight, out-of-mind approach to the kids had been the way Charlie had been treated when he was young. It would certainly account for a lot.

The afternoon dragged on. Katie felt more and more morose and stupid. She couldn't drink because she was driving, and judging by the way Charlie was knocking them back it was just as well one of them was staying in control. Why had she let herself get carried away with the idea that having a party would solve all their problems? She was kicking herself for her stupidity. Marilyn seemed oblivious to the idea that Charlie might not actually be that thrilled about the honour being done him, and despite Katie's efforts to stop her was insisting there was a grand ceremonial cake-cutting and speeches.

'Come on, dear,' Marilyn said as she came bustling up to Katie, who was moodily leaning against the wall, wishing that she was somewhere completely different, 'time to cut the cake.'

The cake, Katie was relieved to see, had been restored to its former glory by one of the kitchen staff, although there was a slight dent in one corner. Marilyn had gone to the trouble of putting the forty candles Katie had managed to rustle up all the way round the cake. Katie wished she hadn't brought them; she had a feeling that Charlie wouldn't be impressed.

Marilyn insisted that Katie walk with her towards Charlie holding the lighted cake, while the band played 'Happy Birthday' again. Katie was swallowing hard. Charlie looked furious, and she knew that he wasn't going to let her forget this humiliation in a hurry.

No one but her seemed to have noticed, however, and there was much laughter and commotion as Charlie tried and failed to blow the candles out. Damn. She'd accidentally brought along some never-ending candles that she'd bought for George's birthday. In the end Charlie simply picked them up and doused them in his beer in disgust.

'Right, is that it?' he said. 'I need another beer.'

'Certainly not,' said his mother, and proceeded to wax lyrical about Charlie's birth and early childhood. If anyone was going to make a speech about her son, it was definitely going to be her. Apparently from day one she'd known Charlie would be a success.

Charlie looked like a worm wriggling on a stick. Katie wished she could get Marilyn to shut up. Was she really that thick-skinned that she didn't realise what torture this was for her son? Eventually Marilyn paused for breath, and Katie darted in with the flowers she'd brought and said a quick thank you to Marilyn for all her hard work. That, she hoped, would be that. But she'd reckoned without the combined might of the Caldwell clan.

'Speech, speech!' the roar went up, and Charlie was thrust forward into the spotlight. A place where she knew he hated to be.

'Right, well. Hmm,' Charlie mumbled. 'I suppose I should say thank you. I wasn't expecting any of this. In fact, I said outright I didn't want any of this, but my mother and wife between them seem to know what's best for me, so here we all are.'

There was a nervous titter at this. People looked at each other questioningly.

'You all think I'm joking, don't you?' Charlie waved his beer around him wildly. 'Well, I'm not. Forty years I've had of this. My mother planning my life down to the last T. And now she's got my wife in on the act too.'

Katie moved forward. 'Look,' she hissed, 'I'm really sorry about this. I got it wrong, but this is neither the time nor place to air our dirty laundry.'

Charlie staggered backwards.

'I think it's the perfect time,' he said. He stood looking at everyone as if working out what he was going to say. 'I'm forty next week,' he continued. 'Quite a milestone, eh? I think it's about time I stopped living the life other people want me to lead, and started to live how I want to, don't you?'

'Charlie, what on earth are you talking about?' Katie felt as if someone had poured a bucket of cold water all over her. She knew what was coming. She'd known it for months.

'The thing is,' continued Charlie, 'my marriage is a sham. It always has been. Turns out women aren't my thing at all. It's taken me forty years to discover I swing the wrong way, but now I've found out, I'm not going to put up with it any longer.'

'What do you mean?' Katie was confused now. What was he on about?

'I'm a friend of Dorothy,' said Charlie.

'Who's Dorothy?' Marilyn looked so puzzled that Katie nearly burst out laughing, though she had never felt less like laughing in her life.

'Dear, dear Mother,' said Charlie. 'You tried so hard to make sure I became a full-blooded male, didn't you? All those sailing weekends, and all that effort to get me in the rugby team. But it didn't work. I'm as queer as queer can be.'

'You're *what*?'

'I'm gay,' said Charlie. 'And, for the first time in my life, I'm proud.'

Chapter Twenty-eight

'You bastard,' said Katie. She was shaking like a leaf, and without thinking she slapped Charlie on the cheek. Then she turned round and stormed out of the room, brushing past people with no thought of anything other than escape. She ran to the car, climbed in it and was halfway home before she gave thought to where she was going.

In her heart of hearts, Katie had known the end was coming. Their marriage had never been brilliant, but since Molly's birth it had limped along while she ignored the warning signs, hoping that if she buried her head in the sand for long enough they'd go away. And now this. Charlie's bombshell had blown their marriage apart. There was no going back now.

Charlie was gay. The words were going round in her head, but what did they mean? How had he found out? Had he been unfaithful to her? The thought made her physically sick, and she had to pull over to the side of the road to retch. She was still shaking and felt alternately hot and cold all over. Suppose he hadn't taken precautions? Suppose he had infected her with something? What was she going to tell the children? Her mind was a whirling maelstrom of questions, and the biggest one of all was, If Charlie really were gay, why on earth had he married her in the first place?

Her whole married life had been based on a lie. She had worked so hard to paper over the cracks, and all the time her husband had been living a lie. As the shock wore away, Katie felt herself filled with a white-hot rage. How could he do this to her? How could he?

The thoughts batted back and forth, back and forth, till she was thoroughly sick of them. She drove and drove with no thought to where she was going, no thought for her future, or what was going to happen now. All she could think of was that she was stuck in a nightmare not of her making and she could see no possible way out.

Mark had gone out somewhere with the girls, so Rob was on his own watching a repeat of *Strictly Come Dancing*. After watching Matt and Flavia's tango, Rob felt inspired to go back to his friend Carlo, and he spent a ridiculous half an hour listening to Carlo telling him how to unleash the sexy beast within. As if there was much point, when there was no one to unleash it on.

Even though Katie wasn't going dancing any more, he hadn't been able to make himself stop. He enjoyed it too much for a start. And he exercised the faintest of hopes that she might come back, eventually. She had to. It simply wasn't the same dancing with someone else. He was still kicking himself that he had let his feelings get the better of him and kissed her. If he hadn't he'd still be seeing her, and though it would have been indulging in the bittersweet pain of knowing they couldn't be together, it would have been much, much better than not seeing her at all. His counsellor, Nina, had said this was the wrong way to look at it, and he should learn from what had happened and move on. The trouble was, Rob didn't want to move on. He just wanted Katie. The counselling was undoubtedly helping him unlock some of the misery in his head, but it couldn't give him the one thing he wanted more than anything else.

There was a ring at the door. Rob frowned. It was too early for Mark to be back. He hoped that it wasn't another doorstepper. Since a new series of *Love Shack* had started airing (special guest commentator: a certain Jasmine Symonds), the press interest in

Mark seemed to have waned, but both he and Rob remained wary. Rob hadn't understood what it meant to have your privacy ripped apart till he was faced with a baying horde of tape recorders and cameras every time he left the house. He sincerely hoped there wasn't some new ridiculous revelation about to hit tomorrow's papers.

Rob glanced out of the hall window before opening the door. To his complete surprise it was Katie. What on earth was she doing here?

'Earth to Gemma, Earth to Gemma,' Mark called, as his daughter sat transfixed by her mobile, seemingly determined to ignore him. He looked at Beth and grinned before grabbing a spoon and using it to fire boiled sweets at his older daughter.

Still wary about media intrusion, Mark had decided to take the girls to Pizza Hut this evening, and bring them home late. They hadn't been to the house much since the storm broke and Mark missed them badly. So far Sam hadn't kept her threat of stopping him seeing the kids, and he'd kept papers out of the house and given them a watered-down version of events. Though, judging by the look in Gemma's eye occasionally, he wouldn't be at all surprised if the tales of his antics hadn't been the talk of the Year Eight toilets. He hoped for Gemma's sake it hadn't, but she seemed spikier than ever when she was with him. She appeared to Mark to be very unhappy, but he had no way of breaking through her hard shell and reaching her. They were all going away to Dorset, camping, at the start of the school holidays. Mark only hoped Gemma would have cheered up by then.

'Dad, you are so sad,' said Gemma witheringly. 'You're all over the papers. No wonder Emily left you.'

'Don't you ever lighten up?' Mark retaliated. 'And Emily leaving me had nothing to do with this.'

'Someone in the family needs to maintain decorum,' muttered Gemma.

'Right,' said Mark. 'Okay, I probably deserved that.'

'You are so embarrassing!' Gemma burst out suddenly. 'Everyone is talking about it. All of Year Eight know what a loser my dad is. I'm the laughing stock of the school.'

'Oh, Gemma,' said Mark. 'I am so, so sorry. Really, I am. If I could do something to change that evening, I would.'

'Why did you have to do it?' asked Gemma. 'Imagine how you'd feel to find out your dad's naked picture had been printed in the papers.'

'Er, gross,' said Beth. 'Were you really naked, Dad?'

'Well, this is one conversation I never imagined myself having,' said Mark. 'Okay, I haven't told you too much about this because I didn't want you to be upset. But what happened was I went out for a drink with my friends, and I think someone must have put something in my drink because I don't really remember much of the evening.'

'You mean you got paralytic.' Gemma's tone was self-righteously accusing. Oh to be young and so sodding sure of yourself, Mark thought.

'No,' said Mark, 'I don't. If I had got drunk I would have known about it. I had a few drinks, but that was all. My lawyer thinks someone might have set me up.'

Beth looked a bit anxious and he kicked himself for having given too much information. It was so hard to know how to handle the situation. He didn't want to lie to the kids, but neither did he want to overburden them either.

'Why do you need a lawyer, Daddy?' she asked. 'Will you go to prison?'

'No, no,' said Mark. 'Nothing like that. It's just one of my patients –'

'Jasmine Symonds,' added Gemma knowledgeably. 'I read all about it in *Heat*.'

'– yes, Jasmine Symonds,' Mark continued, 'hang on a minute, you read *Heat*?'

'Yes, so?' said Gemma. 'Everyone reads *Heat*.'

'Hmm, I'm not sure that's altogether suitable,' said Mark. 'Remind me to have a chat with your mum about that.'

'It's Mum's *Heat* I read,' said Gemma, in unmistakeable teen-putdown tones. 'Besides, I don't think she'll be all that bothered about having parenting lessons from you at the moment.'

Deciding that some battles weren't worth fighting, Mark let the subject drop and went on to explain what Jasmine had accused him of.

'And the reason Emily left me is because she's Jasmine's lawyer.'

'I miss Emily,' said Beth.

'I do too,' said Mark.

'So did you tell on Jasmine?' asked Gemma.

'No, of course I didn't,' said Mark. 'Someone did, but it wasn't me. But because she's made a big fuss about it, there has to be a court case, and that's why I've got a lawyer. But it's nothing at all to worry about.'

Nothing to worry about. How he wished that were true.

Emily was out with Ffion. She'd had two invitations that day, and had blown Ffion out to begin with, but Charlie's party had been so boring, even Katie had suggested she'd better leave. So, finding herself at a loose end, she had decided to drive up to town and go to the club where Ffion was strutting her funky stuff. Emily didn't feel like going, particularly, but it beat sitting at home on her own on a Saturday night, staring at four walls.

It was ages since she'd been out in town, and normally when she came to these things she'd had a fair amount to drink. Ffion was clearly well on her way when Emily arrived.

'Hey, Ems,' said Ffion, giving Emily a huge hug. 'Come and join the party.'

The party included several people that Ffion worked with, and, Emily noticed with a sickening shock, Callum. He affected not to notice her at first, but eventually he looked up and said,

'Hey babe,' before pulling Ffion onto his lap and proceeding to snog her face off.

That was one way of being put in her place, she thought, and she perched reluctantly at the end of the table. Thankfully, just seeing Callum again was enough to make her realise she wasn't missing anything. Ffion was welcome to him.

The talk quickly turned to Jasmine Symonds, who was doing a stonking impression of someone who had managed to pull a rabbit out of a bag. Her guest spot on *Love Shack* was turning out to be inspired, as people were apparently tuning in night after night to hear her talk about the 'trauma' of being abused by her dentist – she had *actually* used the word 'abused'. Emily couldn't believe it.

'He only took her tooth out,' said Emily. 'And it was rotten.'

'Whose side are you on?' asked Ffion. 'That dentist sounds a right shifty sod. He had it coming, I reckon.'

The consensus round the table was fairly united. Between them, they appeared to have read and believed unquestioningly every piece of tittle-tattle about Mark. It made Emily feel inordinately depressed. Maybe a lonely night in on her own would have been a better option.

'What are you doing here?' Rob felt he was being rude, but he was shocked to say the least. Katie was the last person he'd expected to see.

'Can I come in?' She looked dishevelled and slightly wild. There was something in her eyes that made him shiver. And not in a good way.

'Yes, of course,' said Rob. 'Are you all right? Only you look a bit upset.'

'Upset? Upset? Ha. Yes, you could say that.' Katie's voice didn't sound right either, there was a note of rising hysteria in it that Rob recognised from his years of dealing with the various strops of teenage girls.

'What happened?' he asked gently as he sat her down on the sofa. Clearly something was badly wrong.

Katie sat very still for a moment, and then she burst out laughing. But it wasn't a normal laugh, it was a horrible parody of a laugh. A laugh that sounded hollow, without mirth. A laugh that smacked of desperate sadness.

'Katie!' Rob was shocked, wondering whether she needed a slap on the cheek to bring her out of it, then he suddenly realised the laughter had given way to tears, and then she was sobbing in his arms.

'Is it the kids?' he conjectured, wondering what on earth could have provoked this response. 'Or Charlie?'

'The kids are fine,' hiccoughed Katie, 'it's Charlie. He's – oh god, I don't know how to say it – if it wasn't so awful it would be funny.' She took a deep breath before continuing. 'I thought he was having an affair, you see. And he is, I think. Well, I don't know. Maybe he isn't.'

'Katie, you're not making a whole lot of sense,' said Rob, stroking her hair gently.

'I know,' said Katie, 'that's because this doesn't make sense to me. At all.'

'What doesn't?'

'Charlie's gay,' said Katie.

'Expect the unexpected,' said Rob, and whistled slowly. He sat in silence for a few moments, before saying, 'Bloody hell. You're not joking, are you?'

'I wish I was,' said Katie. 'I feel like I'm stuck in a very bad dream. I mean, how could I not have known? It's not as though we've never had sex. We've got three kids, for fuck's sake. How can he possibly be gay?'

'Were there no signs at all?' Rob chose his words carefully. This was the sort of thing you read about in the papers. You didn't expect it to happen to people you actually knew.

Katie sighed. 'I don't know,' she said. 'Though, to be honest,

271

we never had the greatest of sex lives. Sorry. Too much information. I thought it didn't matter, as we were happy in the beginning. Or, at least, I was . . .'

Her voice trailed off.

'I've been kidding myself that everything was okay. I was so determined that my marriage was going to be perfect in a way my parents' wasn't, and now look at me.'

'It's not your fault,' said Rob. He hugged her tightly.

'Isn't it?' Katie asked. 'I think I got so caught up in trying to create the perfect life that I forgot to live a normal one. Any sensible person would have faced up to the truth eons ago.'

'But they wouldn't be you, though, would they?' said Rob. 'What I love about you is your integrity and strength of purpose. You gave it your best shot; it's not your fault you failed.'

Katie looked at Rob wonderingly, as if seeing him for the first time.

'You're right,' she said. 'It's not. And now we can stop pretending, can't we? There's nothing to hold us back.'

She lunged towards him, taking him unawares.

'Woah, Katie,' he said, dodging her kiss. 'This isn't the time or the place.'

'Of course it is,' said Katie. 'I was being loyal to Charlie before. I don't have to be any more.'

Rob couldn't believe it. If anyone had told him he'd turn down the woman he loved, he wouldn't have thought it possible. But he was going to. He had to.

'Katie,' Rob said, 'I have feelings for you. I won't pretend I don't. But you're in shock. And you have a lot of stuff to sort out. I can't believe I'm saying this, but now is not the right time for a quick fling with me.'

'But –' Katie looked so shattered he felt utterly lousy, but her vulnerability made him sure that he was right.

'But nothing,' he said. He brushed his lips across the top of her head. 'Right now, I think you need to get home and sort

272

yourself out. I'll be here if you need me. And I'll do my very best to be a good friend to you. But that's all I can be for now. When the time is right, well, then we'll know.'

'Oh Rob,' said Katie, bursting into tears again, 'why does life have to be so complicated?'

He held her close against him, loving the feel of her in his arms, but knowing she couldn't stay there.

'I wish I knew,' he said sadly. 'I only wish I knew.'

Chapter Twenty-nine

Emily sat at her desk staring at Mark's file. The case wouldn't make it to court till after Christmas, but she'd been charged with the task of following up witness statements. The general consensus in the office was that Mark was guilty as hell. Despite being lawyers, who you might have thought would have looked at the thing with more scrutiny, Mark's appearance in the *Sun* had been enough to convince them, too, that he had broken Jasmine's trust. The trouble with this job, Emily reflected, was that everyone you met was on the make, trying to get something for nothing. It made you cynical, so that when you did meet someone like Mark, who really was straight as a die, you tended to distrust them and not believe they were genuine.

Emily was scouring through the papers to try to find something, anything, which would work in Mark's favour. Maybe if she could find something to make the case collapse she could extricate herself from the mess she had found herself in, not lose her job, and regain Mark to boot. The only thing was, she would have to be incredibly subtle and make it look as though she wasn't sabotaging the case deliberately, otherwise Mel might just get rid of her anyway. Jasmine's star was firmly in the ascendant at the moment – if they won her case then others might beat a path to their door. If they lost it could only harm the company – unless they lost in such a way that Emily could make it look as if they were acting with integrity.

Something was nagging at the back of her mind. Something Ffion had muttered on Saturday about it not really mattering anyway if Mark was guilty, because someone at his surgery was.

Why should it not matter? Maybe Mark was right and he had been set up. Emily decided it might be time she rekindled her friendship with Ffion. Perhaps there were things Ffion knew that the PR company weren't too keen to pass on to their lawyers. Emily knew Ffion of old. She could be incredibly indiscreet. Shove a few vodkas down her neck and it might not be too hard to get her to come up with some hard facts. At least, Emily thought, then she'd feel she was doing something for Mark.

'Katie, you cannot go on like this.' Katie's mum had called round for the third day running to find Katie sitting in turmoil, with beds unmade, floors unswept, and Molly crawling happily through the chaos.

Katie tried to rouse herself out of her stupor. She couldn't even manage to drum up any irritation at her mother for being so absolutely appallingly right. Ever since she'd got back from Rob's on Saturday – he had insisted on driving her home in her car and making sure she sat down and told her mother everything that had happened – she had been in the same stunned state. Charlie had been home once, briefly, to pick up some things, but she hadn't seen him since. For all she knew he'd gone back to Amsterdam. The kids were so used to his absences that thankfully they hadn't picked up yet that their dad had gone. How the bloody hell was she going to explain it to them? How could George, in particular, cope with having a dad who was gay? Kids could be so cruel to each other. She could imagine Mandy Allwick's son having a field day when he found out.

'Sorry,' she said to her mum with a wan smile. 'Would you like a cup of tea?'

'I'll make it,' said her mother firmly. 'And then we're going to tackle this mess. You'll feel better when you're not living in squalor.'

'Says the woman who never ever cleans,' protested Katie. She almost smiled for a moment, before the dull toxic ache that had been residing in her stomach for the past few days returned. What was she going to do?

'Now,' said her mother, returning with the tea. 'You need to start thinking about your position. I could put you in touch with the lawyers who dealt with your dad's and my divorce if you like. They were very good.'

'Yes, weren't they?' The bitterness of Katie's response was a shock to her. It was a new feeling to actually say what she was thinking.

'That's better.' Her mother's placidity was infuriating. 'I thought you must still be pretty angry with me. You shouldn't bottle your feelings up, you know.'

'I'll bottle my feelings up if I want to,' said Katie.

'Yes, and look where it's got you,' her mum replied.

'That's unfair,' said Katie. 'I had no idea that Charlie was gay. Up until recently we've never had any problems.'

'Oh, Katie, is that really true?' Her mum looked at her with great sadness.

Katie was shocked.

'How did you know?' she whispered.

'I'm your mum,' was the answer. 'I've always known. You were such a solemn little child, so brave. Always. You never cried about anything. But it didn't stop me from seeing when you were hurting. I'm sure it's the same for you with the boys.'

It was true. Katie did know when they were upset and not telling her things. It had just never occurred to her that her own mother, who had always seemed so distant, felt the same way about her.

'I knew Charlie was wrong for you from the start,' said her mum, 'but you wouldn't be told.'

It was true, Katie's mum had said the first time she'd met Charlie that she didn't think he was right for Katie. But Katie

276

had still been grieving about her dad, and angry with her mum, and hadn't listened.

'I think,' said Katie slowly, 'that I may have fallen for Charlie on the rebound. I was so devastated by losing Dad, and he was so kind and thoughtful. I muddled up love with something else. Then, as time went on, the children came along, and, well, by then it was too late. I couldn't get out of it. I knew it was wrong, but I kept kidding myself I could put it right.'

'I know,' said her mum. 'And I do understand. I was the same with your father.'

'What?' asked Katie. 'But *you* were the one who pushed for a divorce.'

'I did in the end,' said her mum. 'But only because he'd pushed me too far. I did what you did. I threw myself into work and pretended it was all fine. But it wasn't. I loved him dearly, you know, but it wasn't in his nature to be faithful.'

Katie sputtered into her tea.

'Dad was unfaithful – how – why? How come I didn't know?'

'Yes, constantly,' said her mum. 'And you didn't know because I didn't want you to know. You adored your dad and it would have broken your heart. I would have probably told you eventually, but then he died and . . .' Her voice tailed off. 'I'm so sorry, I shouldn't have said all that, not with what you've just been through.'

Katie's head was whirling. First Charlie. Now her dad. Had nothing in her whole life been real?

'No, Mum,' said Katie, 'I'm the one who should be sorry. I've been condemning you for all these years, when I had no right to.'

'If I'd told you the truth you wouldn't have had to,' her mum said. 'It's just once a lie is in place it's incredibly hard to unpick it.'

'Maybe that's how Charlie's feeling,' said Katie. 'Perhaps I should give him a chance to explain himself.'

277

'Perhaps you should,' her mum agreed. 'He is the father of your children, and whatever's between you shouldn't affect them.'

'I suppose not,' said Katie. 'But it's not going to be easy.'

'No, it's not, but things will get better, you'll see,' her mum assured her. 'Come on, let's get cracking on the pigsty.'

Rob was attending another meeting for the team-building course. Mr Muscles had got up and done another run-through about basic health and safety. Compared to the lack of care taken when Rob had gone to Wales it sounded like the chance of something going wrong was about one in a million. While Rob was clear that what had happened in Wales had been a result of incompetence and too little attention to health and safety, he couldn't help feeling that things had swung too far the other way. Today's children seemed to be wrapped up in cotton wool.

In fact, it was, he felt, rather ironic, that while the pupils he taught, and no doubt the ones at Gemma's school too, were ridiculously mollycoddled, and health and safety was constantly being used as an excuse for cancelling sporting events, when they did have a chance to go away with the school, it was highly likely they'd do an activity that was absurdly dangerous, like potholing. Fortunately there was no potholing to be done around here. Rob hated confined spaces, and didn't think he'd be all that good at scrambling into caves anyway. He had been to the local gym and reacquainted himself with the climbing wall, though. It hadn't felt too hard, and if Mr Muscles was right, the children were going to have so much safety equipment on that no one was likely to be in any danger.

He tuned out Mr Muscles' monotone and started thinking about Katie. She had preoccupied his thoughts constantly since Saturday. Not wanting to crowd her, or to give her the wrong idea, he'd rung just once to see how she was. It was all he could do not to ring her every day, and it had taken all his self-control not to respond to her fumbled kiss. But he had seen the shock in her eyes. She was in no fit state to enter a new relationship, whatever she said, not while the fallout from her current relationship was still rocking her.

Charlie was gay. Well, that was one he hadn't seen coming. He'd thought, on that brief occasion when they'd met, that Charlie had seemed uninterested in Katie, but Rob had put it down to usual married blues. What with Mark's private life being splashed over the papers, Rob was beginning to feel he'd entered a weird parallel universe inhabited by characters whose rightful pride of place should be the *Jeremy Kyle Show*.

'Well, that just about wraps it up for the evening.' Mr Muscles was finishing his talk. Rob had taken scarcely any notes, he'd better crib the rest off Jen, he supposed. 'Any questions?'

Apart from a very earnest English teacher who seemed to be rather terrified about the prospect of kayaking and so wanted to know more about all the issues Mr Muscles had covered, no one had much to say. So it was with relief that Rob sloped off for a quick pint in the Hookers. On his way, he'd ring Katie to see how she was. Two phone calls in a week. That wasn't overdoing it.

'This is a good spot,' said Mark as he started unloading the car. The campsite he'd found was on top of a hill overlooking Poole harbour. The views were pretty stunning, and they'd arrived early enough to get a good pitch. Gemma had bitched all the way about wanting to go to Majorca, like they'd done a couple of years previously, until Mark had bitten her head off and said, 'That was then, this is now.' Gemma had then promptly retreated into a sulky silence and spent the entire journey sending text messages to her friends, no doubt along the lines of what a sad loser of a dad she had. Beth, meanwhile, had asked if they were nearly there yet about half an hour after leaving the house, and continued to ask at half-hourly intervals. It was enough to try the patient of a saint.

But at least they were here. Mark loved the outdoor life and was looking forward to a week's camping. Sam hadn't been keen on it at all, and one of the benefits of the split had been taking the girls away at regular intervals. Normally they enjoyed it, but Gemma was determined to spoil today. She moaned about putting the tent up, that her air-bed was too lumpy, and that she hated being outdoors, till in the end Mark lost patience and shouted at her. Beth promptly burst into tears, and so guilt drove Mark to promise McDonald's. They were probably hungry. He'd forgotten to feed them en route, something he was always getting in a tangle with. He'd forget about food, their blood sugar would drop and then tempers would end up flaring. His mother (who generally was noncommittal about advice) was constantly telling him that he should remember they needed feeding at regular intervals.

They couldn't find a McDonald's, so settled for fish and chips by the seafront instead. Even Gemma cheered up when an over-friendly seagull came and stole their chips. Then they had a run on the beach. It was a blustery day and the sky was filling up with ominous rain clouds, but at least it was warm.

Mark had stocked up on food before leaving, so when they eventually got back to the campsite, towards dusk, he started to sort out hotdogs for tea. The girls, meanwhile, wandered off to the play area, where he knew from past experience they would have a riot, whatever Gemma said about being too old for it. As he lit the gas stove, he felt the first drop of rain. Bugger. He persevered boiling up his hotdogs on his poxy little ring – he kept promising himself he'd get a decent gas stove every time he came camping, and kept forgetting when he got home – after all, part of the joys of the great outdoors included the vagaries of the British weather. It was annoying, but they were well-prepared with cagoules and waterproofs. The drop was followed swiftly by a deluge, and the girls, who hadn't been wearing coats, suddenly appeared wet through. He sorted out fresh clothes for them while they got themselves dry and changed. The weather was now so bad they had to eat their tea inside the tent. It was late by the time they were done, and the rain had clearly settled in for the night. Mark sent the girls to bed, while he tried to read a book under the light of his rather inadequate torch. Eventually he got fed up and decided to call it a day too. He climbed into bed and listened to the steady dripping on his tent. He hoped it was as waterproof as the manufacturers claimed.

With any luck the storm would have passed by morning.

Chapter Thirty

The storm hadn't passed over in the morning. Mark, Gemma and Beth spent a miserable day wandering around Bournemouth in the rain – once they'd done the pier, the aquarium and the arcade there was precious all else to do. Mark spent a fortune on food and fruit machines, and in the afternoon, with nothing left to do, they ended up at the cinema. The next couple of days were the same. They managed one warmish day on the beach, during which Gemma had to be constantly watched as she had a habit of chatting to any vaguely fanciable boy that strayed into her orbit, and a daytrip to Brownsea Island between squalls, before the rain set in in earnest. By day four all three of them were thoroughly sick of being wet and cold. They'd played endless games of rummy and snap, the girls had got bored stiff of the DVDs Mark had brought to watch on the portable DVD player in the car, and everyone was squabbling.

Waking up in the morning to yet more rain, and hearing still more rain was due on the weather forecast, Mark admitted defeat and headed off home. He'd spent a fortune and probably shouted at his daughters more than he'd ever done in his whole life before. It was hardly what you'd call a success.

'I never want to go camping again,' groused Gemma as she and Beth reluctantly helped Mark pack the car.

'Yes, camping sucks,' said Beth, as she poured water out of her wellies.

'We have been pretty unlucky with the weather,' Mark pointed out. 'It might be better next time.'

'Well, I'm not coming again,' said Gemma, looking mutinous. 'I want to go somewhere sunny on holiday.'

'Can't we go to Majorca again?' wheedled Beth.

'I'll see,' promised Mark, packing away the last of the camping gear. Everything was so damp and wet it was going to take days to dry it out. Even he, who loved camping, having fond memories of *Swallows and Amazons* type holidays as a kid, had to admit this had not been fun.

They arrived home bad-tempered and tired after a long drive in the rain on crowded motorways. No wonder people didn't holiday in England, Mark thought. It was such a horrible experience. The girls seemed delighted to be back and promptly sat down in front of the telly while he sorted everything out. There was a message on the answerphone from an old friend, inviting Mark to a fortieth birthday party the following weekend. He rang back to accept straight away. After another few days with grumpy children he was going to be seriously in need of some adult entertainment.

It being the summer holidays, Rob was also home and filled him in on the latest with Katie, who had apparently seen a solicitor about her divorce, and, more importantly as far as Rob was concerned, had been persuaded to come out dancing again.

'So are you and her . . .?' Mark left the question hanging, but Rob brushed it away.

'No chance,' he said. 'I mean, I fancy her and everything, but she's in a mess at the moment. I think it would be a disaster.'

'Blimey, I never thought I'd hear you say that,' said Mark. 'Rob showing some kind of restraint where women are concerned. Wonders will never cease.'

'Yeah, well,' said Rob, 'she's having a rotten time. I think she just needs a friend at the moment.'

Gemma walked into the kitchen. 'Is there anything to eat?' she asked. 'I'm starving.'

'You are not starving,' said Mark, 'children in Africa are starving. Besides, you only just ate.'

'I'm still hungry,' said Gemma.

'You'd better get used to that,' Rob teased her, 'because they don't feed you at all on the team-building course, you know.'

Gemma grimaced. 'I still can't believe you're doing it too,' she said. 'I hope I don't have to talk to you. It'll be so embarrassing.'

'It's all right, Wednesday, I'll make sure I embarrass you as much as possible,' said Rob, and then ducked as she threw a tea-towel at him.

Emily was meeting Ffion in a bar in Crawley. Now Ffion and Callum were apparently an item, which Emily was still getting her head around, they had taken to spending their weekends in Sussex. Callum's ridiculously wealthy parents had gone away on a lengthy cruise, leaving their overindulged son their house to play with for the summer. More fool them, had been Emily's instant response. She wondered if they had any idea quite how feckless their son was, or quite how many drugs were likely to be consumed in their house.

Emily had been hoping to pump Ffion for some information about Jasmine, but so far, apart from imparting the news that Jasmine and Tony were back together, her lips remained tightly sealed. Emily sat listening to an unedifying and seemingly endless account of the doings of zedlebrities who made Jasmine look classy, wondering how soon she could politely call it a day, when Callum came bounding in. He looked a bit wired and seemed raring to go.

'Change of plan, ladies, there's a party over at Lakefield,' he said. 'Fancy a whirl down there in the old man's motor?'

The bar was fairly empty, and the evening so far had not been desperately exciting. Emily didn't have much else to do. Maybe if Ffion got a bit drunker, she might be more forthcoming with some more information.

'You've not been taking anything, have you?' Emily was suspicious. The last thing she wanted to do was get in Callum's car if he was high as a kite.

'Of course not,' said Callum, with that dazzling grin she remembered of old (and which now she was relieved to note had no effect on her whatsoever). 'How could you think such a thing?'

'How indeed?' said Emily drily.

She followed Ffion and Callum to the old man's motor, which turned out to be a Porsche, parked crookedly on the pavement. Unbelievable, that Callum's parents could be so naïve as to let him take their car. Emily wouldn't have trusted him with hers in a million years.

Callum drove fast but, to Emily's relief, reasonably safely towards Lakefield, a small village out near the North Downs. The party itself turned out not to be in Lakefield itself, but in a huge house down a windy drive, halfway up a hill, belonging to the brother of a friend of Callum's. It was a balmy sunny evening, which made a nice change after all the recent rain. The view from the house was across Crawley and beyond, to London twinkling far in the distance. A dramatically large orange sun hung low in the sky, casting long shadows and painting the few clouds vivid purples, reds and yellows. The trees surrounding the house were alive with birdsong. The fields of corn swayed softly in the summer breeze. It was beautiful, but Ffion and Callum barely seemed to notice, when all Emily wanted to do was to stop and stare at the view, the others making instead for the back of the house where a large marquee had been erected, and from whence loud music was pumping.

Emily followed them, but they were soon lost in the crowd. She accepted the glass of champagne offered to her as she walked into the marquee, and then stood like a lemon sipping it, wondering why on earth she'd come.

'Oh my God, it's you.'

Emily turned round and nearly dropped her glass in shock. There, standing before her, was Mark.

'What are you doing here?' they said in unison.

Mark was still reeling in shock. He couldn't believe it when he saw Emily standing before him. He'd forgotten how gorgeous she was, and the months of absence had stripped away any anger he'd felt towards her. Looking at it now, he could see that she was in a difficult position. Maybe he had been a bit harsh. He felt awkward, though, knowing he'd been pretty unkind to her the last time they'd met. They'd had a stilted conversation, before he made his excuses and went off to chat with his friends. From that moment on, Mark decided his best move was to keep out of her way. But it was hard, knowing she was there, and knowing he couldn't be with her.

Emily had disappeared with her friends, which was both a relief and a torture to him. Mark was staying the night, so he spent the rest of the evening getting pleasantly drunk in the company of old friends, and trying to avoid Emily.

Around midnight, Mark was exiting the marquee when he saw Emily having an angry altercation with her friends.

'Oh bugger off then,' he heard her say. 'Go and kill yourselves. See if I care.'

They walked away, presumably going back to their car, while she stormed off looking furious. She came cannoning into Mark, who was standing looking at the view as the bright moon lit the whole valley.

'Oh, hello again,' she said.

'Hello again,' Mark replied. 'Is everything all right? Only I couldn't help noticing . . .'

'Just my divvy ex-boyfriend being a prat as usual,' said Emily. 'He drove us here, and then got tanked up on beer, which on top of all the coke he's probably done means he's ever so slightly over the limit. He wants to go home, but I refused to get in the car with him. Ffion, who I thought had marginally more sense, doesn't seem to care at all. I've a good mind to call the police. That would serve him right.'

'I'd offer you a lift,' said Mark, 'but I'm a bit worse for wear myself.'

'I guess I'll have to get a taxi,' said Emily.

'Oh.' Mark felt a stab of disappointment. Of course she had to get a taxi, it was the obvious thing to do. But he would have liked her to stay. They repaired to the kitchen, where they found the numbers of several local taxi firms stuck to a noticeboard. Emily rang all of them, but to no avail.

'It's hopeless,' she said. 'At this rate I'll have to walk home.'

'Or you could stay,' said Mark. 'If I ask Matthew I'm sure he could squeeze you in somewhere. This place is massive.'

'Do you think it would be all right?' asked Emily, hesitant. 'I wouldn't like to impose.'

'You won't be,' said Mark. 'Matt won't mind putting up a friend of mine. Go on, stay.'

'I suppose I could,' said Emily, still looking doubtful.

'Go on, live a little,' said Mark, nudging her. He looked out to the lawn where the marquee was still full of milling people partying like there was no tomorrow.

Mark fetched them both drinks, and they wandered back out onto the patio, listening to the strains of the music, and they talked and talked and then talked some more.

'Do you fancy a dance?' Mark asked.

Emily shook her head. 'Not tonight,' she said. 'I'm not quite drunk enough to make a fool of myself yet.'

They sat for a little while contemplating the moon, which hung large and red in the sky.

'Isn't it beautiful?' said Emily dreamily.

'You'd get a better view from the back of Matt's field,' Mark told her. 'I can show you if you like.'

Emily hesitated.

'Or is that outside the terms of what we're supposed to be doing? I don't want you to get into trouble at work.'

'Well, by rights I shouldn't be anywhere near you at all,' said Emily. 'But these are exceptional circumstances, so I suppose . . .'

'I've got a picnic blanket and a bottle of champers in the car,' said Mark teasingly.

'Oh go on, then,' said Emily. 'So long as we don't talk about the case, I'm sure half an hour won't hurt.'

As Emily followed Mark down the moonlit path that wound its way to the cornfield backing onto the house, she wondered briefly about the wisdom of what she was doing, then thought, sod it. Life was too short. It might be months before she saw Mark again, and if anything came up about their meeting at work, she could genuinely say they had met by accident.

She felt nervous, though. In the weeks since they'd parted, she had imagined being with him again. Imagined how it would feel to have him close to her, holding her tight, kissing her lips . . .

'Did you say something?' Mark asked, as he found a suitable spot to sit down.

'No,' said Emily hastily, pleased that he hadn't overheard her private thoughts for once. She changed the subject. 'This is a lovely spot.'

'Matt's a lucky bastard,' said Mark. 'But then he always was. Rich parents, clever investment, it all adds up to having a house like this. I should hate him but he's actually very down to earth, plus he's extraordinarily generous. It's quite hard to hate someone like that. Champagne?'

Emily nodded, feeling incredibly awkward as she perched on the end of the picnic blanket. The ease with which she'd been talking to Mark earlier suddenly deserted her. What could she say to him, this man she loved despite everything? Her heart ached with longing. Here they were on a moonlit night, in a field of swaying corn, gazing across a beautiful valley, listening to the distant music from the party. It was a moment ripe for romance, but she couldn't – they couldn't go there. Emily felt absurdly like she was in the middle of a scene from Shakespeare. Any minute now Puck was going to appear with a love potion.

> *How sweet the moonlight sleeps upon this bank!*
> *Here will we sit and let the sounds of music*
> *Creep in our ears; soft stillness and the night*
> *Become the touches of sweet harmony*

She murmured the words as they popped into her head.

'That's beautiful,' said Mark. 'Did you make that up?'

'Don't be daft,' said Emily. 'It's Shakespeare. Are you really such a philistine you can't tell?'

'We dentists don't have much truck with Shakespeare,' protested Mark. 'Though I do remember enjoying *Macbeth* at school. I got to play one of the witches.'

'I can just picture you in drag,' said Emily drily.

The ice was broken and she leaned back, looking at him. Mark lay on his back, gazing at the stars. It turned out he was keen on astronomy and could name most of the constellations.

'There's so little artificial light out here, you can almost see all of Orion,' he said, pointing out the shape of the hunter. 'At home I can only usually see the belt.'

'That's really neat,' said Emily. 'He really does look like he's holding a bow. I've never seen that before.'

The pain of wanting Mark was almost physical. She lay there, wishing she could reach out and touch him, but not daring to.

'If only we could stay like this forever,' she said.

'If only we could,' said Mark. He moved towards her and gently touched her face. It felt like the wind caressing her cheek.

'We mustn't,' she said, pulling his hand towards her mouth and kissing it.

'I know,' said Mark with regret. He pulled slightly away from her.

They'd been there so long, the night was fast fading, and in the east they could make out the first pink rays of the early-morning sun.

'The *rosy-fingered dawn*,' said Emily, wanting him to hold her, then not wanting him to.

'Who's Dawn?' joked Mark.

Emily gave him a look. 'It's Shakespeare again, you idiot,' she said.

'Even I knew that,' said Mark. He was leaning on one side, tearing up pieces of grass. She wondered what was going through his head. She was glad he couldn't see what was going on in hers.

'Bugger it, I'm not made of stone.' Mark sat up and looked at her, and Emily felt herself reduced to jelly. He leaned over and kissed her urgently, and she responded with the fervour of a starving woman who knew this might be her last chance to be fed.

Eventually they pulled apart.

'I'm so sorry, Mark,' Emily said, 'about everything.'

'Me too,' said Mark.

'I don't want to,' said Emily, stroking his face, 'but we have to stop.'

'You're probably right,' said Mark with evident regret. He tucked a stray hair behind her ear in a gesture of infinite tenderness. 'We should stop now while we still can.'

'If I could do something different – if I could make it different, you know I would,' said Emily.

'I know, I know,' Mark replied. He held his finger to her lips and said, 'Hush. We've had tonight. Which was more than we could have expected.'

'But we can't have tomorrow,' Emily said with a piercing sadness.

'Come on, let's go and find something to eat,' said Mark. 'When it's properly morning I'll drive you home.'

They gathered their things up and walked back to the house, holding hands, closer than they'd been for months, yet further apart than ever.

Part Four

Live Like it's Heaven on Earth

Chapter Thirty-one

Katie was nervously pacing up and down the house, the late rays of the autumn sun casting shadows across the lounge. Charlie was bringing the children back after a day out, and Mum was coming to babysit while they went out to discuss the future. She was still in shock about what had happened, but in a way it was also a relief. It was so much less stressful not having to pretend any more, and such a blessing to know that, ultimately, it wasn't her fault that their marriage was over. In the weeks since they'd split, she'd had time to calm down, and she was even beginning to feel sorry for Charlie. He must have been to hell and back.

The doorbell rang and she jumped out of her skin. She was ridiculously twitchy; it was only dinner. Charlie came in looking just as nervous, and she felt her heart go out to him. It must be harder for him than for her. He'd come out in front of his whole family. She could only imagine the way that had gone down in Marilyn's circle.

The boys were full of beans and had clearly enjoyed the day out with their dad, and Molly was gurgling happily in the buggy. Whatever had happened, or would happen, Charlie was a devoted dad.

'Good day?' She spoke with deliberate lightness, trying to keep things buoyant and perky so the kids wouldn't get wind of the tension.

'Great,' he said. 'Could I – would it be all right if I bathed Molly? Only, I've really missed them.'

She let him take Molly upstairs and left the boys watching *X Factor* while she pottered around tidying up. It must be horrible for Charlie being without the kids. She couldn't imagine it. For the first time she saw things from his point of view. He'd lost more than her by his actions.

Her mum turned up soon after, and she and Charlie headed out of the door, towards town.

'Where do you want to go?' asked Charlie. 'The Italian?'

The Italian had been their favourite haunt in happier days. Katie thought with a pang of the time they had gone out for a meal there on Charlie's birthday when she was newly pregnant with Molly. They had had some good times, even if things had ended badly.

'I don't think that's such a good idea, do you?' she said. 'How about the new Thai on the High Street?'

Within minutes they were sitting down in a bright, shiny new restaurant where everything that wasn't gleaming metal seemed to be teak.

'This is nice,' said Charlie, and ordered a Tiger beer for himself and a G and T for Katie.

There was a brief awkward pause before Katie asked, 'How are you?'

Charlie sighed, and put down the menu he'd been glancing at. He rubbed his face in his hands. She could see bags under his eyes, and there were worry lines that hadn't been there before.

'Better, and worse,' he said. 'Better because it's all out in the open. Much worse because I feel like such a shit. I've behaved badly to you. And to the kids. I know what you must think of me, but really I'm not a monster. I never meant any of this to happen.'

Katie sat there not knowing what to say. Charlie was practically in tears. It felt unusual to be this much in control.

'When did you know?' she asked.

'That I was gay?' Charlie looked sheepish. 'I think I've always known. But you know my family. How could I have told anyone that? My parents would have gone ballistic.'

'So you lived a lie and dragged me into it instead?' Katie was veering between sympathy and fury. 'How could you have done that to me? To the kids? Did you ever love me?'

The waitress chose that moment to take their order, so they retreated into awkward silence. Charlie looked on the verge of speaking again, when their drinks arrived.

'Katie, I know if I say I'm sorry every day for the rest of my life, it won't undo the great wrong I've done you,' he said in the end. 'But I am sorry. Truly I am. When we met, I'd convinced myself that the feelings I'd had for other guys were just adolescent yearnings. And you were lovely, really you were. I persuaded myself I loved you – no, I *do* love you, but as a friend. I probably never loved you as a husband should. I'm sorry. It was an unfair thing to do. But I was coming under so much pressure, from Mum in particular, to settle down. You seemed like the ideal answer.'

'Gee thanks,' said Katie. 'I'm so glad that you married me to please your mother.'

Charlie said nothing.

'I deserved that,' he said. 'I can't excuse myself, but I can try to make sure you're financially secure. You have the house and I'll buy myself something smaller. I can give you a reasonable allowance, so you won't have to work.'

'That is generous, thanks,' said Katie. The pendulum was swinging back in Charlie's favour. He had had no business in marrying her, but she could see how hard it must be to live his own life in the kind of family he came from. 'I think maybe I should try to do some part-time work anyway. Being at home hasn't been all that great for me. You weren't the only one lying in this marriage, you know.'

'Oh?'

'Well, I've known for ages you weren't happy,' said Katie. 'That we weren't happy. I just buried my head in the sand and hoped it would all go away. Then I pushed you into having Molly when you'd have preferred not to have another baby. So I'm sorry too.'

'That's another thing,' said Charlie. 'What are we going to tell the children?'

Katie had been dreading that question. So far she had kept it very light, saying that Daddy had to go away for a while, but the excuse was wearing thin. George, in particular, was beginning to twig that something was up.

'I don't know,' she said. 'I think we need to take it slowly, don't you? I mean, they have to know the truth eventually, but there are probably ways we could tell them. I'd rather we handled it sensitively.'

'It's all right,' said Charlie, 'I wasn't planning a repeat of my birthday party.'

Katie burst out laughing.

'I have to say,' she said, 'the look on your mother's face was priceless. Has she forgiven you yet?'

'She may never forgive me,' said Charlie with a grimace, 'but I couldn't have gone on living like that any longer.'

'And is there someone?' Katie asked. She wasn't quite sure if she wanted to know the answer to that one, but her curiosity had got the better of her. Was it better to be left for a man rather than a woman? Or was it being the left that was the hard part? 'I'm guessing there has to be.'

'I think so,' said Charlie. 'He works in the Amsterdam office.'

'That figures,' said Katie.

'He's lovely, you'd like him,' said Charlie. 'His name's Hans. He's kind, sweet, and –'

'Woah,' said Katie, holding up her hand. 'I'm not sure I'm quite ready for all that.'

'No, sorry,' said Charlie. 'But perhaps we can raise a toast to new beginnings?"

To new beginnings,' said Katie, raising her glass, 'and no more lies.'

'So things are looking up a bit?'

Emily had called in on her way home from work and was relieved to see Katie was looking much cheerier than she had of late.

'I suppose so,' said Katie. 'It went better than I could have expected with Charlie last night, but I don't know. I still feel pretty desolate sometimes. It's stupid. I've spent years living a lie, and the effort of keeping it going was killing me. Yet now it's gone I feel as if I've lost direction. Everything I've ever worked towards is meaningless. It's all turned to dust.'

'Apart from the kids,' said Emily.

'You're right,' said Katie, nodding. 'The kids make it all worth-while. Whatever else Charlie's done to me, he's given me them.'

'Talking of the children . . .'

'No,' said Katie. 'I haven't told them yet. Well, we've sat them down and explained that Mummy and Daddy aren't going to be living together any more, but we think it's going to need some careful consideration as to what to say next. I've been looking up websites to find out how it's done. You wouldn't believe the things I've found. *Danny has Two Daddies. Mommy has a Lady Friend . . .'*

'You could try being honest,' said Emily.

'Yes, I'm all for honesty,' said Katie. 'But sheesh. George is ten years old. He's going to get crucified in the playground.'

'Good point,' said Emily. 'And you're sure you're all right?'

'There's a bit of me that's going to take an awfully long time to forgive Charlie, but yes, in a way, I am. It's such a relief to know that my marriage hasn't failed because of something I've done wrong. It's just me that's wrong – well, my gender is wrong. And that makes a difference somehow. Does that sound weird?'

'I don't know,' said Emily. 'I think the whole situation is pretty weird. I think you're entitled to be as weird as you want. In the meantime, I think you need a night out. I've got tickets to see We Five on Friday. I wasn't going to go, because they're crap, but I could use a laugh, and so could you. Can you get your mam to babysit for you?'

'I can try.'

'Then it's a date,' said Emily.

'Where's Gemma?'

Sam was standing on Mark's doorstep like an avenging angel.

'I have no idea,' said Mark, who'd just got in from work and hadn't been expecting to have the girls that day.

Sam looked momentarily disconcerted.

'You mean you don't know where she is?'

'No,' said Mark. 'Why should I? I'm not having the girls till the weekend. Why? Isn't she with you?'

'I thought she was with you,' said Sam shortly. 'Jasmine Symonds is opening our new offices in Regent Street next week and I'm organising the PR, so I was running a bit late and asked her to come here.'

Mark felt a combined tug of worry and exasperation. Sam was always accusing him of putting his job first, but somehow it was okay for her to do it.

'What about Beth?' he demanded.

'She's gone to Amelie's for tea,' said Sam. 'But Gemma was supposed to come here from school. She said she'd rung you.'

The tug of worry became more intense. It was a couple of weeks before the clocks changed, but it was already getting dark.

'Well, she didn't,' Mark said. 'I haven't had a text or a message at work. Nothing. Have you tried ringing her?'

'Mobile's switched off,' said Sam.

'What about Shelly?' Mark asked, trying to still the pounding of his heart. 'Gemma's bound to be with her.'

'I'll ring her now.' Sam had the grace to look embarrassed. So she bloody well should, thought Mark. It was all very well swanning off for the day to London, but she should have let him know what Gemma was up to. Mark wasn't prone to a vivid imagination, but he'd seen enough haunting pictures on the news over the years, of teenagers who'd gone missing, to know he didn't want to face that particular scenario.

Sam stood for a minute with her ear pressed to the phone.

'Bugger, Shelly's switched hers off too,' she said.

'What is the point of them having mobile phones,' muttered Mark. He hadn't been keen for Gemma to get one in the first place, worrying about it rotting her brain, but if she had to have one it would be useful if she turned the damned thing on.

At that moment Gemma and Shelly came strolling down the road, looking as if they didn't have a care in the world. Shelly quickly scarpered when she saw Sam and Mark. Some friend, thought Mark, to leave Gemma to face the music alone.

'Where have you been?' Sam shrieked at Gemma. Mark knew it was relief on her part, but he couldn't help thinking that if Sam had been more organised the situation wouldn't have arisen.

Gemma shrugged her shoulders and said, 'Out with my mates.'

'You were supposed to ring me,' said Mark. He wasn't going to shout, but he had to make her see that she had to be more responsible.

'Sorry,' said Gemma. 'I forgot.'

'Forgot? Forgot?' Sam was like a mad thing. 'You stupid, stupid girl! Don't you realise how worried we've been?'

'I knew I was all right,' said Gemma, which, from her point of view, was probably a reasonable position to take.

'I don't think that's the point, though,' Mark interjected. 'We didn't. And you can't just go round lying to your mum and saying you're coming here when you haven't even told me.'

'Keep out of this, Mark,' hissed Sam.

'I'm only trying to help,' he protested.

'Well don't help!' said Sam. 'She's only like this because of you.'

'What?' The unfairness of the accusation hit Mark hard.

'Imagine what it must have done to her to see you in the papers like that,' said Sam in a loud whisper. 'She's been bunking off school ever since.'

'Hang on,' said Mark. 'Since when has Gemma been bunking off school?'

'Since you were splashed all over the Sunday papers,' said Sam.

'Earth to parents,' said Gemma. 'Hello, I do exist.'

'Have you been bunking off school?' Mark couldn't decide who he was more furious with: Gemma for bunking, or Sam for not telling him.

'S'pose.' Gemma looked down at the floor and stubbed her toe.

'The answer I was looking for was either yes or no,' said Mark.

'Yes, then,' spat out Gemma defiantly.

'May I ask why?'

There was no response.

'Don't badger her,' said Sam, siding with her daughter now she clearly felt that Mark was getting at her. No wonder Gemma was so badly behaved. Between them they'd ensured she'd spent thirteen years with totally inconsistent parenting.

'I wasn't,' said Mark, 'I was merely asking why Gemma thinks she's got something so much more important to do than go to school?'

'It's boring,' said Gemma.

'Yes, I'm sure it is,' said Mark. 'I find work boring too, but I have to go, otherwise you wouldn't have any money to waste down the shops with your friends. That is not a good enough reason to take time off.'

'Oh do stop bullying her,' Sam said. 'I'm sure she's got the picture by now. We've got to go, Amelie's mum will be waiting for us.'

302

Mark waved them off with a heavy sigh. He felt sure there was something more bothering Gemma. She clearly wasn't talking to Sam about it. He wished she felt able to confide in him.

'*Why can't you seeeeee . . . Seee . . . You're the only girl for meeee . . . Meee . . .*'

The dulcet tones of We Five were filling the small exclusive arena where they were launching their first tour.

'We wanted somewhere small and intimate for the boys' first gig,' gushed Ffion when she saw Emily at the door.

'She means they were afraid they wouldn't sell out Wembley, more like,' said Emily, heading for the bar and a drink.

'They are truly dire, aren't they?' said Katie as they watched the boys mime and gyrate their way through a series of increasingly banal and same-sounding songs – if the word 'songs' could actually be applied to the turgid drivel they were coming out with.

'That they are,' said Emily. 'But I don't expect your average ten-year-old will care.'

'I don't much, either,' said Katie. 'I have to confess, although it was a complete nightmare sorting out my life to get out, I am really enjoying the sense of freedom.'

'Good, that was the idea,' said Emily, scanning the room despite herself to see if there was anyone she knew. Her eye caught sight of someone who looked vaguely familiar. Then it came to her. Her face had been splashed all over the tabloids with Twinkle-toes Tony. She was sitting looking very sorry for herself in the corner. As Emily was still drawing a blank with Ffion, maybe it was worth pumping this girl for information instead. 'Katie, sorry to be rude, but will you excuse me for a minute?' she asked, and made her way over to the table.

'Hi,' she said, sitting down next to the blonde. 'I love your necklace.'

The girl looked at her through bloodshot eyes. 'Oh, this,' she said. 'It's just bling that my boyfriend gave me – my ex-boyfriend now – the rotten sod's gone back to his ex.' She hiccoughed.

'More fool him,' said Emily.

'He was famous too,' said the blonde. 'And I was going to be famous. But then he had to go back to her.'

'Oh, what a shame,' said Emily. 'How could he when he had you?'

'Exac'ly,' said Tony's ex, not apparently appreciating irony. 'And I have all my own teeth. Not like *her*. Silly cow. I'm much prettier than she is.'

'What happened to Jasmine's teeth?' Emily asked, her heart thumping.

'One of them fell out and had to be replaced,' said the blonde. 'And, thanks to me, the story got in the papers.'

'Oh, I thought it was thanks to her dentist,' said Emily, trying not to give away her excitement.

For a moment the girl looked suspicious.

'Do I know you?' she said.

'No, I don't think so,' said Emily.

'I only did it for him, you know,' continued the blonde.

'Did what?' asked Emily, unable to believe how close she was finally getting to something concrete.

Jasmine's would-be rival looked at Emily again, the suspicion returning to her face.

'Nothing,' she said. 'Gotta go.'

She tottered in the direction of the loos. Emily waited a few minutes, but the blonde girl didn't return. Damn. Just when it looked like she was about to spill the beans. Still, now Emily knew that Tony and his ex had been involved in the leak. Maybe it wouldn't be too hard to find something to clear Mark's name.

Chapter Thirty-two

'You came.' Rob was really pleased to see Katie. For a couple of weeks she'd been promising him that she would come back to dancing classes, and now here she was.

'Cinderella has finally made it to the ball,' said Katie, giving him a mock bow.

She looked lovely in a simple white top and gypsy skirt. He was pleased to see she'd even bought herself some proper dancing shoes – that must mean she was intending to keep coming. The stress of the past few months had sped up the weight loss that had started some months previously, and the tragedy had given her a slightly vulnerable air. She was a woman still partially on the edge, and it gave her a kind of steely beauty that had been missing before. Rob badly wanted to say something complimentary, but he didn't want it to be misinterpreted, so he just said, 'Well, Cinders, it's nice to see you here again.'

It being the autumn half-term, the class wasn't too well-attended, so Isabella, tonight looking almost like a fairy princess in her floaty pink dress and gold sandals, spent a lot more time with each couple than she did normally. When she got to Rob and Katie she beamed broadly.

'So nice to see you two dancing together again,' she said. 'You were made to dance together.'

Katie blushed, which made Rob grateful that he had kept his

mouth shut. He wanted her very badly, but she was still too vulnerable and he knew he should stay away.

'There is a competition coming soon,' continued Isabella. 'I think it is time you entered, no?'

Rob looked at Katie. 'How about it?' he said. 'I'm game if you are.'

'What do we have to do?' Katie asked, looking a little dubious. 'I'm sure we'd be flattened by proper dancers.'

Isabella explained that there were different categories and that she and Mark could enter the beginners' section.

'You have a good chance of success,' Isabella predicted. 'Your bodies, they move together naturally. Like I said, you two are made for each other.'

Now it was Rob's turn to blush.

'Katie, it's okay,' he said. 'We don't have to if you don't want to.'

'No,' she replied suddenly. 'I'll do it, if only for the chance of seeing you in ruffles and tight trousers.'

'I am *not* wearing ruffles,' said Rob.

'Go on, you know you want to,' teased Katie. 'A blue open-topped ruffled shirt showing off your chest hair would really suit you. I shall have to call you Gethin from now on.'

'Okay, I'll wear that if you wear one of those dresses with tassles that show off your cleavage and leave nothing to the imagination,' Rob shot back.

Katie grinned at him. 'Okay,' she said devilishly. 'It's a deal.'

'Great,' said Rob, and led her into a waltz with a sudden lightening of heart. Katie might well be a long way off being his, but dancing with her every week was better than nothing. Much, much better.

'So you're going to enter a dancing competition?' Mark roared with laughter as he sat in the Hookers with Rob. 'Does that mean you get to wear a silly costume?'

Rob looked a bit huffy.

'That's just what Katie said,' he complained.

'Well, do you?'

'I said I would if she wore a skimpy number,' said Rob.

'Thanks, mate,' said Mark, practically crying into his pint. 'You've given me the best laugh I've had in months. I needed that.'

'Stress levels no better then?' said Rob.

Mark had been wound up for weeks now. Although Fleet Street's finest had found other fish to fry, the court case was still preying on his mind.

'No,' sighed Mark. 'I don't think I'll be able to relax till it's all over, and that could take months, apparently. My lawyer reckons we won't get a court date till after Christmas. I just want it all to go away.'

'What about that other thing?'

'The preliminary hearing at the General Dental Council?' Mark asked. 'That's booked for a couple of weeks before Christmas. I can't believe that Jasmine's so bloody malicious that she put in a complaint about professional misconduct. Well, I can, actually. If she hadn't, all that stuff in the papers would have blown over. As it is, the best-case scenario is I get my knuckles rapped; the worst case, according to James, is I get struck off.'

'Do you think that's likely?' Rob asked.

'I have no idea,' said Mark gloomily. 'Given how crap the rest of my life seems like now, I'm inclined to think it's inevitable. Maybe I should retrain as a plumber.'

'And you still haven't heard from Emily?'

'Not a dickie bird,' said Mark. He had half-hoped their meeting in the summer would have led to her renouncing her career and throwing herself into his welcome arms. He felt he could face all of this with her at his side. 'But if she contacts me, she loses her job. While if she's successful at her job, I may lose mine.'

'You never know,' said Rob, 'things might work out somehow.'

'I can't see how,' said Mark glumly.

'Remember what I always say: expect the unexpected,' said Rob. 'Sometimes miracles do happen.'

'Is Daddy gay?'

Katie nearly choked into her cornflakes. George was sitting looking at her inquisitively from the other side of the breakfast table.

'What makes you say that?' Jeez. How did he even know what being gay meant? The things they learned in the playground these days.

'Jordan Allwick told me,' said George. 'When we went to the park last week. He said that's why Daddy left. He said *everyone* knows.'

George's face was inscrutable as he said this. Katie wondered what was going on in his head. It was so hard to tell.

'What did you say?' she asked, probing, thinking, *Someone give me a bloody hand here, how do I deal with this?*

'I told him that he was lying.'

'Oh,' said Katie.

'But he said he wasn't, he'd overheard his mum talking about it.'

I bet he has, thought Katie grimly. However hard you tried to keep something secret in Thurfield, you didn't have a hope once Mandy sodding Allwick found out. Though quite how she'd found this out was beyond even Katie.

George continued, 'So I hit him.'

'Oh,' said Katie again, not knowing whether to hug him for standing up for his dad, tell him off for unsuitably violent behaviour (even if she totally agreed with it), or cry because any minute now she was going to have to break his ten-year-old heart.

'Did you think that was the right thing to do?' Katie stalled, scrabbling through her brain to remember what exactly it was that *How to Tell Your Children Their Dad is Gay* had said about situations like this. She had an uncomfortable feeling they were

308

rather keen on parents being open about the situation. A naturally private person, Katie would much rather clam up and fudge the issue. But she thought briefly to how her mother had behaved about her father's infidelities, and realised it was no good doing that. Look what a mess Katie was in now as a result of her mother's well-intentioned secrecy.

'No,' said George. 'But Daddy isn't gay. Is he?'

The hopeful look on his face smote Katie's heart. She wished beyond all measure that Charlie was with her so they could do this together, as they had sat down and broached the separation together. But he wasn't. As usual, she was here to face the tough stuff on her own.

'George, do you actually know what being gay means?' Katie asked.

'Of course I do,' said George in scornful tones. 'It's man love man, isn't it?'

'Well, that's sort of it,' said Katie. 'But there's a little bit more to it than that.'

George's face fell. A penny had clearly just dropped very heavily.

'Daddy is gay, isn't he?' he said. He looked shell-shocked and tears glistened in his bright blue eyes. Mummy's little soldier. What a bloody thing to have to tell him.

'Yes, he is,' said Katie. 'But it doesn't have to change anything. Daddy still loves you and always will. And Aidan and Molly. Whatever happens, he's your dad, and that matters more than anything else.'

'My dad's gay?' George repeated again in tones of horror. 'Jordan's going to kill me.'

He slammed his bowl of Coco Pops down on the table and ran off upstairs.

Katie put her head in her hands.

Emily felt furtive. She was quite entitled to be in Andrew's office looking through all the material for the Symonds case, which was starting next week, but the fact that she was actively looking for something, *anything*, to help Mark meant she felt like a character in *Spooks*. Any minute now, MI5 was going to stroll in, in the shape of Maniac Mel, and demand what the hell she was up to.

It was late and the office was slowly emptying – this being Friday night, most of her colleagues had better things to do. Normally, she would have too, but this was too important.

In the weeks since she'd last seen Mark, Emily had come to an important decision. Money wasn't everything. And for too long her guilt about letting down her dad and abandoning her family had made her far too accommodating about the financial mess her mum kept getting herself in. She was going to have to ring her up and explain the situation and see if she could defer a couple of months of payments on the loan. And maybe it was about time she got her mum to face up to the fact that spending loads of money on scratch cards wasn't going to bring Dad back either.

Then she was going to do what she should have done years ago. Namely, get out of the world she had found herself trapped in and go to work for a company with integrity, and do what she'd always planned before she'd got so sidetracked and bedazzled. Emily had been looking online and had found a couple of companies which dealt specifically with litigation cases involving victims who, like her dad, had suffered as a result of malpractice.

Reading some of the cases, Emily had felt more enthused and invigorated than she'd ever done in the seven years she'd been working here. It seemed she could make a difference after all.

But first things first. She had to help Mark. Maybe then they could start afresh. Some things, she realised, were worth losing your job for. She'd been stupid and blind to think otherwise.

After an hour of frantically riffling through every document she could find, Emily was on the verge of giving up. There was nothing that would help. If there was some way of proving Mark's innocence, she wouldn't find it here.

'What are you doing?'

Emily nearly jumped out of her skin. Mel was standing in the doorway.

'Just mugging up on the Symonds case,' Emily said. 'Want to make sure there are no nasty surprises.'

Mel looked suspicious.

'And are there?'

'No, nothing at all. Nada. Zilch,' said Emily. 'Andrew has done a great job. So I'll just put this file away . . .'

'Good,' said Mel. She made as if to leave and then said, 'I hope we can rely on you.'

'Yes, of course,' gushed Emily, resisting the urge to throw a stapler at her boss. 'Little Miss Reliable, that's me.'

'See you on Monday then,' said Mel.

Emily packed her things up and made her way slowly to the door. She'd found nothing. Achieved nothing. She had been no help to Mark at all.

'Psst!' John grabbed her arm as she left the building.

'Not now, John,' she said. 'I'm not in the mood for games.'

'This isn't a game,' he said. 'If you want to help your dentist friend, I'd be inclined to pay a visit to Graham Harker. And I haven't said that, and you haven't seen me.'

John touched the tip of his nose, winked at her and was gone.

Graham Harker? The name was familiar.

Now where had she heard it before?

Chapter Thirty-three

'How are you feeling?' Rob asked Katie as they stood waiting one Saturday night for their turn in the ballroom of a hotel a few miles from Thurfield. It was the first round of the competition Isabella had suggested they enter, and Katie was already wishing she'd said no. Her hands felt clammy, her knees were knocking together, and she felt ridiculously overexposed in the skimpy dress she had somehow ended up wearing.

'Sick,' said Katie. She'd watched the other competitors in awe. Even though they had entered the beginners' section, everyone else looked so much more accomplished than them. She pulled at her skirt. Why had she gone for tassles? Seduced by watching the new series of *Strictly Come Dancing*, now in its fifth week, and persuaded by Rob that they really, really did need to dance in the Latin section, she'd made the mistake of ordering her outfit online: a gold sparkly dress with a halter-neck top and a fringe skirt. The skirt had looked considerably longer in the picture than it was in reality. However much she fiddled with it, it wasn't going to cover more of her legs. The top part of the dress was cut extremely low, and her back felt exposed. What on earth had she been thinking? Although it had to be better than Rob's top. He had gone for exposing his hairy chest in a ridiculously over-the-top blouson-type purple shirt complete with ruffles. His trousers were more subdued, being straight and black, but –

'I don't believe it, you're wearing Cuban heels.' Katie had only just realised. She burst out laughing.

'Of course,' said Rob, giving her a mock bow.

'The next dance is Rob and Katie dancing the salsa, beginner level, first heat,' the compere was saying.

The small crowd clapped and whistled, and Katie and Rob stepped out into the spotlight. They took their positions at opposite sides of the room. Katie swallowed hard.

She vaguely heard a voice say 'Music please', and then she started counting. Rob smiled at her, and, doing the basic step, they swung towards each other as they'd practised.

'Don't forget to smile,' said Rob as he took her in an open hold. 'Three and four, and back and forward, and step and turn . . .'

Within seconds, Katie had forgotten that all eyes were on her and was losing herself in the rhythm of the dance.

'And open and turn,' Rob was reminding her, as for a moment she stumbled and nearly forgot the step. 'And back, and forward, and cha cha.'

Rob stood still as Katie cha chaed around him. This was great. Better than great. All too soon, they had reached the last turn, and Rob executed a dramatic spin they'd spent weeks practising, and she ended up in his arms.

The floor erupted as Rob and Katie took their bows. After hearing their marks – three 9s and an 8 (Katie groaned – that must have been for her mistake) – they were ushered off to wait to hear if they had progressed to the next round.

'That was so much fun,' said Katie. 'I think I could get to enjoy this.'

Rob squeezed her hand. 'Me too,' he said.

Mark sat nervously in the GDC committee room, wondering how on earth he'd ended up here. It was nearly Christmas already, and for the best part of a year he had been fretting about his career. Was he about to find out that it was all over?

James had tried to reassure him that he had nothing to worry about, but Mark couldn't feel as confident as his rep did. It was, after all, their job to present a positive spin on events. They hadn't lain awake all night fretting anxiously about the outcome, or had to fight their way through a media scrum to get to the GDC offices on Wimpole Street, where the hearing was to be held passing a radiant Jasmine giving a fevered account of all of his misdemeanours to Sky News. The tight knot he'd had in the pit of his stomach for weeks now had twisted itself into a new spasm of pain. He didn't think he could take much more of this.

At the front of the room was a long desk, flanked with computer screens, behind which sat three dentists who were going to be his judges, jury and executioners. To either side were the rest of the panel, made up of a combination of his peers and lay people. To his right, sat Jasmine and her medico-legal represent-ative. Mark's fate was in their hands. So far nothing much had happened. Mark had told the hearing who he was and listened while Jasmine's representative outlined his many misdeeds, making him sound like a monster little short of Jack the Ripper. The rest of it had been incredibly boring and, even despite his anxieties, Mark had been on the verge of dozing off.

'Can we hear from Tony Cavendish please?' the chair of the panel said.

With a start, Mark realised that Twinkletoes Tone was taking the stand. He'd almost forgotten the footballer's real name.

'Mr Cavendish,' intoned the chair, who had the most ponderous manner that Mark had ever witnessed in someone who was still awake, 'tell us what happened on the night of February twelfth this year?'

'I'd arranged to meet Kerry,' began Tony.

'And Kerry is –'

'Oh, yeah, right. Kerry's sort of – like – she was my bird for a bit when I split up with Jasmine.' Tony shot an anxious look at his girlfriend when he said this, but she smiled sweetly at him and blew him a kiss.

'I see,' said the chair. 'Carry on.'

'So she says to me, "You seen the papers?" And I says, "No, why?" Then she says, "Your ex-girlfriend. Someone's sold them the story about her tooth, and I know who it is."'

'And who was it?'

'He's sitting right over there,' said Tony, and pointed at Mark.

Mark was fuming. He couldn't believe the barefaced cheek of Tony's lie. But, much as he wanted to leap up and deck Tony one, he could feel James warning him to control his anger.

Mark sat back and listened with increasing horror as witness after witness took the stand to completely and utterly defame his character. Kerry was called, to Mark's dismay. He wondered again, if she had had something to do with all of this. But the incoherence of her evidence, which consisted mainly of Vicky Pollard type utterances like 'yeah, no, but that was what happened, innit?', suggested she knew nothing of import, and were so ridiculous, they elicited the only smile Mark had managed all day.

Someone had found two witnesses from the stag weekend who had seen Mark dancing to White Snake with his trousers round his ankles. And, finally, the scrote of a reporter who had taken pictures got up to report that he had sat at a bar with Mark for several hours, during which Mark had downed whiskies, vodkas, Bacardi Breezers – you name it, Mark seemed to have drunk it – galore. The picture they painted was of a family man whose life started going down the pan after his divorce. Mark sat in silent despair as he watched his career slip away from him.

Emily, who had come along to witness proceedings, and was sitting a little way behind Mark, was horrified as she watched Mark's reputation being destroyed. It was worse than she could have imagined, and made it all the more urgent that she do something about finding out the truth. She'd spent the weekend trying to track down Graham Harker. It was easy to find him by Googling his name. Famous for dozens of exposés of the nefarious doings of the zedlebrity set, he was often used as a talking head in shows about 'stars' who'd fallen from grace. No wonder his name was familiar. It was not so easy to get access to him though – she hadn't managed to find an email address or a phone number for him, but he was, coincidentally, represented by A-Listers.

Was it a coincidence that the reporter who had stitched Mark up so effectively seemed to be involved somehow? Emily didn't quite know whether she was clutching at straws or not, but she definitely smelt a rat. Even more so after Kerry gave her fumbling evidence. It all made sense now. As soon as Emily saw Kerry she recognised her as the girl from the nightclub. Kerry had definitely been hiding something. Maybe it was worth having another go at her. Jasmine and Tony were bound to be on the front covers of the papers tomorrow; it might be worth going to rub some salt in the wound . . .

The end of the day came all too soon, and if Emily had been into gambling she wouldn't have rated Mark's chances too highly. She longed to go to him. He looked so defeated and lonely sitting in his seat, sure, no doubt, that the panel had already condemned him, as indeed they must have after what they'd heard.

Emily scuttled out of the room at the end of the session, determined not to let Mark see she'd been there, but as luck would have it, he and his rep were exiting the building at the same time she was.

'Mark, I'm so sorry,' she said, 'that was awful.'

'I hope you're satisfied,' said Mark. 'I can't believe that your lot have set me up with such a pack of lies.'

'Mark, I had nothing to do with that, honestly,' said Emily in dismay. 'I had no idea they were going to come out with all that stuff.'

'I don't believe you.' Mark looked tense and unhappy.

'Mark, please –' Emily began.

'Just leave me alone, Emily,' said Mark. 'I think you've done enough damage.'

He strode off down the corridor, to the front steps of the GDC headquarters, where the marauding hordes of reporters and photographers lay in wait.

Emily leaned against the wall biting back the tears. Now more than ever, she had to find out the truth.

'Is everything all right, Wednesday?'

It was the last day of the Outward Bound course, and Rob couldn't wait for it to be over. He had enjoyed bits of it, the canoeing earlier on in the term had been fun, but it had taken up far too much time at the weekends, and if Jen so much as suggested he did it again, he was going to have to thump her. Plus they'd saved the worst for last, as he was going to have to face his fears and use the climbing wall. Gemma clearly had as many reservations as he did, because she'd bottled out of their practice session earlier. He had a feeling her rather bitchy friend Shelly might have been giving her a hard time about it.

'Yes, fine,' snapped Gemma. 'Why wouldn't I be?'

'I couldn't help noticing you seemed a bit upset before,' said Rob, 'and I thought maybe Shelly was being a bit unkind?'

'There's nothing wrong, I'm fine,' said Gemma. Her demeanour, as ever, was one of spiky aggression, but he could tell she was fighting to keep control.

'You don't look fine,' said Rob. 'What is it? You can tell me.'

'No, I can't,' said Gemma. 'I can't tell you, because there's nothing wrong. So just leave me alone.'

She flounced off with a defiant air, but Rob wasn't fooled for a second. Mark had mentioned that Gemma had been in a lot of trouble at school recently, and was worried that she might be getting led astray by Shelly. It wouldn't surprise him if that were the case. From what he'd seen, Shelly was a poisonous little cow. But he couldn't help Gemma if she didn't want him to.

He sighed and called the next group to take their turn, and spent the next half an hour shouting words of encouragement as the kids climbed the wall with varying degrees of success. Then it was the turn of Gemma's group. She came back looking incredibly unhappy, and he could see that Shelly was whispering to a girl next to her.

'Right, who's up first?' Rob asked.

'Gemma.' Shelly shot a sly look at Gemma. 'After all, she did so well earlier.'

Gemma blushed, and Rob felt for her instantly.

'I think for that it should be you who goes first,' said Rob. 'Let's just hang on until Chris gets back, though.'

Chris, the course instructor, had just popped out to answer the phone, so Rob spent the next few minutes reminding the girls how to secure their hawsers properly. He was busy showing someone how to tie a figure-of-eight knot for the umpteenth time when he became aware of a scuffle at the other end of the line.

'I am so not a coward, Shelly Osbourne,' shouted Gemma, and ran towards the climbing wall.

'Wednesday, what are you doing?' Rob yelled. 'Come back at once!'

He watched in horror as Gemma swarmed up the wall without a rope, a hat, in fact with no safety equipment at all. Chris had been quite clear that no one was to climb the wall without supervision. She was going to get herself killed.

Gemma was a quarter of the way up when she turned and called to Shelly, 'See who's the coward now?'

'Gemma, come down.' Rob was frantic.

'Oh all right.' Gemma's usual sulkiness asserted itself, and she edged her foot downwards to find a hold. She started her descent, but her foot hadn't engaged properly, and she put it into thin air. Frantically she tried to find a foothold and couldn't. Gemma let out a little whimper and clung to the wall.

'Gem, it's okay.' Rob could see that the bravado was fading and she was beginning to panic. 'I'll come and get you.'

He started to climb up to meet her, trying to talk to her reassuringly, but Gemma was clearly terrified and didn't seem to be listening to a word he was saying.

Rob had nearly reached her. He stretched out his hand and said, 'Gem, it's okay, I'm here.'

She looked down at him, but her fear made her flustered, and instead of reaching for his hand, she attempted to find the foothold again. She swung her foot towards it, but she missed.

'I can't hold on,' she sobbed.

'Yes, you can,' said Rob. 'Come on, grab my hand.'

'I – can't.' Gemma was hysterical now, her fear palpable.

'I'm here,' said Rob, reaching out again. This time Gemma let one hand go and attempted to grab his. She missed, her foot slipped, and she let out a piercing scream.

'No!' yelled Rob. He watched in horror as she fell to the ground. He swarmed back down as fast as he could. Gemma lay on the ground at an awkward angle. She was horribly, horribly still.

Chapter Thirty-four

Mark had just got in from the shops when the phone call came. It was Sam and she was hysterical.

'You have to come now,' she sobbed. 'It's Gemma.'

'Come where? What's happened?' Mark felt sick. What had Gemma done now?

'I'm at the hospital,' said Sam. 'Gemma's had an accident, and she's in a coma.'

'I'm on my way.' Mark only waited for Sam to give him the details of where to go before grabbing his car keys and ran to the car. It took a couple of minutes to undo the lock; his hands were shaking too much. Gemma was in a coma. What on earth had happened?

He drove like a maniac to the hospital – it wasn't their local one, but one about half an hour away, close to the centre where Gemma had gone for her adventure training. It felt like a lifetime had passed since he'd seen his daughter. Was it only Sunday that they'd been together? A quiet fear took hold: suppose she was brain-damaged? Suppose they had her on life support? Fear bubbled under the surface as he tried to concentrate on practicalities: indicate, turn left, slow down for the traffic lights, stay calm. Stay calm. His eldest daughter was injured; how could he possibly stay calm?

Memories flooded back of Gemma's birth – a protracted affair that had taken several days to come to fruition, but then, miraculously, there she'd been, this little scruffy pink bundle looking back at him. The fruit of his loins, the apple of his eye. Then later – pictures of her toddling, learning to speak, being completely and utterly cute, always so cute. Those had been happy days for him and Sam, playing happy families together. Where had it all gone wrong?

And now, lately, the early images of the cute little girl had been replaced by the spiky, difficult teenager who snarled and grumbled her way through life, but nonetheless had remained *his* despite it all. The thought that he wouldn't ever have to tell her off for playing music too loud, or for being rude to him, suddenly seemed too dreadful to contemplate. *Don't go there, don't go there*, he willed his brain. She would get better. She had to.

Eventually, Mark pulled into the grounds of Eastwick Hospital. After some delay, he managed to park the car and ran like a mad thing towards A&E.

As usual in these places, it was packed. He went up to the desk and said, 'My daughter, I think my daughter's here. Gemma Davies?'

The look of polite disinterest became one of overwhelming concern, which Mark didn't think was a good sign.

'Ah yes, Mr Davies,' she said. 'Your daughter was admitted a couple of hours ago. They're about to do a brain scan. Your wife's with her. I can take you to her now.'

'How is she?' Mark felt himself wobble as he asked the question.

'I'm sorry, you'll have to ask the doctor,' said the receptionist, 'but she's in the best hands.'

'Yes, of course,' said Mark, following her down a sterile white corridor. The tawdry Christmas decorations which were clearly meant to brighten it had never seemed more inappropriate.

'Mark, thank God you're here. No one will tell me anything.' Sam ran into Mark's arms and burst into tears.

'Where's Gemma?' Mark asked, holding Sam to him. It felt weirdly natural to have her in his arms again.

321

'In there,' said Sam. 'The doctor's with her now. They want her to have a brain scan. Oh Mark, I'm so scared.'

Mark stroked her hair and made soothing noises. He was as scared as she was, but someone had to be in control.

'What happened?' he asked. 'Do we know?'

'It was an accident,' said a familiar voice. 'God, Mark, I'm so sorry.'

Rob stood there in a state of deep distress.

'I tried to stop her. Honestly I did, but she wouldn't listen. She fell off the climbing wall, and it was all my fault.'

Emily knew she'd found the right house by the number of gaudy Christmas decorations outside – they seemed in keeping with Kerry's character somehow. She paused for a moment, wondering whether she was doing the right thing. It had seemed like the obvious thing to do after she'd seen Mark. She'd rushed back to the office, found Kerry's address in the file, then gone straight to her house. Now she was standing right outside it didn't seem like such a good idea. Still, nothing ventured, nothing gained. Emily rang the doorbell.

There was a long pause before a rather large woman opened the door. She was dressed in a velour tracksuit and her fair hair was slicked back into a greasy ponytail. She could have been anything between twenty-five and forty-five, but given Kerry was in her early twenties, Emily settled on forty. Presumably this was Kerry's mum.

'Yeah?' The woman was hardly welcoming, but then Emily wasn't here to make friends.

'Is Kerry here?' Emily asked.

'She's in the lounge watching TV. Lazy cow. She never goes out now. Not since that footballer ditched her.'

'May I see her?'

Kerry's mum looked Emily up and down suspiciously.

'You're not DSS, are you?' she said. 'Only we've had them snooping around.'

'No, nothing like that,' said Emily. 'I've come about the court case where Kerry's a witness.'

'Oh.' Kerry's mum looked blank, then yelled, 'Kerry, someone to see you.'

She ambled off into the house, and Emily followed her down a dark dingy corridor into a small lounge crammed full of furniture that had evidently been the height of fashion circa 1984 but was looking decidedly ropy now. Kerry was sitting on a beanbag that had seen better days, watching *Neighbours* on the largest plasma TV screen that Emily had ever seen.

'You're that lawyer woman, aren't you?' Kerry looked suspicious.

'Emily Henderson,' said Emily. 'I work at Mire & Innit. Our firm's representing Jasmine Symonds against your old boss, Mark Davies. You remember coming in to sign a witness statement, don't you?'

'So?'

'You do realise, when it goes to court you're going to have a horrible time when they find out your witness statement is a pack of lies.'

'It's not lies,' said Kerry.

'Oh, I think it is,' Emily said. 'And, judging by your performance today, you're not going to make a very credible witness. If you thought that lot today were bad, they'll tear you apart when this gets to court.'

'Don't care,' said Kerry, but Emily noticed she sat up a little straighter.

'You are lying, aren't you?' continued Emily. 'It wasn't Mark who rang the papers, was it? I think it was you.'

'It was Tony's idea,' Kerry burst out sulkily. 'He said that Jasmine needed to be shown a lesson, and that she was too big for her boots.'

'So why did you get involved?' Emily asked.

Kerry looked a little shamefaced.

'I fancied him, didn't I? Besides, Mark was going to give me the sack.'

'I can't think why,' muttered Emily. She felt vaguely dirty. It was horrible doing this, but she had to for Mark's sake.

'So what happened?' asked Emily.

'I stayed after work one night and rang the papers up. Then I emailed a copy of Jasmine's notes to them. I did it from Mark's computer, so it looked like they were from him.'

'Thanks to you, a really decent man is going through hell at the moment,' said Emily, resisting the urge to strangle Kerry. Much as she wanted to, she needed her help. 'So I think it's about time you changed your story, don't you?'

An hour later, Emily triumphantly left the house with a new statement from Kerry saying that not only had she lied about Mark's involvement, and had informed the papers herself, but also that she was fairly sure that Graham Harker had done something to Mark's drink.

Now all Emily needed to do was track Graham down and get him to spill the beans.

Katie was listening to carols and baking mince pies with the children – it was weird how normal and cosy it felt, even though her life had changed so much – when the doorbell rang. To her surprise, Rob was on the doorstep, in a state of deep distress.

'Can I come in?' he asked.

'Of course,' said Katie. 'Rob, are you okay? You look shocking.'

Rob didn't say anything, but followed Katie into the kitchen, where the children had abandoned the mince pies in favour of the tv, where *Home Alone* was showing for the umpteenth time. Molly sat gurgling in her high chair, quite content as long as she had a breadstick to eat.

'Wine or beer?' Katie offered.

'Nothing, thanks,' said Rob. 'I'm not even supposed to be here, but I didn't know where else to go. I couldn't stay at the hospital, obviously . . .'

'Rob, whatever's wrong?' He was shaking now.

'It's Gemma,' he said. 'She's had a terrible accident and it's all my fault. Oh God, Katie, I can't believe it's happened again.'

It took Katie several minutes to prise the whole story out of Rob, and when she had she said, 'But Gemma knew the rules and she didn't listen to you. You told her to stop. Then you tried to get her down safely. It was an accident. It's not your fault.'

'That's what Mark said too,' said Rob, 'which is pretty bloody noble of him. I think if it were the other way round I might be tempted to thump him.'

'No, you wouldn't,' said Katie. 'Mark's not stupid. He knows you'd never do anything to hurt Gemma.'

'Yes, but I did.' Rob looked so bleak that Katie reached out for his hand.

'Rob, it's not your fault,' she said. 'Really, it isn't. It sounds to me as though Gemma was misbehaving. You didn't make her climb that wall. And you tried to stop her. It was just an awful accident.'

'You think?'

'I know,' said Katie firmly and squeezed his hand tightly. 'It'll be all right. You'll see.'

They sat holding hands as it grew dark, and the lights from Katie's Christmas tree sparkled in the conservatory, and shadows gathered in the corners.

Eventually, Rob took his hand away and said, 'I'd better get home. And I should call in at the hospital on the way.'

'Are you okay to drive?' Katie asked. 'Only I could get Mum to come over if you want?'

'No, I'll be fine,' said Rob. He gave her a quick hug, and she watched him go to his car looking so desolate it tugged at her heart. Poor Rob. Poor Mark. Poor Gemma. Poor bloody everybody. She had tried to be positive for Rob's sake. She only hoped she was right.

'Here.' Mark proffered a coffee at Sam. It was just the two of them, as Sam had arranged for Beth to stay with a neighbour. They had been sitting at Gemma's bedside for hours now, and there'd been no change. He'd lost all sense of time. In the end, seeing that Sam looked close to collapse, Mark had persuaded her to take a break. Somehow, seeing Sam, who was always so feisty and in control, in such a state, was stopping Mark from breaking down himself. One of them had to stay strong and in charge. From the minute he'd entered the hospital, a kind of steely determination had taken him over. He had boxed off his emotions concerning Gemma and put them away under lock and key, only to be dealt with when he could. Much as he wanted to cry, he wasn't going to be any use to his daughter if he collapsed in a puddle too.

'It's my fault,' she said. 'If I hadn't been so bloody determined to go to work, none of this would have happened.'

'Don't be daft,' Mark said. 'Whether you went to work or not, Gemma would have still disobeyed orders and climbed that wall. You know what a little madam she's been recently. It's no more your fault than Rob's.'

Mark thought back: he had never seen his happy-go-lucky friend like that before.

'It was an accident,' said Mark, and then repeated what he'd said to Rob. 'If it's anyone's fault it's Gemma's. She should have known better than to go climbing that wall without equipment.'

'But that's my point,' said Sam, sipping her coffee and leaning back against the wall. 'God, that's disgusting. She's been behaving so badly recently. It's my fault. I've not been there for her.'

'Don't you think,' said Mark gently, 'it might be both our faults? I've thought for a while now that she seems to be reacting much worse to the split than Beth has. And, let's face it, we could probably be better at dealing with things than we are. She perhaps doesn't get the consistency she needs.'

'Since when have you become an expert in parenting?' sniffed Sam.

'I'm not,' said Mark. 'None of us are, are we? I just think sometimes we could both handle things better.'

He sat back, half-expecting Sam to launch into a tirade about his inadequacies, which had been a standard feature of their rows towards the end of their relationship, but she sat silently, toying with her cup.

'I think I could,' she said eventually. 'I think you've handled things pretty well considering.'

'Oh.' This was unexpected. Sam wasn't one to take responsibility for her actions.

There was a long pause, then Sam said, 'Do you think maybe we made a mistake?'

Now Mark was truly stunned. The one thing he'd wanted to hear from her for months, and now she'd said it and the only thing he could think about was that he'd rowed with Emily and he wished he hadn't.

'Well, I did,' said Mark. 'What makes you say that?'

'Oh Mark,' Sam burst out unhappily. 'I was so miserable stuck at home, and I blamed you for it. You were always working so hard, and never seemed to be around when I needed you. And then the kids got bigger, and I got that job, and I met Kevin, and it all sort of snowballed. And –'

'You can't turn the clock back,' said Mark. 'What's happened has happened. But if you're not happy with Kevin, you should do something about it. It's not fair on the kids.'

'It's not that I'm not happy with him, exactly,' said Sam. 'It's just he's not very interested in the kids really. And today he barely said anything when I rang him about Gemma. He wouldn't even have Beth for me, which is why Alison picked her up from school. I can't believe how unsupportive he's been. Whereas you –'

'I'm Gemma's dad,' said Mark. 'It's different.'

'No,' said Sam. 'You're different. And it's taken this for me to see what a fool I've been.'

'Let's not dwell on that, eh?' said Mark, putting his arm around her. 'Let's concentrate on getting our daughter better. Gemma's the most important thing right now.'

'She will be all right, won't she?' Sam turned a tear-stained face towards Mark.

'Of course,' he said fiercely. 'She's got to be.'

Chapter Thirty-five

Emily knocked on Mel's door. She felt incredibly nervous, and wondered how Mel would react to what she had to say.

'I hope that you're not going to tell me there's a problem with the Symonds case,' Mel drawled, looking as if Emily was something the cat had dragged in.

'Yes, actually, I was,' said Emily. 'It's one of the witnesses – Kerry Matthews. It turns out her story is a pack of lies. It wasn't Mark who rang the papers, it was Kerry. She did it with Tony Cavendish. There is no case against Mark. It's entirely based on a lie.'

'Holy shit!' For once Mel looked truly rattled.

'Yes,' said Emily. 'I have a revised statement from Kerry and she's kept all the text messages Tony sent her. If the papers get hold of them we're going to look ridiculous.'

'And you're absolutely sure about this?' Mel asked.

'Absolutely,' declared Emily. 'And I feel fairly sure that the journalist who spilled the story about Mark Davies may have been involved in some kind of entrapment.'

'God, this gets worse and worse.' Emily was enjoying seeing Mel squirm.

'Right, you find out what you can about this, and I'm going to do some damage limitation. If what you say is true I want this case dropped like a hot potato,' Mel said. 'Oh, and by the way, good work. I think you can safely say that promotion is in the bag.'

Emily left the room trying not to let out a roar of laughter. In all the time she'd worked here, Mel had never ever praised her. It felt great to have the upper hand for once. Right. Time for phase two. In her search of Andrew's files, she hadn't gone through his emails. Maybe there she might find something to incriminate the firm more. She'd have one last trawl through, and then she was going to go back and tell Mel where to stick her job.

Emily slipped quietly into Andrew's office and started the dull task of tracking back through emails, by a combination of checking those which had been printed and filed and cross referencing with the computer. She searched for Graham Harker's name and got nowhere, so she went back to all the emails he'd received from A-Listers. There were several from Ffion, who had clearly been flirting a lot with Andrew, which was rather amusing. Most of them weren't at all relevant, and then Emily found it. Indiscreet as ever, Ffion had given the game away. Andrew had scribbled a note on it – 'Check this out' – which was dated the day before he went on holiday. Presumably he hadn't had time to follow it up. It was from Ffion to one of her colleagues.

Just to let you know that story we talked about? It's gonna blow this weekend if Graham Harker does his bit properly. But remember he has nothing to do with us . . .

Emily copied the email onto a memory stick, sent a copy to her home computer, and another to her hotmail account. Then she walked back to Mel's office. She stood in the doorway, and said loudly, so that as many people as possible in the office could hear:

'I've had a think about your very kind offer, Mel, and quite frankly I don't think I could live with myself a moment longer if I have to perjure my soul any more than I already have. So you can take your job and put it where the sun shines. I'm out of here. And don't worry about escorting me off the premises. I'm gone.'

Mel sat at her desk, for once in her life speechless, and Emily walked out of her office for the very last time, her head held high, as the rest of the staff rose to their feet in unison and cheered her on her way.

'Way to go,' said John admiringly as she got to the end of the room. 'I always said you were a babe.'

Emily took one last look at the office she had wasted so many years in, and felt an absurd lightening of heart for one whose finances were as precarious as hers were. It was over. A new future awaited her. Maybe, just maybe, now it could involve Mark.

'What happened to your daughter, Mr Davies?'

Mark couldn't believe it. He and Sam had sat by Gemma's bedside all night. There was no change and he couldn't persuade Sam to leave, so Mark had promised to go to hers to pick up some clothes and check on Beth. He'd emerged into a dark, rainy December morning to discover the hospital was besieged by reporters. Didn't they have anything better to do?

'No comment,' said Mark shortly. He put his head down and marched towards his car.

'Whose fault was it?'

'Is she brain-damaged?'

Microphones were thrust in his face; cameras flashed. Mark felt like he was in a particularly vile sort of Hell. How could people do this job day in, day out? Didn't they have any heart?

'Are you going to sue?'

Mark paused and looked at the reporter before him, a weasel-faced little man, with utter distaste.

'Sue? Why would I sue? Who would I sue? What bloody good would that do?'

Mark pushed his way through the crowd and went to put his parking ticket in the machine. It spat out a number. He must be tired, he was sure it said he owed twenty quid. He looked again. It did say he owed twenty quid. Mark looked in his wallet. He didn't actually have twenty quid. Mark leaned against the ticket machine and shut his eyes. The rain came pouring down through a gap in the shelter, and suddenly he wasn't sure if his cheeks were wet with tears or rainwater.

His daughter could be dying and some bastard at the hospital was going to charge him twenty quid for having his car in overnight. Suddenly Mark had had enough. He marched towards the ticket office and wrenched open the door to find a startled car park attendant sitting quietly with a cup of tea and a bacon buttie.

'You want twenty quid for this ticket?' he said.

'You have the car in overnight, that's what it costs,' the man answered.

'Well, I haven't got twenty quid,' said Mark. 'I'm only here because my daughter is lying in a coma in there. I came straight down here last night and haven't been home yet. Don't you people have any conscience?'

'I'm only doing my job,' protested the man.

'That's what they said at Nuremberg,' said Mark. 'Now are you going to raise this barrier or what?'

'What will you do if I don't?'

'I'll drive straight through it,' said Mark. 'Quite frankly, I've had enough. You are my last straw, and I'd advise you not to mess with me if you know what's good for you.'

'Oh, right,' said the man. 'But I'll have to report you for threatening behaviour.'

'Do I look like I care?' Mark asked. 'Report away, and I shall report that you are an obsequious obnoxious little jobsworth.'

'You can't say that about me,' said the man.

'So sue me,' said Mark, walking away. 'Everyone else is.'

It was only when he got back to the car that he realised the utter futility of his actions. The car-park attendant wasn't going to raise the barrier and he still hadn't got twenty quid. He wondered where on earth the nearest cash point might be.

'Do you need twenty quid?' a voice said from behind his car. 'Here, have it.'

To Mark's surprise, the weasel-faced reporter was standing by his car.

'Are you sure?' he said. 'This isn't some kind of trick, is it?'

'I've got kids too,' said the reporter gruffly. 'We're not completely heartless. Go on, hop it before the rest of the pack find out what you just did. They'll have a field day with that.'

'Do you know,' Mark said, 'I couldn't bloody care less what they write. I've got more important things to worry about.'

'So you keep saying,' said the reporter. 'And, having watched you for the last few months, I think, on balance, I'm inclined to believe you. Perhaps it's time people heard the other side of the story.'

Mark rubbed his eyes. This was getting more surreal by the minute.

'Perhaps,' he said. 'Only not now. I'm knackered. I need to get home, see my other daughter, pick up some things for my wife. When my life is less crazy perhaps I'll think about it.'

'You don't want the record put straight?' The reporter was incredulous.

Mark shrugged.

'So much crap has been written about me in the last few months,' he said. 'I don't even entirely trust a version that's written in my favour. And, like I said, I have more important things to worry about.'

'Is your daughter going to be all right?'

Mark flinched and looked away, not wishing to reveal the depths of his feelings. 'I have no idea,' he said. 'I can only hope so.'

Katie opened the door to Emily.

'Oh my god,' said Emily. 'I came as soon as I heard about Gemma. Do you know how she is?'

'There's no change,' said Katie. 'I offered to have Beth for a few days, so that Mark and Sam can stay at the hospital. From what Rob's told me, they don't have much of a support system, and even though I don't know Sam at all, I felt I had to offer. Sorry, I've been meaning to ring you but it's been a bit mad. Who told you?'

'Rob,' said Emily. 'I just went round to see Mark, because I've got some new information about his case. And to let him know that when I'm done, I'm going to hand my notice in. Rob was there. He told me what happened.'

'Is he okay?' Katie asked. 'I haven't seen him since the day it happened, and he was in a terrible state.'

'He didn't look great,' said Emily. 'He's blaming himself.'

'It's not his fault,' Katie insisted. 'It sounds like Gemma just went off on a mad teenage spur-of-the-moment kind of thing. He told her to come back, but she wouldn't listen.'

'She can be difficult,' said Emily, 'but jeez, how terrible. And just before Christmas as well. They're going to have a terrible time.'

'I know,' Katie shivered. 'I can't stop thinking about how I'd feel if it was one of mine.'

There was a pause for a minute, neither of them knowing quite what to say, till Katie changed the subject. 'Come on, this is really gloomy. We're not going to help Mark by sitting here feeling upset. Tell me about this information you've found out. Do you really think it might help him?'

'It turns out Kerry was lying through her teeth,' said Emily. 'If I can only get the information to Mark's lawyers, then the case should collapse. He won't have a charge to answer.'

'That's fantastic,' said Katie.

'It will be if my firm doesn't indulge in some damage limitation. I need more, really. I'm trying to track down this reporter. I think he may have spiked Mark's drink.'

'Quite the super-sleuth, aren't you?' said Katie.

'I don't know about that,' Emily replied. 'I just hope I can find him.'

The doorbell rang again. This time it was Rob. Katie was shocked by his appearance. He looked as though he hadn't slept in a week.

'Come in,' she said. 'Emily's here, planning how to pin down that reporter who stitched Mark up.'

'Do you need any help?' Rob asked. 'I could be useful as muscle.'

'Sounds good to me,' said Emily. 'I just need to track this man down first. I know, I'll ring Ffion. If I'm lucky she may not have found out that I've left work yet.'

Ten minutes later, Emily had the number she needed, and had arranged to see the unsuspecting Graham Harker.

Katie saw her and Rob to the door.

'You won't do anything silly, will you?' she said. She was slightly anxious about Rob's state of mind, which seemed incredibly fragile.

'No, of course not,' Emily replied. 'Besides, with Rob to protect me I can't go wrong, can I?'

Emily paused in the entrance of the bar where they had arranged to meet Graham Harker. His face was easily recognisable from the TV – he was a small, squinty creature with protuberant eyes and rather alarming glasses, and he was sitting at a corner table pretending not to be noticed.

'Graham,' she said, extending a hand with a confidence she didn't feel. 'So good of you to come. Now, I just wanted to go over your statement again, just in case we need to call you.'

'Is this necessary,' Graham said. 'I thought I'd done my bit.'

'You have,' soothed Emily. 'We're just a bit worried the defence may have got wind of, you know – that other business. They may want to call you again.'

'Oh right.' Graham had clearly bitten. 'In that case, fire away.'

'You met with Mr Davies at what time?'

'Around nine, I think,' said Graham.

'And he was already drunk?'

'As a skunk,' said Graham.

'So you plied him with more drinks and got him to spill the beans,' said Emily, smiling sweetly.

'No,' said Graham, but he looked a little edgy. 'I didn't do anything. He kept ordering double whiskies. Like I said in my article, he was a disgrace to his profession.'

'Now that's very interesting,' said Emily. 'Because that's not what I heard. I heard that he was sober until he met you. And that you dropped something in his drink.'

'You don't know that,' said Graham with some alarm.

'Oh, I do,' said Emily. 'The information I have makes for very interesting reading. I should think Mr Davies will have a field day when he finds out. Entrapment; drugging a member of the public. Does your paper know what you get up to in your spare time?'

'I work freelance,' said Graham in rising panic. 'You can't prove any of this.'

'I think you just did,' said Emily. 'Plus, I have a witness.'

Rob got up from behind the table where they were sitting.

'If I were you, mate,' he said, 'I'd listen very hard to what my friend has to say.'

Half an hour later, Rob and Emily left the bar in hysterics, with a written statement to the effect that Graham Harker had not witnessed Mark Davies drinking but that his behaviour was consistent with someone whose drinks had been spiked by persons unknown. Emily would have preferred a full-on confession, but it was better than nothing. And she had a feeling that Mark would be so relieved to be out of it, he wouldn't care about pursuing the matter.

'Thanks for your help, Rob,' said Emily. 'Do you think Mark

would mind me popping into the hospital tomorrow to tell him the good news?'

'It was the least I could do,' said Rob. 'And I'm sure Mark would be delighted.'

Chapter Thirty-six

Mark wasn't sure how many days and nights had gone by since Gemma's accident. He thought it was about three, or maybe four, but they were blurring into one another. When they weren't at the hospital, he and Sam had taken turns to pop over to Katie's to see Beth, who, thanks to Katie's brilliant support, was coping well with the situation and fortunately hadn't picked up on quite how ill her sister was.

For Mark, time had become reduced to endless hours of sitting by Gemma's bedside, holding her hand, talking to her, as the doctors suggested, propping Sam up when she was close to collapse, and bolstering his own fragile emotions by clamping down as hard as he could on them. He had lost sight of everything but a hospital bed, where his daughter lay white and still – even the court case seemed like an unimportant blip on his horizon. His world had shrunk to moments of waiting, listening to the steady sound of her breathing and hoping that today would bring good news.

'She has a good chance of recovery,' Mr Edwards, the consultant, had promised them. 'The MRI scan has shown there's no permanent damage. It's just a question of time now.'

Despite the consultant's upbeat prognosis, Mark had had several dark nights of the soul, wondering if his daughter would ever be the same again. The worst times were always around two or three in the morning, when the darkness seemed all-enveloping, and the thought that morning would never come became curiously real. Mark had insisted Sam slept in the relatives' room while he kept watch over their daughter. And it was then and only then that he gave way to moments of despair, holding her hand and pleading with her to wake up.

So far there had been no response. In his worst moments, Mark wondered if there ever would be again. He never voiced his thoughts, though. Keeping them hidden became like a talisman to him. If he put words to his fears they might actually happen. Shut them out and they never would.

He rubbed his eyes: 4 a.m. Another night was passing and turning towards a steely dawn.

'You've led us a right old dance, Gem,' he said. 'I wish you'd just wake up so I could tell you everything is okay.' He squeezed her hand and held it tight. If only she would respond. If only. But there was nothing. Nothing. What if there was never anything there again?

Suddenly he felt suffocated by this room, by the sound of his daughter's breathing, by the monotonous beeping of the machines monitoring her. Would this nightmare never end?

A howl emanated from somewhere, and he realised to his horror it had come from him. He got up and staggered to the window and looked out as a grey dawn heralded the start of a new day. Tears streamed down his cheeks. It was no good. He was going to lose her. His precious daughter.

'Ugh. Ugh.'

A muffled sound made him turn round. Gemma was moving, and making some spluttering sounds. Mark raced to her bed and buzzed for the nurse.

'Gemma, can you hear me? Please. Wake up.' He held her hand, not daring to breathe.

Gemma sat bolt upright and looked at him.

'Dad,' she said. 'Why are you crying?'

* * *

Emily was practically skipping as she made her way down the corridors of Eastwick Hospital. Rob had rung her with the good news that Gemma was finally awake. She had photocopies of the transcripts of her conversations with both Graham Harker and Kerry. Maybe when she gave them to Mark he would forgive her. She didn't want to think too much about anything else. He'd had so much to deal with that now didn't seem to be the right moment to be considering their future.

She paused as she came to a fork in the corridors, uncertain where to go.

A man in a white coat walked past.

'Are you lost?' he asked.

'I'm looking for Newbery Ward,' she said.

'It's that way,' said the doctor, pointing to the right-hand corridor, and Emily walked towards the end of it.

She had to be buzzed in to the children's ward, which was bright and breezy with pictures on the wall. In a TV room mums sat with small children on their laps, and bored teenagers on crutches hobbled about the place. Upon asking at the nurses' station where Gemma Davies was, Emily was directed to a single room off the main corridor.

Rob had said Mark would still be there. And Emily hadn't given thought to anyone else. It was only when she looked through the window into the room that she realised Mark wasn't alone. He was sitting with his back to her, beside Gemma's bed, with a small, pretty woman at his side. This must be the mysterious Sam. All three were laughing.

Oh God. This was a terrible mistake. She shouldn't have come.

Emily hovered outside the door for a moment, and then watched as Sam leaned against Mark and he put his arm around her.

She definitely shouldn't have come. She was intruding on a private family moment. Mark was clearly going back to Sam.

There was, after all, to be no future with him. She turned and left, tears blinding her eyes. She'd given everything up for nothing.

Rob arrived at Katie's house the Saturday before Christmas, clutching a bottle of red and some dance DVDs.

'I thought you could do with some company as you mentioned that Charlie had the kids this weekend, and I know from Mark that Beth has gone home,' he said. 'And I also thought we could try to start working out a routine for the finals of the dance competition.'

To their amazement, Katie and Rob kept getting through to the next round of the contest, the final of which was in a posh hotel on the Hill on New Year's Eve. 'I've got waltzes, foxtrots, rumba and tango to choose from.' He gave a wicked grin. 'Personally I favour the tango. I understand the Argentinian one is particularly sexy.'

'You would,' said Katie, and shoved him. 'But I'm glad to see you looking more cheerful.'

'I feel more cheerful,' said Rob. 'There will be an inquiry, of course, but Mark's assured me that Gemma has admitted it was her fault, which is a relief. I'm just so pleased she's okay. I mean, she's got a broken leg, but apart from that she's as right as rain apparently. I'd never have forgiven myself if something had happened to her.'

He looked sombre again, and Katie touched him lightly on the arm.

'But it didn't,' she said. 'Gemma's going to be fine. And no one blames you.'

Rob shivered.

'You're right,' he said. 'I just keep going over in my head what might have happened.'

'But it didn't,' said Katie again, 'so you can relax. Go on, shove one of those DVDs on and I'll pour the wine. When we've had enough I'll get a takeaway if you like.'

The sounds of a waltz was soon floating through the house, and Katie and Rob had a hilarious time dancing in Katie's conservatory in front of the Christmas tree, following the instructions of Hank, a laconic Texan, as to how to make the most of three/four timing.

The rumba was equally funny – this time their instructor was Rob's erstwhile online tutor, Carlo. He was about five foot, and despite wearing high black boots he didn't carry off the illusion of height very well. It didn't help that his glamorous supermodel-type partner was nearly six feet tall. Katie and Rob were on the floor every time he suggested they practise their 'sssnake hips'.

'Just as well the boys aren't here,' said Katie as they collapsed on the sofa. 'They'd never let me live this down.'

'How are things?' asked Rob. 'Sorry, I've been so wrapped up in my troubles that I haven't asked you about yours.'

Katie sighed.

'It's two steps forward and three back at the moment,' said Katie. 'Aidan doesn't know what's going on, but poor George. He asked me if his dad was gay, so I told him and now he's so confused. He's convinced all his friends are going to kill him when they find out. And they may well yet. I'm just hoping it will be a one-hit wonder and they'll all forget about it pretty quickly.'

'Unless there's a particularly mean kid, my experience of these sorts of things is that they do blow over eventually,' said Rob.

'Oh, you've come across this one before then?' Katie asked.

'No, can't say I have,' confessed Rob. 'But I'm sure it will be okay in the end.'

'I hope so,' said Katie. 'It seems a really tough break for a ten-year-old boy. I could kill Charlie for putting him through it.'

'And how are you?'

Katie pulled a face.

'Getting there,' she said. 'I have good days and bad days. I think the shock's wearing off, and – does this sound dreadful?

– a part of me feels hugely relieved. But . . . I don't know. It all seems such a waste. Such a terrible waste of time and energy and emotion. I feel like my whole life has been based on a lie. And that is incredibly hard to deal with.'

'It's not a total waste,' said Rob, 'you've got the kids.'

'That's what Emily said,' Katie replied. She paused and had a sip of wine, and sat staring at the sparkling reflection of the Christmas lights in the conservatory windows. It felt cosy and warm and right being here with Rob. For a moment she looked at him and wondered what he was thinking. The last few weeks had brought them much closer together. Was she ready yet to make that commitment towards something more? She'd certainly seen a side to him that had been completely unexpected, but the way Charlie had left her had shocked her to the core. Did she trust Rob enough to start again?

Mark brought Sam a cup of tea, and they sat chatting to their daughter companionably. It took him back to the way things had once been, when the world was young and so were they. In the time since he and Sam had been apart, he had often been so angry with her, he'd forgotten just what he'd seen in her in the first place. And now he was remembering. She was funny and sweet. Despite her feelings of failure, she was and always had been a good mum.

Perhaps the not-unnatural desire to get back into the work-place after years stuck at home had gone to her head a little, but now the chips were down it was clear who was coming first. Sam had made it quite plain to her bosses at *Smile, Please!* that she wasn't going to be back at work anytime soon. Mark applauded the decision. He hadn't planned to be at work this week anyway, because of the GDC hearing – which had gone on in his absence. Funny how something that had felt so important could suddenly seem so immaterial.

'Mum, Dad,' Gemma said suddenly, 'I'm really sorry.'

'What for, sweetheart?' Sam asked, reaching for her hand.

'For this,' said Gemma, indicating the hospital bed and her broken leg.

'We're just pleased you're okay,' said Sam, 'aren't we?'

'Of course,' said Mark. 'Do you remember much of what happened?'

Gemma looked down at her hands, embarrassed.

'I was being a jerk,' she said, fiddling with the bedclothes. 'It was Shelly. She was going on and on about what a coward I am. I just snapped.'

'You're not a coward,' said Mark. 'Why on earth did Shelly think that?'

'Because, well – you know I was bunking off and that.' Gemma was studiously not looking at them. 'Shelly wanted me to shoplift with her. And I said no.'

'Right,' said Mark. 'Well, we think you did the right thing, don't we, Mum?'

'Yes,' Sam agreed. 'Oh, sweetheart. You should have said.'

Gemma looked up at them, her eyes filling with tears.

'I wanted to,' she said. 'I really did. But you're both . . . Well, Mum, you're always working. And, Dad, you were worried about the court case. And –' suddenly it came out in a rush, 'I hate it that you've split up. You're always arguing and you're so mean to each other. I just want things to be like they were.'

'Oh Gemma!' Mark could see his own dismay mirrored in Sam's face. God, how they'd managed to cock this up. 'So you thought by behaving badly we might take more notice of you and get back together?'

'Yes,' sniffed Gemma. 'Shelly read a book where that happened, and she said I should try it. Only then she got all mean and I don't think I like her any more.'

As Shelly had been nowhere near the hospital since Gemma's accident, nor once asked after her (though the rest of the year had sent presents and cards), Mark was inclined to agree.

344

'We're so, so sorry,' said Sam. 'Sometimes grown-ups can be a bit stupid. Can you forgive us?'

Gemma was crying really hard now, and Mark and Sam both sat on her bed with their arms around her.

'It's all right,' they said, as they used to when she was little and having a nightmare. 'Everything's going to be all right now.'

'So are you two going to get back together then?' Gemma asked, her sobs easing slightly.

Mark looked at Sam. She looked away.

'Gem,' he said carefully, 'I don't think that's going to happen. I'm really sorry, but sometimes it's better to say things are over and move on. But I promise – we promise – that we'll try to listen to you more and not fight so much. How does that sound?'

'Mum?'

Sam swallowed, as if taking a slightly bitter pill. Then she squeezed her daughter tight. 'Dad's right,' she said. 'However much we all want it to, it wouldn't work any more. But there's no reason we can't all be friends. And Dad and I will make an effort to change things.'

She looked at Mark again – it was a look that said goodbye, but also one that promised hope of a new beginning. For the first time since they'd split up, Mark realised, they were acting as a team again. And that was the best he could hope for. One good thing to come out of Gemma's accident was that he'd been forced to spend time with Sam again, and remember the things he'd liked about her. But it had also made him realise he really was over her.

Chapter Thirty-seven

Emily stood hovering outside the meeting room where Mark's hearing was being held, holding a file full of all the information she had pulled together. She was waiting for Mark and his rep to arrive and then she was going to hand it to them, but she must have missed them, because the session seemed to have started already.

The Sunday papers had been full of Gemma's accident, and Mark's extraordinary statement about not wanting to sue. She could only imagine the discussions that were going on at work about his naïvety, but to Emily it made him seem like a hero. He must have thought his daughter was dying when he made that statement, and unlike so many people he hadn't been prepared to make any capital out of it. Gemma had been the only thing on his mind.

And Sam.

All weekend, Emily had gone over and over the scene she had witnessed. It was inevitable, she supposed, that what had happened had brought them back together. Nearly losing your daughter must be a life-changing moment, she imagined. And Mark and Sam had years and two children together. What must she appear like to him? A flaky woman he'd met and dallied with, who had put her career above her feelings for him. No wonder he'd gone back to his wife. Who wouldn't?

She would just have to accept that, unpalatable as it was, Mark wasn't going to be a part of her life after all. But at least she could hold her head high, knowing she'd done the right thing.

A secretary exited the room. She disappeared for about five minutes before coming back.

'Excuse me,' said Emily. 'Could you possibly give this to Mr Davies' union rep? It's very, very important.'

'Certainly, madam,' said the secretary. 'Who shall I say it's from?'

'Just a well-wisher,' said Emily, and she disappeared down the corridor.

Rob was attending an emergency session with his counsellor, who'd kindly fitted him in as a last-minute favour even though it was a few days before Christmas. Although he was thoroughly relieved that Gemma was recovering, the events of the previous week had left him reeling. He needed to make sense of all his reactions.

'So do you still blame yourself?' As usual Nina had let Rob chat away without saying a word. He had found this disconcerting at first, but now he was used to it he quite enjoyed it. It felt very self-indulgent, but it was also a great relief to be able to witter on about things, knowing that even if Nina was bored she was being paid to sit there and so it didn't actually matter.

'I do,' said Rob. 'I keep thinking there must have been something I could have done. Like before, with the kid in Wales. That's twice now. I only did this sodding adventure-holiday thing to face up to my past, and now the same thing's happened again.'

'Is that really how it is?' Nina asked. 'Perhaps you're looking at this the wrong way.'

'How do you mean?'

'Don't you think that instead you could use it as a means of putting the past behind you?'

'How can I do that?' Rob asked.

'For a start, Gemma didn't die,' said Nina. 'So that's a positive outcome.'

'That's true,' said Rob.

'And does anyone blame you?'

'No,' said Rob. 'I've been to see Gemma and she was adamant it was her fault, and Mark and Sam were brilliant about it from the beginning.'

'So the people you love don't blame you,' said Nina. 'What about your work colleagues?'

'They all said I was stupidly brave for trying to get her down. In fact,' Rob had only just thought about the stupidity of this, 'the topsy-turvy world we live in dictates that I'm in more trouble for having climbed the wall without a safety harness on myself, than the fact that Gemma actually hurt herself.'

'So no one blames you?'

'No,' said Rob.

'So why keep blaming yourself?'

Rob sat and thought about this for a minute. This was the point in the sessions that he always found the most uncomfortable, where Nina took him to a place where he was stripped bare – where jack-the-lad Rob had no escape, but had to face up to the person he was.

'Because I always have,' he said. 'Ever since Wales. If I hadn't let Suzie distract me. If I hadn't been so in love with her that I could barely keep my eyes off her, couldn't stop thinking about her physically –' He paused and blinked. Suddenly he remembered all too acutely the almost physical pain he'd felt at loving Suzie. He had been in a dazed happiness all that summer; nothing had really entered into that ball of happiness, nothing had broken through their tight, selfish little world, until the accident.

'What do you see when you think about that day?'

Rob didn't say anything for a while, and then he said slowly, 'I see a long summer's day draw to a sudden close and a darkness descend. And the darkness has been there ever since, though I've fought very hard to deny its existence.'

'And what happened last week?'

Rob gulped. His hands were sweating and he felt slightly sick.

'The darkness overwhelmed me,' he whispered. 'That's why I blame myself.'

'And how do you feel now?'

'I don't know,' said Rob slowly. 'Better. Maybe – a bit. I mean, the darkness is still there. I don't think I'll ever get over what happened in Wales, but maybe I can learn to live with it.'

'Excellent,' beamed Nina. 'I think you've done brilliantly today. Hold on to those thoughts and come back to me next week, and see how much better you feel then.'

Rob left the room and set off home. Despite it being December, the sun shone clear and bright. Katie had invited him, Mark and Sam for Christmas lunch, and he felt a lightening of his heart. It was true, he did feel better, as if a great burden had been eased slightly from his shoulders. Perhaps it was time to stop blaming himself.

Katie and Charlie sat down in the headmaster's office. Katie wondered whether Charlie felt as stupidly nervous as she did. She felt exactly as she had done at school the one and only time she'd smoked behind the bike shed, had got caught and had to go to see the head teacher.

'You wished to see me?' Mr Paterson smiled at them both, clearly trying to put them at their ease.

'Yes, it's about, well, it's a rather delicate matter actually,' said Katie. She glanced at Charlie. They had run through this together, but he was looking paralysed with fear. It amazed her now that she had ever imagined she could have been in love with him, but she realised now that the period after her dad's death had been so stressful that she had married Charlie entirely on the rebound. The things that had attracted her to him – his

349

kindness, his apparent honesty, his charm – were the things she'd loved in her dad. Given how much her dad had managed to fool her, was it any wonder she'd been beguiled by Charlie? It was even more of a wonder they'd lasted so long.

'Unfortunately, we are splitting up,' said Katie.

'I see, I'm sorry to hear that,' said Mr Paterson. 'And how are the boys taking it?'

'Not too badly, considering,' said Katie.

'Considering what?'

Charlie looked as though he wished there were a convenient trapdoor in the floor. He was not going to be any help.

'As I said, it's a bit delicate,' said Katie. 'Charlie, do you want to tell him, or shall I?'

Charlie looked at her pleadingly.

'Okay, the thing is, Mr Paterson,' said Katie, 'it transpires that my husband is gay.'

'I see,' said Mr Paterson. 'Right. And the boys know this?'

'George does, Aidan doesn't,' said Katie. 'We think he's a bit young yet.'

'And how is George?'

'Confused.' Charlie spoke for the first time. 'I've tried to talk to him and explain, but I'm not sure I've helped very much.'

'In my experience,' said Mr Paterson, 'children do tend to bounce back. And they do get over things. I think the key is to be as honest as you have been. And also to have two loving parents, which you clearly are.'

Katie cleared her throat.

'The thing we're worried about most –' she said.

'Is whether or not he's going to get bullied, obviously,' said Mr Paterson. 'I shall make sure that the Year Three and Six teachers understand the situation and, rest assured, any difficulty in that area will be dealt with swiftly. You've got to expect some low-level teasing at least. Year Six boys in particular are notoriously silly. But I'll make sure that it doesn't come to anything serious. And if there are problems, I shall of course inform you at once.'

'Thanks, Mr Paterson,' said Katie, shaking his hand, 'you've been most helpful.'

'Yes, thank you,' said Charlie. 'I have to confess to feeling amazed at how understanding you've been.'

'Oh, didn't you know?' asked Mr Paterson as he showed them the door, 'my ex-wife's a lesbian.'

Mark was sitting in the GDC hearing feeling ridiculously light-headed. There was nothing like your child having a near brush with death to put things in perspective. And, suddenly, he felt things were completely in perspective. Gemma was going to get better. Progress, the doctors told them, might be slow, but eventually she would be back to perfect health. And so now the hearing seemed meaningless. So what if he lost his job? Something else would turn up. He knew the truth, even if no one else did. And if the court case went against him too, he'd just have to cross that bridge when he came to it.

Mark looked around the room. He wondered if everyone here was as certain of his guilt as the papers were. Jasmine had given evidence this morning and had given such a convincing account of the pain and distress caused by his apparent actions that he felt sure she would be receiving an offer to star in *EastEnders* as soon as this was all over. One of the panel had managed to get her to admit that her career hadn't exactly been hindered by the revelations that her teeth weren't quite as perfect as the world might have supposed, but Jasmine had been well-primed and hadn't given anything else away.

Mark had half-hoped that he would see Emily again, but there appeared to be no sign of her. Perhaps it was just as well.

The door of the committee room opened, and a secretary came up to James, whispered something in his ear and handed him a file.

James had a quick look at the contents, then whispered to one of his colleagues, before putting up his hand. 'I've just been given some new material which seems to change things significantly,' he said. 'I think the panel should see it immediately.'

The chairperson glanced at the rest of the panel, then said, 'Well, this is a bit unprecedented, but tell us what it is.'

James punched Mark's arm lightly and said, 'You're off the hook, mate.' Then he stood up, held the file aloft, and said, 'This hearing is a travesty, and my client should never have had to come here. I have proof that not only was he not responsible for the leak that led to the story about Jasmine Symonds's teeth coming into the public domain, but his uncharacteristic behaviour at the stag night was just that. Uncharacteristic. Someone spiked his drink.'

'Let me see,' said the chairperson. James passed the file over, and the man quickly scanned its contents before passing it to his colleagues. After a whispered discussion he said, 'Following these revelations, I have no option but to dismiss these proceedings instantly. I find that Mark Davies has no case to answer here, and he can return to his work with no stain on his character.'

The room exploded in uproar. Mark could scarcely take it in. After all the months of worrying, it was finally over.

'How – what – where did this new evidence come from?' Mark turned to James in disbelief.

'I have no idea,' said James, 'the secretary just said a well-wisher gave it to her. Kerry Matthews has signed a new statement to say it was her who rang the papers, and gave details of all the conversations and text messages that went between her and Tony Cavendish on the subject. Oh, and one thing I do have to apologise about – I was a bit dubious about the drink thing, but it turns out you were right. Someone did spike your drink. I'd put money on it being Graham Harker, but our mystery friend couldn't get him to confess, apparently. He did say that you were perfectly sober when you met, and that he thinks he saw someone drop something in your drink.'

Mark sat back and took a deep breath. It was such a relief that the whole thing was over. He had no costs to pay, his reputation was restored, and his daughter was going to be okay. For the first time in months he could sleep easily at night. He only wished Emily were here to share his joy.

Chapter Thirty-eight

Emily was hovering behind a pillar in the foyer of the GDC, desperate to know what had happened. Suddenly the corridor flooded with people jabbering excitedly.

'So Jasmine Symonds has made the whole thing up?'

'And Twinkletoes Tone was behind the leak?'

'I heard Jasmine's lawyers are dropping the court case against Mark Davies too. It will never stand up now.'

It had worked. She'd done it. Emily breathed a sigh of relief, and stood to one side as the excited crowd poured out of the room towards the exit. Although she didn't want Mark to know she was there, she couldn't resist a peek at him, so she hid behind the pillar again and waited for him to come out.

Before he arrived, she was rewarded with the sight of a furious Jasmine and Tony bickering with each other.

And then, there he was, walking out quietly with an air of dignity, smiling that gorgeous smile – the one that sent her heart into her boots – and she longed to reach out and touch him, and tell him she was there. For a moment Emily prepared to throw caution to the wind and call out to him, and then suddenly Sam was there.

'Mark, I'm sorry, I couldn't get here before,' she said, 'but I've just heard the news. Fantastic, darling, absolutely fantastic.'

She flung her arms around him, and he kissed her on the cheek.

'I'm still pinching myself,' he said. 'Come on, I'd better plough my way through the massed hordes of the press, who are doubtless waiting outside for me.'

Emily watched them walk away and felt her heart shatter in two. Stupidly, a little bit of her had been hoping she'd got it wrong. But clearly she hadn't. There was nothing left for her to hope for.

Rob was on his way to watch the annual sixth-form panto when the call came through from Mark.

'So you've got away with it then?' teased Rob. 'How much did you have to pay the judge for that one?'

'Oh, the usual,' joked Mark. 'I offered him my body and he couldn't refuse.'

'Seriously, mate,' said Rob, 'I'm thrilled for you. It must be such a weight off your mind.'

'It is,' said Mark.

'Emily must be delighted,' Rob added.

'Emily?' Mark queried. 'What's Emily got to do with it?'

'Oh shit,' said Rob, 'me and my big mouth. She swore me to secrecy.'

'About what?'

'The fact that she handed her notice in last week and has spent the last few days trying to uncover information that would help you. I went with her to a bar to track down Graham Harker. He wouldn't sign a statement, but he admitted to us that he'd spiked your drink. And Kerry told Emily that she and Tony had cooked up the whole thing together. I hadn't mentioned any of this because Emily wanted to surprise you.'

'Emily did all that for me?' Mark asked slowly.

'She sure did,' said Rob. 'I'd say you're still well in there, mate. That girl seriously has the hots for you.'

'You think?'

'I know,' said Rob. 'Trust your old Uncle Rob for once. She's just yours for the taking.'

'The only trouble is,' said Mark, 'I have no idea where she is.'

Mark came off the phone from Rob with a feeling of elation. Could this day get any better? Emily had given up everything to help him. Rob thought she was Mark's for the taking. As soon as he'd got past the media scrum, been to hospital to visit Gemma and checked on Beth, he was going straight round to Emily's to do what he'd been wanting to do for months: namely, carry on where they'd left off after the dancing weekend, before his life had gone into meltdown.

He and Sam walked out of the GDC building to encounter a raft of photographers and journalists shouting questions and taking photos. For the first time since Mark had been in this nightmare he was enjoying the blaze of publicity surrounding him. It was going to be a lot of fun getting back at his critics.

'How do you feel, Mark?'

'It's Mr Davies to you,' said Mark, spotting his weasel-faced companion from the hospital. 'And I feel great, thanks.'

'What are you going to do now?' another hack shouted.

'Go and visit my daughter,' said Mark.

'Are you bitter about what happened?'

Mark paused. Was he bitter? Probably, a bit. But life was simply too short for bitterness. Gemma's accident had taught him that.

'No, not bitter,' said Mark, 'but I do have this to say. I feel that, thanks to the actions of one brave person, my good name and reputation has been restored to me, as I always knew they would be. I appreciate you people have a job to do, but not all of us who get caught up in the media circus want to be there, and not all of us are guilty of the lies that get written about us day after day in your papers. When my daughter is better, I am going to campaign for greater privacy laws for ordinary citizens, so that this never happens to anyone else.'

'Are you going to sue Jasmine now?' shouted another reporter.

'I think she's in enough trouble, don't you?' said Mark.

'What are you going to do now?' asked another.

'Well, right now I'm going to see my daughter,' said Mark. 'I'm sure Jasmine will be happy to talk to you.'

He pushed his way through the scrum and the press pack surged over to the entrance of the GDC from where Jasmine had emerged belligerently with the Rottweiler by her side. She'd clearly come out with all guns blazing.

'What are you doing next, Jasmine?' someone called.

'I'm gonna sue,' she spat aggressively. 'I'm suing my lawyers. I'm suing A-Listers, and I'm suing Tony Cavendish. We are sooo history.'

'That's right,' added Kayla pugnaciously, 'she's gonna sue.'

The head of Emily's law firm , was standing on the pavement in front of the GDC, smoothly telling reporters that as of today they would be severing all links with A-Listers, whose reputation now lay in tatters.

The head of A-Listers was telling another hack that they would be suing Jasmine and Tony for misrepresentation.

On the opposite pavement, Tony stood looking on forlornly, promising to sue no one. He probably rued the day he'd ever set eyes on Jasmine Symonds.

Mark laughed. 'It's a mad, mad world,' he said. 'I'm so glad I'm out of it. Come on, Sam, time to see our daughter.'

'One last photo,' a photographer yelled, and Mark obligingly put his arm round Sam and posed for the photo. He was feeling so at one with the world and happy, he could give them one picture.

He took his arm away from Sam and suddenly saw Emily in the crowd. He went to call her, but she stared at him with a look of such pain it went right through him. Oh my God – she'd just seen him put his arm round Sam. She didn't think –?

'Emily!' he called.

But she'd already gone.

* * *

'How does that step go again?' Katie and Rob were practising their Argentinian tango for the competition. Katie hadn't been sure if it was the right dance for them, but Rob had persuaded her it was. 'Come on, it's sexy, it's daring, it's different,' he'd said.

'It goes one, two, three, four, and then I turn you, and there.' He swung her round to face him.

'You make it look so easy,' said Katie.

'Well, it is easy,' said Rob, 'when I'm dancing with you.'

'Flatterer,' said Katie jokingly, but she was secretly thrilled. She and Rob were falling into an easy relationship, and now the first shock of the situation with Charlie had eased, she had to admit it was doing her ego enormous good. And dancing with Rob certainly set her pulse racing. Particularly dancing the tango, which, she had to admit, was incredibly sexy. Charlie had never set her pulse racing like that.

More and more of late, she'd taken to wondering how much more her pulse might race if she and Rob took things a little further. But, as yet, he hadn't shown any inclination to, which was disappointing, but perhaps expected. He had behaved like the perfect gent, and fulfilled his promise to her not to take advantage of her vulnerable state. The trouble was, she wasn't feeling quite so vulnerable any more, and she'd quite like to be taken advantage of. But, having got it so badly wrong the last time, Katie wasn't about to suggest that she and Rob gave it a go. She was rather hoping he'd decide to say it first . . .

Chapter Thirty-nine

On Christmas Eve, Emily stood in the snow on a chilly Welsh hillside at her dad's grave, holding a wilting bunch of freesias, which was all that she'd managed to find at Paddington Station. It had taken all her strength to come, but it was something she knew she had to do.

Alun Dai Henderson
15 June 1942 – 28 November 2007
Dearly beloved husband, father and brother
In God We Trust

Even now, after a year, seeing it carved out in the stone it seemed almost impossible to think it was her beloved dad lying there, but she had to finally face up to the fact it was.

It was the first time Emily had been here since the funeral. She'd made excuses of time pressures before, but really she knew it was the fact that she'd felt she'd failed all his expectations that had stopped her from coming. And now that she finally felt she was getting to grips with her life, it seemed important that she put the past to rest, and made something of her future.

She knelt down in the snow and laid the flowers on the grave.

'I'm sorry, Dad,' she said. 'I let you down. I didn't become the woman you wanted me to be. But I think I'm ready to be that person now. I won't let you down again.'

It was time to say goodbye. Blinking back the tears, Emily picked up her backpack and headed down the hill for home. The snow blew in her face, but as she reached the bottom of the hill, the clouds parted and sunshine briefly filled the valley. Somehow, she just knew her dad was telling her everything was going to be okay.

'Happy Christmas, Happy Christmas!' Katie felt quite surreal as she ushered her soon-to-be ex-husband, his lover and her potential lover into the lounge. But, as she'd said to her mum, if you couldn't be forgiving at Christmas, when could you? The children were going to have to get used to the situation one day, so it might as well be sooner rather than later. Besides, it didn't seem fair for them not to see both their parents at Christmas. As soon as Katie had learned from Charlie that his mother still hadn't forgiven him, she'd immediately asked him over on Christmas Day. When he'd said Hans would be in town, she'd been a little shocked, but decided to go with the flow. Finding out that Rob, too, was going to be on his own, she'd decided she might as well ask him too. She'd asked Mark, Sam and Beth, too, as Gemma was still in hospital, but they'd said they would rather all spend the day round Gemma's hospital bed.

'Well, this is the oddest Christmas I've ever had,' said Rob, as he came into the kitchen to see if Katie needed any help. 'Expect the unexpected indeed.'

'If you'd told me at the start of the year that I would be entertaining my husband and his male lover on Christmas Day, I'd never have believed you,' laughed Katie. 'But it does have its advantages.'

'Doesn't it just.' Rob moved tantalisingly close to her, but the moment was broken by Aidan running in to say that Molly had fallen over.

Somehow Katie didn't mind, though. She felt sure their time would come.

* * *

'Happy Christmas!'

'Happy Christmas!'

Mark, Sam and Beth sat on the edge of Gemma's bed, chinking glasses and eating chocolates.

'Have we got crackers?' Gemma wanted to know.

'We not only have crackers,' said Mark, 'your very clever and versatile mother has brought us cold turkey a day early.'

'I couldn't quite run to a roast,' said Sam. 'Sorry about that.'

'When can we do presents?' Beth asked.

'Now, please say now,' Gemma pleaded.

'Well, maybe one now,' teased Sam, 'and some more later. I'm afraid the big ones will have to wait till you get home.'

The next ten minutes was spent in an orgy of ripping paper. The girls whooped and shrieked as they found CDs, clothes and make-up they'd requested.

'Oh thanks, Dad, you're the best,' said Gemma, finding herself in possession of the latest Amy Winehouse CD. 'Sorry I haven't had a chance to buy you a present yet.'

'I know this isn't quite the Christmas we were supposed to have,' said Mark, 'but I think your mum and I agree that the best Christmas present is having you here with us.'

Sam smiled through her tears and squeezed his hand, and then they all fell silent as the staff, who were touring the wards singing Christmas carols, launched into a heart-rending rendition of 'Silent Night'.

'Happy Christmas, Gemma,' said Mark, and raised his glass. 'And here's to a great New Year.'

'Are you feeling a bit better, love?' Emily's mum had been tenderly solicitous over Christmas. At first Emily had felt as though she was using her mum – her mum had enough troubles of her own, she didn't need her youngest daughter coming home with her tail between her legs having made such a catastrophic mess of her life. But her mum had been brilliant. 'That's what I'm here for,' she'd said. 'Being a Mam is the one job you can never stop doing. Besides, I need to have someone to look after. Since your dad died I've felt completely useless.'

So Emily had spent a restful week, eating home-cooking and going for long coastal walks. It was good to feel the wind in her hair and the spray on her face, as she walked her mum's new dog on the beach – 'Your sister suggested it,' her mum had told her, 'it's nice to have the company.' Emily had enjoyed catching up with relatives she hadn't seen for years, including Auntie Mabel, who'd always been so suspicious of 'Lunnon' – 'I always knew you'd come back,' she said. 'No good ever came of people who went to Lunnon' – and cousins who had stayed in the area, worked in Swansea, and had had their kids young. She'd seen the future she would have had if her dad hadn't insisted that his bright little girl worked hard and went into law.

'I feel much better, thanks,' said Emily. 'Though I think I've put on a stone since I've been here.'

'About time you did,' said her mum. 'You'd got far too thin.'

Emily laughed. Her mum, who was built like a little round barrel, always thought everyone was too thin. She regarded it as her job in life to fatten up all those around her – as if the quality of her love could be measured in the size of the portions she doled out.

'And you're sure you're okay for money,' said Emily, 'because even if I get this new job I'm going for, I'll be earning less, and I can't help as much with the loan as I could.'

'Yes, yes,' said her mum. 'I'll be fine. It was a good idea of your sister's, persuading me to go back to work.'

Thanks to her dad's illness, her mum hadn't worked for years, and being a full-time carer had rendered her practically housebound. Now she was going out to work at the local M&S, Emily could detect a change in her. She was more confident – vivacious, almost – the jolly mother that Emily remembered from her childhood, before Dad's accident had robbed them all of a decent family life.

'Besides, I told you about that letter I got, didn't I?' said her mum.

'Which letter was that?' asked Emily.

'The one from your dad's company. It turns out there's been a campaign started since your dad died. People liked him, you know, and they liked the fact that he always spoke up about what had happened. Anyway, they're going to give us some money. Not much, but it's something. It should be enough to pay off my debts.'

She passed over the letter, and Emily scanned its contents.

'Oh no. Mam, you can't accept this,' she said. 'It's way too low. I know, I'll see if I can get my new firm to let me represent the patients' group. Dad's company is doing the right thing badly. I'm sure we can get them to do it well.'

'You're sure?'

'Oh yes,' said Emily with a sudden happy grin. Finally, here was a case worth fighting. 'I have a few media contacts. I'm sure I can get a story out there that Dad's firm won't like to hear. I reckon we can get far more out of them.'

'Is that legal?' her mum asked.

'Yes,' said Emily, 'it's perfectly legal. Moral? Perhaps not. But sometimes I think the end justifies the means, don't you?'

'Let's just go over it one more time.'

Rob had arrived at Katie's with his dance DVDs and more wine. It was only three days until the competition and he was determined they were going to win. Katie wasn't taking it nearly seriously enough, in his opinion, teasing him constantly about his male ego.

'But there's no point in doing anything if you're not going to be the best,' said Rob.

'And you're the best?' Katie asked.

'Oh yes, and one day you are going to know it,' Rob said, then regretted it. He'd been trying very hard to keep a lid on his feelings, but it was becoming more and more difficult. Every time he saw Katie, every time he danced with her, he knew he was falling deeper and deeper in love. Yet he still wasn't sure if she was ready for a new relationship, and he didn't want to rush her, so he held back. It was a new experience for Rob, getting to know a woman first before sleeping with her. And one he was rather enjoying. He'd met her mother, spent Christmas Day with her family, and seen an awful lot of the kids – who, to his relief, seemed to accept him easily.

It was, he also discovered, a way of utterly inflaming desire. The more he saw of Katie, the more he wanted her. The more he touched her while dancing, the more she inflamed him. She was becoming everything to him. He hoped that one day he might be everything to her.

'Okay, if you insist,' said Katie, 'but do we really have to do the tango?'

'Of course we do,' said Rob. 'It's the dance of lurve – it's the one where we can really show the judges our passion and commitment. I think we've got a much better chance of winning with this.'

'Okay, if you insist,' Katie agreed, but she looked awkward.

They cleared a space in the lounge, Rob put on the music, and soon they were lost in the dance itself. Sometimes, when he was dancing with Katie, Rob felt as though he were somewhere far away, and all that connected them was the throbbing music and the way it flowed through them and in them as they fell into the dance. Dancing with Katie was like dancing with no one else.

The dance came to an end and she lay in his arms for a moment. He felt her tenderly lying against his chest, and longed to pull her to him to kiss her, to take her to bed. But she had seemed awkward and out of sorts earlier. He wasn't sure if she was ready for a new relationship. Or whether he should push her.

'That was great,' he said lightly, pulling away from her. 'I think one more practice should do it.'

'You're a hard taskmaster, Rob Dylan,' said Katie.

'It's why you love me,' said Rob, wondering if one day soon he'd say that knowing it was true.

Chapter Forty

'I'm sorry, I tried to leave them behind, but they refused to stay,' said Rob, arriving at Katie's house the day before New Year's Eve for one last run-through. Mark, Gemma and Beth followed him into the lounge.

'Gemma's insisting on watching us practise,' he said apologetically.

'And I wanted to come and see George,' said Beth shyly.

'And I'm just here for the ride,' said Mark. 'I hope you don't mind the invasion.'

'Not at all,' said Katie. 'You can all have a laugh at our expense. I'll call the boys down.'

Luckily Katie's lounge was large enough to accommodate everyone, and they all squeezed on the sofa and laughed their way through Katie and Rob's routine. Though that was mainly because Rob was goofing about and getting it wrong, pretending to step on Katie's feet, spinning her in the wrong direction and generally cocking things up.

Katie had a feeling she knew why he was doing it. There had been a moment earlier in the week when she had felt as certain as she could be that he'd been about to kiss her, and then he'd pulled back. She'd spent every day since wondering why. Was it his misplaced sense of chivalry, or was it simply that he didn't fancy her anymore?

Because now she knew, without a doubt, that she did fancy

him. He made her laugh, he bolstered her ego, and dancing with him was sublime. The effort of not being with him was beginning to get to her. Any minute now she was going to spontaneously combust, her feelings spilling out for the world to see.

'Are you going to come and cheer us on?' asked Katie as they repaired to the kitchen for a cup of tea, leaving the kids watching repeats of *Strictly Come Dancing*. 'Sorry about the mess, by the way.'

Katie's kitchen was rather less shiny these days, but, she felt, somewhat more homely.

'Mess?' said Mark. 'What mess? Don't forget I live with Rob. And I'd love to come and see you.'

'Shame Emily's still away,' said Katie. 'I was going to ask her too.'

Mark looked a little awkward.

'That would be all right, wouldn't it?' said Katie.

'I'd love to see her,' Mark answered. 'I'm just not sure that she'd love to see me.'

'Why?' Katie asked. 'I haven't spoken to her since before the hearing, but look what she did for you.'

'And then she saw me putting my arm around Sam to have my photo taken,' said Mark. 'I'm worried she might have got the wrong idea.'

'Right,' said Katie. 'Hmm. Well, next time I see her, I'll put her straight.'

George and Beth wandered in for snacks and Katie administered biscuits and drinks. As they left she was amused to hear Beth say, 'Having a gay dad isn't *that* weird. Did you know Mr Paterson's wife is a lesbian? And at least you don't have to live with your dad's boyfriend.'

Katie nearly spat out her tea. The things kids said. George seemed much happier these days. Perhaps he was at last coming to terms with things.

She sat happily in her kitchen. Maybe something would happen with Rob. Maybe it wouldn't. But it was certainly fun being in a situation where it was a possibility.

Emily got off the train at Thurfield and looked around her. It was good to be back, nearly a year to the day since she'd come home from Wales after the previous Christmas. And what a year it had been. Thurfield had never seemed more welcoming. Her cottage never more cosy. She was brimming over with energy and enthusiasm for her new job. Her new boss, whom she'd spoken to a couple of days after Christmas, had been as enthusiastic as she was to take on her dad's firm.

'I love being David against Goliath,' he'd said. 'These companies get away with murder.'

The other bonus was that John was joining her in the company. It turned out he was as disillusioned as she was with Mire & Innit, and was keen to get started in his new role.

The only blot on the landscape was Mark. Emily knew that one day she'd come to terms with it, but it hurt like hell right now.

She let herself in and picked up her mail. There were dozens of messages on the answerphone, including one from Katie telling her that she and Rob were taking part in a dancing competition tonight, and would Emily like to come? Tonight – 8 p.m.? Hell, it was already half past seven. But it would be good to see Katie, and she felt obliged to cheer her on. Katie was her best friend, and Emily knew she had been unforgivably silent over the Christmas period.

She picked through her mail and then picked up a brown jiffy bag that looked like it had been hand-delivered. She opened it and a DVD of *Green Wing* fell out.

There was a note from Mark inside.

Dear Emily,
I was given the second series for Christmas. I need someone to watch it with? I'd really like it if that someone was you.

Love Mark

PS I think you may have got the wrong idea about Sam and me. We're not back together.

Underneath he'd written:

> *Dance like no one's looking*
> *Love like you've never been hurt*
> *Work like you don't have to*
> *Live like it's Heaven on Earth.*

I think I'd like to try the last one, wouldn't you?

The phone rang, but Emily ignored it as she held the letter and read and reread it. Mark wasn't with Sam. Mark wasn't with Sam. Hallelujah! Emily danced round the room in delight. Mark wasn't with Sam, and he wanted to see her again. Life didn't get better than this.

It was only then that she realised Katie was leaving a message for her.

'We're all here, so I hope you can make it,' she was saying. 'Mark's coming. Oh, and by the way, just so you know, he isn't going back to Sam.'

Emily picked up the phone. 'You try stopping me, girl,' she said.

Rob felt ridiculously nervous as he and Katie took to the dance floor. The couples before them all seemed to have danced better, been better, looked better than he and Katie did. Well, Katie looked gorgeous in a shimmery turquoise dress, but he was feeling a bit of a prat in his DJ and red cummerbund.

The music started gently, and he softly led Katie by the hand. When they reached the centre of the room, he pulled her towards him, she stroked his head, and then pulled back. His heart was

369

pounding as he felt himself getting lost in the sensuality of the music. Katie glided her way around the dance floor, sliding against and then away from him. She pressed her body against his and lifted her leg up for him to spin her around. He pulled her back to him and then they faced each other while dancing side by side, low and dirty to the sexiest of all dances. Every moment by her side, the thrum of the music, the closeness of her to him, the whiff of her perfume, increased his feelings. He could deny it no longer and then suddenly, when he spun her round and she fell back in his arms, he looked into her eyes and knew she felt the same way.

'I feel like I'm in that scene from *Dirty Dancing*,' he said.

'Me too,' said Katie. 'How dirty can we go?'

'Very,' said Rob with a grin, and then pulled her to him and snaked his body against hers. It felt so right, so comfortable.

'We should be together,' he said.

'I know,' Katie replied.

'You do?'

'I thought you'd never ask,' said Katie.

'I was waiting for you to be ready,' Rob told her.

'Oh, I'm ready,' Katie assured him, as they executed the last spin of the dance and they ended by collapsing together onto the floor.

The crowd erupted in cheers and claps, and as Rob lifted Katie to her feet, he pulled her to him and kissed her passionately.

'There,' he said, 'I've been wanting to do that for ages.'

Mark was sitting cheering with the rest, watching Rob and Katie make the dance floor their own. They moved in such perfect sinuous, sensual rhythm, he felt almost voyeuristic watching them. If ever a couple were meant to be together, it was Katie and Rob.

He wondered if he would ever feel that way about anyone again.

Katie and Rob returned to their table, flushed and happy with their success. They had scored maximum points for execution and delivery, and had just lost a couple of marks for timing lapses. They had stormed into the lead, and the couples that followed them were going to be hard-pushed to match them.

'Well done, you two,' said Mark. 'I really admire you both. I wish I could dance like that.'

'You could always try dancing like no one's looking.'

Mark looked up in shock. Emily was standing before him.

'Emily,' said Mark. He was stunned. For weeks he'd thought of nothing but Emily, and here she was standing before him in all her heart-stopping gorgeousness.

'Talking to yourself is a really bad habit, you know,' said Emily.

'I must have picked it up from you,' said Mark. The noise and chaos of the dance competition had faded into the background. All that mattered was that Emily was here.

'We'll just go and powder our noses or something,' said Rob, but Mark barely noticed when he and Katie discreetly slid away.

'I thought you didn't care,' said Mark.

'I thought you didn't,' Emily replied. She looked embarrassed. 'I just assumed – I thought you'd got back together with Sam.'

'No, not now,' said Mark. 'Never, after you. Nothing compares, and all that.'

'Doesn't it?'

'Now and for always,' said Mark. 'There's only ever going to be you. There was only ever you.'

'I got your note,' said Emily.

'So what do you think?' Mark asked.

'I think it's time,' she said, 'that we lived like it's heaven on earth, don't you?'

And she kissed him. The sounds of the room faded away as he held her in his arms, right where she belonged.

Suddenly he was aware of a loud roar and a huge commotion.

'I hate to break you two lovebirds up,' said Rob, tapping Mark on the shoulder, 'but Katie and I appear to have won a gold medal.'

'That's fantastic!' Emily hugged Katie and kissed Rob. Mark gave Rob a manly handshake and pecked Katie on the cheek.

'Congratulations to Katie and Rob,' the compere was saying, 'and now we'd like everyone on the floor for the dance-off.'

The first strains of 'The Time of My Life' started playing.

Rob was straight onto the floor with Katie. He motioned to Mark and Emily to follow them.

'I'm still a crap dancer,' said Mark, 'but do you fancy it?'

'Me too,' said Emily, 'but I don't think anyone's looking, do you?'

2 FOR 1 DANCE SESSION

CEROC

Visit our website, www.avon-books.co.uk and print out your own 2 for 1 dancing session voucher with Ceroc. Ceroc is the world's largest dance organisation with 55,000 people attending classes every month in the UK. Ceroc teach modern jive – a funky fusion of salsa and swing dancing without complicated footwork which makes it a popular choice for the social dancer. There are 120 dance nights in operation every week all over the UK including more than 20 in London alone.

- Visit www.ceroc.co.uk for a list of participating dance venues
- Contact your chosen dance venue in advance of your visit, stating that you are in possession of a 'TLC 2 people for the price of 1 dance session voucher', to check availability, discuss the usage of the offer (restrictions may apply) and book your session.
- You will find the voucher at www.avon-books.co.uk. Hand in your voucher on arrival at the venue.
- Proof of purchase is required, therefore a copy of the book 'Strictly Love' and the book's till receipt must be presented along with the voucher. If this is not produced, you must pay the full price for your dance session.
- Please read the terms & conditions on the voucher.
- Voucher valid until 31st December 2008.

TERMS & CONDITIONS
1. This offer is open to all UK residents aged 18 years or over for non Ceroc members only. This offer is not available to employees of HarperCollins or its subsidiaries, TLC Marketing plc or agencies appointed by TLC and their immediate families.
2. The voucher entitles the bearer to one free dance session, when accompanied by another person paying the full price.
3. Proof of purchase is required, therefore a copy of the book 'Strictly Love' and the book's till receipt must be presented along with the voucher. If this is not produced, you must pay the full price for the dance session.
4. Only one voucher may be used per person. The voucher claimant may not claim another voucher at a participating venue.
5. Offer excludes existing members.
6. All additional customers will pay the full price and all future bookings will be charged at the full price.
7. Voucher valid until 31st December 2008.
8. Offer excludes Public Holidays and Bank Holidays.
9. The offer is based on advance bookings only and is subject to promotional availability at participating venues.
10. Voucher cannot be redeemed at a venue you already have dance sessions at.

11. Customers must call the venue in advance of their visit, stating that they are in possession of a 'TLC 2 for 1 dance session voucher', to check availability, discuss the usage of the offer (restrictions may apply) and book their session.

12. The instructions listed at the back of the book and on the website form part of these terms and conditions.

13. If you fail to cancel your booking within 48 hours of the appointment, or do not show at the venue, a cancellation charge may be incurred.

14. The list of participating venues remains subject to change. Please contact your chosen venue to confirm continual availability of the offer.

15. Participating venues are all contracted to participate in the 2 for 1 dance session offer.

16. Participating venues reserve the right to vary prices, times and offer availability (e.g. public holidays).

17. Prices (if any) and information presented are valid at the time of going to press and could be subject to change.

18. Neither the Promoter, nor its agents or distributors can accept liability for lost, stolen or damaged vouchers and reserves the right to withdraw or amend any details and/or offers.

19. The voucher may only be used once. Photocopied, scanned, damaged or illegible vouchers will not be accepted.

20. The 2 for 1 dance session voucher has no monetary value, is non-transferable, cannot be resold and cannot be used in conjunction with any other promotional offer or redeemed in whole or part for cash.

21. In the event of large promotional uplift, venues reserve the right to book voucher holders up to 4 months from date of calling to make a promotional booking.

22. Neither TLC, its agents or distributors and the promoter will in any circumstances be responsible or liable to compensate the purchaser or other bearer, or accept any liability for (a) any non-acceptance by a venue of this voucher or (b) any inability by the bearer to use this voucher properly or at all or (c) the contents, accuracy or use of either this voucher or the venue listing, nor will any of them be liable for any personal loss or injury occurring at the venue, and (d) TLC, its agents and distributors and the promoter do not guarantee the quality and/or availability of the services offered by the venues and cannot be held liable for any resulting personal loss or damage. Your statutory rights are unaffected.

23. TLC and HarperCollins Publishers reserves the right to offer a substitute reward of equal or greater value.

24. The terms of this promotion are as stated here and no other representations (written or oral) shall apply.

25. Any persons taking advantage of this promotion do so on complete acceptance of these terms and conditions.

26. TLC and HarperCollins Publishers reserves the right to vary these terms without notice.

27. Promoter: HarperCollins Ltd, 77–85 Fulham Palace Road, Hammersmith, London, W6 8JB.

28. This is administered by TLC Marketing plc, PO Box 468, Swansea, SA1 3WY

29. This promotion is governed by English law and is subject to the exclusive jurisdiction of the English Courts.

30. HarperCollins Publishers excludes all liability as far as is permitted by law, which may arise in connection with this offer and reserves the right to cancel the offer at any stage.

WIN TICKETS TO SEE CHICAGO!

We are offering 1 lucky AVON reader a pair of tickets to see CHICAGO, plus a free show programme and an interval drink. Having celebrated 10 glittering years in the West End, smash hit musical CHICAGO continues to dazzle audiences night after night. This multi-award winning production is filled with stunning choreography inspired by Bob Fosse and a sizzling score that includes the classic *All That Jazz*.

This fantastic prize is valid for all performances excluding Saturday evenings until 31 March 2009. Prize is subject to availability and travel is not included. No cash alternative is available.

CHICAGO THE MUSICAL - Cambridge Theatre, Seven Dials, London WC2
To book tickets call 0870 890 1102. www.chicagothemusical.co.uk

To enter this free prize draw, simple visit www.avon-books.co.uk and answer the question below or send your postal entry to Avon Chicago Competition, Harper-Collins Publishers, 77–85 Fulham Palace Road, Hammersmith, London, W6 8JB.

In *Strictly Love*, what does Emily do for a living? Is she:

    A) A lawyer
    B) A doctor
    C) An accountant

TUESDAY, 12 FEBRUARY 2008

Dance like no one's looking

Today I was given a mission by my editor.

In order to properly research my latest book I have agreed to undergo dancing lessons.

Given that I have two left feet and no sense of rhythm, this could be highly amusing.

On the other hand I do love to dance . . .

So tonight I am going to attend my first ballroom dancing lesson.

At the heart of my latest book are these four lines, which are attributed to everyone from Mark Twain to a Chinese proverb.

I don't care where they're from.

I just love them.

Love like you've never been hurt
Dance like no one's looking
Work like you don't have to
Live like Heaven on Earth

I sincerely hope no one is looking too much tonight . . .

FRIDAY, 15 FEBRUARY 2008

First Steps . . .

Well I survived my first dance lesson.

What am I talking about 'survived'?

I had an absolute blast.

I did feel quite nervous as I walked through the doors of the studio. Was I too old for all this? Too awkward? And when I saw the calibre of the sexy young couple strutting their stuff on the dance floor, too amateur by half?

However, I needn't have worried, as my dance teacher, Izobela was not only delightful, but instantly put me at ease.

On discovering that I wanted to get the feel for several dances (I have worked out rumba standing on my own in front of a computer screen, and tried to waltz with a nine-year-old following a DVD, but it isn't quite the same) she kindly showed me the basic steps of rumba, tango and social foxtrot.

In rumba apparently the thing to do is to keep the top half of your body straight and tall, but the bottom half should be lithe and lissom, so you can perfect your snake hip-type movement. Like most things in life, if you relax it's easier. To start with nerves were making me stiff as a post and I was so worried about not getting the basic steps – back, side close, forward side close, trying to keep your feet in between your partner's WITHOUT tripping up takes some doing, I can tell you.

After mastering a simple routine, Izobela then took me on to the tango. Here I felt like a complete prat, I have to say. It was, however, very funny learning how to stretch myself right back with my head flung back, before coming forward again and doing this funny rocking thing (which if I did with my husband I wouldn't be able to cope without falling into fits of giggles), before doing that wonderful side-stepping bit which the tango is famous for and then ending it in a spin.

Finally I moved onto the social foxtrot. This apparently is a good one to use when you're in a crowded room. When proper competitive dancers do it, they should, so Izobela told me, simply glide around the room (and she demonstrated this brilliantly with her next pupil), but it's common for beginners to fumble and for the men not to lead properly. Again. I haven't had such fun in a while.

And however hopeless I am, I do love to dance . . .

WEDNESDAY, 27 FEBRUARY 2008

Invisible

On Monday it was my husband's birthday. I had intended to buy him and me a dancing lesson, but Izobela was away last week and rather inefficiently I hadn't got round to booking one with her before she went.

My husband, like a lot of men I suspect, mostly stands on the side drinking a pint when I hit the dance floor. This is not because he is too embarrassed to show off his dad dancing, but because he needs several pints to give him the confidence to go up and strut his funky stuff. I have been very keen to get him dancing ever since I went to salsa lessons a few years ago, but time, inclination and not enough beer has prevented him from taking me up on the offer.

As it was his birthday, we went out for dinner with several friends on Saturday night to a tapas bar. We eventually staggered home at just gone midnight, opening a bottle of wine, and listening to my husband's new Alison Moyet CD.

At that point, enough red wine and good cheer had been consumed for him to suddenly realise that Alison Moyet just begged to be danced with. I was trying really really hard to remember Izobela's strictures about ¾ time and whether it is back step, side, close, forward, and spin, while trying to impress on my husband the importance of him following me into dancing heaven without falling over.

I am pleased to report, we didn't fall over, I did feel like I'd got the hang of snake hips (in vino muchos exagiteras, me thinks) and it was ever so much fun.

Just as well you can't see me dancing from here . . .